D0846533

MANSLAYER

DWARF TROLLSLAYER GOTREK Gurnisson and his human companion Felix Jaeger continue their adventures in this latest tale by the author of *Orcslayer*.

Returning to the Empire from their latest sojourn overseas, Gotrek and Felix stop off in the Imperial city of Nuln. There, they bump into Gotrek's old friend the Slayer Malakai Makaisson, who is helping the Imperial war effort by transporting cannons to the frontline in his airship the *Spirit of Grungni*. After a series of mishaps it becomes clear that traitors are at work, trying to sabotage the Empire's artillery production. Can Gotrek and Felix expose the culprits before time runs out for the beleaguered armies of the Empire?

More Gotrek & Felix from the Black Library

GOTREK & FELIX: THE FIRST OMNIBUS
by William King
(Contains books 1-3: *Trollslayer, Skavenslayer & Daemonslayer*)

GOTREK & FELIX: THE SECOND OMNIBUS
by William King
(Contains books 4-6: *Dragonslayer, Beastslayer &*
Vampireslayer)

Book 7 – GIANTSLAYER
by William King

Book 8 – ORCSLAYER
by Nathan Long

More Nathan Long from the Black Library
BLACKHEARTS: THE OMNIBUS

(Contains the novels *Valnir's Bane, The Broken Lance* and
Tainted Blood)

Gotrek and Felix

MANSLAYER

Nathan Long

To Anthony, a Slayer if ever there was.

A BLACK LIBRARY PUBLICATION

First published in Great Britain in 2007 by
BL Publishing,
Games Workshop Ltd.,
Willow Road, Nottingham,
NG7 2WS, UK

10 9 8 7 6 5 4 3 2 1

Cover illustration by Geoff Taylor
Map by Nuala Kinrade.

Thanks to Alison and Doug Lister for their help with Malakai's
dialogue. 'Ah couldnae done it wi'out ye.'

© Games Workshop Limited 2007. All rights reserved.

Black Library, the Black Library logo, Black Flame, BL Publishing,
Games Workshop, the Games Workshop logo and all associated
marks, names, characters, illustrations and images from the
Warhammer universe are either ®, TM and/or © Games Workshop Ltd
2000-2007, variably registered in the UK and other countries around
the world. All rights reserved.

A CIP record for this book is available from the British Library.

ISBN 13: 978 1 84416 509 4
ISBN 10: 1 84416 509 4

Distributed in the US by Simon & Schuster
1230 Avenue of the Americas, New York, NY 10020.

No part of this publication may be reproduced, stored in a retrieval
system, or transmitted in any form or by any means, electronic,
mechanical, photocopying, recording or otherwise, without the prior
permission of the publishers.

This is a work of fiction. All the characters and events portrayed in
this book are fictional, and any resemblance to real people or
incidents is purely coincidental.

See the Black Library on the Internet at
www.blacklibrary.com

Find out more about Games Workshop
and the world of Warhammer at
www.games-workshop.com

THIS IS A DARK age, a bloody age, an age of daemons and of sorcery. It is an age of battle and death, and of the world's ending. Amidst all of the fire, flame and fury it is a time, too, of mighty heroes, of bold deeds and great courage.

AT THE HEART of the Old World sprawls the Empire, the largest and most powerful of the human realms. Known for its engineers, sorcerers, traders and soldiers, it is a land of great mountains, mighty rivers, dark forests and vast cities. And from his throne in Altdorf reigns the Emperor Karl-Franz, sacred descendant of the founder of these lands, Sigmar, and wielder of his magical warhammer.

BUT THESE ARE far from civilised times. Across the length and breadth of the Old World, from the knightly palaces of Bretonnia to ice-bound Kislev in the far north, come rumblings of war. In the towering World's Edge Mountains, the orc tribes are gathering for another assault. Bandits and renegades harry the wild southern lands of the Border Princes. There are rumours of rat-things, the skaven, emerging from the sewers and swamps across the land. And from the northern wildernesses there is the ever-present threat of Chaos, of daemons and beastmen corrupted by the foul powers of the Dark Gods. As the time of battle draws ever nearer, the Empire needs heroes like never before.

'On we pressed, north through the Blackfire Pass, to tread at last on Empire soil for the first time in twenty years. And though my heart sang to be home, it was a grim time in the land of my birth, and it grieved me to see it so wracked with panic and privation.

'Gotrek was eager to reach Middenheim and find his doom in battle against the great hordes of Chaos that had again swept south to threaten the lands of men. In this desire, however, he was to be frustrated, for, passing through Nuln, we stumbled upon a vile and far-reaching conspiracy intended to destroy the beating heart of the Empire from within at the very hour when its greatest enemy attacked it from without.

'While in pursuit of these foul villains, it chanced that Gotrek met an old friend, and I an old love – and never could two reunions have been more different; for Gotrek's was fond and fortuitous, while mine was both sweet, and more painful than I can express.'

– From *My Travels with Gotrek*, Vol VII, by Herr Felix Jaeger (Altdorf Press, 2528)

ONE

'By Sigmar's golden beard, brother!' cried Otto. 'You haven't aged a day!'

'Er...' said Felix, as Otto's butler took his sword and his old red cloak and closed the front door behind him, shutting out the warm rays of a late summer morning.

Felix would have liked to return his brother's compliment, but looking him over top to bottom, the words stuck in his throat. Otto's once blond hair had retreated from his head and turned to silver on his chin – chins, rather. And though he was exquisitely dressed in perfectly tailored velvets and brocades, the best tailor in the world couldn't have hidden the prodigious swelling of his belly.

Otto limped forward, gripping a gold-topped walking stick, and brushed some of the road dust off Felix's shoulders. Gods, he walks with a cane now, Felix thought.

'And you haven't matured a day either, I see.' Otto chuckled. 'Same ragged cloak. Same patched breeches. Same cracked boots. You vagabond, I thought you were going to find your fortune.'

'I have found it,' said Felix. 'Several times.'

Otto wasn't listening. He waved a hand at the butler, who was wrinkling his nose with distaste as he hung Felix's cloak in a closet at one side of the entrance hall.

'Fritz!' Otto called. 'Wine and cold cuts in the study!' He motioned to Felix with a pudgy hand as he stumped down a cherry-panelled corridor towards the back of the townhouse. 'Come, brother. This calls for a celebration. Will you stay to lunch? Annabella – you remember my wife? She will be most interested to see you again.'

Felix followed, stomach growling at the mention of food. 'Lunch? Thank you, brother. You are most generous.'

It had been a lean journey from Karak Hirn, up from the wild lands of the Border Princes through Blackfire Pass then down the Old Dwarf Road into Averland and on. In this time of war even the breadbasket of the Empire had been stripped bare – all its wheat, wool and wine sent north to supply the army fighting to stop Archaon's encroaching hordes. Its men too had gone north, sometimes unwillingly. As he and Gotrek had boarded the riverboat *Leopold* at the Loningbruck docks for the long meander down the Upper Reik to Nuln, Felix had seen companies of miserable, pinch-faced farm boys sitting on their packs, all kitted out with spears and bows and cheaply made uniforms in the colours of their lords. Burly sergeants in well-worn breastplates had watched over them like prison guards, making sure none of them slipped off home before the barges came to ship them north. Felix had shaken his head at the sight. How was it possible that these untrained boys, most of whom had never been away from their villages, could turn back the supernatural might of the numberless armies of the Wastes? And yet, for centuries, they had.

'Now then, brother,' said Otto, settling noisily into a high-backed leather chair by the open window of his opulent study. Sunshine and the droning of contented bees filtered in from the garden. 'How long has it been?'

Felix sighed as he sat in the opposite chair. He felt as if he was sinking into a leather cloud. Sigmar! He had forgotten such luxury existed. He smiled wryly to himself. There might be a war on, and privation all around, but one could always trust Otto to do well for himself. In that regard he was just like their father. 'I haven't been keeping track,' he said. 'How long has it been since the ratmen attacked Nuln?'

'Ratmen?' said Otto, looking up as the butler set wine and meat and fancy pastries on a table between them. 'Beastmen, you mean. That was twenty years ago.'

Felix frowned. 'The ones who came up from the sewers and destroyed the College of Engineering and spread plague and ruin? Those were ratmen.'

Otto chuckled. 'Yes, yes. I read your book when it came back from the printers. Very entertaining. But really, there was no need to embellish the truth. The beastmen were bad enough.' He took a sip of wine. 'It sold very well for a time, by the way. As have the others.'

Felix gaped, Otto's absurd insistence that the ratmen were beastmen forgotten. 'You... you published my journals? But...'

Otto smiled, his eyes almost disappearing behind his round cheeks. 'Well, you wouldn't accept my money, and I had some foolish notion that you wouldn't make any yourself.' He gave another amused glance at Felix's threadbare clothes. 'So I took it upon myself to provide for your old age. Annabella read them as you sent them to us, and thought they were quite good. Absolute rubbish of course, daemons and dragons and vampires and whatnot, but just the sort of tall tavern tales that sell these days. Certainly went over better than your poetry ever did.' He helped himself to a pastry. 'I put aside the profits, just in case you ever returned. Of course I had to deduct the printing costs and what not.'

'Of course you did,' muttered Felix.

'But I believe there's still a tidy sum, enough for a man of your, ah, frugal nature to live on for a bit, I should think.'

Felix could feel the blood rising in his cheeks. Part of him wanted to leap out of the chair and strangle Otto for his presumption and condescension. How dare he? Felix had often thought about publishing his journals – about turning them into books – but he had meant it for a time when he was settled, when he would have time to edit them properly, to check his facts, to compare notes with other learned men. He had thought to make them scholarly treatises on the lands and cultures and monsters he and the Slayer had encountered, not a series of penny dreadful melodramas. People would think he was a hack! On the other hand – a tidy sum? There was certainly something to be said for that. He rolled up a slice of ham and stuffed it into his mouth. Sigmar, that was good! He sipped his wine. Heaven!

'How much exactly, is a "tidy sum"?'

Otto waved a hand. 'Oh, I don't know. I haven't looked at those ledgers in years. Come by the office later this week and we'll–'

'Father?' said a voice from the corridor.

Felix looked around. A tall, blond youth with a thin, serious face stood in the study door. He had a stack of books under one arm, and wore the robes and skull-cap of a university student.

'Yes, Gustav?' said Otto.

'I am going to the Verenan debating society meeting tonight. It may run late.'

'Very well. I'll send Manni with the coach to wait for you.'

Gustav made a face. He looked about seventeen, perhaps eighteen. 'I don't need the coach. I can make it home very well on my own.'

Otto's face went red. He opened his mouth to speak, then shot a look at Felix and thought better of it. 'Very well, very well. Just don't walk alone until you get to the Kaufman Gate.'

'I know, father,' said Gustav, with infinite disdain.

Otto forced a smile. 'Come and meet your uncle Felix.'

The boy's eyes widened. 'The… the dead one?'

'Only a long away from home,' said Felix, standing and extending a hand. 'A pleasure to meet you, nephew.'

The boy advanced hesitantly and gave Felix a limp hand.

'Gustav studies theology and law at the University of Nuln,' said Otto. 'And he has published poetry.'

'Really?' said Felix. He coughed modestly. 'I once published some poetry. In Altdorf. Perhaps you've...?'

'I don't write old-fashioned stuff like that,' said Gustav airily.

'Old... old fashioned?' stuttered Felix, trying to keep his voice level. 'What do you mean by...'

'I am of the new school, the School of the True Voice,' said Gustav. 'We eschew sentiment, and speak only of what is real.'

'Sounds highly entertaining,' said Felix dryly.

Gustav sniffed. 'Entertainment is for plebeians. We edify. Our philosophy–'

'Gustav,' said Otto. 'You'll be late for your lecture.'

'Ah.' Gustav nodded. 'Of course. Good day, uncle. Father.' He inclined his head solemnly and left.

Otto rolled his eyes at Felix and shrugged.

'I didn't know you had a son,' said Felix, resuming his seat.

'No? He was born... Oh yes, that's right. He was born a year after you left Nuln. Very grave, isn't he?' Otto chuckled. 'Reminds me of you at that age, actually.'

'Me?' said Felix. 'I was never such a...'

'You were worse.'

'I wasn't.'

Otto raised an eyebrow. 'Have you read those poems lately?'

Felix snorted and took another sip of wine.

'So, what brings you back to Nuln?' asked Otto. 'Are you still playing valet to that surly dwarf?'

'I am his Rememberer,' said Felix stiffly. 'And we're on our way to Middenheim, to help turn back the Chaos invasion.'

Otto made a face. 'Bit old for that now, surely. Why don't you stay here and work for me? You can help the soldiers up north and add to your nest egg at the same time.'

Felix sighed, amused. It seemed every time he came to Nuln, his brother offered him a job. Poor Otto. He didn't give a damn about helping Felix 'add to his nest egg.' He just wanted him to get a respectable job and stop being an embarrassment to the family. 'You're helping with the war effort?' he asked, avoiding the question.

'Oh yes,' said Otto. 'Jaeger's of Altdorf won the contract to ship raw iron from the Black Mountains down the Reik to Nuln. We are sole suppliers to the Imperial Gunnery School.' He chuckled to himself. 'Neat bit of negotiating, that. There were three shipping companies with lower bids, but I footed the bill for the Countess's annual Weaver's Guild Ball and buttered her up something shocking and, hey presto, I got the nod.'

Felix scowled. 'So you're not helping the war effort. You're gouging the cannon makers for everything you can get.'

Otto shook his head impatiently. 'Not a bit of it. Our bid may have been higher, but our service is better. Jaeger's is the best in the Empire. Everyone knows that. It just took a little oil to get the Countess to award the contract on merit rather than price. That's the way it is with business.'

'And that's why I'm not in business,' said Felix, a bit more snootily than he had intended. 'I'll pass, thanks. Why don't you ask your son?'

'Him?' Otto snorted. 'He's too much like you. Too high-minded and honourable to get his hands dirty in the real world. Father always did want us to become nobles. Looks like he succeeded, at least with you, and his grandson. Well, I wouldn't want to compromise your ideals, m'lord.'

Felix gripped the arms of the chair. The veins pulsed in his neck. He was no noble. He had nothing but contempt for the nobility. He opened his mouth, then closed it again. If he didn't stop he would say something he regretted, and there was that tidy sum from the sale of his books to consider. He eased back in the chair, forcing himself to relax. Twenty years gone, and he and his brother still couldn't carry on a polite conversation for more than five minutes.

'These books of mine,' he said at last. 'Can I see them?'

'Certainly,' said Otto. 'I think we still have a few copies lying around somewhere.' He lifted a delicate silver bell on the table and shook it.

LUNCH WAS VAST, and would have been a grim affair, had it been just the brothers at table, for despite his attempts to be civil, Felix had found himself boiling at his brother's every other word. He was such a pompous ass, so ignorant and incurious of the true state of the world, so sure that life was ordered for his pleasure and that he deserved every luxury he had.

Fortunately, they had been joined by Annabella, Otto's Bretonnian wife – as plump and silver as Otto these days, though still a handsome woman – and she had kept up a constant stream of questions about Felix and his adventures, giggling and gasping at all the appropriate moments. This sweet and flattering babble had done a marvellous job of hiding that he and Otto hardly spoke to each other once during the meal.

The only awkward moment had come when, overwhelmed with the spirit of hospitality, Annabella had asked Felix if he wanted to stay with them while he was in Nuln. Otto's head had snapped up at that, and he had glared across the table.

He needn't have worried. Felix felt the same. If this was how he and his brother got along after only a few hours together, a few days under the same roof and they would be at each others' throats. He politely declined Annabella's offer, saying that he and Gotrek were very comfortably lodged in an inn and wouldn't think of imposing.

At the front door after the meal, as Felix collected his sword and cloak from the butler and tried to find room in his pack for the leather-bound books with his name on them, Otto coughed.

'You might want to stop home in Altdorf on your way north,' he said. 'The old man is on his last legs.'

FELIX'S HEAD SWAM as he walked through the Kaufman district towards the High Gate. He had received too much news too fast. Apparently a lot could change in twenty years. Otto had a son who was attending university. Felix's poetry was old-fashioned. His adventures had been made into books. His father was dying.

The tall, gabled townhouses and walled and guarded estates of wealthy merchants passed unnoticed as he wound through the cobbled streets. The sniffs of prosperous burghers and their plump wives as they stared at his shabby clothes went unchallenged. Otto had a son. His father was dying.

His father was dying.

Felix was surprised that news was affecting him so much. He was surprised, actually, that his father was still alive. How old must he be? Seventy? Eighty? Just like the grasping old miser to wring every year he possibly could out of life, just to make sure he got his money's worth.

If there was one person in the world that Felix got on with less well even than his brother, it was his father. The old man had disowned him when he had decided to become a poet instead of joining the family business. He had said Felix was wasting the education he had paid for. Funny really, when it was that education that had opened Felix's eyes to the beauty and variety of life and introduced him to the worlds of literature, philosophy and poetry. Gustav Jaeger had wanted his sons to have all that knowledge, had wanted them to be able to spout it on command, but only because such learning was one of the qualities of refinement that marked a man as noble, and Gustav had desperately wanted his sons to be the first noble Jaegers. As tight-fisted as he was, the old man had poured gold into the coffers of the high and mighty of Altdorf like it was water, trying to buy a title to pass onto his sons – apparently to no avail.

Felix had hated his father for his crassness, his narrow-minded pragmatism that left no room for art or beauty or romance. Gustav Jaeger had sacrificed his childhood to claw his way out of the gutter, becoming one of the richest merchants in the Empire. And, having reached that eminence, he had seemed determined that his sons would sacrifice their childhoods as well. He had made no allowances for youthful follies or indiscretions.

Perhaps that was one of the reasons Felix had extended what should have been a passing fancy into a lifelong sidetrack.

Felix sidestepped a rushing carriage and passed under the iron portcullis of the High Gate without looking up. Should he go see him? Should he try to make amends? Should he spit in his face? Should he flaunt the books that had been made of his life? That would show him! Or would it? The thought of seeing the old buzzard, even sick in his deathbed, was daunting. He'd never been able to look him in the eye. Even full of youthful confidence after the publishing of his first book of poems and being the toast of Altdorf University, Gustav had been able to make him feel like he was seven years old and had just wet the bed.

The deep bark of a cannon firing woke Felix out of his reverie. He looked up, wary. Had something happened? Was Nuln under attack? No one else seemed to have noticed. They continued on with their errands as if nothing had happened. Hadn't they heard? Had he imagined it?

Then he remembered. This was Nuln, forge of the Empire. The Imperial Gunnery School test fired new cannons several times a day. When he had lived here before, he had become so used to it that he too had never looked up from his daily round when they sounded.

He looked around him, seeing for the first time the streets he passed through. Nuln, outside the wall that separated the old city from the new, was a noisy, busy place. The war may have impoverished much of the rest of the Empire, but Nuln made cannons, guns and swords. It thrived in war. Everywhere he looked there was bustle and industry. Wagons hauled heavy loads of coal or saltpetre or finished guns through the maze of streets and tall, soot-blackened brick and timber houses. Grimy workers trudged wearily home from their shifts in the manufactories of the Industrielplatz. Fat merchants trundled by in palanquins, their bodyguards jogging in front and behind.

Sausage and pie sellers shouted their wares from carts fitted with sizzling grills, and the smell of cooking meat mixed with sewer stench and the acrid reek of smoke and black powder to create what was, in Felix's mind, the signature smell of Nuln.

But though Nuln's men of industry were doing well, the same could not be said for the lower classes. Those sizzling pies and sausages were selling for triple what they should have been, and looked to have been made of sweepings from the slaughterhouse floor. The stalls of the fruit sellers and costermongers that fringed the market squares were mostly bare, and the prices for the meagre produce on display were shocking. The press gangs of the state militias were out in force, and there were few able-bodied young men on the street.

On the other hand, there were more beggars than Felix could remember ever seeing in Nuln. They thronged the streets, and lifted their palms in every doorway. He saw whole families camped in alleys and courtyards.

Patrols of the city guard, uniformed in Nuln's colours of charcoal and yellow, sauntered through the shuffling crowd, eyes moving and truncheons swinging. Jugglers and singers jostled elbows with broadsheet sellers, doomsayers and demagogues on the street corners. Sisters of Shallya asked for alms for the upkeep of their hospitals and temples.

'The end times are upon us!' cried a wild-eyed Sigmarite ascetic who carried a hammer fashioned out of wood that was the size of an anvil. 'The wolves of ruin swarm down from the steppes to devour us all! Beg almighty Sigmar for forgiveness before it is too late!'

'We must send the children north!' wailed another, who wore nothing but a loincloth. 'Their purity and innocence is the shield that will turn the sword of Chaos! They are our hope and salvation!'

A group called the Ploughmen called for the shutting down of the foundries. 'We must turn our swords into ploughshares. We must make peace with our neighbours to the north.' They weren't getting much of a crowd.

Another group, The Silver Chalice, was calling for the closing of the Colleges of Magic and the death of all magicians in the Empire. 'The corruption comes from within!'

A young man in a mask that was a bright yellow headscarf with eye holes cut in it held aloft a lit torch while a similarly masked compatriot passed out cheaply printed leaflets. They wore tabards over their jerkins, emblazoned with a crude symbol of a flaming torch. 'The cleansing flame will burn away the corruption that chokes Nuln like the smoke from the foundries!' declaimed the youth. 'No more will the fat priests shear their flocks! No more will the forge owners and factors underpay the brave men who pour the iron that makes them rich! No more will the landlords raise rents on hovels not fit for dogs to live in! Raise the torch, brothers! Join the Brotherhood of the

Cleansing Flame and burn them out! Burn the city clean!'

As Felix watched, the masked men caught sight of the watch patrol pushing towards them and they quickly gathered up their leaflets and disappeared into an alley.

Felix continued on. As he got closer to the river and the area known as Shantytown, the buildings became flimsier and taller, and the streets – neatly cobbled within the old city and around the universities – were here unpaved swamps of mud and filth. Felix noticed the symbols of the various agitator groups scrawled more often on the walls of buildings the further he went – the wedge-shaped plough of the Ploughmen, the chalice of the Silver Chalice, the flaming torch of the Cleansing Flame. That last symbol made him shiver, for he remembered the fire that had burned this neighbourhood to the ground during the attack of the ratmen, all those years ago. He found it hard to believe that any organisation advocating flame as a tool of change would gain followers here, but one never knew. People had short memories.

At last, in the very heart of Shantytown, he came to a rundown and ramshackle tavern. The weathered sign over the door was painted with a picture of a pig with a blindfold tied around its head. A few rough mercenaries lounged on benches outside the narrow door, sipping ale and basking in the late summer sun. A pair of towering bouncers nodded to him as he approached.

Felix ducked through the low door and looked around the tavern's dim interior. Gotrek sat at the bar, his squat, massive form perched on a high barstool, his towering crest of red hair aflame in a solitary shaft of sunlight. He hunched forward, massive, muscular arms resting on the bar top, as Old Heinz, the owner of the Blind Pig and an old comrade from Gotrek's mercenary days, filled two tankards from a keg of ale. He handed one to Gotrek and they raised them solemnly.

'To Hamnir,' said Heinz.

'To Hamnir,' agreed Gotrek.

They drank deep, draining the tankards.

Heinz wiped his mouth with the back of a meaty hand. 'But he died well at least?' he asked.

Gotrek frowned and coughed into his mug.

'Aye,' said Felix, stepping forward and taking a seat beside the Slayer. 'He died well.'

'Good,' said Heinz, and turned to draw them all another pint.

Gotrek gave Felix a look that was almost gratitude. The Slayer didn't like to lie, but telling Heinz the truth obviously wasn't appealing either. Hamnir had not died well. He had died betraying his race, and it had been Gotrek that had killed him. This wasn't the first time Felix had saved him from telling this uncomfortable truth. He hoped it was the last.

Gotrek stuck a thick finger under his eyepatch and rubbed his empty socket. 'Heinz says the war will be won or lost at Middenheim. We leave tomorrow at dawn.'

'Right.' Felix sighed. So much for a few days with a roof over their heads. But he wasn't surprised. Gotrek had been like a hunting dog that had scented a fox ever since they had learned at Barak Varr that the hordes of Chaos had once again come down from the wastes to threaten the lands of men. Nothing was going to stop the Slayer from getting north to challenge another daemon.

'Remember the time Hamnir tried to save the entire library of Count Moragio while the orcs were breaking down the doors?' said Heinz as he set tankards in front of Gotrek and Felix. 'Never seen a dwarf so worried about a bunch of books. Mad, he was.'

'Aye,' grunted Gotrek. 'Mad.' He snatched his ale off the bar and stumped angrily off to sit in a dark corner.

Heinz peered quizzically after him with rheumy eyes. The old mercenary was still a big man, but old age had stooped his shoulders, and the bulk that had once been muscle now sagged off his bones. 'What's got into him?'

'Old wounds,' said Felix.

'Aye,' said Heinz, nodding sagely. 'I know the kind.'

'DID you SEE the burning today?' asked the harlot.

'What did you say?' shouted Felix.

It was later that same night. The Blind Pig was crowded now, and filled with noise and smoke and the reek of close packed bodies. Boisterous students from the universities and colleges yelled boasts and challenges at each other. Mercenaries and soldiers hunched around tables, telling tall tales at the top of their lungs. Apprentices and smoke-blackened iron workers from the forges across the river bantered with giggling harlots and barmaids eager to strip them of their pay. Slumming nobles' sons kept their backs to the wall and laughed too loudly as they tried to soak up the atmosphere without getting their clothes dirty. Tilean traders talked business with dwarf craftsmen in one corner. A halfling oversaw a dice game in another.

'The burning. Did you see it?' asked the girl, a chubby thing with her hair in red ringlets and rouge caking her round cheeks. 'One of the guards at the Gunnery School. The witch hunters found out he had a mouth under his left arm and burned him on Tower Isle this afternoon.'

'You don't say,' said Felix, disinterestedly.

The girl had squeezed in beside him at the bar hours ago, thinking him an easy mark, and he had fed her wine just to have something to do. Truth to tell, he would much rather have been upstairs in the room Heinz had given him, reading the books his brother had made from his journals, but Gotrek had sunk into one of his blacker moods and Felix had decided that it would be a good idea to stay nearby and keep an eye on him. The Slayer hadn't moved since he had walked away from Heinz, only drunk tankard after tankard of ale and stared all night at nothing with his single angry eye.

He had been this way since he had killed Hamnir deep below the mines of Karak Hirn, grimmer and angrier than Felix had ever known him. Gotrek never spoke of his feelings, so Felix didn't know what was going through his head, but seeing someone who had once been one's best friend succumb to the lure of Chaos and then killing him for it would be enough to make even the most cheerful soul bitter, and Gotrek hadn't exactly been a ray of sunshine to begin with.

'He screamed almost like a human when he burned,' said the girl.

'Who did?' asked Felix.

'The mutant. It made me shiver.'

'Very empathetic of you, I'm sure,' said Felix.

'What does emfetic mean?' asked the harlot. 'Is it something dirty?'

Felix didn't answer. He had heard someone say the word 'Slayer', and turned his head to find the speaker.

A group of drunk students, still in the long sleeve-less robes they wore to lectures, were staring openly at Gotrek.

A chinless one with thin blond hair was frowning. 'A Slayer?'

A dark-haired one with a haughty sneer nodded. 'Aye. I've read of them. They are dwarfs who have vowed to expunge some great shame by dying in combat with a terrible monster. There are trollslayers, dragonslayers, what-have-you slayers.'

Chinless guffawed. 'This one looks like a flagon slayer!' he said loudly. 'He's had his nose in that mug since we got here.'

The others burst out laughing at this witticism. Felix cringed and looked at Gotrek. Fortunately, it seemed the Slayer hadn't heard. Now if only the fools would pass on to another target all would be well.

It was not to be. The others liked Chinless's joke so much they felt the need to repeat it, louder.

'Flagonslayer! That's rich!'

'How about aleslayer?'

'Aye! Aleslayer, bane of the taproom!'

'Hoy, Aleshlayer!' called one with jug ears, his words slurring with drink. 'Shlay another flagon for ush! Show ush yer might!'

'Come now, fellows,' said Felix. He pried himself from the harlot and stepped forward, but it was too late. Gotrek had raised his head and fixed the students with a blank, baleful stare.

Most of them paused at that, suddenly aware that the bear they were poking wasn't dead after all. But Jug Ears was apparently dimmer, and drunker, than the rest. He giggled and pointed.

'Well at leash he'll never get crosh-eyed drunk. He only hash one eye!' He raised his glass in mock salute. 'Hail flagonshlayer! Mighty cyclopean drainer of kegsh!'

Gotrek stood, tankard in one hand, knocking the heavy oak table he sat at to the floor. 'What did you call me?'

Felix stepped between them. 'Easy, Gotrek. They're very drunk and very young. We don't want any trouble.'

'Speak for yourself, manling,' said Gotrek, pushing him gently but inexorably out of the way. 'Trouble is exactly what I want.'

The other students backed away uneasily as Gotrek stumped forward, but Jug Ears stood where he was, grinning foolishly. 'I dub thee Flagonshlayer! Aleshlayer! Pintshlayer!' He laughed. 'Thas' it! The pint-shized pintshlay–'

Gotrek's fist connected with Jug Ears's jaw with a crack like a gravestone snapping in two. The boy flew through the air and crashed into a table full of burly Hochland handgunners, knocking their drinks to the floor and soaking them all in ale. Felix's harlot squealed and ran, disappearing into the crowd.

The leader of the handgunners, a black-bearded giant of a man with leather bracers on both wrists, lifted the unconscious Jug Ears off the table by his shirtfront as the other students rabbited for the door. 'Who threw this toff?' he growled. His eyebrows dripped with ale.

'I did,' said Gotrek. He grabbed an entirely blameless smith's apprentice by the front of his leather apron. 'You want another?'

'I want these drinks paid for, is what I want,' said the giant. 'And a cleaning for my best uniform.'

'I'll clean the floor with it,' said Gotrek and, still holding his tankard in his left hand, hurled the apprentice with his right with less effort than Felix would have flung a sack of onions.

The apprentice hit the mercenary high in the chest, knocking him backward through the table and sending his Hochlanders diving in all directions. They leapt to their feet, roaring, and charged at the Slayer, fists and brass knuckles raised high. Gotrek ran to meet them, his drink held protectively behind him, bellowing incoherent insults.

Within seconds the whole tavern was fighting, violence splashing outward from Gotrek and the handgunners like ripples in a pond as elbows were bumped, drinks spilled, then insults and blows exchanged. The dwarfs and Tileans fought a gang of weaver's apprentices. Barmaids and harlots shrieked and dived for cover. A dozen dock workers scrapped with three nobles and their six bodyguards. Students of the university brawled with students of the School of Engineering. A company of Bretonnian crossbowmen seemed to be fighting each other. The halfling gambler rode the shoulders of a red-bearded Talabecman, banging on his skull with a pewter dice cup. Everywhere mugs flew, bottles smashed and furniture splintered. Old Heinz beat on the bar with an axe handle – roaring ineffectively for order while his bouncers grabbed the collars of anyone they could get their hands on and chucked them out of the front door.

Felix fought back to back with Gotrek in a ring of Hochlanders, cursing all the while. Another stupid bar fight over nothing. And Gotrek had started it. He should let him fight his own battles. This was the last thing he wanted to be doing. And yet, in the state Gotrek was in, one of these villains just might get in a lucky shot, and getting trounced in a tavern would do nothing for the Slayer's mood.

He ducked a black jack and rabbit-punched the mercenary who swung it in the kidneys. The man groaned and doubled up. Felix kneed him in the face. Gotrek back-fisted the captain, sending a spray of yellow teeth flying. The giant's knees buckled and he fell forward. Gotrek jumped back, holding his tankard out of the way. Another mercenary grabbed him around the neck, trying to strangle him. Gotrek reached up and caught him by the top knot and flung him over his shoulder into three others. They went down in a heap.

Four more leapt for the dwarf. Felix tripped one and shoulder blocked another. Gotrek kicked and elbowed the others to the ground.

The captain was up again, a long wooden bench raised over his head for a smashing blow. Gotrek lurched forward and punched up, driving his fist between the man's legs. The captain squeaked like a rat-man and tottered back, eyes wide.

All around the bar the fight was slowing down, the combatants too battered or too drunk to continue.

Heinz's hoarse bellow rose above the moans and groans. 'Who started this? Who smashed up my tap-room?'

The giant mercenary toppled backwards and crashed to the floor like a felled tree, revealing Gotrek, swaying in the centre of a pile of unconscious bodies, still holding his tankard of ale. He hadn't spilled a drop.

Heinz's brow lowered. 'Gurnisson. Did you start this?'

Gotrek drained his drink in one swallow, then smashed the tankard on the floor. 'And what if I did?' he asked.

'And you were bouncers here once.' Heinz shook his head, disgusted. 'Get out.'

Gotrek stumped towards him menacingly. 'And who's going to make me?'

The bouncers started moving in.

Felix stepped beside Gotrek and leaned down to speak in his ear. 'You don't want to fight old Heinz, do you? Your old companion? Your blood brother?'

Gotrek shrugged him off. 'Who says I don't?'

'*You* will, tomorrow morning,' said Felix. 'Come on. If you want to fight, let's go find a tavern where you don't know the owner. There's nobody left here worth fighting anyway.'

The Slayer stopped unsteadily and squinted around the room, taking in the crowd of groaning drunks and battered bouncers. He sneered. 'You're right, manling. Nothing here but a bunch of cowards. Let's find another place.' He turned and aimed himself at the door, then started forward, rolling like a sailor.

As he reached the door, Heinz called after him. 'It was a quiet twenty years, Gurnisson. Don't come back for another twenty.'

AFTER A QUARTER of an hour of meandering through the cramped, overhung streets of Shantytown – deserted at this late hour – with Gotrek muttering and cursing under his breath and changing his mind about which way they were going every few minutes, the Slayer stopped in a small square with a fountain in the centre. The fountain had once been grand – Magnus the Pious holding aloft the hammer of Sigmar with griffins at his feet spouting water into a circular pool. Now the pool was dry, the griffins' beaks cracked, revealing their copper pipes, and Magnus's hammer missing its head and most of its haft. The forms of sleeping beggars and vagrants clung to the walls of the surrounding buildings like dirty shadows.

Gotrek swayed for a long moment in the middle of the square, as if lost in thought, then stepped to the fountain and plopped down on the rim of the pool.

Felix joined him. He was feeling a bit worse for wear and it was a relief to sit. There hadn't been many opportunities for drinking on the road from Karak Hirn, and all the unaccustomed alcohol had gone to his head somewhat.

Gotrek lay back and looked up at the sky, still muttering to himself.

Felix frowned down at him. 'If you want to sleep, we should find an inn.'

'We'll find an inn, manling,' said Gotrek, with every indication of lucidity. 'I'm just thinking.'

'Fine,' said Felix. After a moment he found himself lying back too. The wind was picking up and it was getting too cool for comfort, but lying there was very peaceful. Mannslieb was full and bright, casting a delicate silver glamour over rooftops that by day would have looked shabby and poorly patched. Stars shimmered in the sky like fireflies pinned to black velvet. Felix picked out the constellations. The Hammer, the Wolf, the Dove. His eyes closed, and after a long moment opened again. Then closed again. His breathing grew heavier.

He fought to open his eyes again. 'We really should find some place–' He stopped, blinking up at the sky. A huge black shadow was pushing across his vision, blotting out the stars. Now it was eclipsing Mannslieb! He gaped, frozen with dread and confusion. What was it? Was he dreaming? Was it some strange swift storm? Was it a daemon come to devour them all? Was it...

Gotrek sat bolt upright beside him, staring straight up. 'It's the *Spirit of Grungni*!'

TWO

GOTREK AND FELIX caromed through the twisting, uncooperative streets of Shantytown like lunatics, trying to keep the receding airship in sight. It was heading due east, and all the streets seemed to head every direction but. They were constantly having to zigzag and double back as the black oblong shape disappeared behind tall, gabled tenements and massive crenellated warehouses, only to appear again as they turned a corner and found it drifting away from them above the moon-washed rooftops.

Harlots and other late-night walkers shied away as Gotrek and Felix staggered drunkenly past, shouting commands and obscenities at the sky. An undermanned watch patrol almost moved to block them, then thought better of it and let them pass. Cats and dogs and rats scurried into the shadows at their approach.

The *Spirit of Grungni* led them out of Shantytown and through the government buildings and trading houses of the Neuestadt towards the Universitat. There the streets became wider and the way easier, and the airship seemed to be slowing. This was good, for Gotrek and Felix were slowing too. Felix was gasping and sucking wind, weakened by too much wine. Gotrek showed no signs of losing his breath, but he was groaning and holding his belly with each step. Felix thought he could actually hear the ale sloshing inside the dwarf, but it was probably his own stomach he heard.

At last, with a roar they could hear from the ground, the airship reversed engines and came to a slow halt over the high grey stone turrets of the massive, castle-like central building of the College of Engineering. Lights on the roof underlit the brass gondola and Felix could just see ropes dropping from it.

Gotrek and Felix fetched up panting and gasping against the College's intricate iron gates a few moments later. Four wary guards stepped out from a guard house just inside, spears at the ready. More watched from the tops of the fortified walls.

'Mak…' said Gotrek. 'Mak…' then vomited a vast quantity of ale all over the wrought iron bars.

'Hoy!' said the guard captain, stepping forward. 'Get away, you filthy drunks! I'm not cleaning that up. Go home and sleep it off!'

Gotrek's hand shot through the bars and caught the captain by the belt, then pulled him down to his level. 'Makaisson,' hissed Gotrek, as the other guards shouted and stepped forward, drawing their weapons. 'Fetch Malakai Makaisson. Tell him Gotrek Gurnisson wants to see him.'

The other guards shouted at Gotrek to let their captain go, but Gotrek wrapped his powerful fingers around the man's neck and he frantically waved them off.

'It's too late,' squeaked the captain. 'College is closed for the night. No visitors. You'll have to come back in the morning.'

Gotrek shook him. 'Fetch him now or I'll come in there and feed you your sword, pommel first.' He shoved him back into his men.

The captain choked and recovered himself as his men started forward again. For a moment it looked like he was going to let them try to chase Gotrek off, then he reconsidered and called them back.

'Leave him, but watch him,' he said, massaging his bruised throat. 'Brugel, go ask Professor Makaisson if he'll see a filthy drunk named Gotrek Gurnisson.'

AFTER WHAT SEEMED like several hours to Felix's foggy brain, he and Gotrek looked up at the sound of approaching footsteps. Out of the shadow of the entry of the college's massive central building came a small squad of guards escorting a short, broad figure in a thick, fleece-lined leather jerkin. He wore a peculiar leather cap with goggles pushed up over his shaggy brows, and a slot at the top to make room for a short crest of bright red hair. It looked like he had just come off the airship.

'Whur's the liar claimin' tae be Gotrek son of Gurni?' spat the dwarf in his strange, thick accent. 'Whur's the eejit dinnae know the Daemonslayer's been deid these seventeen–'

He broke off in mid-sentence as he caught sight of Gotrek standing at the gate. He stopped and stared. 'Weel noo, ye look like him, right enough.' He shot a glance at Felix. 'And this looks like young Felix an' aw.' He crossed his arms over his massive chest. 'But Maximillian Schrieber said ye went intae some hell-gate in Sylvania and never returned. How am ah tae be sure ye ain't some daemons of the void in disguise?'

Gotrek roared and plucked his axe from his back. He slashed left and right, making a big X in the air with it, then held it at the ready and stumped towards the gate, shoulders lowered. 'Are you calling me a daemon, Malakai son of Makai?'

The guards shouted and advanced, lowering their spears. The captain drew a pistol from his belt and aimed it through the bars, but Malakai just grinned and waved them back. 'Put it awa', boys. Put it awa' and open yon gates. There's but the one who can wield yon axe!'

The guards hesitated, but at last their captain motioned them forward and they drew the bolts and pushed on the bars.

Malakai threw his arms wide as the gates swung out and Gotrek and Felix stepped in. 'Gotrek Gurnisson, I'm grieved tae see ye hivnae met yer doom, but ah'm glad tae see ye no' the less.'

He clasped Gotrek's hand and slapped him on the shoulder.

'Well met, Malakai Makaisson,' said Gotrek gruffly. 'I hope you have some ale here. I lost some just now and I've got a bit of a thirst.'

* * *

'WHY AM AH here?' Malakai shrugged as he lit an oil lamp and set it on a low desk. 'Ach weel, wae one thing an' another, I'm no' welcome in the dwarf holds at the minute, so here ah came an' offered ma services. Made me a professor, if ye can believe it.'

Gotrek and Felix sat on an unmade day bed in the middle of a vast, high ceilinged workshop that was apparently Malakai's office, located on the third floor of the college's main building. It was chilly in the room, for it had no roof and the east wall was only half-built. Scaffolding rose before the unfinished wall, and building stones and sacks of mortar were stacked at its foot. Night air and moonlight poured in through it, while high overhead, a canvas tarpaulin snapped in the breeze like the sail of a ship.

In the moonglow beyond the yellow light of the lamp, Felix could make out the looming shapes of partially assembled machines, strange weapons, odd bits of pipe, scrap metal and glass tubing, short-legged tables covered with scribbled-upon sheets of vellum, and what looked like an enormous metal horse. Felix thought he recognised one of the machines as a drill of some sort, and another as a lathe, but the rest were far beyond his understanding.

Malakai pottered about among it all like a gardener seeing to his prize roses, straightening and checking and adjusting things all around the room, and chattering all the while.

'Ah'm sorry for the state o' the place, but ah heard the skaven made a wee mess o' things here at the college some twenty years past and they hiv niver got around to fixing it up again.'

'Er, yes,' said Felix, face flushing. 'We'd heard about that.' *And had a hand in the destruction*, he thought guiltily. He didn't say anything, however. The whole incident was a bit embarrassing.

'That'll change noo ah'm here,' Malakai continued. 'Have this place straight in a jiffy. And better than it was afore.'

'So Max Schrieber survived Sylvania,' said Gotrek, sipping the mug of ale Malakai had found for him. 'And Snorri Nosebiter?'

'Oh aye,' said Malakai. 'They both of them made it back to Praag, ready t'fight the hordes come spring, just as ah wis. But it niver happened. The marauders milled outside the city for a few mair weeks, then just turned aroon an' went back hame. Seemed tae've lost all heart, somehow.' He sounded sad at the memory. 'Max thought it might hae somethin' tae do with the vanishin' of them tae wee sorcerers, but nobody ever really learn't the why of it.'

'Are Max and Snorri still alive?' asked Felix.

'Max is – weel when ah saw him four days ago he wus. He's at Middenheim, wi' the defenders, where ah've just come frae.' His brow creased. 'As tae Snorri, ah dinnae noo for certain. After the spring thaw came tae Kislev that year, he went aff wi' some Empire mercenaries, chasin' a herd o' beastmen south towards the Middle Mountains. No' heard o' him since. Grimnir grant that he met his doom.' He looked pensive for a moment, then shrugged and grinned. 'But enough about aw that. Whur hae ye been these seventeen years? I'll wager that's a tale worth the telling.'

'Well,' said Felix, frowning. 'I'm not sure where to begin.' He looked over at Gotrek and saw that the

Slayer was lying back on the day bed, his one eye closed, snoring gently.

Malakai looked over and clicked his tongue. 'Och, the laddie's fallen asleep. Ach weel, no' a bad idea at that. Save yer story, young Felix. It'll keep. Come on. Ah'll find ye a bed.'

FELIX WOKE WITH the familiar feeling of opening his eyes in an unfamiliar place that he had experienced so many times in his travels with Gotrek. He was in a small, clean, cell-like room, lying on a narrow but comfortable bed. His head pounded and, strangely, the pounding seemed to echo through the waking world. For a long, disorienting moment he had no idea where he was. The place was too nice to be a jail. He tried to think back. There had been a tavern, and a fight, and then a drunken walk. He had laid down beneath a fountain. Had he fallen asleep there? No! The *Spirit of Grungni*!

Suddenly it all flooded back. He was in the dormitory of the College of Engineering. The pounding in his head was from last night's drinking. The pounding that shook the room was the morning artillery practice at the Imperial Gunnery School, a few streets away. Felix sat up and rubbed his temples, groaning. Did they have to start so early? It was hardly civilized.

After pulling on his boots and breeches and finding the wash room and water closet, he asked directions of a fresh-faced and much too chipper engineering student, then shuffled at last back into Malakai's enormous workroom. Felix squinted painfully in the blaze of sunlight that streamed through the unfinished wall, and looked around. A work table had been cleared off

42   *Nathan Long*

and Malakai and Gotrek were wolfing down a breakfast of eggs, sausage, bacon, black bread, ham, griddle cakes, pale lager, and that vile Tilean import that some called the black oil of Nuln, coffee.

Gotrek's appetite seemed none the worse for last night's excesses, but Felix's stomach churned at the sight of all the greasy food.

'Welcome, young Felix!' called Malakai, much too loud. 'Sit doon and dig in before Gurnisson eats the lot.'

Felix fought down the urge to heave. He wiped his clammy brow. 'Is… is there some tea, perhaps?'

'Ah'll have one of the lads brew up a pot,' said Malakai, then shouted towards the back of the room. 'Petr! A pot of Cathay fur oor guest!'

Felix clutched his head, certain it was going to shatter.

A moonfaced youth with wild blond hair and a chinstrap beard poked his head up from the innards of a dismantled steam tank. He had wide, watery blue eyes that he blinked rapidly. 'Aye, professor,' he said. 'Right away.' He clambered out of the tank, but caught his foot on a valve and sprawled face-first on the floor. He was up in an instant, blood leaking from his nose. 'No harm done,' he piped. 'No harm done.' He scurried out of the room, bumping into a telescope as he went.

Malakai shook his head. 'Poor wee lad. My best student. Can set the calibrations on a pressure gauge near as weel as a dwarf, but cannae see past his haund, and he could trip o'er a dust mote.' He chuckled as he stuffed a chunk of ham in his mouth. 'He'll be coming to Middenheim to help oot in the engine room. But he's noo allowed on the bridge. He'd wreck us.'

Gotrek looked up, his single eye bright. 'You're flying to Middenheim?'

'Aye. The Imperial Gunnery School has asked me tae tak a shipment of cannon there.'

'You're taking me,' said Gotrek. 'I want to be there before the end.'

'O' course,' said Malakai. 'Always happy tae help a Slayer find his doom.'

'Can we leave today?' asked Gotrek.

Malakai chuckled. 'Much as ah'd like it, laddie, nae. The last cannon won't be test-fired till tomorrow morning. We'll leave jist as soon as it's loaded.'

Gotrek grunted unhappily, but Felix hid a grateful smile. Another night in a proper bed would not go amiss.

'Ye'll still get there mair than a fortnight quicker than if ye marched,' said Malakai, amused.

Petr rushed into the room with a teapot in one hand and a cup and saucer in the other. He wove successfully around a jewellers stove, but his feet got tangled in a block and tackle and he flew forward with a cry. He managed to twist as he fell and landed on his shoulder, saving the teapot and cup from destruction, but slopping scalding tea all over his hands.

He sprang up again and set the teapot and cup before Felix, wincing. 'Sorry! Sorry!' he said. His hands were lobster red.

'Go soak those in cold water, laddie,' said Malakai. 'Ye dinnae want blisters.'

'Aye, professor,' said Petr.

He hurried away. Felix couldn't bear to watch him go.

'Cack-handed pillock,' muttered Malakai. He turned to Gotrek and Felix with a sigh. 'When ye've finished wi' yer breakfast, ah'll take you o'er to the Gunnery School tae meet Lord Groot, who runs the place. As the trip is Imperial business, he has final approval on all ma crew. But dinna worry.' He winked. 'Ah'll put in a good word for ye.'

IF THE COLLEGE of Engineering was big, the Imperial Gunnery School was enormous, a vast complex of workshops, firing ranges, forges, and dormitories surrounding the soaring black granite majesty of the school building itself, which rose above the city like an unimaginably large engine of war, all spires and spikes and saw-toothed crenellations. Fearsome soot-blackened gargoyles jutted from every corner and cornice. Tall, narrow, red-glassed windows gleamed between towering buttresses like the vents in the iron door of some infernal furnace.

Lord Julianus Groot did not look like he should be in charge of such a forbidding place. A thick, cheerful, pot-bellied man with greying mutton chops and a few wisps of hair trailing across his round, bald head, Groot looked more like a village smith than the High Chancellor of the Imperial Gunnery School, which was his official title. He wore a singed leather apron over his black brocade robes of office, and had his trailing sleeves tucked into heavy leather gloves.

'Any friend of Malakai Makaisson's is a friend of mine,' he said, crushing Felix's hand in a powerful grip. 'A better ally the Empire could not have.'

Felix and Gotrek stood with Lord Groot and Malakai in a sweltering forge room where ranks of sweating smiths pounded and shaped steel on regimented rows of anvils as overseers moved among them, observing and criticising. It did nothing for Felix's headache.

Felix was surprised to hear the chancellor speaking with the flat, common accent of the Handelbezirk – the mercantile neighbourhood that was the heart of Nuln's ever-spreading network of trade. He would have expected a man with a title to speak in the more refined and cultured speech of the nobility. Perhaps Groot had bought his way into his title. Rumour had it that the Countess had done stranger things for money.

'It'll be good to have seasoned warriors escorting our guns,' he said, gripping Gotrek's hand. 'When you're up against the Ruinous Powers even a flying ship isn't safe. Some of them beasties have wings. You'll have some sorcerous help too, Makaisson.'

'Oh?' said Malakai, squinting suspiciously. 'And jist who might that be?'

Groot turned and called back into the haze of smoke that veiled the room. 'Magus Lichtmann, come meet your travelling companions!'

Gotrek, Felix and Malakai looked up. Felix wasn't sure what he expected. Some malefic figure striding out of the smoke with glowing eyes? A wizened old man in a pointy hat? What he saw was a tall, beardless man of middle age, bent over an anvil, observing intently as a smith shaped a cannon fitting. He glanced up and firelight winked off his spectacles. 'Hmmm? Oh. Terribly sorry, my dear Groot.'

The magus picked his way through the forges to the chancellor. He was thin to the point of being skeletal, with a prominent throat apple, a weak chin, and a beaked nose beneath a mushroom cap of reddish brown hair. He wore the orange and red robes of the Bright College, and like Groot, he protected his attire with a sooty leather apron. His spectacles were made of delicate steel wire, and his eyes, behind them, were green with flecks of gold.

'Terribly sorry,' he said again in a clear, educated voice as he nodded around at them all. 'Julianus and I have been attempting to develop a new alloy, using magical flame to smelt together metals at temperatures impossible to achieve with mundane fire alone. I was just observing how our latest sample behaved under the hammer.' He smiled at Groot. 'Very malleable, Julianus, but not yet as strong as it could be, I believe.'

'I'll have a look in a moment, Waldemar,' said Groot. He turned to the others. 'Professor Makaisson, Slayer Gurnisson, Herr Jaeger, may I present Magus Waldemar Lichtmann, a Magister of the Bright College, and also an engineer of great renown.'

Magus Lichtmann bowed and extended his left hand, and it was only then that Felix noticed that the magus didn't have a right hand. His right sleeve was pinned up just below the elbow. 'A distinct pleasure, professor,' he said, shaking Malakai's hand. 'Your advances in engineering are well known to me.'

He grinned sheepishly as he turned to shake Gotrek's hand and then Felix's. 'Apologies for the left-handed handshake,' he said. 'People often find it a bit unnerving. I lost the right in a fire. Highly embarrassing for a bright wizard, but I was young then, and hadn't yet learned control.'

Malakai raised an uneasy eyebrow. 'I hope ye have the noo. Airships are a wee bit flammable.'

The Bright Wizard laughed, a loud, horsy bray. 'Oh yes, I've gotten a bit better since then, thank you. I can keep my flames to myself.'

'Magus Lichtmann is going to Middenheim to help in the fighting,' said Groot.

'I am very much looking forward to it,' said Lichtmann. 'It has been a long time since I have been in battle, and never anything on this scale. But a man of conscience cannot, at a time like this, continue to hide in the halls of academia. He must act. He must do his part for his homeland and his people. And I am hoping to put some of the new ideas that Groot and I have been developing to the test of war.'

'Weel, yer welcome aboard, magister,' said Malakai. 'Ah'll be happy to hiv someone tae blether wae. This alloy sounds interestin'.'

'It certainly is,' said Lichtmann, his eyes brightening. 'It's a simple idea really, but hard to execute without a Bright Wizard's ability to control the temperature of fire. You see...'

As Lichtmann began to explain – and Felix's eyes began to glaze over – a young man in the colours of the college poked his head through the door of the workshop, saw Groot, and hurried to his side, his face tight with tension. 'My lord,' he murmured in the chancellor's ear. 'Might I speak with you?'

Groot nodded and turned to the others. 'Would you excuse me a moment?'

He stepped away and listened as the student whispered urgently in his ear. Felix and Gotrek waited, sweating in the heat, while Magus Lichtmann continued to babble to Malakai about melting temperatures and tensile strength, whatever that was.

After a moment Groot nodded and said, 'Aye, that's bad,' then rattled off a rapid series of orders and sent the youth running back the way he had come.

The chancellor sighed and returned to his guests. 'Sorry about the interruption. There's been a theft. I'm afraid your flight might be delayed, Malakai.'

'What?' barked Gotrek. His single eye blazed.

'Whit happened?' asked the engineer.

'A barge full of gunpowder was stolen during the night,' said Groot. 'Gunpowder meant for the cannons you will be carrying. The Dwarf Black Powder Guild delivered it yesterday to our landing near Glory Bridge in preparation for loading it onto the *Spirit of Grungni* tomorrow. It was under heavy guard all night, but by morning the guards had vanished along with the barge and the powder.' He shrugged and scratched his bald head violently. 'Wish they'd told me sooner, but they wasted two hours running about seeing if someone from the City Council had ordered the barge moved.'

'You can't leave without the powder?' asked Felix.

'The cannon are useless wi' no powder tae fire them, lad,' growled Malakai. 'Wi'out it they're jus' pretty pieces of iron, an' no reason tae take 'em to Midden-heim.'

'Sabotage,' said Magus Lichtmann. 'This is vile. Someone has done this to weaken the defences of the Fauschlag.'

'It's worse than that,' said Groot. 'The fiends could have done that by setting fire to the barge and blow-ing up the powder. Instead they've stolen it. That means that, whoever they are, they plan to use the powder for their own purposes.'

'And I'm guessin' it won' be tae make fireworks,' said Malakai, grimly.

THREE

A STRONG WIND knocked cold spray off the oily waves of the Reik and blew the pungent stinks of the Industrielplatz across the water. Felix wrinkled his nose and fought down nausea. He smelled burning oil, sulphur, tanning hides, rendering fat, dead fish, and other odours he couldn't name and didn't care to learn the source of. Out in the centre of the river where the current was swift, long, flat barges and high-prowed merchantmen manoeuvred to and from the main docks, further west. Gulls screamed overhead, much too loud for a man in his condition.

Lord Groot had asked Malakai and Magus Lichtmann to accompany him to the river to view the site where the theft had occurred, and Gotrek and Felix had tagged along for want of anything better to do. Now they were waiting while Groot and Malakai and Lichtmann and a few other members of the Gunnery

School argued with a gaggle of city officials and a representative of the Dwarf Black Powder Guild on the embankment above the stone landing from which the barge had been stolen the night before.

Felix leaned dully on a piling off to one side, still suffering from his hangover, and watched Gotrek prowl restlessly about on the landing below him, looking down into the water and examining the pilings intently.

'I find it very suspicious,' a trim man in the colours of the city watch was saying. 'The barge was tied up here, in the open, and yet there were no witnesses to its theft, and the crew and the guards have not been found.' He sniffed. 'They were Gunnery School guards, yes?'

Lord Groot drew himself up. 'Surely you can't be suggesting that our guards stole the barge.'

'Not at all,' said the man, in a tone that made it clear that he was indeed suggesting that. 'I just find it peculiar, is all.' His name was apparently Adelbert Wissen, the Ward Captain of the Neuestadt, a position that gave him authority over every watch station north of the river and south of the Altestadt wall. He held himself like he thought he had authority over the winds, the tides and the movement of the sun – a handsome, black-haired dandy in an immaculately tailored uniform and polished steel breastplate, with the haughty, damn-your-eyes look of one noble born. Felix was sorely tempted to splash mud on his perfectly polished boots. 'What need for guards if the powder had been unloaded at once? Then the theft would not have occurred.'

'Didn't I just tell you that we are forbidden by edict of the Countess to store so much in the school?' asked

Groot, exasperated. 'Would you have me break the law? And why are you wasting time talking to me? Why aren't you looking for the barge. Surely it can't have vanished.'

'I have men looking for it on both sides of the river,' said Wissen. 'The situation is well in hand.'

'What I want to know is, will I have to pay twice for the same powder,' said a pinch-mouthed older man in chocolate velvet and a mink cloak. 'I only agreed to finance these guns once. If there is more outlay now I will have to charge Middenheim more interest.'

'If you think we're going to give you free powder when you've gone and lost what we've just sold you, you've got another thing coming!' barked a stout red-bearded dwarf in green doublet and brown boots. 'Carelessness, I call it.'

'What patriotism, Lord Pfaltz-Kappel,' said Magus Lichtmann, gesturing with his single hand. 'And such a spirit of cooperation, Guildmaster Firgigsson. It is so heartening to see the peoples of the Empire putting aside their petty grievances and coming together to help fight our common enemy in this time of war.'

Neither the noble or the dwarf seemed to note the sarcasm in his voice.

'I've done my part,' said Lord Pfaltz-Kappel. 'You'd have no cannons at all were it not for me. It would be just like the dwarfs to steal the powder back and make us buy it twice. Gold-hungry little misers.'

'Who are you calling miser, you tightfisted old penny pincher?' retorted Firgigsson. 'I marked down my price almost to half because it was going to the aid of Middenheim. Most like you stole it so you could get two barges for the price of one!'

'Why dinna ye leave the name callin' fur later?' said Malakai, dryly. 'Shouldnae ye be decidin' what yer goin' tae dae about findin' the powder and them what stole it?'

'Agitators stole it,' said Ward Captain Wissen. 'And I do not doubt they mean to use it. I have sent to the Countess and the High Constable to ask that men be placed around the granaries and the palace. And judging by events, perhaps some men should be assigned to the Gunnery School as well, since they don't seem able to mount their own defence.'

Felix saw Gotrek's shoulders tense as the argument got louder and louder. Finally he stomped up the stairs and glared at them. 'Shut up!' he bellowed.

The men all turned to him, looks of surprise and outrage on their faces. Malakai grinned.

Ward Captain Wissen put a hand to his polished breastplate. 'You dare speak to a commander of the watch in such a–'

Gotrek cut him off. 'What colour was this barge?'

The men looked at each other, confused.

Guildmaster Firgigsson raised a shaggy eyebrow. 'It was red and blue, Slayer,' he said. 'With a stripe of gold between. Our guild colours, if it's any business of yours.'

'You interrupted us for that?' sneered Lord Pfaltz-Kappel. 'Groot, is this person a guest of yours?'

Gotrek ignored them as their babbling erupted anew and stumped back down the stairs. Felix followed him, curious. The Slayer began looking at the pilings again, muttering 'red gold blue, red gold blue,' over and over.

Felix stared at him, concerned. Was the Slayer still drunk? Had he gone mad at last?

'Ha!' Gotrek raised his head, grinning. 'Red gold blue!' He turned to Felix. 'Look here, manling. The paint from the barge has scraped off onto the pilings.'

Felix leaned out over the water and looked at the river side of the rough wooden posts. They were covered in faint streaks of paint – layer upon layer of red, green, white, black, blue, yellow, grey and brown. 'Uh, I see red, gold and blue. But I see other colours too. How can you…?'

'Humans are blind,' growled Gotrek. He stabbed his blunt fingers at three points on the post. 'Here, here and here. The red, gold and blue are over the other colours, and much fresher.'

Felix shrugged. 'I'll take your word for it. But what good does it do us?'

'Blind and thick-skulled,' Gotrek snorted. He pointed to the white-capped water. 'Look at that chop. I'll wager its been that way since the wind freshened last night. No matter where the thieves tied up the powder barge, it will have left its mark.' He looked west. 'Now all we have to do is check every dock and tie-up down the river until we find red, gold and blue again.'

Felix laughed. 'Is that all? That could take days.'

'It better not,' Gotrek grunted.

'Why don't we tell Ward Captain Wissen,' said Felix. 'It'll take less time if we have the watch looking.'

Gotrek spat into the water. 'Do you think they see any better than you? I want to be away tonight, not a month from now. Besides…' he shot a glare up at Captain Wissen. 'I don't care for that one's manners.'

The Slayer stomped up the stairs and started off down the embankment without a word or gesture to Malakai or Groot, his head down like a bloodhound's. Felix sighed and started after him. Gotrek was one to talk about manners.

FIVE HOURS LATER they were still looking at pilings. Gotrek had examined every inch of the riverside; every landing and tie-up, every side branch and canal, and the underside of every bridge, and they were only just now reaching the official commercial docks that bordered Shantytown. Felix would not have believed there were so many nooks and crannies and hidden backwaters branching from the Reik's stone banks. His back ached from bending over docksides. His eyes hurt. He was hungry and he needed a drink.

'This is impossible. We'll never find it,' he said.

'That's the trouble with humans,' muttered Gotrek. 'They're not thorough. No patience.'

'That's because we don't live for five hundred years.'

The commercial docks stuck out into the river like cracked grey fingers. The weathered wood boomed hollowly under their heels as they paced each one, out and back, checking both sides. Felix didn't see any red, gold and blue paint, but he saw another crudely drawn torch symbol scrawled on a piling. He had seen scores of them during their search, as well as the symbols of the other agitator groups. They were all over the waterfront.

Longshoremen and carters stepped around Gotrek and Felix as they lugged goods from ship to wagon and from wagon to ship. Cargo guards glared at them as if expecting them to steal something or try to stow away. Felix felt foolish and in the way. This was a bad plan. It wouldn't work. The sun was setting behind the looming ranks of brick warehouses that fronted the river. Soon it would be too dark to see. Felix's aching eyes were already having difficulty distinguishing between the faint streaks of paint. That one, for instance. Was it red or orange? And that one, gold or green? And the one below it, blue or black?

'Red, gold and blue!' rasped Gotrek. He got down on one knee and leaned forward, sniffing like a bloodhound. After a moment he ran a stubby finger down a crack between two warped planks. Grains of black stuck to his fingertip. He sniffed them. 'Black-powder,' he said. He lifted his head and looked around, taking in the ships, the warehouses, the saw-tooth silhouettes of Shantytown tenements rising behind them.

Felix groaned. If the barrels had been offloaded here they could be anywhere by now. And if Gotrek was going to be 'thorough', it could be a very long night.

'You,' said Gotrek, to a passing longshoreman. 'Did you see someone unloading barrels from a red and blue barge here this morning?'

'This morning?' said the man, without breaking stride. 'I was asleep. I start at sunset.'

Gotrek cursed and strode towards the warehouses, glaring speculatively at the men they passed.

Felix followed. 'Let me try,' he said, afraid Gotrek's brusqueness was going to land them in a fight.

He looked around the dockside. There was a tavern here somewhere. He remembered it from his days carousing with the other sewer jacks, when he and Gotrek had last lived in Nuln. Ah, there it was.

A placard painted with a laughing bear standing on a red and yellow ball swung in the breeze just a few hundred yards to the east, and as he had expected, half a dozen shifty looking men lounged around outside it, sipping from leather jacks and watching the comings and goings of the docks with eagle eyes.

Felix felt in his belt pouch until he found a gold crown, one of his last, then sidled up to a likely looking villain with a three day beard and a greasy forelock over one eye.

'Evening, brother,' Felix said, twirling the coin in his fingers. 'Were you here this morning?'

The man turned and stared at the rotating coin. 'Could have been.'

'Did you see some men unloading some barrels from a red and blue barge at the dock over there?' He pointed with the hand that held the coin.

Forelock looked at Felix's face for the first time, and his eyes went as blank as buttons. 'I don't see nothing for no jagger.' He turned away and started into the tavern.

Gotrek grabbed the man before he reached the door. He spun him around and slammed him against the wall, holding his axe an inch from his forelock. 'Do you see this axe?'

The man choked, face pale and eyes wide. The other men stood up from their benches, crying out and reaching for daggers. Felix drew his runesword and faced them. The men paused, considering their chances, then shrugged and slouched with feigned nonchalance into the tavern.

'Please don't kill me,' mewled Forelock.

Gotrek jerked his bearded chin towards Felix. 'Answer his question.'

'But… but they'll kill me.'

'I kill you now. They kill you later. Take your pick.'

Forelock swallowed. Sweat ran down his brow. 'I-I-It was Big Nod's boys! Offloaded this morning 'fore dawn, then set the barge adrift down river.'

'Where are they?'

'I can't…' The man hesitated, then his eyes came back to the axe. 'Cold Hole Lane, by the dog pit. Just follow the docks until…'

Gotrek jerked him away from the wall and shoved him forward. 'Take us there!'

'But they'll see me!' pleaded the man.

'They'll see you dead if you don't move.'

Forelock bit his lip, miserable, but then turned and led the way through the twilight gloom. Felix trailed behind Gotrek, unreasonably annoyed that the villain had marked him as coming from wealth. How had he guessed? It had been ages since Felix had been wealthy. His clothes were as ragged as those of any man in Shantytown – worse in fact. Then he understood. His voice. He still spoke like an educated man. He had been so long out of the Empire that he had forgotten how much accent mattered here.

FORELOCK BROUGHT THEM to a cobbled square that abutted the river. The fish market was closing up for the day. Fishwives and whelk sellers dumped their heads and bones and shells in the river and gossiped as they packed up their carts. All along the north edge of the square wide ramps sank down into the ground, angling back under it. At the bottom of each ramp was a high, wide, arched door, open, but covered with soiled leather curtains. Men rolled carts and barrows up and down the ramps. Though he had never been in one before, Felix knew what they were – commercial cold cellars, built with one wall against the river so that it would transfer its constant chill to them. The cellars were used to store ice, ale, fish and other perishables.

Forelock stopped at the west end of the square and pointed, his hand shaking. 'The third one in. That's Nod's. I don't dare go no farther. They'd see me.'

Gotrek looked at him suspiciously, then sneered and pushed him aside. 'Run away, then.'

He started forward. Felix joined him.

'Hoy,' came Forelock's voice from behind them. 'What about that Karl?'

Felix sighed, then flipped the coin over his shoulder.

Gotrek stopped at the top of the third ramp. A sign over the door said Helder's Ice House. It looked no more criminal than the others. Men were lowering a fully laden ale wagon down the ramp using a block and tackle. Others were sliding still struggling sturgeon down a wet canvas chute to men at the bottom who gaffed them with billhooks and flopped them onto a low cart.

A set of shallow stairs went down one side of the ramp. Gotrek and Felix walked down them and pushed through the leather curtains. It was dim inside, and cold. Haloed torches glowed in the moist air and Felix could see his breath. As his eyes grew accustomed to the gloom, he saw that the cellar was one long, cavernous tunnel that ran under the market square above, all the way to the river wall. The tunnel

was about thirty feet wide, with a double row of crumbling stone columns forming an aisle down the
centre. Crates and barrels were piled to the left and
right of the aisle, pushed up against what Felix at first
thought were towering stacks of baled hay. Then he
saw that the bales were blocks of ice, wrapped in hay
to keep them from melting. The entire room was
lined, floor to ceiling, with walls of ice. Below the
arched ceiling was a lattice of wooden beams and
struts. These supported a crane and winch that could
be moved the whole length of the tunnel to facilitate
the loading and unloading of carts.

A second ale wagon was being unloaded as they
entered – huge man-high kegs winched up and swung
across, then set down gently on top of others. To the
wagon's left, men in winter coats were laying the
twitching sturgeon in beds of crushed ice while,
deeper in the tunnel, other men climbed all over the
piles of crates, shouting and whistling to each other as
they placed inventory or cut ice from the great blocks.

Gotrek marched up to a burly bearded man who
stood next to the ale wagon, checking a manifest.
'Where's Big Nod?' he growled.

The man looked down at him, sizing him up, then
shrugged and turned back to the wagon. 'Never heard
of him.'

Gotrek punched him in the stomach, smashing the
air of out him in a rush. The man collapsed to his
knees, white and wheezing.

Gotrek grabbed him by the beard and yanked his
head up. 'Where's Big Nod?'

'Get… get stuffed,' whispered the man.

Gotrek slapped him to the ground.

Felix winced. Violence was all very well if the man was a thief, but what if he really never had heard of Big Nod? What if the weasel with the greasy forelock had lied to them? All over the underground room men were turning to look at them. Some moved between them and the door.

'Hie!' came a piercing voice. 'What's the trouble?'

Felix looked over his shoulder. A ginger-haired halfling with bushy mutton chops stood in the door of an office, hands on his hips. An enormous man with pig eyes and a slack jaw stood behind him, scratching himself idly.

'Where's Big Nod?' said Gotrek.

'Y've got the wrong place,' said the halfling. 'No one here by that name. Now away with ye before I call the watch.'

The workmen edged closer, hefting billhooks and cudgels.

Gotrek strode forward. 'Where's the black powder? Where are you hiding it?'

'Uh-oh, Nod,' said Pig-Eyes, dully. 'They know about the powder.'

The halfling's cheek twitched, and he kicked Pig-Eyes in the shin. 'Shut yer pie hole, ye cloth-headed orc!'

Pig-Eye cringed away. 'Sorry, Nod. Sorry.'

The halfling shot a nod towards the doors. They began to creak closed. 'Right, lads,' he said, drawing an icepick as long as his arm. 'Now that Hollow Head's let the cat out, looks like we'll have to teach a nosy dwarf to mind his own business. Bleed 'em!'

The warehouse men swarmed in, weapons swinging, as the big doors boomed shut. Gotrek and Felix were surrounded. Felix drew his sword and parried a long pole with a cruel hook at the end. A gutting knife stabbed at his stomach. He twisted away. Gotrek picked up the man he had flattened and heaved him at the crowd. Four men went down, but more surged around them, slashing with barrel hooks, daggers and clubs. Brass knuckles glinted on meaty fists. Big Nod screeched encouragement behind them.

Felix blocked a cudgel, but checked his riposte, even though he had an opening. He felt constrained. He had no compunction about wholesale slaughter when it was orcs or bandits in the mountains, or Kurgan or beastmen in the wilds of Kislev, but this was Nuln. This was the Empire. There were laws here, consequences. Even though these villains were trying to rip his entrails out with their hooks and long knives, he didn't feel right murdering them somehow.

Gotrek too did not kill, fighting only with his fists and whatever sticks and poles he could take from their attackers. He dealt terrible damage regardless. Men lay moaning and writhing all around him, eyes blackening and broken noses gushing blood. He snapped the arm of a man twice his height with a flick from a stolen club. Another's knee bent sideways from a savage kick.

'Practising mercy?' gritted Felix as they fought back to back.

'Mercy? Bah!' said Gotrek. 'These scum are not worthy of my axe.'

A man in an apron roared and charged Gotrek with a barrow loaded with a huge side of beef. The meat caught the Slayer amidships and drove him back, smashing him into the tubs that held the iced sturgeons. He went down and the barrow went with him, tipping on its side. The half-carcass slid across the stone floor on a smear of blood.

A dozen men leapt on the Slayer, flailing with their hooks and cudgels. One dived from the top of the ale wagon.

'Gotrek!' Felix slashed around with his sword, fanning back his attackers as he attempted to reach his companion. Maybe they should have been killing these hoodlums after all.

Gotrek surged up, kicking and punching, a barrel hook buried in the meat of his left arm. The men dodged back, then darted in again, stabbing and swinging. Gotrek reached behind him, pawing for weapons, and found the tails of two sturgeons. He snatched them up and swung them like clubs. Each was longer than Felix's sword and weighed more than a halfling. The Slayer caught one man on the side of the head with a wet smack that knocked him flat. He took another's legs out from under him.

Gotrek grinned savagely. 'Ha! Now we'll see!'

He strode into the mob, the two massive fish whirling around him in a silvery blur. Warehouse men flew left and right, their heads knocked sideways, spit and teeth flying. Felix caught up a cudgel and followed behind him, cracking the heads and hands of those who had managed to dodge the deadly onslaught.

The tide turned. More than half the workmen were down, and the others were hanging back, wary. Gotrek's left fish slapped a man in the stomach. His right clubbed another in the back of the head. Bits of slimy fish flesh flew everywhere.

Felix slashed with his club and blocked with his sword. His attackers danced back, eyes wide. Was he truly that frightening? Why were they looking over his shoulder?

A hard hand shoved him roughly to the floor and something big whooshed by his ear. He looked up in time to see Gotrek knocked flat by an enormous keg of ale that swung at the end of a rope and pulley. The keg caromed on, mowing down a handful of men, then smashed into one of the stone support pillars in an explosion of ale, smashed staves and tumbling stones.

The ale slopped to the ground in a great spreading tide as men staggered to their feet. The halfling screamed a war cry and ran at the unmoving Slayer, ice pick raised. Felix tried to stand, but slipped in the swamp of ale, blood and filth that covered the floor. His sword flew from his fingers as he tried to steady himself. He wasn't going to make it in time.

'Die, ye nosy dirt eater!' cried the halfling, and jabbed down with the pick.

Gotrek's hand shot up and caught Big Nod's wrist. The halfling screamed in the dwarf's iron grip. Gotrek got to his feet as the little villain scrabbled and kicked at him ineffectually. Still holding him by the wrist, Gotrek raised the halfling over his head, then flung him. He splashed down in the lake of ale.

Gotrek waded in after him and sat on his chest. His fingers closed around the halfling's throat. 'Where is the powder?'

'Please, no…' he sputtered.

A mortar-crusted stone as big as a pumpkin bounced into the ale, drenching them both. The halfling looked up. Felix followed his gaze. The pillar that the keg had struck was falling apart. Men were picking themselves up and running from it. As Felix watched, a huge mass of stone and mortar broke free and sloughed to the ground in an avalanche. The network of rafters groaned. Dribbles of dust rained down from the ceiling above.

Gotrek didn't look up. 'Where is the powder?'

Felix backed towards the wall, staring up warily. 'Gotrek, get away…' He paused, frowning. Was there someone in the rafters? He thought he had seen a white-haired, black-clad figure ducking under a crossbeam, but there was so much dust in the air he couldn't be sure.

The rest of the pillar exploded in a shower of dust and stones as the weight of the roof finally became too much. The rafters warped and splintered with the strain. Men ran for the doors and threw them open, trying to escape.

'The powder,' repeated Gotrek, implacably, as stones crashed down all around him.

A hole was opening in the roof.

'Are ye mad?' squealed Big Nod. 'We'll be killed! Let me up!' A stone impacted inches from his head. He shrieked.

Gotrek didn't even flinch. 'Tell me and I'll let you up.'

'But I don't know where it is!'

Gotrek's hand tightened around the halfling's neck. The hole in the ceiling was getting wider as more stones and mortar peeled away and dropped to the floor. Felix could just see stars in a deep blue sky through the clouds of dust. A rock the size of a fist bounced off Gotrek's back. He didn't seem to notice. Another smashed Big Nod's outflung hand.

'Curse ye!' he wailed. 'I sold it! I sold it to them that ordered it stolen! I don't know where they took it!'

Gotrek surged up and dragged the dripping halfling to the wall. A huge chunk of masonry crashed down right where they had been. Nod gulped, eyes bulging.

Gotrek pressed him against the wall and leaned a forearm across his windpipe. 'Who bought it?'

'I don't know.'

Gotrek pressed harder. Nod's workmen pressed past them, too intent on escaping to be concerned about their boss.

'Come on, Gotrek,' said Felix. 'Bring him outside. It's time to go.'

'Not until he talks.'

'I don't know! Truly!' squealed Big Nod. 'They wore scarves and hooded cloaks. I never saw their faces!'

'It's the truth, dwarf,' said the burly, bearded man Gotrek had first spoken to. 'Came to us at night. Never stepped into the light.'

Another huge chunk of stone slammed down to the floor beside them. Felix felt the impact through the soles of his boots. Big Nod wailed.

Gotrek grunted and dragged the halfling towards the doors. Felix hurried after them, relieved. Halfway there, a flash of white drew his eye upward. There *was* someone up there. A black-clad figure was climbing the rafters. Felix barely registered it before it disappeared through the hole in the roof, its white hair flashing in the starlight. Felix frowned. There had been something disturbingly familiar about the figure, something he was sure he should recognise, but the memory stayed tantalisingly out of reach.

As soon as they were outside the leather curtains, Gotrek pinned Big Nod to the wall again.

'What now?' cried the halfling. 'We already told you. We didn't see their faces. Leave me be!'

'I don't believe you,' Gotrek growled. 'Thieves always make sure of their employers.'

Burly shook his head and made the sign of Taal. 'They was dangerous men. Magickers for certain.' He swallowed. 'Said they could kill us in our dreams if we crossed them.'

'And they paid twice what the job was worth,' said Big Nod. He glared back towards his cellar. 'Won't be enough to fix this though, curse ye. Ye've ruined us!'

'You've ruined yourself,' grated Gotrek.

'Were they Nulners?' asked Felix. 'Could you tell that much?'

'They weren't Shantytowners,' said the halfling. 'I know that. Talked posh, like you. Big words.'

That was something at least. Felix was going to ask another question when he heard shouts and the thud of blows from the top of the ramp. He looked up. Men in the uniforms of the city watch were coming down it, trying to collar scurrying workmen.

'Sergeant!' cried Big Nod, waving frantically in Gotrek's grip. 'Arrest these villains! They attacked my men and smashed up my place! Look at my roof!'

The watchmen started towards them.

'These are the thieves that stole the black powder from the Imperial Gunnery School,' countered Felix. 'They've just confessed to us.'

'We never!' said the halfling. 'They're lunatics, sergeant. Mutants, I shouldn't wonder.'

'Now now,' said the sergeant, a square, stocky fellow with greying hair and enormous moustaches. 'One at a time. And put that halfling down.'

Gotrek glared at him for a moment, then reluctantly lowered Big Nod to the ground and let go of his neck.

The halfling staggered back, gasping and clutching his bruised neck as he glared at Gotrek. 'Y'black-hearted wreckers! Now you'll see! It's the Iron Tower for you, you filthy…!'

'Pipe down if you please, sir,' said the sergeant. 'None of that. You'll have your say.' He turned to Felix. 'Now then, who might you be? And what's your interest in who stole what from the Gunnery School?'

Felix hesitated for a heartbeat, remembering that he and Gotrek were wanted men in the Empire – he for vandalism and incitement, Gotrek for killing Imperial cavalrymen during the window tax riots. Then he chided himself for being foolish. All that was a long time ago, and in Altdorf, not Nuln. Surely no one would remember, would they? It seemed impossible. 'I am Felix Jaeger. My companion is Gotrek Gurnisson. We are guests of the College of Engineering, and…'

The sergeant blinked. 'You're Felix Jaeger?' he interrupted. 'And this is Gotrek the Slayer?'

Felix's heart sank. They *did* remember them. After all these years there was still a price on their heads. Incredible. His hand dropped to his hilt. Gotrek reached for his axe.

But the sergeant laughed and turned to his men. 'Look here, lads! It's the "Saviours of Nuln" come back to protect us from some new menace!'

His men laughed too, dark and nasty, repeating 'the Saviours of Nuln,' derisively.

'You've quite an imagination, Herr Jaeger,' said the sergeant, smirking. 'Ratmen in the sewers of Nuln – skavlings did you call 'em? You and your friend the only ones who could save the day. The watch a lot of incompetent blunderers. Make for a good laugh around the watch station of an evening, your books.'

Felix gaped. This was the last thing he had expected. 'You've… you've read my books?'

'Captain Niederling read 'em to us, as he can read. Never heard taller tales in all my life.'

'What books are these?' growled Gotrek, his single eye turning on Felix.

Felix flushed. He had meant to tell Gotrek the night before, but the dwarf had been in such a foul mood that he had put it off, then forgotten it. 'I… I'll explain later.'

'I don't care who they are,' said the halfling. 'They smashed up my business. Lock 'em up!'

'We were looking for the black powder,' said Felix. 'They stole if from the Gunnery College, then sold it this morning.'

The sergeant cocked an eyebrow. 'Playing out one of your books, Herr Jaeger? Maybe you ought to keep your adventures on paper in the future.' He held up a hand as Felix and the halfling both started talking at once. 'Now now, I think both of you better come down to the watch station and explain it all to the captain.' He grinned. 'Captain will be right pleased to meet you, Herr Jaeger. He loves your books. Highly imaginative, he calls them.'

Gotrek growled in his throat and Felix shot him a warning glance. It would not do for the Slayer to murder an officer of the watch. They had only just returned to the Empire. Felix wasn't keen on going into exile again so soon. On the other hand, an axe through the forehead of this sergeant and his captain might be just the thing. Highly imaginative, indeed! Every word he had put in his journals was the truth. Skaven *had* attacked Nuln. And he and Gotrek had had some part in defeating them. Did they think he was some purveyor of low melodrama? Some Detlef Sierck? How dare they!

'WHAT ARE THESE books, manling?'

Felix swallowed, nervous. He had been waiting for the Slayer to ask that question.

It was many hours later. Gotrek and Felix were walking back to the College of Engineering, trailing behind Malakai Makaisson and Lord Groot, who were talking eagerly about tomorrow. Apparently Lord Pfaltz-Kappel had found more funds, the Dwarf Black Powder Guild had found more powder, and the flight of the *Spirit of Grungni* was back on schedule.

In the end, it had taken the intervention of Groot and Makaisson, and the reluctant confessions of the halfling and his henchmen, before the watch could be convinced to let Gotrek and Felix go. They had been released into Lord Groot's custody like naughty children returned to their father, and told to leave the investigating to the authorities.

Gotrek had been remarkably well behaved throughout the whole ordeal. Not that he was cooperative in any way. He had cursed Nuln and the watch and refused to surrender his weapon or answer any questions, but on the other hand, he hadn't killed anyone, or wrecked the furniture, or punched the captain in

the face when he laughed at the sergeant's witticism
about them being the 'Saviours of Nuln,' and called
Felix's stories of ratmen 'amusing fancies'.

Indeed, every time Felix's books had been mentioned, Gotrek had turned that baleful glittering eye
upon Felix, and stared silently at him. Felix quivered
each time. It had reminded him of when Gotrek had
attacked him in the tomb of the Sleeper, an experience
he was not eager to repeat.

Now Gotrek had at last asked the dreaded question.
'Ah…' said Felix. 'Well, as you know, over the years
I've kept journals of our journeys – notes for the epic
poem of your death, you see. And… and whenever
we've found ourselves in a friendly port, I've sent those
that I've finished home to my brother for safe keeping.
And he… well, he published them without my knowledge.' He swallowed. Gotrek just continued to stare at
him. Was he going to attack him here and now? 'I– I
meant to tell you last night, but somehow…'

'So you've already begun to tell my saga?' interrupted Gotrek.

'Ah, yes,' said Felix. 'In a way. Although I can't speak for
the quality. I haven't begun to read them yet myself, and
I have no idea what kind of editing my brother–'

'Good,' said Gotrek, cutting him off again. 'If my
fame is great enough, my doom may seek me out and
save me hunting for it. I owe your brother a debt.'

He stumped on without another word. Felix gaped
after him. He had expected anger, dismemberment
even. Never had it occurred to him that the Slayer
might approve. On the other hand, he *had* asked him
to write the epic. Why should he be surprised that
Gotrek was pleased that he had begun?

FOUR

FELIX WOKE AGAIN to thunder. This time it was all outside his head, and much louder than previously. The blast brought him bolt upright in bed. Was it a cannon firing? If so, it must have been much closer. Perhaps one of Makaisson's inventions had exploded. It wouldn't be the first time.

He blinked around sleepily in the pre-dawn light as the reverberations of the explosion faded away and people in nearby rooms raised their voices in alarm. He had not slept well. His mind had been restive. Images of the black-clad, white-haired figure in the rafters of the cold cellar had spun endlessly through his head, trying to resolve themselves into a memory that wouldn't come.

People were running in the halls now. He moaned and climbed wearily out of bed. By the time he had found and pulled on his clothes and stepped into his boots, someone was knocking sharply on his door. He opened it. Gotrek and Malakai stood without, looking grim.

'There's been an explosion on the Gunnery School's testing field on Aver Isle,' said Malakai. 'The last gun of our shipment was tae be tested this morning. We're off tae see what's what.'

GOTREK GRIPPED HIS axe like he meant to butcher someone with it. His face was rigid with rage. 'The gods conspire to keep me from my doom,' he rasped.

Felix nodded. It certainly seemed that some unearthly agency was trying to stop Gotrek from reaching Middenheim in time for the siege. He and the Slayer stood on the neatly clipped green lawn of the Gunnery School's test range, which was situated on Aver Isle, a small island in the centre of the River Aver, and linked by bridges to the Neuestadt district to its north, to the Halbinsel district to the south, and to the west, the forbidding Island of the Iron Tower, the notorious prison of the witch hunters. The testing range was a cool and strangely peaceful place at this time of the morning, silent and wreathed in swirling mists from the river, but evidence that terrible tragedy had recently shattered that peace smouldered before them.

An enormous iron cannon sat broken upon the lawn, its lavishly decorated barrel split into five splayed sections, peeled back so that it resembled some black orchid from the jungles of Lustria. The wooden gun carriage the cannon had been mounted on was shattered and smoking, and the grass all around it was scorched. Patches of red remained on the ground where the bodies of the crew had been flung when the gun had exploded.

Malakai and Lord Groot and other men from the Gunnery School and the College of Engineering circled the cannon, examining it closely and talking amongst themselves. Behind them, a sturdy wagon was being wheeled onto the field in preparation for carrying the gun back to the school. Magus Lichtmann stood to one side, murmuring incantations and making strange gestures with his left hand and the stump of his right arm. By the armoury building, Ward Captain Wissen talked with the administrators of the range. A company of city guard waited near the gate.

Lord Pfaltz-Kappel paced behind Lord Groot, a sour look on his face. 'I suppose I'll have to pay for this too,' he whined.

'Certainly not,' said Groot sharply. 'The school guarantees all its work. You paid for the finest gun the Empire can build. You'll get it. No matter how many times we have to cast it.'

'How long to make anither?' asked Malakai.

'From start to finish, shaping and casting a gun takes fourteen days,' said Groot. 'Twelve if we rush it.'

'Twelve days,' growled Gotrek under his breath. His axe twitched.

'Fortunately,' continued Groot, 'we have a gun just ready to be poured. It is meant for the garrison at Carroburg, but they can wait. Middenheim's need is greater. If we pour it this morning, it can be ready four days from now at dawn.'

Gotrek grunted angrily but said nothing.

'Ah've niver before seen a gun explode wae such force,' said Malakai shaking his head. 'It's almost as though the muzzle wis plugged. Groot, were ye using some experimental ammunition?'

Groot shook his head. 'We would never do that for a test fire. It was loaded with plain iron shot.'

'Perhaps it was loaded wrong,' said Pfaltz-Kappel.

Groot wheeled on him, eyes blazing. 'The crews of the Imperial Gunnery School are the best in the world. The men who died here today were fifteen-year veterans. Great soldiers and personal friends of mine. They did not "load it wrong".'

Magus Lichtmann joined them, frowning. 'I detect no residue of magic,' he said. 'No spell caused this to happen. It seems it may have been an accident after all. Some hidden fault in the iron.'

Lord Groot made a face.

Lichtmann shrugged. 'These things happen, Julianus.'

'Not to my guns,' said Groot. 'I want to look at it more closely when we bring it back to the school.'

'It was saboteurs,' said Captain Wissen, crossing towards them. 'I'll stake my reputation on it. The same villains who stole the powder. Someone from within the school, most likely. Secret cultists among the gun shapers. They want to delay the shipment to aid their masters in the north.'

'There are no cultists in the Gunnery School!' bellowed Groot.

Wissen's lip curled. 'There are cultists everywhere.'

The men stepped aside as workers from the school lowered planks from the back of the wagon and attached chains to the wounded cannon. Four men manned cranks and, with a clattering of gears, began to drag the massive gun inch by inch up the planks.

Groot watched in sad silence, like he was at a funeral.

A grey and gold palanquin carried by four men in the livery of Countess Emmanuelle, Elector Countess of Wissenland and ruler of Nuln, came through the high iron gates of the firing range and crossed the lawn. Murmurs rippled through the nobles, and they turned towards it expectantly, waiting to see who it carried. Could it be the Countess herself, Felix wondered? He hadn't seen her since she had thanked him and Gotrek for their help in defeating the ratmen and saving her city twenty years ago. She had been beautiful then. Had she kept her looks?

It was not the Countess.

The bearers set down the palanquin, and one of them opened the door. Out stepped a tall, stooped, delicate old man in severe but exquisitely-tailored black. He had a long, horsy face and thick white hair. The murmurs from the nobles grew louder. Felix frowned when he saw him. He looked familiar, and he knew he had met the man before, but couldn't remember where.

'Greetings, gentlemen,' he said in a soft voice. 'I have come at the request of the Countess. She has heard of the school's troubles and wishes to know what is being done.'

Felix knew him as soon as he spoke. It was Hieronymous Ostwald, the Countess's personal secretary, though he was much changed since he had last seen him. Twenty years ago, when the courtier had called Felix to his offices in the Countess's palace during the skaven crisis, he had been a dark-haired, slightly fleshy man in his fifties. Now he looked like a frail and kindly old grandfather.

But judging by the wary glances Lord Pfaltz-Kappel and Lord Groot and the others gave him, he was more dangerous than he looked.

'I understand that there has been a theft and sabotage,' Ostwald continued. 'I would like to hear the details, and also who the suspects might be. Have the cults been investigated? Have you entertained the possibility that it might be the...' He paused and looked around furtively, then lowered his voice. 'That it might be our "enemies below". I...' His eye fell on Felix and he paused, frowning. 'By Sigmar! Is it... are you related to Felix Jaeger? The bearer of the Templar's Sword? His son perhaps?'

Felix bowed. 'I am Felix Jaeger himself, sir,' he said. 'A pleasure to see you again.' He stifled a smile. It was funny how easily the old courtesies came back.

'Impossible,' said Ostwald, goggling at him. 'You haven't aged a day. You must have drunk from the chalice of youth!'

Felix blushed and didn't know what to say. 'No, sir. I... I feel every one of my years, I'm afraid.'

'My friends,' said Ostwald, turning to the others. 'You know not who you have in your midst! This is Felix Jaeger, who, with the help of his stout – er, stout-hearted – companion, helped turn the tide against the ska... the *beastmen* who invaded our fair city all these many years ago.' He looked at Wissen. 'Captain, I would request that you ask the High Constable to allow Herr Jaeger and Herr Gurnisson to assist you in your investigations, and to share with them all information you have about these crimes.'

Wissen looked appalled, but hid it by bowing and clicking his heels together. 'As you wish, excellency.'

The others looked at Felix and Gotrek with raised eyebrows. He couldn't tell if they were impressed or amused.

Gotrek chuckled almost inaudibly.

Groot stepped forward. 'My lord, if you will come back with me to the school I will tell you what we know.'

'Of course, of course,' said Ostwald. He motioned to Felix as he started back to his palanquin. 'Come, Herr Jaeger. Walk beside my chair so that we may talk. I am no longer able to walk long distances.'

Groot and the others lined up behind the wagon carrying the exploded cannon, and followed it out of the test grounds and onto the stone bridge that connected Aver Isle with the north bank of the Reik. Felix paced next to Lord Ostwald's palanquin with Gotrek beside him. The old man sat at the window and pulled a sable rug around his knees, as if the late summer weather was too cold for him.

A host of memories flooded Felix's mind as they walked, brought on by Ostwald's sudden reappearance in his life, the scenes and emotions coming to him as if they had happened yesterday – killing von Halstadt, the burning of the Blind Pig, Elissa's dark curls, and her betrayal, hideous rat-faces coming out of the dark, the terror of the poison gas, the horror of the diseased skaven in the cemetery, the doctor who had given him the pomander that had protected him from their noxious stew. Felix paused. The doctor was the same man who had introduced him to Lord Ostwald. The two of them had belonged to a secret order of some kind. What had his name been? Oh yes.

He turned to Ostwald. 'Do you still see Doctor Drexler, my lord?' he asked.

'Doctor Drexler?' said Ostwald. 'Oh, but I'm terribly sorry, my dear boy. Doctor Drexler passed away, many years ago.'

'Oh. I'm sorry to hear it,' said Felix. And he was. The old physician had been one of the wisest, most learned men he had ever met, a great healer with a deep understanding of human nature.

'Yes,' said Ostwald. 'He never truly recovered from his fight with that vile skaven warlock. His health remained feeble for a few years, then he succumbed to a cancer of the brain and died.'

'That is sad news indeed,' said Felix, but Ostwald's mention of the skaven sparked another question. 'Tell me, my lord, why no one believes that it was ratmen who attacked the city? Everyone, even men who were there and fought the vermin, seem to remember them as beastmen.'

Ostwald leaned closer to the window and put a finger to his lips. 'Quietly, Herr Jaeger. Quietly.' He looked around, then continued. 'It is strange, I know, but it is for the good of the Empire.'

'The good of the Empire?' Felix looked around too, though he couldn't imagine who would be eavesdropping on their conversation. They were halfway across the bridge now, moving very slowly behind the wagon that carried the huge shattered gun. The only person near them was Gotrek, who was spitting over the balustrade into the water.

'Yes. Don't you see?' continued Ostwald. 'The morale of the people is low enough as it is, and the knowledge that the entire land, from the wilds of

Kislev in the north, to the Border Princes in the south, is riddled and undermined by the burrows of an innumerable, implacable foe bent on our utter destruction, would cause widespread despair. So, though we know of their existence, for the good of the people, those of us in possession of this dangerous knowledge must remain silent and fight them in secret. Therefore, the Countess and her advisors tell the people that it was not skaven they fought, but beastmen, and those who say otherwise are arrested – for the good of the community, of course.'

'And this works?' asked Felix, confounded.

'I have found,' said Ostwald, with a sad smile, 'that if you tell a lie long enough and loud enough and from a high enough position of authority, that most people will come to believe it, even with the truth staring them in the face. And those who don't believe it can be disposed of as traitors or madmen.'

'I... I see.' Felix wanted to say that he thought that this was a despicable practice that would only cause the people to come to mistrust the Emperor and his servants, but since Lord Ostwald was one of those servants he decided it was probably in his best interests to hold his tongue.

'I do not approve of this practice,' said Ostwald, pursing his lips. 'For I believe that the skaven thrive in this secrecy. I believe it would be better if we were to speak openly–'

A sound like the gabbling of a thousand geese interrupted him. It came from ahead of them, further down the bridge. Felix looked up, but could see nothing around the great bulk of the cannon. Captain Wissen and his troops were edging around its wagon as Groot and Lord Pfaltz-Kappel craned their necks and asked what was happening.

Gotrek started forward, pulling his axe from his shoulder. 'Trouble,' he said.

'Excuse me, my lord,' said Felix, ducking his head to Ostwald. He drew his sword and followed the Slayer.

The gun wagon was so wide that there was little room between it and the stone balustrades on either side of the bridge. They pushed around it and stopped behind Wissen's men, who had formed a line before the wagon.

Beyond them, an angry mob of Shantytown working men and young men in students' robes was flowing onto the bridge, screaming slogans and waving cudgels, staves and lit torches. Many of them wore yellow strips of cloth around their foreheads or arms. There were hundreds of them. They filled the street beyond the bridge.

'Grain for the people, not the army!' shouted some.

'Iron workers starve while gun makers grow fat and consort with sorcerers!' cried others.

'Smash the guns! Smash the guns!' roared still others.

Standing on his toes, Felix could see men in yellow masks amongst the mob, chanting and shaking their fists with the rest.

As the crowd got closer, the men at the front began to throw bricks, torches and paving cobbles at Wissen's men. The watchmen dodged and ducked. They had no shields, and no bows or guns, so they couldn't retaliate.

'You see?' said Wissen. 'Agitators. Did I not say? Hold your line, men.' He looked back at Groot and

Magus Lichtmann and Lord Pfaltz-Kappel, who were peeking around the gun wagon. 'Return to the isle, my lords, and ask Lord Ostwald to do the same. There will be violence.' He glanced at Gotrek and Felix as his men set their spears. 'You too, meinen herren,' he said with a sneer. 'I would hate to be responsible for the deaths of the "heroes of Nuln".'

'Worry about your own hide, watchman,' said Gotrek, sheathing his axe and smacking his fists together as the crowd swarmed closer. He caught Felix's look and snorted. 'There's no honour in slaughtering untrained fools.'

But that wasn't what Felix had been thinking about. He was wondering if there was any honour in fighting the mob at all. Uncomfortable memories flooded his mind. Hadn't he led the mob during the window tax riots? Hadn't he thrown bricks through the windows of the rich? Hadn't he urged the poor to storm the Lord Mayor's office? Hadn't he fought the watch in the streets? It felt very strange to be on the other side of the spears. He had more sympathy for the mob than he did for the men around him. He agreed with the agitators, at least in principle. The poor should be fed. Working men should be paid a fair wage.

On the other hand, smashing things and fighting the watch never got anyone anywhere, and he doubted these fellows were going to wait for him to explain that he was on their side before they caved his head in. He pulled his sheath from his belt and slid it down over his sword. Gotrek's way seemed best. There was no honour in slaughtering untrained fools, but at the same time, there was no honour in letting them slaughter you either.

In the middle of this reverie, a familiar shape caught the corner of his eye. A figure dressed all in black with a white shock of hair peeking from a voluminous hood, watching from the embankment. He lifted his head up to get a better look, but a flying stone skipped off the top of his head and he flinched down, cursing. By the time he stood again, vigorously rubbing his crown, the figure was gone – if it had ever been there in the first place.

A last volley of cobbles rattled all around them, and then the mob smashed into the watch's line. Wissen's men gored dozens, but they were but one thin line before an unstoppable battering ram of humanity. They were driven back by the sheer mass of the crowd. Some of the agitators squirmed past them, shouting, 'Smash the gun! Smash the gun!'

Gotrek clubbed these to the ground with his heavy fists. Felix laid about him with his sheathed sword, using it as a club. But there were too many. More and more were pushing through and slipping around them. Felix saw a watchman take a brick to the temple and fall. Three workmen dragged down another, even while his spear ripped out the guts of one of their companions. More workers pushed forward, trampling the bodies. They threw glass bottles at the gun wagon. Oily liquid splashed as the bottles shattered. Torches followed, and the wagon burst into flames.

Wissen fired point blank into a protester's face with his pistol and lashed about him with his sword, but he stepped back with every swing. 'Fall back! Fall back!' he cried. 'Use the gun as a barrier!'

'It's the gun they're after,' growled Gotrek.

The watchmen didn't hear him. They backed away, following Wissen as he retreated around the gun.

Gotrek and Felix were suddenly alone in a sea of howling workmen. They flattened everyone they could reach, but they were but a small rock in a wide stream. The mob flowed around them on both sides and began clambering onto the gun, some perilously close to the flames, hitting it ineffectually with their clubs and rakes, still shouting 'Smash the gun! Smash the gun!'

'Push it in the river!' shouted someone from further down the bridge. 'Push it in the river!'

The mob took up the cry and began to rock the gun wagon back and forth. 'Into the river! Into the river!'

'No you don't,' said Gotrek, and spun towards the mob around the gun, pulling them off and throwing them aside.

Felix helped, braining the rioters with his sheathed sword and kicking them left and right. He heard glass smash beside him and something spattered his arm and cheek. He turned. Gotrek was drenched in oil. Shards of sticky glass glittered in his crest and slid down his naked back.

Gotrek looked over his shoulder. 'Who…'

A torch sailed over the heads of the mob. Gotrek whipped his axe off his back and blocked it. It spun and glanced off his right shoulder, then bounced into Felix.

Fire bloomed on Gotrek like an orange flower, flowing up the side of his head and wreathing his crest in flame. Felix's cloak and jerkin went up as well. The rioters flailed at them with their cudgels and staves.

'Flame-throwing cowards!' roared Gotrek. 'Come and face me steel to steel!'

He and Felix slapped at the flames as the mob battered at them. They only succeeded in setting their hands on fire. The fire stuck to everything. Felix cursed, his fingers a fiery agony. Heat blasted his face. Gotrek howled with rage. He slashed around with axe, decapitating clubs and severing hands, then surged for the balustrade. Felix followed. The rioters leapt back from their flames.

Gotrek dived off the bridge. Felix was right behind him. The world spun around him – bridge, river, shore, sky, Gotrek on fire – then, with a wet slap, he plunged into the waves. The cold shocked a cry out of him and he sucked in a mouthful of water.

He kicked and flailed in a confusion of bubbles and murk. After a moment of blind terror he broke the surface, choking and retching, eyes tearing.

Gotrek bobbed beside him, throwing his dripping crest out of his eyes. One side of his face was covered in blisters. 'That's what I get for being merciful.' He looked up, then his one eye widened. 'Swim!' he barked.

Felix followed his gaze. The bridge rose up beside them, and looming out over the balustrade, directly above them, was the exploded cannon. It was sliding off the rapidly tipping gun wagon. Felix stared, frozen, as it let go entirely, smashed through the balustrade in an explosion of granite, and began to topple off the bridge.

'Swim, manling!'

Felix snapped out of his paralysis and kicked forward, trying to get under the bridge. Gotrek was ahead of him, swimming strongly. Felix kicked and flailed for all he was worth, but it seemed like he was treading water. He wasn't going to make it.

With a sound like a battering ram hitting an iron door, the cannon smashed into the river. Felix felt himself being drawn back as the big gun opened a vortex in the water, then he was pushed forward again as the water surged back up. His shoulder slammed into a bridge pillar and he spun away on a roiling hill of water.

As they shot out on the other side of the bridge, Gotrek caught him and kept him afloat. 'Can you swim?'

Felix rolled his shoulder and flexed his arm. They were sore, but nothing was broken. 'I… I think so.'

'Then come on.'

Gotrek struck out for the north bank. Felix followed, then paused and looked up. On the bridge, the rioters were dispersing, running for the shore as they whooped and cheered at their victory, Captain Wissen's men chasing after them. Felix cursed them, his earlier sympathy entirely evaporated. The maniacs had set him on fire. He hoped they all roasted alive.

FIVE

'IT WAS A great loss,' Lord Groot said, as he and Magus Lichtmann, Malakai and Gotrek and Felix watched the pouring of the new gun with a group of Gunnery School officials from a metal platform above the casting room floor. 'Not in iron, though that is not cheap these days, with the shippers gouging us with "wartime prices", but in men and honour. Not only did we lose one of the best crews in the Empire, we lost the body and spirit of Johannes Baer, whose ashes were mixed with the iron of the gun.'

'His ashes?' asked Felix.

The heat from the forge was making the burns on Felix's face sting, and his left hand was sweating and itching under his bandages, but the honour of being invited to watch the pouring of a great cannon was not to be refused, so he merely stepped back a pace and hoped it would be over soon.

Felix's left hand had been salved and wrapped, and he was wearing clothes borrowed from a student at the College of Engineering, to replace his cloak and jerkin, which had been badly scorched, and everything else, which was soaking wet. The hand still throbbed, but he didn't dare complain. Gotrek's entire right arm, the right side of his neck, his right ear and part of his back were swathed in bandages, and his Slayer's crest was several inches shorter than usual where the Gunnery School's barber surgeon had cut away the blackened parts, and yet Gotrek bore his pain and indignity with stoic silence.

'Aye,' said Groot. 'It is a long-standing tradition, and a great honour. Artillery men of distinction are cremated when they die, and their ashes added to a new cannon. It is thought to imbue the gun with the fortitude and spirit that the men had in life. Johannes Baer was such a man. A great gunner and a brave soldier who died defending his gun when his position was overrun.' He bowed his head. 'The men who died today will soon be joined with their own guns. Today...' He looked towards the enormous glowing crucible that hung over the casting pit. 'Today, Leopolt Engle will be wed to his gun. He died four months ago in the siege of Wolfenberg, when the city wall collapsed under the bombardment of one of the enemy's hell cannon. He had destroyed two of the foul machines with his marksmanship.'

A bell chimed below. Groot stepped forward. 'They are ready.'

The others joined him. Felix stayed where he was. He could see just fine, and Groot and Gotrek's thick frames protected him somewhat from the waves of brutal heat.

Men in heavy leather aprons and leather hoods that covered their faces and necks stepped back from the casting pit, a square hole in the stone floor that was filled with sand. In the centre of the pit, at the bottom of a slight depression, was set a wide white ring. A shallow groove had been made in the sand, leading to the ring.

'That opening,' said Groot, pointing, 'is the tip of the cannon mould, made of clay, and buried upright in the sand pit. The thick rod that hangs straight down into the centre of it is the bore mould. The molten iron is poured into the mould, then when it cools, the bore mould is removed to make the gun's barrel chamber. We use secrets taught us by dwarf gun makers to make sure that both the gun mould and the bore mould are perfectly vertical and perfectly aligned. This ensures that the cannon shoots straight and is of uniform thickness all around when finished.' His chest puffed up. 'Consequently, our guns are the most accurate in the Old World.'

Above the casting pit was a sturdy wood and metal gantry from which hung the massive crucible that held the molten iron that would be poured into the mould. At the moment the crucible sat over a super-heated coal furnace. Foundry workers stood around it in heavy leather, scooping impurities off the top with long steel spoons and dumping them in sand-filled stone buckets. Another bell clanged and the men stepped back. A door opened behind them and onto the gantry stepped a priest of Sigmar and two initiates. These too wore the heavy scarred leather of the forge men, but their gear had the shape of temple vestments, and was stitched upon the breast with the symbols of the hammer and the twin-tailed comet. Their faces were uncovered however, and Felix wondered how they stood it.

The priest held an iron-bound Book of Sigmar folded in his arms. His face, hellishly under-lit by the liquid iron's crimson light, was pocked with circular burn scars. He had obviously performed this duty many times before. One of the acolytes carried a gold-headed hammer, the other carried a stone urn. They too had burns on their faces, but not so many.

The workers on the gantry bowed their heads as the priest took the hammer from the first acolyte, then opened the book and began to read aloud. Lord Groot and the other men from the school who watched the ceremony lowered their heads as well. Felix did not. The ceremony was too fascinating not to watch. Gotrek and Malakai watched too. The priest's words were lost in the roar of the furnace, but whatever the invocation was, it was brief – necessarily so, Felix thought. When he finished, he stepped back and nodded to the second acolyte.

The man stepped forward, his face running with sweat. His lips moved continuously as he opened the stone urn and upended it over the crucible. The dust that poured out glittered as it drifted down into the molten metal, and a swirl of flames and sparks shot up when it touched, splashing the holy men. The acolyte with the urn flinched back and almost dropped it as a spark struck his cheek. With an effort he controlled himself and stood solemnly as the priest finished the ceremony and closed the book.

As they backed away, the forge men stepped forward again, unlocking the crucible from its mooring and then pulling on chains that rolled it forward until it hung over the sand pit. Other chains lowered it until the bottom of the massive container was only inches above the sand. Two heavily gloved men stepped to it and grasped long handles that sprouted from its side. With long-practiced motions they tipped the crucible slowly forward until molten iron began to spill from its spout into the groove in the sand. Sparks leapt in all directions. The men poured carefully, making sure the stream was smooth and constant. It wound down the groove and into the mould like a glowing red snake slipping endlessly into a hole.

Felix blinked to moisten his eyes. The blast of heat from the pouring metal made the room even hotter than before, and they were as dry as eggshells. The entire front of his body felt on fire. He looked over at the others. All were sweating, but none showed any sign of discomfort, curse them.

'Leopolt Engle,' intoned Lord Groot. 'May you, in death, bring victory to the Empire and defeat to her enemies as you did in life.'

'May Sigmar so grant,' said the other men of the school.

For another interminable ten minutes the forge men trickled the metal into the mould while Felix's face felt like it would shrivel up and peel off. At last the mould filled to the brim and the men tipped the crucible back upright.

As the priest stepped forward to say one final blessing, Felix noticed that the initiate who had been burned had fainted. He lay on the gantry, still clutching the urn, while his fellow acolyte knelt over him, shaking him.

Groot and the other men of the school bowed to the cooling gun and made the sign of the hammer, then turned to depart.

Groot smiled at Gotrek and Felix. 'Come,' he said. 'The heroes who defended Johannes Baer's cannon when Wissen and his cowards turned and fled must be honoured. You will feast at my table tonight.'

'Will there be ale?' asked Gotrek.

'Of course!' said Groot. 'As much as you like.'

'Good,' said Gotrek. 'I'm parched.'

As much as *Gotrek* likes, thought Felix. Groot may come to regret those words.

As THEY WALKED through the grounds of the school towards Groot's quarters in the main building, they saw guards in the uniform of the school leading away another guard. The man was raving.

'The guns,' he cried. 'They were looking at me! They want to kill me!'

Groot stopped the strange procession, holding up a hand. 'Sergeant Volker, what is this? What has happened?'

The sergeant looked pained. 'It's Breyermann, sir, who guards the guns before they're shipped. He's come to believe that the guns are alive, and that they mean him harm.'

'They stare at me!' wailed Breyermann from behind him. 'They hate us all!'

Groot shook his head. 'Terrible. First Federeich mutates, and now Breyermann goes mad. What are the odds that such misfortune strikes two of our lads in one week?'

'We thought perhaps that Breyermann caught his madness from Federeich, sir,' said the sergeant. 'Wouldn't be surprised if he shows stigmata soon.'

Groot nodded. 'Aye. You undoubtedly have the right of it. Very sad. Inform his family. And give him to the Sisters of Shallya. Perhaps they can cure him before it becomes a matter for the witch hunters.'

The sergeant saluted and he and his men led the madman away. Groot sighed and continued towards his quarters. Felix looked back at the sad procession, a jumble of half-formed thoughts churning in his head. He noticed that Gotrek was looking back too.

LATE THAT NIGHT, as Gotrek and Felix staggered with Malakai towards the College of Engineering after Groot's lavish feast, Gotrek stopped and turned in the direction of Shantytown.

'I want to go to the Blind Pig,' he said, slurring only a little.

'You want *more* to drink?' asked Felix, amazed. The Slayer had put away an enormous amount of ale at dinner. Felix had seen Groot wince as the third keg had been broached. He supposed Gotrek might be trying to numb the pain of his burns – as Felix had been doing – but then he often drank like that, so who could say?

Gotrek shook his head, then steadied himself. 'I want to talk to Heinz.'

'I'm not sure he wants to talk to you,' said Felix, but Gotrek was already stumping away into the night.

Felix sighed and waved goodnight to Malakai, then followed him.

'Watch out for the big 'un, young Felix,' called Malakai. 'He's liable to get intae trouble.'

Felix snorted. There was no other possible response.

'YER NOT TO come in,' said the big bouncer who stood, his arms folded across his broad chest, in front of the Blind Pig's door.

'Try stopping me,' growled Gotrek, aiming himself at the door.

The bouncer braced himself, then wavered before Gotrek's mad, one-eyed glare and stepped aside. He shrugged. 'Ah, go on. There's no one to fight anyway.'

Felix followed Gotrek into the tavern and saw that it was true. It was empty but for one lonely barmaid and old Heinz, half asleep on his elbows behind the bar.

The barman's head came up as he saw Gotrek. 'I told you not to come back, you wrecker!' He didn't seem at all surprised that Gotrek was wrapped in bandages.

'I stayed away last night, didn't I?' said Gotrek. He tossed a gold coin marked with the sigil of Karak Hirn onto the bar. 'Charge me double for my drinks,' he said. 'That'll pay the damages soon enough.'

Heinz looked at the coin for a long moment, then picked it up and pocketed it. 'Suppose I can use all the business I can get.' He turned and drew two pints.

'What happened?' asked Felix. 'Where is everyone?'

Heinz sighed as he set their pints before them. 'It's Ward Captain Wissen and his thugs. Since that ruck on the bridge they've been prowling Shantytown and the Maze, roughing up anyone they find on the streets, trying to find the leaders of the Cleansing

Flame. All my regulars are holing up until it blows over.' He snorted. 'I could tell Wissen he's looking in the wrong place. Those troublemakers ain't from around here.'

'Where are they from?' asked Gotrek. He sounded suddenly much less drunk.

'They're toffs,' sneered Heinz. 'Altestadt brats with too much time on their hands. See themselves as do-gooders, standing up for the common man. The Torch, their leader calls himself. Gives fiery speeches about how the poor should rise up and kill the priests and the nobles and the factors. But when the folk start smashing things up and the watch come down on them, where are the Torch and his rich mates? Nowhere. They take off their masks and disappear. Cowards, I calls 'em.'

'I call them worse,' rasped Gotrek.

'So why aren't the watch looking in the Altestadt?' asked Felix.

'They don't know,' said Heinz. 'They think they're all Maze-born rabble rousers.'

'Why don't you tell them different?'

Heinz scowled at Felix. 'No Shantytowner would tell the watch nothing. No matter what it was, they'd find a way to turn it against us.'

'We'd find them in the Altestadt, then?' asked Gotrek.

'If you knew who they were,' said Heinz. 'But nobody knows that. Not even their followers. They have a meeting house in the Maze though. Hidden.'

'Where is it?' pressed Gotrek.

Heinz turned and looked at him, then shook his head. 'No, Gurnisson. I don't want to lose the Pig.

They live up to their name, the Cleansing Flame, with them what cross them. Set fire to the houses of many a man they thought betrayed them. Why do you want to know?'

Gotrek raised his bandaged arm. 'They set me on fire.'

Felix touched his face. 'Me too.'

Heinz looked from Gotrek to Felix and back. His lips pulled back in a snarl. 'No one sets my friends on fire and gets away with it!' Then he paused, uncertain. 'They're dangerous men though. A snake with many heads. You've friends in the palace, if I recall. Maybe they could help you. Save us all some strife.'

Gotrek just grunted and drank his ale.

Heinz rubbed his whiskery chin, visibly melting in the heat of Gotrek's withering silence. 'Of course, there's no connection between us anymore,' he said. 'Been twenty years since you worked for me. And I threw you out two nights ago. Nobody would think it was me who sent you.' He chewed his lip thoughtfully then sighed. 'All right. It might stir up trouble, but I've weathered trouble before, and I hate them muckrakers almost as much as I hate the watch.'

He looked around warily, despite the fact that there was no one in the place, then leaned forward and lowered his voice. 'I overheard one of them telling a new recruit how to get there once. They're in the middle of the Maze, behind a place called the Broken Crown. The fellow said that the building looks like just another old tenement, but it's built atop an old brewery, and the cellars go down and down. The Flame boys keep an eye on it night and day, so watch yourselves when you get close.' He dipped his finger in a puddle of ale and began to draw a map on the bar. 'I'll show you how to get the Broken Crown. After that, you're on your own.'

FELIX WAS LESS than eager to enter the Maze, which was known as the roughest part of the roughest neighbourhood in Nuln, particularly not in the dead of night, particularly with Gotrek weaving drunk and him not much better. But he knew nothing could stop a Slayer bent on vengeance, so he followed along warily, one hand on the dragon-figured hilt of his runesword, and his eyes searching every shadow they passed.

The Maze was the haunt of gangsters and cultists and wanted men. There were no street lamps here, and few lights of any kind. Though Mannslieb and Morrslieb were out, the buildings were so crowded together, and so tall – some looming five and six storeys above the alleys – that the moons' light rarely reached the street. Some of them sagged against each other over the street like drunk lovers and blocked the sky altogether.

In most places, the lanterns over the doors of the lawless taverns and gambling halls and low rent brothels that filled the lower floors of the rickety tenements provided the only illumination. Most of the back alleys were pitch black and Felix had to rely on Gotrek's keen tunnel-bred vision to lead them safely through the dark. In some places, new structures, even flimsier than the old, were built upon the rubble of the buildings that had burned down during the skaven invasion, twenty years before. In other places the charred timber bones still stood, patched tents and makeshift lean-tos rising in their midst.

Hard-eyed men watched Gotrek and Felix from doorways and windows. Women in low-cut dresses made kissing noises as they passed. Groups of villains lounged outside open-fronted beer stalls, their legs splayed out into the street, deliberately blocking the way.

Gotrek stumped past them all, ignoring them, his one eye looking for the landmarks Heinz had told them to watch for, and turning where he had told them to turn.

After a quarter of an hour they came to a filthy, rubbish strewn street. On the left was a tavern beneath a crude painting of a broken crown. An alley ran down the side of the tavern. Heinz had said that the Cleansing Flame's meeting house was in a tenement that faced the alley behind the Crown.

'On tiptoes now, eh?' said Felix, thinking of the men Heinz had said watched the area night and day.

Gotrek clomped forward as if he hadn't heard, his boots echoing down the alley. Felix sighed and followed. So much for subtlety. He drew his sword.

Behind the Crown was a crooked alley, so narrow Felix could have reached out and touched both walls at once, if he had cared to soil his hands. To the left and right the alley disappeared into shadow, but across from the rear entrance of the Crown, a slanting slash of moonlight illuminated a dilapidated tenement with a dingy junk shop in its bottom floor, smashed and smoke-blackened furniture and crockery spilling from its unlit but open front. Was this the place? Was it the tenement to the left? The one to the right? Unfortunately Heinz's knowledge had ended at the Broken Crown. They would have to start sticking their noses into doors and looking around. Felix's skin crawled at the prospect.

As Gotrek crossed to the junk shop and looked into it, Felix peered left and right, trying to see into the shadows of the alley, looking for watchers. He gave up. It was too dark, and if there was anything to see, Gotrek would have seen it.

The Slayer jabbed a thumb at the open junk shop door. 'A trap,' he said. 'An open door, but no footprints.' He studied the ground again. The alley floor was hard-packed earth, like all the streets in the Maze. Gotrek followed the prints leading to a closed door, then moved further left, to a spot where it looked like scrap lumber had been used to patch a hole in the wall. 'Here,' he said, and pulled on the boards.

They resisted. As Gotrek stepped forward to pull harder, Felix heard a whistle from somewhere above and behind them. He turned and looked up. Someone was backing away from an unshuttered window. Below it, the back door of the Broken Crown slammed open and seven men swaggered out, swords and daggers dangling casually from their hands. Each of them wore a yellow cotton mask over his face.

'Y'need a key fer that door, stuntie,' said a tall man with the build of a longshoreman, as the others spread out to encircle them.

'I have one,' said Gotrek, drawing his axe and holding it so it glinted in the moons' light.

Some of the men murmured nervously at the sight of it, but the big man sneered, waving them on. 'Come on, lads. They was looking for the Cleansing Flame. Let's not disappoint 'em.'

The masked men lunged forward, swinging their weapons. Gotrek shattered the big man's sword with a slash, then gutted him with a backhand and turned to face three more. Felix backed into an angle of the alley wall so he would only have to face two. He blocked one and kicked at the other as a third tried to find space between them to attack.

These were alley-bashers, not trained swordsmen. Felix countered their attacks with ease and blooded both his opponents on the first pass. But as he recovered to guard, something buzzed past his ear and stuck in the plaster wall beside him. He flinched away. It was a crossbow bolt.

He risked a look up. Someone was reloading in the second floor window. Then, in an eyeblink, they were gone – vanished! Someone or something had yanked them savagely backward out of sight.

Felix was so surprised he almost took the left-hand basher's sword through the belly. He lurched right and the blade grazed his hip. The man on the right was stabbing straight for his eyes. Felix batted his sword aside at the last second and it stuck in the plaster wall next to the crossbow bolt. He kicked the man between the legs, then ducked another thrust from the man on the left and ran him through.

As the dead man fell, Felix slashed at his companion, who was still clutching his groin, and cut halfway through his neck. He turned to face the one who had been trying to push through the other two, but to his surprise, the man was falling forward. A crossbow bolt sticking out of his spine.

He looked up to the window again. There was nobody there.

Gotrek was looking up too. All his opponents were dead as well, one from a bolt behind the ear.

'We have a friend, it seems,' said Felix.

'No one in this place is a friend,' muttered Gotrek. He sidled to the hidden door, keeping his eye on the dark window, then reached back and yanked sharply on the planks. They jerked open with a *ping* of snapped metal, revealing a pitch black opening. Gotrek stole a quick glance inside, then nodded to Felix while returning his gaze to the window. 'In, manling.'

Felix stepped cautiously to the opening. He felt equally reluctant to step into the darkness or stay out in the alley at the mercy of a marksman. With a curse he strode across the threshold and into a narrow corridor. Gotrek backed in after him and closed the door behind him. The darkness was absolute, at least for Felix.

Gotrek shifted around in front of him. 'Put your hand on my shoulder, manling,' he said. 'We'll go without a light.'

Felix reached forward and touched the cloth of Gotrek's bandages. He switched to the opposite shoulder. Gotrek started forward confidently, the wooden floor creaking beneath his feet. Felix followed behind, fighting the urge to put his sword hand in front of his face to shield off any unseen obstacles.

'Stairs down,' said Gotrek, after a few paces. Felix gripped tighter as Gotrek descended, and felt for the edges of each step.

'There would have been a guard behind the door,' he said. 'He must have gone to warn the others.'

'Aye,' said Gotrek. 'They know we're coming.'

At the bottom of the steps, Gotrek froze, holding perfectly still. Felix tried to do the same. After a moment Gotrek started forward again.

Felix let out a breath. 'Do you hear them ahead of us?'

'No,' said Gotrek. 'The front door opened.'

Felix swallowed, and the flesh of his back crawled as he imagined the mysterious sharpshooter from the alley padding down after them in the dark.

Gotrek turned a corner and Felix saw in the distance a faint sliver of flickering orange from under a door. It gave just enough light for Felix to see that the corridor leading up to it had no doors.

'Keep to the walls,' said Gotrek. 'And tread softly.'

The Slayer began edging down the left side of the corridor. Felix went down the right, trying to step on the boards as close to the walls as possible, where they wouldn't creak so much. When they reached the door, Gotrek put his unburned ear to it and listened. Felix held his breath.

'Empty,' breathed Gotrek. He tried the latch. It was locked. He put his palm and shoulder against the door and pushed. The door was much sturdier and better mounted than the hidden door above. Felix could hear the deadbolt groaning with complaint as Gotrek pressed harder and harder. Finally, with a sharp *pang*, the lock gave way and the door flew open. Gotrek jumped forward and caught it before it slammed against the wall. Then he stepped cautiously inside, his axe held at the ready. Felix followed.

The room within was little more than a wide space in the hall. It looked to Felix like a guard station. A low table and two stools sat along one wall. They had not been abandoned long. There was a charcoal brazier on the floor next to them with two sausages cooking on it. A half-eaten loaf of bread sat on the table. A yellow mask was crumpled beside it.

Gotrek glanced around at the walls. 'Hidden panels everywhere,' he muttered.

He stepped forward, peering down the hall beyond the room, then froze and looked back over his shoulder towards the corridor from which they had just come. He motioned Felix to hide to the right of the open door, then took up position to the left. He put a finger to his lips. Felix nodded.

They waited for what seemed to Felix an eternity. From where he stood he could not see through the door, and though he strained his ears, he could hear nothing but the sounds of an old building: creaks and groans, a faint sound of muffled voices, either far above them or far below them, the drip of water from somewhere nearby, the scrabbling of rats inside the walls.

And yet Gotrek remained tensed, axe ready, legs bent to spring, his eye fixed firmly on the frame of the open door. He must be hearing something, but what?

Then, with a movement too swift to see, Gotrek's free hand shot forward through the doorway and pulled a figure into the room, spun it around and slammed it into the side wall. His axe was at its neck. Just as swiftly, a stiletto was at his.

Felix gasped. It was the white-haired figure – the mysterious phantom he had seen in Big Nod's cold cellar and at the riot on the bridge. It raised its shock-haired head, revealing ice-blue eyes and skin like white silk. It smiled, revealing gleaming incisors.

'Hello, Gotrek,' it said, in a voice like honey and sand. 'Hello, Felix. You haven't aged a day.'

It was Ulrika.

SIX

FELIX STARED AT her, a hundred conflicting emotions warring within him: surprise, longing, loathing, anger, regret, nostalgia, bitterness, hope, happiness, grief.

She was beautiful – more beautiful, perhaps, than she had been in life. All her flaws had been polished away. Her skin glowed with the soft lustre of alabaster. Her short-cropped hair, once a sandy blonde, was now snow-white, her eyes were a more piercing blue, her lips a wanton red. A black neckerchief was knotted loosely around her graceful, corded neck. She was as tall as ever, and both slimmer and harder under her tight-fitting black doublet and breeches, and looked the same age as when he had seen her last – twenty-one or twenty-two years old. A bone handled rapier hung low at her trim waist, and black leather cavalry boots encased her long legs to mid-thigh. The hand that held the needle-thin stiletto to Gotrek's throat wore black kid-skin gloves of the finest quality.

And yet, for all her beauty, there was something subtly repellent about her as well. Her perfection was that of a statue, lacking entirely in humanity. And as mesmerising as her eyes were, they were equally as unnerving. They looked at him with the unwavering intensity of a hunting cat's – like she saw him only as prey. She smelled wrong as well. The cloying scent of cinnamon could not hide the coppery tang of blood that hovered about her, nor the faint echo of cold, wet earth.

'The bloodsucker.' Gotrek spat on the floor. He did not lower his axe.

'You spared me once,' she said, calmly. 'Will you break your oath and kill me now?'

Felix noted that she still had her slightly slurred Kislevite accent. It was still bewitching.

'Have you broken *your* oath?' countered Gotrek.

'I made no oath,' said Ulrika. 'I was unconscious at the time, if you recall. But if you mean the promise that my mistress made, to teach me to harm no one...' She smiled again, showing long incisors. 'I wager I have killed one for every hundred you have slain in the last eighteen years. And none that didn't deserve it.'

Gotrek snarled and pressed his axe closer to her neck. At the same time, her stiletto pricked the skin of his. A bead of blood ran down and disappeared beneath his beard.

'It would be a shame,' she purred. 'To end so illustrious a career in a spat over the meaning of a word.' She glanced around the room. 'Particularly when our goals appear to be the same.'

'What do you want with the Cleansing Flame?' asked Felix. He could have wished that his first words to Ulrika after eighteen years had been something more personal. He also wished that she and Gotrek would lower their weapons, but he doubted asking would do any good.

'Surely you want what I want,' said Ulrika. 'To discover where these villains have hidden the black powder.'

'The Cleansing Flame have the black powder?' asked Felix.

Ulrika raised an eyebrow. 'You don't know that? Perhaps, then, I can be more useful to you alive than dead?'

'How did you learn this?' asked Felix.

Ulrika shrugged. 'I would find it much easier to talk if your dwarf friend would remove his axe from my neck.'

Gotrek didn't move.

'Gotrek,' said Felix. 'It's Ulrika.'

'Not anymore,' Gotrek rasped.

'Will you break an oath?' pressed Felix.

'She has killed.'

'Then take it up with her mistress,' said Felix.

'I will,' Gotrek growled. 'When I've finished with her.'

He leaned in, looking as if he meant to saw Ulrika's head from her shoulders, but then, from all around them came the sound of running feet. Even the ceiling resounded with footsteps.

Gotrek stepped back from Ulrika, going on guard.

The vampire drew her sword. 'Cockroaches,' she hissed.

Felix turned in a wary circle, scanning the walls and ceiling. Hidden panels, Gotrek had said, but where? The whole place was so patched together and makeshift anything could be a door.

The wall in front of him flew out like the shutters of a cuckoo clock, and four masked men surged out, slashing at him with daggers, axes and cleavers. There were more behind them. At the same instant, panels in the other wall and the ceiling slammed open. Men charged Gotrek and Ulrika. More dropped down in their midst, stabbing in every direction. The tiny guard room was suddenly more crowded than the Blind Pig during Powder Week.

Felix parried and blocked the men in front of him. A dagger from behind gashed his burned shoulder. He hissed in pain and tried to return the attack, but his long sword was cumbersome in this tight space. Still blocking the three men in front of him, Felix twitched away from another backstab and kicked behind him like a mule. The attacker grunted and doubled up, and a back swing from Gotrek's axe took off the top of the man's head.

A man with a short, curved cutlass thrust at Felix and he ran him through. A cutlass! A much better close quarters weapon. Felix left his runesword in the man's guts and stripped the cutlass and dagger from his slack hands. He used them to parry cuts from his other two attackers, then glanced over his shoulder for danger from behind.

A blink took in the rest of the room. All the men who had dropped from the roof were dead, their limbs and heads lopped off – Gotrek's work. The Slayer fought five men who were pushing forward through the far wall. More were dead at his feet. Ulrika stood at the mouth of the inner corridor, teeth bared, her rapier and dagger flickering like humming birds in the brazier-glow. Men fell away from her, blooming red from the chests, necks and groins. A knife was buried to the hilt in her stomach. She appeared not to notice.

Another blink and he was back to his own opponents. He ducked a heavy cleaver swinging for his head, then stabbed the cleaver-man with his dagger and used his cutlass to gash a wrist behind a lunging knife. He had no idea who the wrist belonged to. His vision had narrowed to just the blades coming towards him. A short sword thrust at his groin. He smashed down on the fingers holding it and it clattered to the floor. A hand axe hacked at his head. He ducked and slipped left, shouldering someone in the ribs, and gutting someone else. The hand axe cut his shoulder – the same shoulder the dagger had hit! He hissed and stabbed back angrily, and was gratified to hear a scream. A knife grazed his cheek and he lashed out with his cutlass. The knife-man crumpled, his neck open to the bone.

The last two men backed away from him, squeezing back through the trap and running into the darkness beyond. Felix started forward, snarling.

'Don't be drawn, manling,' said Gotrek's from behind him.

With an effort, Felix restrained himself from chasing the men. It always amazed him how, when his blood was up, he found himself ready to do things you couldn't have paid him to do when he was calm and thinking clearly.

He turned. All the men who had attacked them were dead or fleeing. The room was a charnel house. The bodies were knee deep. Gotrek had a few minor cuts, but was otherwise unwounded. The Slayer was glaring at Ulrika as she drew the dagger from her stomach and tossed it aside with a sniff of annoyance.

'My Tilean doublet,' she said. 'That will take some…' She paused as she met Gotrek's gaze, then rolled her eyes. 'Do you still wish to slay me, Slayer?'

'You are a monster,' growled Gotrek.

'A monster that you allowed to come into existence.'

Gotrek bared his teeth. 'That makes it worse.'

'Perhaps we should settle this later,' said Felix, looking around uneasily as he recovered his runesword from the stomach of the man it had killed.

Ulrika's chin came up. She cocked her head. 'Good idea. More are coming.'

'Where?' said Gotrek eagerly.

She nodded towards the left wall. 'We should elude them.'

'Elude them?' Gotrek sounded as disgusted as if she had suggested he kiss an orc.

Ulrika sighed. 'You were never long on strategy, were you, Slayer?' She continued as if speaking to an unusually slow child. 'If we fight every step of the way, the leaders will have time to sneak away or move the powder.'

Now even Felix could hear footsteps, and they were coming from more than one direction. 'Then let's go.'

But Gotrek was still glaring at Ulrika.

'What?' she snapped, impatient.

At last he snarled and turned towards the inner corridor. 'Follow me.'

Ulrika gave Felix a quizzical glance, as if to say 'did he mean me?' Felix shrugged and they followed the dwarf into the corridor.

Felix could see almost nothing, but he heard men coming ahead of them.

'You call this eluding them?' said Ulrika.

'Shut up, leech,' growled Gotrek. He felt along the walls with his fingers. The composition of the walls changed with almost every pace – brick, wood, plaster, stone. These cellars had obviously been rebuilt countless times. Gotrek turned a corner. The footsteps got louder, and there were more approaching from behind them.

'Ha!' said the Slayer, then felt up and down a section of brick. 'I knew there would be another.'

Felix looked up and down the corridor anxiously. It sounded like both groups of men were almost on them.

With a grunt of satisfaction, Gotrek used a thick fingernail to pry out what looked like a loose chunk of mortar. There was a click and a section of the wall swung back, revealing a stairway going down. 'In. Quick,' said the Slayer.

Felix and Ulrika slipped through the secret door and Gotrek pulled it closed, enveloping them in darkness. Just as it clicked shut again, boots rumbled up from both directions just outside.

'Where are they?' said a harsh voice.

'They were heading towards you,' said another. 'Don't tell me you let them slip by.'

'No one got by us!' said the first voice. 'You must have lost them. Search back the way you came!'

The two groups split up again and the bootsteps faded into the distance.

'A hole even the roaches don't know of,' said Ulrika. 'Interesting.'

Gotrek sniffed. 'I smell smoke and meat. They are below.' He stepped to the stairs. 'Hand on my shoulder, manling.'

They started down the stairs, Gotrek and Ulrika in front, Felix stumbling along behind. He ground his teeth in frustration. Why was he always the one who couldn't see in the dark?

'So, how was it that you learned that these madmen had the black powder?' Felix asked after they had descended a few flights.

'Countess Gabriella hears many things,' said Ulrika. 'Among them was a rumour that the Cleansing Flame would soon make an attack on the Imperial Gunnery School that would be the beginning of the burning of all of Nuln.'

'What!' said Felix. 'They mean to blow up the school?'

'Aye,' said Ulrika. 'When the countess heard that the black powder had been stolen, she wondered if it might be the Cleansing Flame who had purchased it from the thieves. She sent me to investigate. While you were going for your swim in the Reik, I pulled aside one of the yellow-masked agitators who was leading the rioters and questioned him. He told me that the countess's suspicions were correct.'

'He talked?' said Felix, surprised.

'Oh yes.' Ulrika chuckled. 'I bled him for everything he knew.'

Gotrek spat, disgusted. 'And what does your mistress care for the safety of Nuln,' he asked.

'She cares for Nuln precisely the way a shepherdess cares for her sheep,' came Ulrika's prim reply.

Gotrek growled in his throat, but said nothing.

After another flight, the Slayer stopped at a landing. 'Keep back,' he said, and shrugged out from under Felix's hand.

Felix listened, trying to understand from the soft sounds that followed what Gotrek was doing. Then suddenly there was a thin line of torch glow illuminating Gotrek's ugly face, and casting a dim light on the rest of the landing, revealing that the stairs continued further down.

Gotrek peered through the cracked door with his one good eye. Felix stepped behind him and looked over his shoulder.

Though he could only see a narrow sliver of the room beyond, he saw that it was big, with a high ceiling and a far wall more than thirty paces away. There was a large square of yellow cloth on the left wall above what appeared to be a stage of some kind – planks laid over an under structure of old barrels.

'They must have escaped,' echoed a plaintive voice from the room. 'We searched all over the cellars.'

'Escaped?' said an upper class voice. 'I find that hard to believe. Search again. From top to bottom. They cannot be allowed to interrupt us now. Go!'

'Yes, brother. Right away, brother.'

Gotrek closed the door. 'Further down,' he said.

They resumed their descent.

Four flights later, the stairs ended at another hidden door. Gotrek listened at it, then tugged on the catch and pushed it open a crack. He peered through, then opened it wider. There was a hanging of some kind in

front of the door. Gotrek drew his axe, hesitating. Felix
strained his ears, listening for movement.

'Worry not,' said Ulrika. 'I smell nothing with a
pulse in this room.'

Gotrek shot her a look, then eased through the door
and looked around the edge of the hanging. He
motioned his companions out. Felix and Ulrika
stepped through and pushed past the curtain. They
were in a small room that looked something like
Felix's father's office in his counting house. A desk
with pigeon holes and ledger shelves stood on the left
side of the room, a horn lamp illuminating it. The
hanging was a yellow banner with the torch symbol of
the Cleansing Flame stitched onto it. An armoire
stood against the right wall. The far wall had a stout
door in it.

Gotrek crossed to the door, listened, then tried it.
Felix and Ulrika stood behind him as he opened it. A
short corridor ended at a large, well-lit warehouse
room. Felix could see men rolling barrels past the
door under the direction of masked overseers.

'The black powder,' murmured Ulrika.

'Aye,' said Gotrek. 'But where are they taking it?'

He crept into the corridor with Felix and Ulrika on
his heels. They stopped just out of the square of light
that shone from the high, vault-ceilinged room. It
looked like the store room at a garrison fort. Boxes of
steel shot were piled next to pyramids of cannon balls,
racks of spears, swords and bows, a small deck cannon
that looked like it had been stolen off an Estalian gal-
ley, and… the stolen barrels of black powder.

On the right-hand side of the room was a wooden
loft. Stacked upon it were sacks of flour, racks of long

guns, kegs of ale, barrels of salted beef and butts of water, as well as small barrels of pitch and paraffin.

The work crew was rolling the black powder barrels out from under the loft, and through a ragged hole in the far wall that led into a brick walled tunnel. The sewers. Felix could smell them from where he stood. Small boats bobbed in the channel of liquid filth. The men loaded two barrels on each boat and then other men poled them away. Only half a dozen barrels remained.

'Destined for the Gunnery School?' asked Felix. 'We should go back and tell Lord Ostwald,' said Felix.

'Go back?' Gotrek snorted. 'Wait ten minutes and you can tell him it's over.' He strode forward into the light.

'Fool! Wait!' hissed Ulrika. 'Have you never heard of subtlety!'

It was too late. One of the masked overseers was looking directly at Gotrek. He pointed, shouting an order. The men pushing the barrels righted them, then drew weapons and charged. More men poured out of side rooms, snatching up spears and swords from the weapon racks. On the loft platform, others began taking the long guns from the racks and feeding them powder and shot. The masked overseer started shouting arcane phrases.

Gotrek grinned, his one eye glittering. He ran forward, bellowing a dwarfish warcry.

Ulrika stared after him. 'He's insane.'

Felix shrugged. 'He's a Slayer.' He raced in after Gotrek, screaming wordlessly.

Ulrika ran right beside him.

The two sides came together with a clash of steel in the centre of the big room. Gotrek killed five men instantly, his fell axe shattering spears, swords and bodies with equal ease. Felix hacked down through the shoulder of a spearman and into his ribcage. Ulrika lunged, recovered and lunged again in a blur, killing two men in the time it took Felix to pull his sword from the spearman's chest.

Then they were surrounded – three whirlwinds fighting back to back in the eye of a hurricane of steel. Spears and swords and hand-axes stabbed in at them from all sides. A sword opened a shallow gash in Felix's chest, tearing and bloodying his borrowed shirt. A spear tore his thigh. This was madness! Why wasn't he wearing his trusty mail? Because he had thought he and Gotrek were going out for a drink, that's why!

More men poured in from the entrances – patrols returning from hunting the passages, Felix guessed – and surged forward to join the press, pushing the melee into the shadow of the loft. Gotrek slew them as they came, wreaking terrible carnage with every stroke. Ulrika floated and flowed like a dancer, her sword everywhere at once. Bodies toppled in her wake, dying from wounds that barely bled. Felix hacked and blocked, more concerned with keeping the spears and swords at bay than with killing anyone. Attacking was too dangerous. Every lunge was an opportunity for five enemies to find an opening and run him through.

The masked overseer finished his incantation and thrust his hands towards the centre of the fight. Nothing happened. Perhaps Gotrek's axe had protected them, thought Felix. It had dissipated spells before. Or perhaps Ulrika could counter magic now that she was a vampire. It gave Felix a good feeling knowing his companions were so powerful – a sense of security. With them at his side he knew he could face the greatest armies and come out on top. Gotrek was unstoppable, and Ulrika appeared to have become an even better swordswoman than she had been when she was alive. In fact, they were so good that Felix didn't really have to do anything. He was tired anyway. Why didn't he just lower his weapons and watch the two of them work? They would protect him. He had nothing to worry about. All was well. Everything would be…

'Wake up, Felix!'

A sharp pain in his cheek snapped his eyes open. Half a dozen spear and sword blades were stabbing towards him. He yelped and leapt back wildly, and smacked into one of the wooden posts that held up the loft, knocking the wind out of him.

To his left Ulrika shouted at him as she impaled one attacker and elbowed another to the ground. 'Beware!' she snapped. 'The mage tries to glamour us.'

Felix growled, furious at the violation. His mind was his own! He renewed his attacks, glaring at the masked sorcerer.

A tattoo of deafening bangs sounded from above. Men screamed. Felix felt hot agony sear his neck. He looked up. The gunners in the loft had got off a volley. They had hit some of their own men, but both Gotrek and Ulrika had been shot as well. Gotrek had a bleeding stripe just above his ear, and Ulrika was clutching her breast.

'Cowards!' roared Gotrek. 'Come down here and fight!'

He lashed out at the support post and chopped it in two with one strike. The platform groaned and sagged in the middle. A flour sack slid off a stack and dropped down into the melee, smacking an agitator on the head. Gotrek pushed for the other post, cutting a swathe through his attackers.

'Gotrek, don't!' cried Felix.

But it was too late. With a fierce backhand, Gotrek smashed through the second post.

'Run!' roared Felix, and bulled into the men in front of him, trying to get clear. They shouted and backed away, tripping over each other as the planks and beams of the loft twisted and snapped above them. Ulrika danced through the mob. Gotrek laughed maniacally, shoving the men aside and grinning back over his shoulder.

With a splintering roar, the loft gave way all at once. The front edge slammed down in a rain of men, guns, kegs, barrels of water and sacks of flour, and crashed right through the ancient warehouse floor, collapsing the supports that held it up, and sending the cannon, the cannon balls, and all the crates of shot smashing into the level below. The sagging planks slanted steeply under Felix's feet as he tried to run, and suddenly he and Gotrek and Ulrika, and all the men that surrounded them, slid backwards down into the hole and fell on top of the heap of debris at the bottom. Felix thudded shoulder first – the *same* shoulder again – into the corner of a wooden gun case, buried under a squirming, moaning, coughing pile of bodies. All around, men called orders and shouted questions. Somewhere nearby, Gotrek chortled madly.

Felix clawed and elbowed his way to the surface. He could see nothing. A cloud of choking dust obscured everything.

Ulrika sat up out of the mound, shoving a body aside. She was covered in dust, making her black clothes match her white skin. She spat. 'Well done, Slayer. Well done.'

'Get them!' the sorcerer's voice rang out from above. 'Kill them!' He began chanting another spell. Felix cursed and tried to stiffen his mind.

All around, men were pushing themselves to their knees and groping for their weapons, their cloaks of dust making them look like some strange snow tribe on the warpath. They turned haltingly towards Gotrek, Felix and Ulrika, groaning as they attacked. The vampire slashed around her, killing all within reach, then helped Felix to his feet. He chopped to his left and right. Every inch of his body felt battered and bruised. His sword weighed as much as a cannon. Sigmar! It *was* heavy! He could barely lift it off the ground, let alone block with it. Beside him, Ulrika was having the same difficulty, losing her balance with every swing of her rapier. Their opponents were not having the same trouble.

'Sorcery!' Ulrika cursed, and tried to scramble back up the slanting floor towards the sorcerer. A thrusting spear tripped her and she slid back.

A man split in two in front of Felix, and Gotrek stepped through the pieces, glaring up at the masked sorcerer.

'Enough of your noise!' he barked, then plucked a cannon ball the size of a cantaloupe from the debris at their feet and hurled it at the magician.

The magician squawked and ducked, but not fast enough. The cannon ball crushed the side of his head like an eggshell and he fell into the hole, as limp as a sawdust doll.

Immediately Felix's sword was lighter again, and he attacked their foes with renewed energy. Ulrika did the same.

The dust in the air settled as they fought, and the outlines of the chamber they had landed in slowly emerged into clarity. The mound under their feet was a grisly, treacherous jumble. Bloody limbs and crushed heads stuck up out of the mess of shattered timber, spilled long guns, cannon balls and bags of shot. The deck cannon had pinned half a dozen men. They squirmed under it like squashed bugs. The screams were unbearable.

More figures were creeping out of shadowed arches at the edges of the chamber, and at the far end...

Felix froze, and almost took an axe in the knee because of it. He stumbled back as the air cleared and the thing at the far end of the chamber was revealed. 'Sigmar save us,' he choked.

Gotrek and Ulrika glanced up from their fights. Gotrek grunted. Ulrika snarled.

At first it seemed to be a twisted tree, growing from a stone altar and hung with bodies, but then Felix saw that the tree was a sculpture – at least he hoped it was a sculpture – made entirely of bones, of a giant, bird-headed deity, four bodies hanging from its four outstretched hands by hooks that pierced their flesh. The bones of the sculpture were human – leg bones, arm bones, hip bones, skulls and ribcages – all fused together as if they had melted in a furnace. There was no order to the construction. Each of the sculpture's arms and legs was made of hundreds of random bones – skulls and ribs, fibia and tibia – every one of them decorated with swirls of beaten gold. The thing's head was long and narrow and came to a beak-like point. Two gold-sheathed skulls served it for eyes. Dozens of finger bones – still attached to skeletal hands – were its teeth. From the eyeholes of the skull-eyes glowed a sickly greenish light.

The same light shone down into its torso, a lacy, ovoid cage of bones. There was something within the cage, something that writhed and twisted. The bodies that hung from its hands swayed like heavy fruit.

Felix shivered with dread. It appeared that the Brothers of the Cleansing Flame were not mere agitators.

SEVEN

'FOOLS,' GROWLED GOTREK, cutting down two men.

'Dupes of Chaos,' agreed Ulrika, impaling another.

'They must not leave here!' said a new voice from above. 'Slay them, changed ones! Slay the unbelievers!'

Felix looked around. *Changed ones?*

The figures emerging from the temple doors roared and surged forward, clambering up the mountain of debris and clawing at the companions. Felix flinched as he fought them. It was as if he were looking at them through warped glass. Their limbs were stretched and bent, their heads lopsided and bobbing on elongated necks. Hideous goitres and lumps grew from their skin. Some had new limbs – stumpy arms or tentacles or claws growing from their torsos. Some had eyes or mouths where they shouldn't.

But there was worse to be seen beyond them. The bodies hanging from the bone god stirred and pulled themselves free of the hooks to drop, cat-like to the ground. The thing in the bone cage uncoiled and slithered out through a hole near the pelvis. It was pink and blind and foetal, but had stilt-like spider legs that carried it swiftly towards the fight, and the coiled, flexing proboscis of a butterfly.

These new troops swarmed in behind their twisted brethren. Felix's stomach churned as he buried his blade in the spongy head of a man with scaly, seven-jointed fingers. He hated fighting mutants. It was hard to fight something you felt pity for. It was like killing someone with the plague – a necessary, but soul-crushing, task. Not all mutants had dabbled in the black arts. With some, the mutations just came, and there was nothing they could do about it. And once they came, the revulsion of their family and friends, and the persecution of the witch hunters, drove them underground to seek out their own kind. Small wonder that they gravitated to the cults of the Ruinous Powers. They were the only ones who would welcome such creatures with open arms, the only ones who would shelter them and promise them a future.

That was the trouble. It was hard to kill a man when, in the same circumstances, you might have followed the same path. Of course, it became much easier when that man was trying to rip your guts out with a mouth full of shark teeth, but it still didn't make Felix happy to do it.

Neither Gotrek nor Ulrika seemed to have any second thoughts. Gotrek stood on the butt of the fallen cannon, butchering any that came within reach and roaring for the thing from the bone cage to come and taste his axe. He split a mutant with skin like a lobster from head to crotch. The four men who had dangled from the statue leapt to take its place. They appeared to have been skinned. Their exposed muscles were glistening crimson. They bled endlessly.

Ulrika was a blur of black and grey, out of which shot the silver lightning of her blade. Mutants died all around her. A man leapt on her from the warehouse above, stabbing at her chest. She caught his wrist and pulled him off her back, then sank her jutting fangs into his neck, ripping out meat and veins in a spray of blood.

Felix whirled madly, hacking off a clawed hand, ducking a horned fist, then gutting a man with translucent flesh. A tentacle curled around his left ankle. He slashed down at it, but too late. It jerked his legs out from under him, and he fell hard on a bag of shot, hissing with pain. A thing with praying mantis arms and a face of melted wax leapt on his chest. He knocked it off with his arms, then lashed at it with his sword, but the tentacle was still pulling him down the mound, and he missed.

He looked down. The tentacle belonged to a woman dressed like a Shantytown harlot. It came out from under her short skirt. Felix shuddered at the implication. The woman raised daggerlike hands, licking her lips as she dragged him closer.

Suddenly there was a flash of steel and the harlot's head rolled from her shoulders in a spout of blood. It thudded to the floor and her tentacle went slack. Felix looked up. Ulrika was smirking down at him.

'In case you have any compunction about killing a lady,' she said.

The praying mantis thing lashed out at her from behind. She stumbled forward, grunting, and it sprang at her like a flea. Still on his back, Felix thrust up with his sword and gutted it in mid-leap. It landed on him, dead.

Ulrika kicked it off him, then grasped his hand and hauled him to his feet while fending off three others. Her strength was frightening.

'Thank you,' she said.

'The same to you,' said Felix. He returned to the fray. His hand tingled where they had touched. His thoughts flashed unbidden back to other times they had touched. He fought the memories off as desperately as he fought the mutants.

The skinned things were dead, but Gotrek was soaked in their sticky blood. It seemed to be clotting as Felix watched, slowing the Slayer's movements.

The foetal spider clicked forward and lunged at Gotrek. Faster than the eye could see its curled tongue straightened and jabbed. The Slayer blocked with his axe and missed, slowed by the swiftly drying blood, then staggered back, a hole like a gun wound in his right arm. He roared in pain.

Felix beckoned to Ulrika. 'Come on.'

They fought forward to guard Gotrek's flanks, holding off mutants to his right and left as he launched a barrage of attacks at the foetal thing with his axe, crusted blood exploding from his body like brick dust. None struck home. The creature's spider legs seemed to have the ability to jerk its torso out of harm's way in the blink of an eye. Gotrek lashed at a leg, but the thing whipped it away, backing down the mound.

The Slayer cursed, frustrated, then threw his arms wide, cracking off more blood. 'Right then. Have a go.'

The thing lunged in again, snapping out its needle-like snout straight for Gotrek's heart. The Slayer's free hand blurred and he caught the spike at its fleshy root. The spider foetus keened like a newborn and tried to jerk away. Gotrek held it fast, laughing, then brought his axe down in the centre of the creature's unformed body. It disintegrated in an explosion of gelid pink flesh.

Felix heard a ripple of dismay go through the mutants. 'The blessed one is dead,' they whispered, falling back. 'He killed the favoured of the Changer.'

Above them a voice called out. 'Brothers, escape! This place is lost! You will be contacted in the usual ways! The plans proceed!'

Gotrek spun, glaring up towards the voice. 'Get him! He knows what's what!'

Gotrek, Felix and Ulrika tried to run up the broken slanted floor as the mutants scattered for the exits, but just then a black powder barrel toppled into the hole and bounced down the planks, a length of match cord fizzing and sparking from its top. Felix threw himself right. Gotrek and Ulrika went left. Another barrel rolled by. They careened across the floor of the unholy temple and smashed into the statue of the Changer of Ways, toppling it.

'Down!' shouted Gotrek. 'Behind the pile.'

Felix scrabbled over the mound of crates and guns and dived for the ground on the other side.

A thunderclap punched him in both ears, and a wave of blistering air lifted him up and slammed him into the wall behind the mound. A boiling cloud of fire roiled above him as a rain of bricks, boards and body parts battered him. Something struck him on

the head, and for an instant all went black. His whole
world was noise, heat and pain.

After a moment the noise and blackness receded,
though the heat and pain remained. He looked up.
Through the hole above him he could see that the
warehouse room was on fire. Another explosion
rocked it as he watched. Smoke obscured the vaulted
brick roof. The temple was ablaze too. Fire licked up
the plaster wall beside him, waking new pain in the
burns he had taken on the bridge. On the other side
of the rubble heap, mutants howled in agony. The
hideous statue was gone, blown to pieces, and that
end of the chamber was engulfed in flame.

Gotrek staggered to his feet and brushed dust and
glowing cinders off his shoulders. He looked like he'd
lost a fight with a dragon. 'Time to go, manling.'

'Go where?' asked Felix. They were surrounded by
fire.

'The sewers,' said Gotrek.

Ulrika pushed up to her hands and knees, dislodg-
ing a long plank. Her beautiful doublet was ruined.
The hair on the left side of her head was singed and
black. 'A wise plan, Slayer. You surprise me.'

Gotrek grunted, apparently disappointed that she
had survived.

'We go through that?' asked Felix, pointing up at the
warehouse inferno.

Gotrek shrugged. 'Better than staying here.'

Felix nodded and stood wearily. He didn't feel like
he could walk a step, let alone run through a burning
cellar, but staying here was death. The sense of where
he was and what lay between him and fresh air suddenly pressed down on him like a cart sitting on his

chest. His limbs went weak. He was five floors below ground in a burning building, the walls of which were a jumble of old, rotting timber, poorly mortared stone, brick and cheap, dry plaster. He had been far deeper in dwarf mines, but there he had had some confidence that they had been shaped by master masons. This place had been built by a succession of slum lords and criminals. Suddenly he wanted to see the sky more than anything in his life.

He scrambled up the slanted floor behind Gotrek and Ulrika into the burning warehouse, forcing his trembling, exhausted limbs to move. Flames were everywhere. The heat beat on Felix like a hammer. Every breath was like inhaling glass. The sewers were only ten paces away, and the path clear. Only a few steps and they would be safe.

Gotrek started forward, then stopped at a sound from above and looked up. 'Back!' he said, throwing his arms out. 'Back!'

With a rumbling and snapping, the brick ceiling above the hole to the sewers caved in, followed by timbers from the floors above it, all on fire. The debris blocked the hole to the sewers, and the ceiling kept coming down, a rain of bricks, timber and fire, that advanced on Gotrek, Felix and Ulrika like the leading edge of a storm. Dust billowed out towards them in a flaming cloud.

'The hidden stair!' cried Ulrika.

Gotrek made no argument, only turned and ran with Ulrika for the office with the secret door.

In his years with Gotrek, Felix had become used to shortening his stride to match the Slayer's. Not here. Fear lent him wings, and he nearly beat Ulrika to the office, and bested Gotrek by ten paces.

The office was filled with smoke, but was only just beginning to catch fire. Ulrika tore down the banner that hid the door and felt up and down the wall.

'Yebat!' she cursed, scrabbling desperately. 'Where is it.'

'Stand aside, parasite,' said Gotrek. He jabbed a finger at a nail head in a support beam and the door swung open. Ulrika pushed in first, her face rigid with panic. Gotrek and Felix filed in after her and Gotrek closed the door.

The stairs were dark, but at least free of smoke and fire. They hurried up them as the building roared and moaned and creaked all around them.

Felix heard Ulrika mumbling something that sounded like some Kislevite prayer.

'Scared, bloodsucker?' asked Gotrek.

Ulrika laughed, high and tight. 'Swords, daggers, pistol balls; they cannot kill me. But fire, fire means the true death.'

'I'll keep that in mind,' Gotrek growled.

As they raced up, Felix saw firelight glinting through cracks in the walls. Sometimes smoke trickled through and the walls radiated heat like an oven, and more and more smoke was filtering up the stairwell from below. Felix coughed, his eyes watering and his throat raw.

Five flights up, an orange light flickered from above them, and Felix could hear the crackling of flames.

Gotrek stopped. 'Blocked,' he said.

'Back down, then?' asked Felix. They looked over the railing. The smoke below them glowed from within with a hellish red, and the light seemed to be getting closer by the second. The stairs groaned and shifted under their feet, then suddenly dropped several inches and lurched to one side.

'I don't think so,' said Gotrek.

'We're trapped!' whimpered Ulrika.

Gotrek snorted and turned to feel the building's exterior wall, an unplastered mess of thinly mortared brick. Felix copied him. It was cool to the touch.

Gotrek flipped his axe around so that the square end faced out. He smashed it into the wall. Bricks flew. He swung again.

'Ha!' said Ulrika, grinning with relief. She stepped back and kicked at the wall with her boot heel. Mortar crumbled.

Felix joined her, kicking and stabbing at the bricks with his runesword. Sacrilege, no doubt, to use so grand a weapon for so pedestrian a purpose, but if Gotrek was using his sacred rune axe, and if it saved his life...

A hole opened up in seconds, Gotrek smashing through the two layers of brick with ease. Felix and Ulrika's kicks helped him widen it as the flames from below and above crept closer. Felix sucked in great breaths of the cool, clear air that blew in from the hole. He had never tasted sweeter.

At last the opening was wide enough for Gotrek's broad shoulders and they clambered though into another cellar; this one blissfully free of fire.

But as they reached the ground floor it became clear that the building had not escaped the blaze. The narrow corridor that led to the street was filled with weeping, wailing people, all trying to get out at once. Felix could hear crackling and screaming from the upper floors.

The alley, as Felix, Gotrek and Ulrika pushed out into it, was just as crowded. The nearby tenements had emptied and people milled around in panicked circles. Others ran away. Men in the masks of the Cleansing Flame were dotted through the crowd, shouting orders that no one listened to. The cult's meeting house was a roaring hell of flame and blackened beams, half its original height. The buildings to its left and right were burning too, and the wooden shingles of the building that housed the Broken Crown were smouldering.

People in further tenements were spreading wet blankets on their roofs, trying to protect them from the flurries of fiery sparks that whirled up and away over the gables. Others were forming bucket lines that trailed to a small well where two men were hauling up a single bucket and lowering it over and over again. The meagre splashes of water that the men at the front of the line threw on the fire were doing little.

'Sigmar,' breathed Felix. 'All of Shantytown is going to burn!'

Gotrek grunted, his massive fists balled in anger.

Ulrika shook her head in dismay. 'What terrible villainy.'

Gotrek sneered at her. 'What's the matter? You don't like your dinner cooked?'

She drew herself up, offended. 'I'm beginning to think that you are deliberately misunderstanding the Lhamian way.'

'Or maybe you are,' said Gotrek. He started for the well. 'Find a big tub, manling,' he said over his shoulder. 'We need to draw more water.'

Felix nodded, and was about to enter an unburned tenement, when a voice screeched nearby.

'There they are! There are the murderers who started the fire!'

Felix turned with Gotrek and Ulrika to see one of the masked men pointing directly at him.

Another cultist joined the first. 'Get them!' he cried. 'String them up! Throw them in the fire!'

'It wasn't us!' shouted Felix. 'It was them!' But his voice was lost in the roar of the crowd as they turned angry eyes on them.

'Kill the fire starters!' bellowed a man.

'They burned my baby!' shrieked a woman.

All at once the crowd surged in from all sides, snatching up stones and bits of smoking wood.

Gotrek bared his teeth in fury and frustration, and Felix was momentarily afraid that he was going to lash out at the mob, but then, with a dwarfish curse, he turned and made for a narrow alley, shoving the shouting people in front of him roughly aside. Felix and Ulrika followed him, hunching their shoulders against a rain of sticks and stones. Felix didn't want to hurt the poor souls in the crowd, but they were trying to tear him apart. He kicked and elbowed them aside, men and women alike.

They reached the alley mouth. Gotrek let Felix and Ulrika in first and then followed. Here, the mob could only press them from behind. Alone, Felix could have outdistanced them easily, but Gotrek, with his short legs, was too slow, and they railed unmercifully on his back with their makeshift weapons, the cultists urging them on. The Slayer cursed and grunted, but did not strike back. The end of the alley was rapidly approaching. They would be surrounded again.

They dodged around a rickety exterior stairway. Gotrek stopped suddenly. His axe lashed out – once, twice – chopping through the stair's supports, then ran on with Felix and Ulrika.

The crowd flooded after them, but then, with a squeal of tortured nails and twisting wood, the stairway peeled away from the outside of the tenement.

The crowd screamed and backed away, pushing back against their comrades who were continuing to press down the alley as the stairs accordioned down on themselves and crashed to the ground. A dozen or so Maze residents had made it past the crash. They ran out of the alley after Gotrek, Felix and Ulrika.

Gotrek spun on them as they spread out, baring his teeth. Felix and Ulrika drew too. The men and women slowed, uneasy.

'Go back,' said Gotrek. 'Fight the fire.' He raised his axe. It flashed red in the light of the inferno. 'You do not want this death.'

He turned again and the companions ran on. The crowd did not follow.

The Maze was filled with people and noise. Bells rang. People shouted. Men and women ran away from the fire or towards it. Teams of men ran past with ladders. Two women pushed a sloshing hogshead of water on a barrow. Others carried empty buckets, old blankets and brooms.

Felix's heart hung as heavy as a lead brick in his chest as he and Gotrek and Ulrika dodged through them all. He felt useless and miserable. He wanted to do something to help the innocents who were dying and losing their homes because of the Cleansing Flame's callous arson, but he couldn't think of a thing. He and Gotrek were very good at killing and destroying things. Ask them to fight a troll or a dragon, or bring down a corrupt king, or smash some eldritch temple and they would get to work with a will, and more than likely succeed, but ask them to protect someone from hunger or disease, or to save their home from fire or flood, and they were as powerless as the next man. You couldn't slay hunger with an axe. You couldn't kill fire with a sword.

As they came around a corner near the edge of the Maze, they saw Ward Captain Wissen hurrying towards them with a company of the watch. His polished breastplate glinted yellow with reflected fire.

His eyes widened as he saw them. 'You!' he cried, pointing. 'Is it you at the bottom of this?'

Gotrek didn't slow down. 'Out of my way, fool!'

'Arrest them!' shouted Wissen.

The watchmen spread across the road, lowering their spears.

Gotrek stopped, growling and staring them down.

'The culprits are the Cleansing Flame, ward captain,' said Felix quickly. It wouldn't do to have the Slayer slaughter the watch. 'Your agitators are cultists, worshippers of the Changer of Ways. It was they who started the fire. And they plan worse. They mean to blow up the Imperial Gunnery School with the stolen powder.'

Anger flashed across Wissen's face. Jealousy perhaps? 'And how do you know this?' he sneered.

Felix looked around to get confirmation from Ulrika, and realised that she was no longer with them.

He looked back over his shoulder. She was nowhere to be seen. Where had she gone? When had she left? 'We heard it from the cultists themselves,' he said, facing Wissen again. 'And we saw them taking the powder into the sewers.'

'But you have no evidence of this?' asked Wissen.

Felix grunted with frustration. 'I don't understand you, ward captain. All along you have suspected agitators of having been behind the thefts, but now that we bring you word that your suspicions are correct, you question it? What is the difficulty?'

'The difficulty is *you*,' said Wissen, stepping forward and jabbing his finger. 'I have had the Cleansing Flame under observation for these past several months. My men have come very close to discovering who their leaders are, and what their ultimate goals are. We were this close!' he held his finger and thumb less than a half inch apart. 'This close to scooping them all up in a bag and jailing the lot of them. We might have uncovered a vast network of agitators and collaborators had we been able to put the screws to them, but then here come the "Saviours of Nuln," waltzing into town like a pair of drunken ogres, and smash up everything they touch. We'll never catch them now! You've scattered them to the four winds!' He cursed and turned to his men. 'Arrest them!' he cried. 'Arrest them for interfering with the work of the constabulary.'

Gotrek went on guard. 'You'll take me when I'm dead.'

Felix groaned. This was bad. Gotrek was going to kill a captain of the watch and they would have to go on the run again before they could warn Groot and

Makaisson of the Cleansing Flame's plans. 'Captain,' he said, fighting to keep his voice calm. 'Ward captain, be reasonable. Do I need to remind you that we have been ordered by Lord Hieronymous Ostwald himself to assist you in your investigations? How will you explain to him our arrest? Should you not at least consult with your superiors?'

Wissen paused, grinding his teeth. His men hesitated.

'We were on our way to tell Lord Groot of the danger to the Gunnery School,' Felix continued. 'If you would care to accompany us, I'm sure that the truth of our story will be found below it.'

A nasty smile spread slowly across Wissen's face. 'Ha!' he said. 'I'm sure it will.' He bowed elaborately to Felix. 'Very well, sir. Lead on. Lead on and we will see.'

EIGHT

LORD GROOT UNLOCKED a heavy, iron-bound door and threw it open. 'These are the lowest rooms in the school,' he said in a cross voice. 'And the last that we have not examined – a dungeon we have never found it necessary to put to use.' He stepped aside and let Gotrek, Felix, Malakai, Magus Lichtmann and Captain Wissen step in.

Groot had been roused from his bed more than an hour ago, and was not in the best of moods. He had all of Felix's sympathy. Felix was so tired and sore from all the night's fighting and falling and battering that he could barely put one foot in front of the other. His eyes kept crossing and it was an effort to focus them again.

The dungeon was a very small affair. A guard room with ten cells beyond it, and a 'questioning' room beyond that. It looked indeed like it had never been

used. The corners of the few sparse furnishings were
sharp and unblunted by use, and everything was furred
in a thick coat of dust. None the less, the party made a
dutiful tour of the place, poking their heads into each
cell and scanning the questioning room. Gotrek and
Malakai made a more careful examination, running their
hands over every wall, and scrutinising the floors and
ceilings closely, while Magus Lichtmann muttered and
gestured with his single hand. Groot and Wissen waited
for them to finish with exaggerated patience.

At last the two Slayers exchanged an unhappy glance
and returned to the door.

'Nithin',' said Malakai with a sigh. 'Nae hidden
doors, nae hollow walls, nae trapped floors. Same as
a' the rest.'

Wissen gave a little snort of triumph.

'And you'll agree that we've seen everything there is
to see?' asked Groot.

'Aye, that ah dae,' said Malakai. 'Naught's been left
oot. We've seen it a'.'

'And I detect nothing hidden with magic of any
kind,' said Magus Lichtmann.

Groot nodded. 'Then let's return to someplace
warmer and wait for the sewer detail's report.'

He led the way back up through the many cellars to
the receiving room of the school. Leaders of the sewer
detail were waiting for them – a captain and a sergeant
of the school guard standing at attention at the
entrance with a hunched, haggard man in filthy
clothes who carried a lantern, a long-poled hook, and
a short sword and dagger on his belt.

Felix recognised the man's accoutrements instantly.
He was a sewer jack. A host of memories flooded his

mind at the sight – Gotrek and he carrying those very implements, the other men of their patrol – Gant, Rudi, Hef and Spider, the twin brothers who had shared the same girl. He also remembered the vile smell that had taken forever to scrub from his skin and his hair. The memory was so vivid that he thought he could smell the odour even now.

No, no, he thought as he saw Magus Lichtmann wrinkling his nose, it wasn't the memory after all. It was the sewer jack.

'What have you to report, captain?' asked Groot.

The guard captain saluted him and stepped forward. 'Nothing, my lord. Steiger here took us through every tunnel and channel that crosses under the school. There was nothing. No barrels. No loose powder. No fuses. No evidence of digging or recent construction. We even…' He coughed. 'We even had him probe the stew for anything hidden under the surface. There was nothing there either.'

Groot nodded. 'Very good, captain. You are dismissed. Get some rest. And give this man a crown for his pains.'

'Aye, my lord,' said the captain.

The sewer jack touched his forelock to Groot as the captain and the sergeant led him out. The light of early dawn shone into the entry hall as they opened the door.

'You see, Lord Groot?' said Wissen, eagerly, as he and the others followed Groot into the receiving room. 'Nothing! No powder. No sign of the Cleansing Flame.'

Groot only groaned and sank wearily into a deep leather chair.

'Could be it hisnae been placed yet,' said Malakai.

'Or it was never sold to the Cleansing Flame in the first place, perhaps,' suggested Magus Lichtmann.

Captain Wissen scowled at Gotrek and Felix. 'I begin to wonder if any part of their story is true. We only have their word that they found the Cleansing Flame's quarters. Or that the Flame are cultists.'

Gotrek rounded on him, his fists balling. 'Do you think I got these cuts falling down stairs?'

'Falling off a barstool, perhaps,' sneered Wissen.

Gotrek surged forward, lowering his head. 'Right. That's it.'

Malakai stepped in his way and put out a restraining arm. 'Easy laddie, easy. You'll no' catch yer villains like this.'

'You see?' cried Wissen, backing away. 'You see? Whatever acts of heroism these two might have performed in the past, they're mere taproom brawlers now. It may be true that they uncovered sorcery and mutation among the Brotherhood of the Cleansing Flame, but it could be just as true that they were carousing in some Maze ale cellar and kicked over a lantern, then thought to tell this wild tale to cover their villainy.'

Gotrek pushed at Malakai's arm. 'Do you call me a liar?'

'Not at all,' said Wissen. 'I merely say that we can't know, because you burned all the evidence, and we found nothing below the school.'

'We didn't burn it!' snapped Felix, his anger finally winning out over his exhaustion. 'The cultists burned it when they saw that we were in danger of exposing them!'

'And does that make it any less your fault?' asked Wissen. 'If you had not entered their lair they would have had no need to destroy their idols.' He pointed to the line of tall windows that ran along the front wall of the room. 'Look there! Look!'

All heads turned to the windows. Through the dia-mond panes Felix could see, smudged across the shell-pink dawn like a black smear of dung upon a lady's ball gown, a twisting pillar of smoke that rose from the centre of the Shantytown district. The orange glow of fire still underlit it at its base.

'That is your work,' said Wissen. 'Whether you set it or no. Scores dead. Hundreds without homes. Victims to your bullheadedness.'

Felix couldn't tear his eyes from the rising smoke. He felt as if the words were being stacked on top of his heart like stone slabs, one at a time, crushing it. As much as he hated the man, he couldn't help but think that Wissen was right. It *was* their fault. They had barged in as they always did, and innocents had been hurt. He looked over at Gotrek, expecting him to be trying to push past Malakai for Wissen again, but the Slayer was looking at the floor, his hands clenched. It seemed the words had hit him too. Somehow that made it worse.

Wissen turned to the others, bowing. 'My lords, I will place men in the sewers below the Gunnery School, just in case Herr Jaeger's story is true. It is only prudent. But may I suggest that he and Gurnisson be confined to the College of Engineering at least until the matter of their actions can be put before Lord Ostwald.'

'I think that is wise,' said Magus Lichtmann, his spectacles winking in the dawn light. 'It is a terrible pity. Much as I admire their zeal, I fear that the Slayer and his companion have been perhaps too hasty. If they had reported what they had discovered to Ward Captain Wissen, instead of trying to destroy the cult – if that is indeed what it was – single handed, much tragedy could have been avoided.'

Lord Groot nodded. 'Aye,' he said. 'Maybe it's best. These sort of tactics no doubt work well enough in the lands of our enemies, but this...' He shook his head sadly. 'This took the lives and livelihoods of honest Nulners. That can't be allowed.'

Malakai banged a side table with his huge fist. His face was as red as his crest. 'Ye empty-headed eejits!' he barked. 'Have ye nae more sense than a bunch o' hens? Yer locking up the wrong lads!' He swept his hand towards Gotrek and Felix. 'Who wis it found the thieves that stole the powder? Who uncovered the vermin who bought it, and learned o' their wicked plans?'

'We have only their word for that,' piped up Wissen, raising a finger.

'Shut it, yoo!' said Malakai. 'I'm talkin'.' He turned to Groot. 'And as to who's tae blame for the fire. Do ye think this wee mannie,' he pointed at Wissen, 'and his lads would hae' fared any better? By Grungni's beard, them Flame boys would have heard 'em coming before they walked down three flights, and set the whole works ablaze. Ye would ha' lost a full company o' the watch as well as all those poor wee beggars in the warrens.' His finger moved to Gotrek and Felix. 'Gurnisson an' young Felix hae come closer than any to catching these lunatics. And it's them yer going tae lock up? Awa 'n boil yer heids!'

Groot raised his hands placatingly. 'Not locked up, Malakai,' he said. 'Not locked up. Only, erm, taking a rest, let's say, until Lord Ostwald can review what's happened. I don't doubt he'll approve of all they've done, and set them on the trail as soon as he's spoken to them.'

'And when can Lord Ostwald see us?' asked Felix.

'Ah,' said Groot, scratching his head violently. 'Well, he's been sent for.'

Lichtmann stepped forward. 'Pardon, Julianus, but I believe Lord Ostwald is closeted with the City Council today and tomorrow, reviewing some sort of fiscal matters.'

Groot looked at Gotrek, Felix and Malakai, embarrassed. 'So, a day or two then? The rest will do you good. You do look a bit the worse for wear.'

Gotrek growled. 'I make no promises.'

Groot and Wissen looked about to protest, but Malakai stepped forward.

'I do,' he said. 'Neither Gurnisson nor young Felix will pass through the gates of the College of Engineering until Lord Ostwald comes tae see 'em.'

Groot frowned and exchanged glances with the others, as Gotrek glared at Malakai.

'You will vouch for their good behaviour?' asked Groot at last.

'Aye,' said Malakai. 'If they step through that gate, ah'll take full responsibility for their actions.'

Groot nodded. 'Very well. Then I release them into your custody. And thank you, Malakai, for your understanding.'

Malakai snorted. 'Oh, I understand fu' weel.'

* * *

As THEY STEPPED out of the gates of the Imperial Gunnery School and started down the street towards the College of Engineering, Gotrek shot a sidelong glance at Malakai.

'You truly mean to try to keep me locked up?' he asked.

Malakai chuckled. 'Eh? O' course no'! Oh, ye'll no' leave by the gate. A dwarf does no' break a promise. But there's a wee hole down tae the sewers. I said naught about wee holes.'

WHEN THEY GOT to the college, Felix went to his room, closed his shutters and his curtains and lay down in bed. But tired as he was, he had difficulty getting to sleep. His mind remained filled with Wissen's damning words. Malakai had made a spirited defence, but Felix still could not convince himself that the fire hadn't been, at least in part, their fault. Should they have gone back and told the authorities instead of wading in? Should they have fought the cultists in a different way? Was there something else they could have done?

When he did fall asleep, his dreams were haunted by the sounds of crackling flames and the screams of the dying.

FELIX WOKE TO a gentle tapping on his door. When he raised his head from the pillows, a man in the robes of a physician was poking his head in. He smiled at Felix.

'Sorry to wake you,' he said. 'But Professor Makaisson asked me to look in on you and change your bandages.'

Felix mumbled for the man to come in and tried to sit up to receive him. He was so stiff and sore he could barely move. The physician came in and helped him up, then went gently but firmly about his work. Felix smiled through his grunts and groans. Makaisson might be mad, but he did well by his guests.

Once all his burns and cuts had been salved and dressed and he had gone about the slow, painful process of pulling his clothes on, he hobbled through the school to Malakai's workshop. Once again he found Gotrek wolfing down an enormous breakfast while Malakai pottered among his inventions. The Slayer too had fresh bandages, but not nearly as many as yesterday. Felix shook his head. Though he had seen evidence of it many times before, he was yet again amazed at how quickly the dwarf's wounds healed. Many of his burns were only shiny pink spots, like punctuation marks among his tattoos.

Felix stepped to the unfinished room's missing wall and looked out over the city. The fires in Shantytown seemed to have died down for the most part, but there was still an ashy pall above the skyline that was not clouds. He sighed and sat down at the table and helped himself to ham, black bread and tea.

'The best cure for yer gloom, young Felix, is to catch yon madmen before they dae worse,' said Malakai. He snorted. 'Ward Captain Wissen willnae catch 'em, that's certain. 'No doubt e's out there now, flogging any poor soul he can catch, but gettin' nae answers, I'll warrant ye.'

Felix nodded, but was not convinced. The best cure would have been to not let the madmen start the fires in the first place.

Petr appeared in the door as Felix took his first sip of tea. He hurried forward, tripping over a coil of rope, then stopped at the table and pushed his wild hair out of his face.

'Good news, professor,' he said, beaming myopically. 'Meyer at the Gunnery School says that the new cannon has cooled and seems to be without fault.'

'Aye. Good news indeed,' said Malakai.

'All that remains,' continued Petr, 'is for the sprue to be cut and the barrel to be smoothed within and cleaned and polished without.'

'And how long will that take?' asked Felix.

'Meyer said that the smiths are aware of the urgency of the situation and will work around the clock to get it done,' said Petr. 'They say it will be done two mornings from now.'

Malakai shook his head sadly. 'Men rush things. Dwarf smiths would take a fortnight tae do it, at the least.' He shrugged. 'But as we have tae be awa' as soon as can be, I suppose quicker may jist be better.'

'Two days.' Gotrek grunted. 'Time enough to find those masked cowards. Eat faster, manling. I want a look in the sewers.'

'Petr,' said Malakai. 'Gae tae the steward and get the key to the sewer door.'

'Aye, professor,' said Petr. He turned and ran out of the room, tripping over the same coil of rope again as he went.

Felix shook his head. How had the boy survived as long as he had?

* * *

Felix shivered as he and Gotrek stepped through a
doorway into the sewers from a cellar under the College of Engineering. It was all as it had been twenty
years ago, the crumbling brick walls, the low arched
ceiling, the river of filth flowing sluggishly between
the two narrow ledges, the rats scurrying away into
darkness, the constant echoing plops and drips, the
moist reek that flooded his nostrils. Memory once
again overwhelmed him – it was here that the fight
with the skaven in the College of Engineering had
ended all those years ago, with the steam tank crashing through the floor and coming to rest half
submerged in the stew. He shivered. No good ever
came of entering the sewers.

'Good luck, sirs,' said Petr, as he pushed the heavy
door closed behind them.

The boom of it closing was drowned out by a shriek.

Gotrek and Felix spun back, drawing their weapons
and holding up their lanterns. There was nothing
behind them.

'All right, Petr?' called Felix as the door inched open
again.

'It's nothing,' squeaked Petr. 'Nothing. Just pinched
my finger a… a little. Good luck.'

The door closed more slowly this time, and they heard
locks and bolts clacking shut, and a soft moaning.

Gotrek grunted. 'A dwarf so clumsy would have
been smothered at birth.'

Felix frowned. 'How would you know he was
clumsy at birth?'

'That one? I've no doubt he tripped coming out of
the womb.' He started down the sewer tunnel. 'Come,
manling, the Gunnery School is this way.'

They continued down the tunnel, travelling slowly as Gotrek examined the walls on both sides, crossing back and forth over the granite slabs that bridged the stew at regular intervals. The Slayer muttered under his breath from time to time, but said nothing out loud.

A short while later, Gotrek looked up. 'Someone ahead.'

He crept forward, readying his axe. Felix got a better grip on his sword. All manner of possible horrors rose up in his mind as they rounded a curve in the tunnel and the flickering glow of a torch grew stronger before them. Was it ratmen? Cultists of the Cleansing Flame? Mutants?

'Halt!' said a voice. 'Who goes there?'

A trio of Nuln city watch came round the curve, torches held high. They stopped when they saw Gotrek and Felix and thrust their spears nervously before them.

'Who's there?' called the sergeant. 'State your business!'

Gotrek grunted, annoyed. Felix sighed. He had forgotten that Wissen had said he was going to place patrols down here. This was going to be a bit awkward.

'Perhaps we should retire,' he murmured to Gotrek, as the watchmen came closer.

'We need to find the powder,' said Gotrek.

'Aye,' said Felix. 'But we can't kill the watch to do it. We're in enough trouble as it is.'

'Come forward, curse you!' said the sergeant. 'Into the light. What are you doing down here?'

'We can return later,' continued Felix. 'Now we know they're here, we can avoid them next time, once their guard is down.'

Gotrek growled, but finally nodded and began backing away.

'It's the Slayer and the other one,' said one of the watchmen. 'Them that burned Shantytown!'

'Why so it is,' said the other.

'Stop, you!' called the sergeant. 'You're not meant to be outside the College!'

He and his men started forward at a trot.

Gotrek cursed and stopped. Felix groaned and lined up beside him.

The sergeant halted before them and pointed his spear. 'Hand over your weapons and come with me. Watch Captain Wissen will want to hear about this.'

'Tell him about this,' said Gotrek. His hand shot forward and caught the shaft of the sergeant's spear. He twisted it and the sergeant staggered left, then toppled into the stew with a thick splash.

Gotrek advanced on the other watchmen, as the sergeant came to the surface gasping and choking and covered in filth.

'You want to join him?' the Slayer rasped.

The watchmen backed off, wide-eyed, then turned and ran, calling and whistling for reinforcements.

The sergeant slogged after them, waist deep in the flow. 'Come back, cowards! How dare you desert a senior officer!'

Gotrek chuckled nastily and made to continue forward, but there were answering cries and whistles from further down the tunnel. He cursed again and turned away.

'Right, manling,' he said. 'We'll return later. Let's see what we can turn up in the Maze.'

Felix frowned. 'The Maze? Is that wise? We're not well liked down there at the moment.'

'And where are we liked?' asked Gotrek.

FELIX WALKED THROUGH Shantytown with a heavy heart. The men and women of the Maze were wheeling their charred belongings through the streets on barrows and dog carts, their children tailing behind them. Larger wagons were carrying fresh timber, bricks and plaster in the other direction. Priests of Morr carried burned bodies away on carts and stretchers.

Felix wore the hood of his cloak up to hide his face, but Gotrek walked openly, his singed crest and his burn scars showing, and just as Felix had feared, they were getting a lot of looks. People glared. Some whispered behind their hands to each other, but none approached. Perhaps, in the light of day, with the fires of hate somewhat cooled, they didn't relish confronting a dwarf as fearsome looking as Gotrek. Felix was not reassured. It wouldn't take much to spark the Shantytowners to violence again. One voice raised in anger, one pointed finger, and they would be swarmed again.

He held his breath every time they passed another street corner orator. Each was telling the crowds that clustered around them that it was the Countess, or the nobles, or the merchants, that were to blame for the fire – that the rich were burning the poor out to make room for new warehouses and manufactories. The orators urged the Shantytowners to rise up and smash the merchants and the nobles and the fat priests who supported them.

Gotrek stopped at the edge of one such crowd and listened to the speaker, staring intently at him. The man stood on a wooden crate near the mouth of an alley. A handful of other men surrounded him, handing out leaflets and talking in low tones with the listeners. Felix hovered beside him uneasily, anxious to move on before somebody noticed them and started calling for their heads.

'Did we hear that voice last night?' Gotrek asked.

Felix closed his eyes and listened. The voice sounded familiar, but he couldn't be sure. 'I don't know. The message certainly sounds like what the Cleansing Flame were preaching, but these men don't wear masks.'

Gotrek started pushing forward. 'If it squawks like a goblin, and it smells like a goblin…'

'Gotrek, wait,' whispered Felix. 'We'll have the whole neighbourhood after us! We're already getting looks.'

Gotrek paused, considering, then nodded. 'Aye. We need to get one alone.' He rose up on his toes and peered through the crowd. 'This way,' he said, and started down the street, away from the orators.

Felix followed him around the block and then into an alley. Gotrek strode unerringly though the zigzag labyrinth of back streets and mews until they stood in the shadows of an alley just behind the orator and his fellows.

'Right,' said Gotrek. 'Lure one in.'

'Lure…? How?'

Gotrek shrugged. 'You're the subtle one.'

Felix groaned. 'All right. I'll try.'

He edged to the mouth of the alley and looked around. He was standing behind and a bit to the left

of the agitators. From this angle he could watch the
faces of the crowd as they listened to the speech. The
orator was stirring them well. They cheered on cue.
They shook their fists. They were angry, and looked to
be spoiling for a fight. One of the speaker's fellows
was facing the crowd just in front of Felix, holding a
fistful of leaflets.

Felix tugged his hood down over his eyes, then
stepped out of the shadows and waved at the man.
'Hoy. Let me see one of those.'

'Certainly brother,' said the man. He crossed to Felix,
holding one out. 'Did you see the fires last night? Did
you lose your home to the villainy of the landlords?'

'Oh yes,' said Felix, taking the leaflet and in the same
motion pressing the tip of his dagger against the
man's stomach. 'And I saw who started them too.'

The agitator looked down, then up, meeting Felix's
eyes under his hood. 'You!' he gasped.

'Shout and you're dead,' said Felix. 'Now, into the
alley.'

The man hesitated, and made to back away. Felix
caught his arm and twisted it, pressing harder with the
dagger.

The man whimpered, eyes wide.

'Shhhh,' said Felix. 'Come on.'

He turned with the man into the alley, bending over
the leaflet as if he was discussing it with him, all the
while keeping the tip of the dagger pushed firmly
against his abdomen.

'What do you want with me?' whispered the agitator, as the shadows swallowed them.

'Me?' said Felix. 'I want nothing. It's him that wants
to speak to you.' He nodded further down the alley.

Gotrek stepped forward, the light from the end of the alley glittering in his single angry eye.

The agitator flinched back, almost escaping Felix's grip. 'The dwarf!' he cried. 'Powers of darkness protect me!'

Gotrek's hand shot out and caught him by the neck. He yanked him down to his knees. 'Who are your leaders?' he growled.

'Leaders?' said the agitator. 'I don't know what you...'

Gotrek's thick fingers tightened, and the man's sentence ended in a strangled squawk.

'Who are your leaders?' the Slayer repeated.

'I... I...' squeaked the man. 'I don't know.'

Gotrek slapped him across the ear. It sounded like a branch snapping.

The man wailed in pain. Gotrek clamped a hand over his mouth until he stopped, then let up. 'Who?'

'I swear I don't know!' gasped the man. 'We never see them without their masks!'

'What about the man speaking?' asked Felix.

'He is above me,' said the man. 'But he is only the leader of thirteen men. He only does what he's told, like the rest of us.'

'And who tells him what to do?'

'The leaders,' said the man. 'The masked ones.'

'Maybe he knows who they are,' said Felix.

'No one knows,' said the agitator.

'I'll hear it from him.' said Gotrek. He looked around. There was a flimsy wooden door opening into the back of a tenement beside him. 'Open that,' he said to Felix, then dragged the cultist closer to the mouth of the alley.

Felix tried the door. It wasn't locked. He held it open.

Gotrek shook the agitator. 'Call a name,' he rasped.

'A name?'

'One of your "brothers". Call his name. Ask him to come here.'

'Er, I…'

Gotrek slapped him again. 'Call!'

The man cried out in pain. 'Harald,' he whimpered.

Gotrek raised his fist. 'Louder!'

'Harald, come here!' squealed the man. 'Hurry! I need you!'

'Good,' said Gotrek, and snapped the cultist's neck with a twist of his hands.

The man slumped bonelessly to the ground, dead. Gotrek left him in front of the door, then entered the building and pulled his axe from his back. Felix stepped in after him.

'Close it.'

Felix pulled the door shut and drew his sword. He looked at Gotrek. 'You killed him.'

'Aye.'

Gotrek pressed his ear to the door. Felix frowned, then joined him.

They heard steps and a question, then a cry of alarm.

The steps came closer.

'Dolf!' came a voice, right on the other side of the door. 'Dolf! What happened?'

Felix tensed.

'Not yet,' murmured Gotrek.

The steps ran off again and Felix heard raised voices from beyond the alley. The orator's rant faltered, then continued in the background. The voices got closer. It sounded like four men.

'What happened to him?'

'I don't know. But I think he's dead.'

'Was he attacked?'

'I see no wound.'

'Perhaps his heart just stopped.'

'Come on. Let's get him up.'

'Now,' said Gotrek. 'And stay quiet.'

He pushed the door open. Four men hunched over the body of the dead cultist, lifting him. Gotrek cut down the two nearest before they even had a chance to look up. Felix lunged at a third and ran him through as he let go of the body and reached for his sword. The fourth opened his mouth to scream. Gotrek split his head down to his neck before he made a sound.

'Inside,' said the Slayer. 'Leave the first.' He grabbed two bodies by their collars and dragged them into the tenement.

Felix caught another by the wrists and hauled at it. The body bumped heavily over the lintel and he let it drop next to the others. Gotrek threw the last on top of the others. Felix's stomach felt queasy. He could not remember killing anyone as unprepared as the men who had just died. It did not feel honourable or heroic. He and Gotrek had quite literally caught them stooping.

'That was…'

'Quiet,' said Gotrek. He closed the door and pressed his ear to it again, his axe at the ready.

It took a few minutes, but finally another questioning voice called down the alley, and then another cry of alarm. This time the orator's speech stopped, and Felix heard him calling to the crowd to excuse him for a moment.

His voice rose again in the alley. 'What do you mean, vanished? How could they have vanished? What…?' Footsteps stopped right outside the door. 'Is he drunk? Dolf! Get up! Bah. Get him up. Harald! Feodor! Where are you?'

Gotrek opened the door. Two men were bent over the body, while a third, the orator, stood behind them, hands on his hips. Gotrek slashed left and right, killing the first two cultists, then leapt at the orator and punched him in the stomach. The man folded up with an explosion of breath, and collapsed moaning over the Slayer's shoulder. Gotrek turned back to the door, carrying him.

A chorus of cries came from the mouth of the alley. Felix looked up and saw a clutch of curious crowd members pointing and shouting. They called behind them and started down the alley.

Gotrek stepped through the door. Felix closed it. Gotrek threw the orator to the ground, then began piling the dead cultists against the door. Fists pounded on it from the other side, but could not budge it.

Gotrek picked up the orator and slung him over his shoulder again. 'Come on, manling.'

He carried the orator through the tenement and out onto the street, then immediately entered another tenement on the opposite side and found the stairs to the cellar.

They went down, and Gotrek dropped the man onto the dirt floor amid heaps of trash and broken furniture. He knelt on his chest with one knee and lowered his axe to the man's neck.

'Who are your leaders?' he rasped.

The orator blinked up at him, dazed and frightened. He swallowed. 'I... I have no leaders. I am the leader.'

Gotrek broke his nose with his bony fist. 'Who are your leaders?'

Blood spilled across the orator's cheeks like a red river. 'I... I don't know! They wear masks!'

Gotrek raised his fist.

Felix winced and stepped forward, holding up a hand. 'Who do you *think* they are?'

The man's eyes went wide. 'I dare not! I cannot!'

Gotrek punched him again, further shattering his nose. He screamed.

'Do you dare now?' growled Gotrek.

The orator spat blood and glared up at Gotrek. A mad light had come into his eyes. 'Do your worst, dwarf. Pain ends with death, but if I betray my masters, death is only the beginning of pain.'

Gotrek leaned forward, crushing the man under his enormous weight. He pressed the blade of his axe into the man's neck. 'And what if death is a long time coming?'

'It comes now!' cried the orator, then thrust his head forward and twisted, so that he cut his own throat against the axe blade.

Felix gasped as the man's head slumped back and the clean-edged wound gaped open like a second mouth. Blood pumped from it in a torrent.

Gotrek sat back, annoyed.

Felix let out a breath. He disliked this sort of business. 'A wasted effort,' he said. 'We know nothing more than when we started.'

'Killing seven servants of the Ruinous Powers isn't a waste,' said Gotrek, standing. 'But you are right. These rankers know nothing. We will learn nothing of their masters from them.'

Felix nodded. 'And I don't think we'll find their masters in the Maze.'

Gotrek cleaned his axe on the shirt of the orator, his brow furrowed. 'They have protected themselves well, curse them.' He put his axe on his back and turned to the stairs. 'Come on, manling. A drink will help me think.'

As THEY TURNED the corner onto the street that the Blind Pig occupied, Gotrek grunted as if he'd been shot. Felix looked up, then gaped. The tavern was gone – reduced, along with most of the other buildings around it, to charred beams and mounds of smouldering black rubble. In the street before it, sitting slumped on an overturned water bucket, was Heinz, his face buried in his arms. His clothes were stained with soot. The backs of his hands were burned.

Gotrek stopped in the middle of the street, staring at the sad tableau. Felix stopped behind him. A carriage pulled to an abrupt halt behind them.

'Someone will die for this,' said Gotrek.

Felix nodded, but a nagging voice in his head wondered again if he and Gotrek were responsible for the fire. And if they were, would the Slayer kill *them*?

'Hello, Felix,' said a familiar voice behind them. 'Hello, Slayer.'

Felix turned. Leaning out of the window of the carriage behind them was a heavily hooded and veiled figure. A shock of white hair shone through the black lace of the veil.

'Ulrika,' said Felix. 'What are you doing here?'

'I have been looking for you,' she said. 'My mistress wishes to speak to you. To ask a favour of you.'

Gotrek tore his eyes from the ruins of Heinz's tavern and glared up at her. 'The oath breaker wants a favour?' There was a dangerous note in his voice.

'It pertains to the Cleansing Flame, and may help uncover their leaders and what they have done with the powder.'

NINE

GOTREK STARED LEVELLY at Ulrika for a long moment, then turned back to the Blind Pig. 'You go,' he said to Felix. 'I have things to do.'

'Me?' Felix didn't like the idea of walking into the den of the vampire countess alone. She had dealt honourably with him before, but one never knew with vampires. 'But this might be the information we have been looking for.'

'You're better off without me,' said Gotrek. 'I don't trust my axe in her presence.'

'I don't trust my neck in her presence,' said Felix, but Gotrek was already stumping towards Heinz and didn't look back.

'All right, I… I suppose I'll go, then.'

Felix turned back to the carriage. Ulrika was holding the door open for him. He could see her sharp white teeth smiling through the veil. He swallowed, dread and excitement warring in the pit of his stomach, then shrugged and climbed in.

Ulrika rapped the ceiling with her knuckles and they started forward. She closed the blinds against the twilight, then removed her hood and veil and leaned back, looking at him, her eyes twinkling in the light of a horn lantern. Her hair had been trimmed very close in order to cut out the sections that had been burned the night before, and she looked even more androgynous than usual.

Felix shifted uncomfortably, uncertain what to say or where to look. She was so beautiful, and yet so unnerving. So much like the woman he had once known and loved, and at the same time nothing like her at all.

'I remember you with fondness, Felix,' she said after a moment. 'Is that how you remember me?'

Felix frowned. His memories of their times together rose up before his eyes and he could feel desire stirring within him. At the same time, the smug smirk that had twisted her mouth as she asked the question reminded him unpleasantly of her inborn sense of entitlement, which had always rubbed him the wrong way. There had been so many fights, over so little. She had been so foreign to him, even then. A noblewoman. A Kislevite. A born warrior. She had so little in common with an overly educated merchant's son from Altdorf, who thought himself more poet than soldier. Their ideas of the world had been so dissimilar they might have been different species.

Now they were.

And yet, his most lasting memories of her were not the fights and the sullen silences, nor the jealousies and sadness at the end when things were falling apart, but instead of laughing with her, riding with her, rolling with her, fencing with her, both with sword and word, and most of all, of enjoying the challenge of her.

'Yes,' he said at last. 'For all our troubles, I still think of you... fondly.' He coughed as another thought came to him. 'Ah, have you spoken to... to Max since...'

Her wide grin flashed again. 'Still jealous, Felix?'

'Not at all!' said Felix, hotly. 'I was just wondering what he thought of... of what has occurred.'

'Of course,' she purred. 'Of course. No, I have not spoken to Herr Schreiber since my... "demise". He is in Altdorf, I believe. Teaching. I am not sure he would welcome a visit and, to be honest, I have not thought to seek him out.' She frowned and touched her breast. 'My heart no longer works as it did. Nothing can touch it now.'

For the first time her mask of sly amusement seemed to slip a little and Felix thought he saw a ghost of pain flit across her face.

'Uh,' said Felix, into the silence. 'So, how have you been?'

Ulrika snorted, then chuckled, then doubled over with laughter. At last she flopped back in her seat and looked at him through half-closed eyes. 'Oh, Felix, I *have* missed you.' She sighed, then gazed up at the red damask ceiling, her long white fingers trailing aimlessly across the leather bench. 'It is not an easy thing, becoming one of night's dark masters,' she said. 'One must learn first to master oneself, one's appetites. This is difficult. The hunger is at times... overwhelming.

The urge to rend and kill and drink one's victims dry…' She licked her lips and her eyes flicked to Felix's neck, then swiftly away. She coughed. 'Well, it is constantly with one. Fortunately, I have had a very wise, very patient teacher, who has opened the wisdom of her centuries-long life to me without stint. Countess Gabriella, despite what your surly companion believes, has lived up to her vow and taught me how to control my animal hungers, how to sip and savour, rather than guzzle and slaughter. She has taught me how to use my newborn powers, and also, more importantly, how to hide them. And she has tutored me in the twisted family trees of the Nehekharan bloodlines, and in the feuds and internecine jealousies that threaten them.'

Felix frowned. A family tree where no one was related was a strange thing to imagine.

'She has not always been the kindest mistress,' Ulrika continued, and a flicker of some emotion came and went in her eyes that Felix thought might have been pain or anger or fear. 'She is sometimes cruel. It is, I think, part of our nature. And there have been times when I have cringed under the lash of her displeasure. She is wary, as anyone in her precarious position must be – always on guard against betrayal, or incautious words and actions that might expose what she really is. Because of these concerns, she has occasionally scolded me for taking unnecessary risks, or for befriending people not fully under my control.' She shrugged. 'But I owe her my life – or my undeath, rather. For had she not taken me under her wing after that mad idiot Adolphus Krieger turned me, I would have been dead – truly dead – within the day, either by the sun, or Gurnisson's dread axe, or some peasant's bonfire, so I cannot speak too harshly against her.' She chuckled. 'In that, I suppose I feel for her like any daughter feels for her mother, eh?'

All at once, she leaned forward, her face troubled. 'Listen, Felix. You have met her before. Indeed, you knew her before I did. She was cautious then. But you should be aware before you speak to her again that, due to the crazed schemes of Adolphus Krieger and other deluded madmen among our aristocracy, this tendency towards caution has grown. She is, in her way, as suspicious as the Slayer, and extremely unwilling to let live those she feels threaten her existence. So...' She hesitated, then shrugged apologetically. 'So, be polite, eh, Felix?'

Felix swallowed. 'I... I will do my best.'

'Thank you,' she said, then chuckled. 'I must say, I am very glad Gotrek decided not to come.'

AFTER RIDING EAST on Commerce Street through the Reik Platz and on past the squat grey pile of the Nuln town hall, Ulrika's coach turned south into the tidy streets of the Handelbezirk, still alive with wealthy merchants closing up their offices and walking to their clubs or homes, or chatting and drinking in the cafes and taverns that lined the streets.

Another turn to the east, and the coach was rolling down a quiet side street, flanked on both sides by prosperous, well kept townhouses. The warm glow of lamp light shone from diamond-paned windows. The coach made a right down a side alley and pulled at last through a coach yard gate.

Felix stepped out of the carriage behind Ulrika and looked up at the rear of a sturdy, respectable four storey townhouse. He wasn't sure what he had expected, but it wasn't this. It was certainly nothing like Krieger's vast, brooding castle in mist-shrouded Sylvania. There was a distinct lack of towering basalt walls and leering gargoyles and dark foreboding.

Ulrika led the way to the rear door as grooms came out of a coach house and began unhitching the horses. 'It would have been more correct to receive you at the front door,' she said. 'But there are prying eyes everywhere, as the countess says, and she doesn't want any connection to be made between you, for both your sakes.' She paused with her hand on the latch and looked back at Felix. 'One more thing I forgot to mention. Here in Nuln, the countess is not Countess Gabriella of Sylvania, but Madame Celeste du Vilmorin, late of Caronne, a Bretonnian noblewoman.'

'Very well,' said Felix, unsure what he was to make of this information.

Ulrika opened the door and led him into a small room with dark passages leading off into shadows. From further in the house Felix could hear female laughter and quiet music. Ulrika stepped to a narrow winding stair in the left wall and began to ascend. Felix followed.

'The countess...' He caught himself. 'Sorry, Madame du Vilmorin is entertaining?'

'Her ladies are,' said Ulrika.

'Oh,' said Felix. He blushed. 'Oh, I see.'

Ulrika smiled. 'There is no better thief of secrets than a harlot.'

The stairs wound past three more floors, and at each Felix could hear laughter and singing and more intimate sounds.

The fourth floor was much quieter. A thick red Araby carpet ran down the centre of a wide, panelled hallway. Beaded crimson lamps hung from the walls at regular intervals, casting a ruby glow over every surface. Ulrika stepped to a door halfway along the hall and tapped softly at it. After a short wait, the door opened and a young girl in a blue silk dress looked out. Felix almost gasped. She was the most beautiful girl he had ever seen, a little porcelain doll with blonde ringlets, a knowing smile, and enormous blue eyes. She couldn't have been more than fifteen.

'Herr Jaeger,' murmured Ulrika, ducking her head.

The blonde girl curtsied to Felix. 'Welcome, sir. You are expected. Please come in.'

Felix looked uncertainly at Ulrika.

She smirked. 'Perfectly harmless, Felix. I assure you.' She started down the hall. 'I'm going to get out of my hunting clothes. I will join you shortly.'

Felix hesitantly followed the diminutive beauty into a lushly appointed ante-chamber. Tiny, feminine chairs were gathered around low, lacquered tables, all crowded with vases of lush flowers and exquisite statuettes. Crystal chandeliers cast shards of gentle light across the accoutrements of the life of a woman of leisure – a harpsichord, an embroidery frame, a book open to an illustration of a flower. Everything seemed too delicate to be touched.

'Please have a seat, Herr Jaeger,' said the blonde girl. 'I will inform madame that you have arrived.'

She disappeared into a further room and Felix lowered himself warily into one of the filigree chairs, trying to keep his scabbard from bumping into anything. The chair held. He let out a breath, and looked around. There was something wrong with the room. Though it appeared calculated to seem peaceful and exquisite and feminine, it unnerved him somehow, and he didn't know why. What was the discordant element? His eyes roamed from place to place. An enamelled clock ticked quietly on the mantelpiece. Paintings of young lovers walking down sunlit lanes and girls in flower-garlanded swings hung on red brocade walls. A golden ewer and cups sat on a sideboard.

Then it struck him. There were no windows. It wasn't just that the windows had been blocked or curtained. They had been removed entirely.

The inner door opened. Felix turned and made to stand, then stopped, halfway to his feet, paralysed by the sight that met his eyes. Filing out of the inner room was a line of young women, all in simple, elegant white dresses, like novitiates at a Shallyan convent, except that their heads were uncovered, and that they were all astonishingly, painfully, beautiful.

Felix's heart stopped as the first in line looked him in the eye. She was the most gorgeous girl he had ever seen, a dark eyed brunette with lush red lips and a figure to match. Then his gaze was caught by the eyes of the girl that followed her. His heart stopped. She was the most beautiful girl he had ever seen, an ethereal blonde with the regal nose and statuesque bearing of a princess from a fairytale. The girl behind her...

He tore his eyes away and gathered up his jaw. He was making a fool of himself. But what man would not? Each was more bewitching than all the others, and each in an entirely different way. Where had they come from? And why were they here? He couldn't help looking after them as they glided by and sashayed out into the hallway.

'Madame will see you now, Herr Jaeger,' said a voice behind him.

Felix jumped and turned guiltily, nearly knocking over a spindly little table which held a Cathay vase. He grabbed at the vase as it tottered, and nearly succeeded in upsetting it entirely before he managed at last to steady it.

The little blonde girl held the inner door open, a hand over her mouth to hide an amused smile. 'This way, Herr Jaeger,' she said.

Felix followed her through the doorway into a warm, candle-lit boudoir. This was a much darker, more sombre, room, though no less feminine. Books and paintings of beautiful women in ancient dress lined every wall. Rich velvets and brocades in burgundy and cobalt upholstered graceful couches and chairs. A massive canopied bed stood like an altar upon a dais at the far end. Its canopies were closed.

To one side, before a grand fireplace surrounded by a baroquely carved mantelpiece that rose, urn upon corbel upon pillar, all the way to the ceiling, was a luxurious tasselled and fringed chaise longue, upon which reclined the woman Felix knew as Countess Gabriella of Nachthafen, dressed in a robe of crimson silk that spilled off onto the floor like a flow of blood. She had not changed physically in the slightest since the last time he had seen her. She still appeared to be an alabaster-skinned beauty of perhaps thirty, with thick black hair and sparkling black eyes. Her figure was petite but exquisite, and her smallest move full of fluid, feline grace.

'Welcome, Herr Jaeger,' said the countess, her voice silky with soft Bretonnian consonants. 'You have not aged a day.' She raised her hand to him.

'Nor have you, madame.' Felix smiled as he took her hand and bent over it. She had had an Altdorf accent when last they met. It appeared she took her Bretonnian imposture seriously.

The countess motioned behind him. 'Please sit.'

'Thank you, madame.' Felix sank into a velvet covered chair.

'Astrid,' said the countess, as the little blonde girl appeared at Felix's side and placed a glass of wine and a tray of sweets at his elbow, 'Please make sure that Captain Reingelt still slumbers, and then you may retire.'

'Yes, my lady.' The girl curtsied, then stepped to the canopied bed. She drew aside one of the curtains and looked within, then turned back to the countess. 'He does, my lady.'

'Very good,' said the countess.

The girl curtsied again and then drifted silently out into the antechamber. Felix stared uneasily at the hidden bed, alarmed. What had happened to poor Captain Reingelt, whoever he might be?

He turned back to Countess Gabriella and found her gazing upon him. He flinched. She smiled. 'Are you comfortable, Herr Jaeger?'

Felix chuckled. 'I don't know if I have ever been more comfortable and at the same time uncomfortable in all my life.'

The countess laughed, a silvery waterfall of delight.

'You are not the first, Herr Jaeger,' she said, 'upon whom this place has had that effect.'

'Ah,' said Felix, motioning back over his shoulder. 'Those… young women. Were they all…?'

'Not a one,' said the countess. 'We of the sisterhood do not grant the blood gift in so profligate a manner. They are merely girls – children made victims of their own beauty – whom I have rescued and brought here so that they may learn the womanly arts at my… hmm… my atelier.'

It took a moment for Felix to fight his way through the flowery phrasing to the meaning of her words. 'You kidnap pretty little girls and train them to be harlots?'

Countess Gabriella smiled with practiced ease. 'It amuses you to be blunt, Herr Jaeger. But no, the girls are purchased from orphanages or saved from the street, and though it is true that the least of them may indeed find employment within these walls, the best will become the wives and mistresses of the richest, most influential noblemen and merchants in the Old World, and live lives of luxury and leisure of which, in their previous lives, they could never have dreamed.'

'All the while spying for you and your "sisterhood",' said Felix.

The countess nodded. 'But of course. One likes to see a return on one's investment.'

Felix opened his mouth to make a witty reply, but all at once the countess's smile vanished as if it had never been.

'But now to business,' she said.

Felix sat up and waited for her to speak, but despite her words, she paused, her eyes boring into him like a Sigmarite witch hunter trying to see into his soul.

'Before we begin,' she said at last. 'I must ask you a question.' She sat a little forward, her robe falling open to reveal the soft white contours of her breasts. 'I have information to impart to you that will help us both in our fight against these vile cultists, but first I must know that you and your fell companion do not mean me and mine any harm, and will not expose or attack us after our mutual foe is defeated.'

Felix hesitated. For reasons of etiquette and manners, he was glad Gotrek was not present – had he been here there would almost certainly have been bloodshed already – but the Slayer should have been here to answer this question for himself. 'I mean you no harm,' he said at last. 'But I cannot speak for the Slayer. He has said that he feels you forswore the oath you made that you would teach Ulrika to do no harm.'

Countess Gabriella's eyes flashed. 'Does he indeed? And why does he believe such a thing?'

Felix coughed. 'Well, both of us witnessed her kill several men last night.'

The countess waved a dismissive hand. 'She defended herself, and you. It is less than the Slayer does himself. Did he think I would make a sister of Shallya of her?' She raised her chin, defiant. 'Since I accepted her as my get, Ulrika has not killed a single man while slaking her thirst. This was the sum of my promise. More he cannot expect. Ulrika is a warrior. She killed scores of men before entering my service, some of them while fighting at the Slayer's side. In the course of her duties as my bodyguard and my envoy, she has killed to defend me and to protect my interests. Would the Slayer consider these things a breach of my oath?'

Felix pursed his lips, remembering Gotrek's feud with Hamnir, and many others. 'I cannot say, but I know Gotrek has demanded that those who make vows with him honour their most minute points, sometimes beyond all common sense.' He shrugged. 'He is a dwarf.'

The countess slapped the arm of the chaise, annoyed. 'You cannot say? Then why is he not here to speak for himself?' she asked. 'The information I have may be the key to destroying these fiends. But I dare not reveal it to you without protecting myself.' She glared at Felix. 'Can you not give me a guarantee for the dwarf's behaviour?'

Felix laughed, then recovered himself as she saw her anger flare. 'Forgive me, countess, but Gotrek obeys no one but himself. He would not honour any pledge that I or anyone else made in his name.'

The countess's jaw clenched.

'On the other hand,' said Felix. 'The Slayer does not hesitate once he makes up his mind. If he had decided that you had truly broken your vow, he would already have acted. He would be here, and you would be… defending yourself.' He had almost said, 'you would be dead,' but decided at the last second that that would not be very diplomatic.

As the countess mulled this over, the door opened behind Felix and a tall woman in a corseted green satin dress entered and took a seat on a chair near the chaise. She had long wavy auburn hair that hung almost to her waist and a trim, elegant figure. Felix found it hard not to stare at her. Another beauty! Was there no end to them? This one seemed more mature than the rest of the countess's students – a woman, not a girl – but as graceful as a leopardess and as proud as a swan. She met his gaze steadily, then winked an ice blue eye at him. He jerked back in his seat, surprised. It was Ulrika! The auburn hair was a wig. She grinned at his surprise, and put a finger to her lips.

Felix stared anew. He hadn't seen her dressed in so womanly a fashion since their first night together, back on her father's estate. The memory of it made his heart skip a beat.

'So,' said Countess Gabriella, finally. 'You don't think the Slayer means me harm?'

'I cannot say, countess – er, madame,' said Felix, pulling his eyes away from Ulrika and his mind back to the present with difficulty. 'His temper is changeable, to say the least. I do know that at present he wants two things above all others. He wishes vengeance on the Brotherhood of the Cleansing Flame for the burning of the tavern of his friend, and he wishes to reach Middenheim and die facing a daemon in battle. If you can aid him in achieving either or both…'

'Mistress,' said Ulrika, interrupting. 'If I might make an observation.'

'Of course, daughter,' said the countess.

'I think it is perhaps impossible to remove the risk from this venture. I do not think the Slayer will give you the guarantee you wish. But…' she said, raising her voice as the countess opened her mouth to interrupt. 'But, I think that the risk is justified. The

Cleansing Flame want no less than the destruction of the Empire and the end of our way of life. They have sided with the Ruinous Powers, and will undoubtedly call upon them for aid. They will bring sorcerers and beasts and daemons against us. They will summon their dark gods to smite us. These are foes that the followers you currently command, loyal though they may be, cannot prevail against.'

'Even yourself, daughter?'

'Even myself,' agreed Ulrika, then continued. 'If we want to ensure the destruction of these evil men, and the defeat of their vile masters. If we want to preserve the life we have now and the future we crave, then we must risk this alliance. Herr Jaeger and Slayer Gurnisson have won battles against the deadliest of foes. I have seen Herr Jaeger kill a dragon. I have witnessed the Slayer destroy daemons. Tides of beastmen have fallen before them. They are our best weapon against these corrupters.'

Felix swallowed. No need to lay it on so thick, he thought. Just because they had fought all those things and won didn't mean they could do it again, or wanted to do it again. Well, he didn't anyway.

Countess Gabriella pressed her fingertips together, her eyes turned inward, thinking. As the silence lengthened, Felix caught Ulrika looking at him. She spread her hands in a pleading gesture.

Felix grunted. He didn't want to convince the countess to dig them deeper into this mess. He didn't like this kind of fight – where one never knew who one's enemies were. He didn't care to guess which of the men around him had worn a mask the night before and tried to blow him up with black powder. He didn't like wondering when a friend or companion might turn on him, dagger raised, the mad light of fanaticism blazing from his eyes. The more he thought about it, the more flying off to Middenheim and fighting enemies out on an open battlefield seemed like the most appealing option.

But he knew it was useless. He had seen the look in Gotrek's eyes when he had found Fritz sitting before the blackened ruins of the Blind Pig. They were going nowhere until the Slayer had found the men responsible for hurting his friend, so if the countess could help them get it over with more quickly, so much the better.

Felix coughed politely. 'Countess, there was a time, some years ago, when you asked *me* to trust *you*. When I was forced to overcome my fear and distrust of your kind so that we could work together to defeat a common foe. I was as hesitant then as you are now, and yet, when, against every instinct, I agreed and we joined together, we triumphed.' He spread his hands. 'As I said, I can make no vow for Gotrek, but I know he hates these men as much, if not more, than you do. If you give him a way to confront them, he will take it. That, you can trust.'

The countess nodded, still unseeing, then at last sighed and looked up, fixing Felix with a stare as cold and bottomless as the depths of Black Water Lake. 'I suppose I have no choice,' she said. 'Particularly since I can do nothing with the information I have without you, at least not quickly or without weakening my position. But know this; you will not betray me and live. You may be a great hero, and your companion a fell warrior, but the daughters of the deathless queen are everywhere, behind every beautiful smile, and they seldom strike from the front.' She glanced meaningfully towards the canopied bed, then smiled at him. 'You would not die in battle.'

Felix shuddered. 'Threats are not necessary, madame,' he said. 'Your reputation is enough.'

'Good,' said the countess. She looked to Ulrika. 'Tell him.'

Ulrika lowered her head, then turned to Felix. 'As I was ripping out the throat of one of the cultists last night, this came away with his flesh.'

She lifted a golden chain from her bodice, unhooked the clasp and passed it to Felix. He took it reluctantly, but it seemed she had removed all traces of gore. He looked at it. On the chain was a small golden pendant, in the shape of a shield emblazoned with a wolf's head. He vaguely recognised the device, but couldn't remember from where.

'What is it?' he asked.

'A signet chain worn by members of Wulf's, a private gentlemen's club in the Handelbezirk,' said Ulrika.

'Ah, of course.' Once she said it, Felix recognised it instantly. Back in the days when he and Gotrek had been bouncers at the Blind Pig, he had from time to time thrown out members of Wulf's who had come in looking to start trouble. The club had originally been a club for rich merchants, but when the more elegant Golden Hammer had opened, the merchants began to go there instead, and Wulf's was taken over by their sons, idle layabouts with too much money and too much time on their hands. They aped the manners of the nobility and liked to prove their superiority over their poorer brethren with the point of a rapier.

Strange that one such would belong to a group that seemed dedicated to overthrowing the established order.

'We want to learn if other members of Wulf's also belong to the Cleansing Flame,' said Ulrika. 'But it is a gentlemen's club. No women are allowed. Even the servants are all male.'

'And you know no men but me?' asked Felix, incredulous. 'Unless I have the purpose of this establishment entirely wrong, you must know half the rich men in this city. None belong to Wulf's?'

'My customers are not my confidants,' said the countess, as if explaining something to a child. 'I extract secrets from them without their knowledge. Asking them openly to spy for me would expose to them my true purpose. Those few men who *are* my confidants and servants...' She nodded towards the bed. 'Some are so besotted that I cannot trust their judgement. Others... well, I will not bore you with internecine intrigues and tales of divided loyalties. Suffice to say that there is no man already within my circle upon whom I can entirely place my trust. So...' She raised her eyes to meet his. 'That leaves you.'

Felix frowned, still confused. 'But I don't understand. I can't help you either. I'm not a member.'

'No,' said the countess. 'But your brother is. Though he no longer dines there, he has never resigned his membership.'

'Wha... How... How do you know that?' gabbled Felix.

The countess smiled. 'As you said, Herr Jaeger, we know half the rich men in this city. And the other half too.'

'Otto comes here...?' Felix was dumbfounded, though he couldn't think why. Why should his brother be any different from any other rich man he had ever known?

'You will ask him to take you to dinner there,' said the countess, placidly. 'Once inside you will hopefully hear a voice you heard in the burning cellar, or recognise someone by their walk. And then...' she smiled prettily. 'Well, you're the hero. I expect you'll know what to do.'

Felix groaned, recalling how he and his brother had left things at the end of their last conversation. How in the world was he going to get Otto to take him anywhere, let alone to a club he no longer frequented?

'You will report to Ulrika all you find, is that clear?' asked the countess. 'I want to know everything before you act.'

'Yes, countess. Certainly,' said Felix, distracted. He rose to go, playing out different ways he might approach his brother, and not liking the outcomes of any of them.

The countess raised a tiny golden bell, but Ulrika stood and held up a hand.

'No need, madame. I'll see him out.'

The anteroom door slammed open. The little blonde girl tumbled in and hit the carpet chin-first as two silhouettes filled the doorway. More figures crowded the anteroom behind them. Felix's hand dropped to his hilt.

'What's this!' Countess Gabriella was on her feet instantly, a dagger in her hand. 'Who dares enter my chambers uninvited?'

Ulrika too gripped a dagger, and was looking like she regretted having changed into womanly garb. She stepped protectively in front of Felix. The little blonde girl was crabbing backwards away from the door, wide-eyed, a smear of blood on her lip.

Two women stepped into the room – well, one of them was a woman. Felix wasn't sure the other was even human – or ever had been.

'Good evening, Madame du Vilmorin,' said the more human of the two, throwing back a rich, velvet cloak. She was beautiful – as beautiful as any of the countess's students – an olive complexion like an Estalian, with pouting lips and heavy lidded eyes as black and cold as a winter sea. Thick waves of glossy black hair spilled down past her bare shoulders to a wide-skirted dress of oxblood satin and black embroidery, so exquisitely made that a queen might envy it.

'What is the meaning of this intrusion, Lady Hermione?' snapped the countess. 'And you, Mistress Wither?' The countess's robe had fallen open entirely and her naked white curves shone in the dark room like alabaster lit from within. 'Give me a reason why I should not set Ulrika upon you,' she said as the little blonde girl clung to her right leg.

'We heard a rumour,' said Lady Hermione coolly, as she tugged off black lace gloves one finger at a time, then tucked them into a beaded drawstring purse that matched the colours of her dress exactly. 'That you thought to bring an outsider into our business.' She ran her eyes up and down Felix with a dismissive sneer. 'It seems we heard correctly.'

The other woman – Mistress Wither – rasped wordlessly at this in a voice that sounded like water splashing on a hot stove. She was tall – taller than Felix by half a head – and appeared skeletally thin under the hooded shroud that hid every inch of her and hissed against the carpet as she glided from place to place. Long sleeves hung down past her hands. Her face was covered with a thick black veil that made it look like there was nothing within her hood but shadows.

'What business is it of yours,' asked the countess, 'what tool I use to achieve my ends?'

Tool, thought Felix. Well, good to know her true opinion of him, he supposed.

Lady Hermione flicked an eye over Felix again. 'He has never been tasted. You have no hold on him. You treat with him as an equal. We heard you.' She gave the countess a sad look. 'You know better than this, sister. We do not use men that are not fully bound to us. You cannot allow him to leave like this. He will betray us. He will expose us to all of Nuln. Our work will be undone.'

Felix opened his mouth but Ulrika touched his arm with a warning hand.

'Our work will be undone if Nuln falls to the barbarians,' said the countess. 'Our lives will be undone. This man can do what we cannot. Go where we cannot.'

'What?' sniffed Hermione. 'To Wulf's? Yes, we heard that too. Don't be ridiculous.' She motioned behind her. 'Any number of my gentlemen are members of Wulf's. You had but to ask.'

Felix looked through the door. Lounging languidly on the fragile chairs in the anteroom were a handful of dashing, mustachioed heroes, each as handsome as a statue of Sigmar, and certainly just as much a work of art. They did indeed look the sort that would belong to Wulf's.

It was Countess Gabriella's turn to sneer. 'Do you think I would trust any of your creatures? Whose interests would they serve, I wonder?'

'Surely all our interests are one in this calamity,' said Hermione. 'There can be no rivalry when all our lives are at stake.'

'Can there not?' asked the countess. 'If this victory were *yours*, and not *ours* or *mine*, would you not rise in the esteem of our lady, while I sank? Would you not come one step closer to winning my position, as you have been trying to do all these decades?' The countess waved an impatient hand. 'Oh, enough of this. It matters not, for your "gentlemen" cannot win the information that Herr Jaeger can. Only he can do it.'

'Is he so great a hero as all that?' asked Lady Hermione, raising a sceptical eyebrow. 'My gentlemen are some of the finest duellists in all the Empire.'

'No doubt,' said countess as if she didn't believe a word of it. 'But they were not in the burning cellar under the Maze. They did not hear the leaders of the Cleansing Flame order their followers to attack. So how can they hear the voice of a clubman and know that in another part of town he wears a yellow mask and consorts with mutants?'

Lady Hermione sniffed, frustrated. 'Surely there must be another way to learn who these men are!'

'There might be, but there is not time to find one,' said the countess. 'The madmen could burn Nuln at any time – tonight perhaps!'

Lady Hermione exchanged a glance with Mistress Wither, then turned back to the countess. Her face was set and hard. 'Be that as it may, you must still find another way,' she said at last. 'Because this man will not leave here alive having seen us and heard our names.'

TEN

'You DARE MAKE demands in my house!' cried Countess Gabriella. 'I still rule here in Nuln, no matter how much it might pain you.'

'You won't after she gets word of this foolishness,' said Lady Hermione. 'Trusting cattle. No good ever comes of it.'

Behind her, her exquisite companions were getting to their feet and resting their hands on their hilts.

'Ladies,' pleaded Felix. 'There is no need for this. I and my companion leave in a few days for Middenheim, where we are very likely to die in the fighting. Your secret will die with us.'

The vampiresses ignored him utterly.

'The foolishness,' said the countess, 'is allowing Nuln to die to preserve your standing in it. Will you be queen of the ashes?'

'There will be no ashes. We will find another way. Now stand aside. Mistress Wither thirsts.'

The tall shadow glided towards Felix, arms raising.

Felix stepped back, drawing his runesword.

Ulrika snarled and advanced, drawing a second blade from her sleeve – a bone handled stiletto that gleamed like captured moonlight in the dark room. 'Come end your misery, mistress,' she said.

Mistress Wither shrank back from the blade, hissing.

'Silver!' gasped Lady Hermione. 'You would use poison against your own?'

Hermione's gentlemen drew their rapiers and pushed in through the door behind her. At the same time, the curtains of the canopied bed were thrown roughly open, and a powerful looking man stumbled out, entirely naked, brushing the hair out of his eyes and groping for a long sword that was propped against a side table. 'Is m'lady threatened?' the man slurred.

'Peace, captain,' said the countess, holding up her hand as he drew his sword.

The man stayed where he was, but remained on guard.

The tableau held for a long moment as the two sides sized each other up.

At last the countess laughed. 'Sisters, you amuse me. To preserve your secrecy you will start a fight that all the gentlemen of the Altestadt who are at their leisure one floor below us will hear. Will you then kill all of them when they come to see what is the matter? Your secrecy is in greater peril if you attack than if you withdraw. Now come, lower your weapons.'

The women stayed where they were.

'The fight may be over quicker than you think,' said Lady Hermione.

'Aye,' said the countess. 'And with at least one of us truly dead. What do you think she will say of that? Has she not said that murder among us is the greatest sin?'

'It is you who drew silver!'

'And you who forced silver to be drawn,' said the countess. She lowered her dagger. 'Now, come, listen to reason. The man will go and learn who these cultists are and what they plan, and he will be watched. Indeed, you may watch him, if that is your wish. If he speaks of our existence before he leaves Nuln, then do what you will.'

'And after he leaves Nuln? How can you guarantee his silence then?' asked Lady Hermione.

Countess Gabriella looked from Felix to Ulrika and smiled. 'Though he is not bound to us by the blood kiss, there are other ties that will stay his hand.'

Lady Hermione curled her lip. 'And all know how great is the constancy of man.'

'Greater than that of sisters, so it seems,' said Ulrika disdainfully.

Lady Hermione remained on guard, glaring at Felix, and though he could not see Mistress Wither's eyes, Felix felt certain that they were fixed upon him too.

'Sisters,' said the countess quietly. 'We fight while our enemies light their fuses. We must act. Now. Let us resume this argument when we know that Nuln is safe.'

Lady Hermione and Mistress Wither exchanged a glance, then at last stepped back. Lady Hermione's men lowered their swords. Ulrika hesitated, then sheathed the silver stiletto.

'It seems it must go as you say,' said Hermione, bitterness dripping from each word. 'But after, we will see. After, we will bring all before the lady, and we will see.'

Countess Gabriella inclined her head. 'So long as the Empire stands, I will be content with her verdict.'

Lady Hermione snorted. 'Oh, the nobility. It moves one to tears.'

Mistress Wither laughed like a steam piston.

The two vampiresses stepped to the right and left of the door. Hermione curtsied to Felix and swept a hand to the door. 'Go then, oh fair and gentle knight. Save us from the machinations of our enemies. But know, champion, that our eyes will ever be upon you.'

Felix's flesh crawled as Ulrika led him forward between them and out through the antechamber under the glowering scrutiny of Lady Hermione's gentlemen. He didn't like this at all. What guarantee did he have that the women wouldn't strike out of spite once he had outlived his usefulness? And would they watch him everywhere? When he slept? When he went to the jakes? He groaned silently. It might have been better to have had the fight then and there and gotten it over with.

'I APOLOGISE,' SAID Ulrika, as the coach swayed smoothly through the streets towards Shantytown. 'Family can be embarrassing.'

'Who are they?' asked Felix.

Ulrika pursed her lips. 'Lady Hermione is the countess's chief rival here in Nuln. She has been longer in the city – almost fifty years. And so was understandably upset when the countess, who though she does not look it, is younger than her by several centuries, was given the ruling of Nuln instead of her. But it is her own fault. Though she has no equals when it comes to seduction, she is quick to anger, and unwilling to compromise. She hasn't the temperament to lead.'

'Yes, I saw that.'

'Mistress Wither...' Ulrika shook her head. 'Mistress Wither is a caution to us all. She was too flagrant in her youth. Too violent. She was caught by hunters, and left naked and shackled to a rock to await the rising sun. She was rescued by her thralls, but not before dawn had come.' Ulrika shivered. 'It might have been better had she died then. Her skin is like burned paper. It never heals. She is in agony every moment of her eternal life. Only feeding gives her some relief, but not much, and not for long. She hates men beyond all reason.'

'Wonderful,' said Felix. 'And do you trust them not to attack us after this is over?'

'I do not know.' Ulrika sighed and looked out of the window into the torchlit night. 'Sad as I will be to see you go, I think it is good that you are leaving soon.'

'Aye,' said Felix. Running towards the daemons to escape the vampires. What a life.

Ulrika dropped Felix off in Shantytown where she had picked him up. As he walked towards the remains of the Blind Pig, he saw a swarm of activity under the yellow glow of bright lanterns. A wagon had been drawn up beside the ruined tavern, and Heinz and his bouncers were throwing blackened timbers onto it.

''Ware below!' came a familiar voice, and a section of the tavern's roof folded in on itself and crashed to the ground.

Gotrek was revealed on the remains of the upper floor. He was black with soot from head to toe, and had a kerchief tied around his nose and mouth.

'This is why dwarfs hate trees,' he called down to Heinz as he chopped through some ruined beams. 'Trees burn. Stone does not.'

'Aye, well, not all of us can afford to build with stone,' said Heinz.

'You can now,' said Gotrek.

'I won't take your gold, curse you!' said Heinz, standing straight and glaring up at the Slayer. 'I told you once already.'

Gold, thought Felix. Gotrek still has gold?

'You think I'm giving it to you?' asked Gotrek. 'I'm paying for my next thousand drinks.'

'That bracelet is worth a thousand thousand drinks,' said Heinz peevishly.

'I'll bring some friends.'

Heinz snorted and turned away to lift another burned board. 'And what friends have you got, you miserable grouch?' he muttered to himself, but he was smiling in spite of himself.

Gotrek saw Felix coming and swung down a ladder to join him by the wagon. There was an open half keg of ale next to it. Gotrek dipped a mug in it and drank deep, then wiped his mouth, smearing away a thick layer of soot.

'What did the parasite say?' he asked.

Felix hesitated, considering how much to tell him about his visit to the countess's brothel. Did he mention the countess's attempt to force a promise of Gotrek's good behaviour from him? Did he mention Lady Hermione and Mistress Wither and their intention to murder them if they revealed their existence? Perhaps it was better to let sleeping dogs lie. On the other hand, he should know the other players in the game.

'The countess is as wary of you as you are of her.'

'She has reason to be,' growled Gotrek.

'And she has allies – rivals, really – who don't want us involved at all.'

'Allies?'

'Two other vampire women,' said Felix. 'A beautiful seductress and a… a shrouded thing, burned by the sun, apparently, and hiding it under robes. The countess convinced them in the end that we were needed to defeat the cultists, but I think they would sooner kill us.'

'Let them try,' said Gotrek. 'I made no vow with them.'

Felix coughed. 'All the same, the countess may have provided the link to the Cleansing Flame we have been seeking. It might be politic to stay your hand, at least until we find them and the powder.'

'Politic.' Gotrek spat out the word as if it was the vilest profanity. 'What is this link?'

Felix pulled the wolf's head pendant from his pouch. 'Ulrika took this from one of the cultists last night. It's an insignia worn by members of Wulf's, a club for rich burghers. She and the countess think that some of the other cult leaders might be members of the club too. They want me to go there and listen, in hopes I will hear a voice I recognise from the fight.'

'That is a slim hope, manling. Not worth the alliance.'

'I agree,' said Felix. 'But it's the only hope we have at the moment.'

Gotrek grunted, dissatisfied. His gaze travelled back up to the tavern's skeletal upper floor.

'I'll see my brother about going to Wulf's tomorrow night,' said Felix. 'He is a member.'

Gotrek nodded, distracted. He finished his mug of ale in a single swallow and started back towards the ladder. 'Doesn't sound like my sort of work. Come back when you've found me something to kill.'

'Ah, Gotrek,' called Felix after him.

Gotrek stopped and turned. 'Hey?'

'You're... you're giving Heinz gold to fix the Blind Pig?'

'Aye.'

Felix frowned. 'You said we were broke. We didn't eat our last two days before Nuln.'

'We are broke,' growled Gotrek. He held up his thick left wrist, full of gold bracelets, letting them glint in the lamplight. 'Some gold's not for spending.'

'Unless a friend's tavern burns down,' said Felix.

'Aye,' said Gotrek, and started towards the ladder again.

Felix watched as the Slayer climbed it and moved carefully through the ruined upper storey, expertly choosing the next parts to demolish. There was a sat-isfaction on his ugly face that was almost happiness. Felix suddenly remembered that Gotrek had been an engineer before he shaved his head and took the Slayer's Oath. A strange melancholy passed over him when he thought that, if whatever tragedy had caused

Gotrek to become a Slayer hadn't happened, this is what he would have been, a builder of houses and halls. Would he have been happy with just that? Had there really been a time when simple labour could have fulfilled Gotrek's heart?

FELIX VISITED THE Nuln office of Jaeger and Sons the next morning just before noon. The long, dim room was filled with rows of bookkeepers, perched on high stools and bent over their ledgers like an army of hunchbacked storks, quills flying from ink pot to parchment and back. Young boys scurried among them carrying account books nearly as heavy as themselves. The air smelled of candlewick and dust.

'May I help you?' asked a pale man with spectacles and heavy jowls who sat at a high desk near the front door. He had ink stains on his fingers and his lips.

'I'm looking for Otto Jaeger. I'm his brother.'

'Do you have an appointment?'

'No. I'm his brother.'

The bookkeeper sniffed as if this made no difference whatsoever. 'I'll see if he's receiving.' He shouted over his shoulder. 'Rodik! Ask Herr Jaeger if he will see his brother.'

A thin little boy saluted, then scurried back through the rows of tall desks and disappeared around a corner as the bookkeeper went back to his accounts, ignoring Felix. The scritch of quill nibs on paper filled the room as he waited. It sounded to Felix like a hundred rats clawing at the walls of a hundred cages. A shudder went through him. Imagine if he had remained on the path his father had set for him. He would have spent his life in a room like this, adding up accounts, fretting over the delivery of goods, worrying about the price of oats and about how much to bribe the local authorities.

A thought made him smile. Why was it that, when faced with a horde of howling orcs he wished so dearly for this life, and when faced with this life, he wished so dearly for a horde of howling orcs? A truism could have been found somewhere in that conundrum, if he had had any energy for that sort of thing anymore.

The little boy popped his head around the corner. 'He says he'll see him, sir!' he squealed.

The bookkeeper slapped his desk and stood, roaring. 'Don't shout, you little goblin! You disturb the others! Come up and tell me politely, like a gentleman.' A vein throbbed in his pale forehead.

The little boy cringed and hurried forward, head down, as the clerks stifled amused laughter and shot sly smirks at each other.

'Sorry, Herr Bartlemaas,' said the little boy, his eyes on the ground. 'Herr Jaeger will see, er, Herr Jaeger.'

'Better,' said the head clerk. 'Now show our guest back to Herr Jaeger's office. And no more shouting, or you'll not get your penny today.'

Felix followed the boy's slumped shoulders through the office, fighting the urge to draw his sword and chop the whole place to flinders.

'YOU'LL HAVE TO be brief, brother,' said Otto without looking up from the papers spread across his massive desk. 'I'm expecting representatives from the bargemen's guild at any moment. I cannot keep them waiting.'

In comparison with the opulence of his home, Otto's office was as plain as a monk's cell – a small room with an iron stove in one corner, a pair of chairs before the big desk, and floor to ceiling bookshelves on every wall, all filled with massive ledgers, each with a month and year printed neatly on the spine. Otto's pens and blotters and ink bottles were all of cheap manufacture. The lantern he used to light his work the same as any farmer would have. Felix wondered if his brother dressed his office down on purpose in order to be able to plead poor mouth to his business associates. He certainly wouldn't put it past him.

'Well, I…' Felix paused, then summoned his courage and continued. 'I've been thinking about your offer.'

Otto raised his eyes in mock surprise. 'What's this? You wish to get your hands dirty, m'lord? You wish to descend from your lofty perch and join us mere mortals in the real world?' He chuckled, then continued in his normal tone. 'What happened? Has the little maniac with the axe fired you at last?'

Felix bit his tongue. A smart reply wouldn't get the job done. 'Fired me? No. But he almost got me burned to a cinder. I'm growing tired of collecting scars.'

'Don't tell me you were behind those fires in Shantytown last night?' said Otto, his eyes widening.

'Not behind them, exactly,' said Felix. 'But certainly in the middle of them.'

Otto shrugged. 'Well, you got out of it at least. And you've done me a good turn. I'll make a tidy profit selling bricks and timber to rebuild it all.'

'At wartime prices,' said Felix dryly.

'Naturally,' said Otto. 'So, what would you like to do?'

The vile little profiteer, thought Felix. Was it any wonder cults like the Cleansing Flame flourished when men like Otto preyed on the poor and the unfortunate? He took a deep breath and relaxed his clenched fists.

'That's what I'd like to discuss with you,' he said at last. 'But I don't want to take up your time here. Perhaps…'

A knock came at the door and the little boy looked in. 'The bargemen are here, sir,' he said.

'Thank you, Rodik,' said Otto. 'Tell them I'll see them in just a moment.' He stood and came around the desk as the boy disappeared again. 'Come have dinner with me tonight at the Golden Hammer,' he said to Felix, then looked him up and down. 'Have you got a good suit of clothes?'

'Ah, no. Mine were singed somewhat. And these are borrowed,' said Felix. 'And I don't suppose we could eat at Wulf's instead?'

Otto made a face. 'Wulf's? Why would you want to go there? It's a dreadful place.'

'I hear it's more, ah, sporting than the Golden Hammer,' said Felix.

Otto sneered. 'Bunch of preening jackdaws who've never done a day's work in their lives. A lot of Gustav's schoolmates go there.'

'Does Gustav go there?' asked Felix, suddenly hopeful. That would make things easier. He could ask the boy about the other members. Perhaps he would have noticed something.

Otto shook his head. 'Not Wulf's. He thinks it represents the antipathy of true speech, or whatever he calls it. Besides, they bully his sort there.'

'I still want to see it,' said Felix. 'If I'm going to live here, I want to know what sort of amusements are on offer.'

Otto smirked knowingly. 'I see how it is. Tired of the privations of the road and want to live a little. Well, I don't blame you. Wulf's is certainly sporting. The evening isn't complete there until some young fool is carried to the surgeons by his friends. But if you want to go...'

'Sounds amusing,' said Felix, with what he hoped was a properly snobbish voice.

'Very well.' Otto fumbled in his pouch. 'Go see my tailor. You remember where he is? Good. Tell him it's on my account. I'll subtract it from your book profits later. And take this and get yourself a shave and a trim. You look like a Kurgan.' He dropped a handful of coins in Felix's hand – gold, silver and copper. 'Rodi!' he shouted.

After a moment the little boy looked in. 'Aye, sir?'

'Show my brother out and ask in the bargemen.'

'Aye, sir.'

'Come by my house at seven, Felix,' said Otto. 'We'll go from there.'

'Right,' said Felix. 'See you tonight.'

He followed Rodi out into the office.

Before they got to the front Felix paused. 'Rodi,' he said.

'Aye, sir,' said the boy, stopping.

'Do you want to be a clerk?'

A terrified expression flashed across his face, and he shot quick looks towards Herr Bartlemass and Otto's office. 'Oh, yes, sir! More than anything, sir.'

Felix scowled. 'I see,' he said. 'And if you didn't want to be a clerk, what would you want to be?'

'A sailor on a ship,' said Rodi instantly. 'My cousin Lani was a mate, sir. He told the most wonderful stories. Been everywhere, my cousin has. Do you know what apes is, sir? My cousin seen one once.'

Felix shuddered, remembering a night under jungle moons, with huge, shaggy shapes lumbering up the steps of a ruined temple towards them. He pushed the scene away and smiled at Rodi. 'A sailor, eh? Well, in case you ever change your mind about clerking, here's something towards your sea chest.' He picked a silver coin from those his brother had given him and handed it to Rodi.

The boy's eyes grew wide as he stared at the coin. 'Thank you, sir!' he said, then darted a wary look at the other boys in the room and slipped the coin quickly into his belt pouch.

Felix shrugged as he wove through the streets towards Otto's tailor. The money would most likely go to Rodi's mother or father and the boy would never leave Otto's office, but at least Felix had tried. He wondered if he would have given him the money if he had said he wanted to be a soldier or an adventurer.

Probably not.

WULF'S OCCUPIED A grand brick and stone building on Commerce Street in the heart of the Handelbezirk. Golden light spilled from its tall windows, each decorated with a stained glass wolf's head. Wide stone steps led up to its stout oak doors. A huge, uniformed man with the look of an ex-soldier pulled them open for the garishly dressed young men who came and went, chatting boisterously with each other. He seemed to know them all by name, and joked with them as they passed.

The giant sized Otto and Felix up as they stepped out of Otto's enclosed coach and Otto told his coachman and two bodyguards to wait for them down the street. Felix blushed under his scrutiny. He was certain the man had seen in an instant that his doublet and breeches were brand new, and that his gaze could see through the finery to the penniless wanderer beneath. He felt an utter fraud in these clothes, an actor masquerading as a rich man. An uncomfortable actor at that. The stiff lace of the collar chafed his neck. The tight green velvet of the doublet constricted his chest. The glossy, knee-high boots pinched his feet. His face felt dry and hot where the barber had scraped his chin and cheeks clean.

'Your names, meinen herren?' rumbled the giant deferentially as he and Otto mounted the steps.

'Otto Jaeger and a guest,' said Otto.

'Herr Jaeger,' said the giant, bowing. 'Forgive me for not recognising you at once, sir. It has been some time since you visited. Welcome.' He pulled on a huge brass ring that was clamped in the jaws of a brass wolf's head, and the door swung open. 'Please remember that guests are only allowed in the dining room and smoking room, sir.'

Otto nodded and they stepped inside. The entry way was clad in dark wood. The banners of several mercantile guilds hung from the walls. Young men laughed and gossiped on a wide stairway that rose up to upper floors. A deafening torrent of merriment and clinking plates poured from a door to the right.

After depositing their cloaks and swords with a porter, Otto and Felix passed through the door into the dining room. Something flew past Felix's face and he flinched back, wary. The missile hit a young diner in the back of the head and plopped to the floor. It was a hunk of black bread. Laughter erupted to Felix's left.

The diner jumped up, armed with a hunk of bread of his own. 'Who threw that?' he called, eyes flashing. 'Mieritz! Was it you?'

A young man in orange and green velvet spread his hands, grinning. 'Me, Fetteroff? Why would you suspect me?'

Fetteroff flung his bread. Mieritz snatched it deftly from the air and took a bite. 'My thanks, sir,' he mumphed as he chewed. 'My bread seems to have fallen on the floor.'

His friends erupted at this witticism, as did Fetteroff, and everyone returned to their dinners.

'I warned you,' said Otto out of the side of his mouth.

A steward in a high collar bowed and led them to a table for two against the far wall. The dining room was large and high ceilinged, with roaring fires in grand fireplaces at both ends. Rich tapestries – all of them depicting wolves on the hunt – hid the plaster walls, and gold stencilled wooden pillars rose to carved and painted beams. Large circular tables filled the centre of the room, all crowded with preening, posturing young men, each apparently trying to outdo all the rest in the richness and elaborateness of their clothes. Felix had never seen so many colours under one roof. It was as if a rainbow had been violently sick.

'Sigmar's beard, what a cacophony,' said Otto, wincing as loud laughter erupted again from one of the tables. 'Do you really prefer this to the Golden Hammer?'

'I'm not sure I do,' said Felix. 'But I wanted to see for myself.'

A server came. Felix ordered duck in plum sauce while Otto ordered roast beef, and Bretonnian wine for the two of them.

Felix tried to listen to his fellow diners while Otto talked about what job he might do for Jaeger and Sons. He wished he could close his eyes in order to concentrate better on their voices, but Otto would remark on that, so he kept them open. He cursed at the constant din. The room was too loud and echoed too much.

He tried to concentrate on picking one voice out from the hubbub, then another, but found it hard to focus on them without getting caught up in their conversations, and the more he heard, the more his teeth clenched and his hackles rose. It wasn't the noise or the high spirits of the young men at the tables that made him angry – in his travels with Gotrek he had seen more than his fair share of wild taverns and boisterous inns. In fact he liked carousing now and then; singing bawdy songs, arm wrestling, dancing with ladies of less than sterling reputations, having deep philosophical conversations with total strangers that he forgot entirely the next day. He had met Gotrek on such a night.

This was different. There was a cruelty to the laughter, a hatefulness to the jokes and jibes that were bandied between the tables, that was peculiar to the idle rich. These young men were not friends, they were rivals, and deadly rivals at that, for all their blaring bonhomie. Their jokes were not meant to entertain, but to belittle their victims and bolster themselves. They chose their companions not because they liked them, but because knowing them offered some advantage. The symbol of the wolf had been well chosen for this place, Felix thought, for the society of its members seemed based on the pecking order of the wolf pack, where the biggest, meanest, and most cunning predator savaged those below him, and they in turn savaged those below them.

Felix had always despised such behaviour, ever since his days at the University in Altdorf when the nobles had sneered at him for his mercantile upbringing and denied him entry to their clubs and fraternities. It distressed him to see the sons of merchants aping precisely this vile behaviour. One would have thought that, having been snubbed and condescended to by their 'betters', they would have wished to belong to a more egalitarian society. Instead, they were worse snobs than the nobility, exaggerating their viciousness and vainglory until they were little better than beasts in velvet.

The wine came. The server poured glasses for them and retired.

Otto had a sip of his and made a face. 'Gods,' he said. 'Their cellar isn't what it used to be either. Their importer must be cheating them.'

Felix took a sip. It tasted all right to him, but then, after all his years with Gotrek, he was more used to ale.

'Ah well,' said Otto. 'As I was saying…'

Felix turned his attention to the other diners again, trying to blot out their words and concentrate on their timbre and tone while thinking back to voices of the Cleansing Flame. He groaned. Why had Ulrika and the countess invested so much hope in so tenuous a thread? There might be no connection between Wulf's and the Brotherhood of the Cleansing Flame except that they shared one member in common – the man Ulrika had killed when she took his pendant. This whole evening might come to nothing. He might be subjecting himself to dinner with his brother for no reason at all.

He gazed around at his fellow diners, hoping some quirk of gesture might spark a memory. He sighed. They all looked like villains to him, but he tried to measure them objectively. It was difficult. That fop in the purple, with the rouge on his cheeks and the ruff so wide it nearly hung over his shoulders, he certainly looked like the member of some sort of debauched cult. And that fellow in the lemon yellow, with the permanent sneer and the earring. Felix could just imagine him performing blood sacrifices when Morrslieb was full. And the rogue in red and gold who was playing cards with his companions, was he using magic to change the cards? And the handsome, sallow-cheeked dandy who was coughing convulsively into his handkerchief. Was he spreading the pox through every brothel in Nuln? And that fellow...

He almost spat out his mouthful of wine as he saw a man watching him suspiciously from across the room. Was it a cultist? No. Wait a moment. He recognised him. But from where? Where had he see that strong jaw before? That perfectly curled moustache?

That proud nose? Then he knew, and almost laughed. It was one of Lady Hermione's beautiful gentlemen, keeping an eye on him. Almost literally. He couldn't have been more obvious if he tried. Perhaps that was the point. Lady Hermione was reminding Felix of her omniscience. Suddenly he didn't feel like laughing anymore.

He gave the man a glare and continued to survey the room. Then stopped again as he saw another almost-familiar face peeking out from behind the nearest pillar. Who was this? He knew the hair, which hung down before the man's sleepy eyes, but the clothing was unfamiliar. Of course! That was because the last time he had seen him, he had been naked. It was the Captain Reingelt, the countess's current swain. It seemed she didn't trust Lady Hermione to share information. And why should she?

Their dinners came, and Otto tucked his linen napkin under his chin and dug in. Felix gave up his search and joined him. Trying to pick out cultists by sight seemed as impossible as trying to recognise them by their speech. He was no witch hunter. He didn't know how to differentiate normal human villainy from the baser horrors of daemon worship. He could recognise a mutant if it looked at him with two heads, but until their corruption showed he was as lost as the next man.

'I know you're not much for sitting at a desk all day,' Otto was saying. 'But we have plenty of jobs that would have you out and doing in the fresh air. Someone needs to go to Marienburg every spring for instance. We buy many of our dyes for our wools there from Bretonnians, Estalians and Arabyans. Araby makes the best indigo. But getting the best prices and making certain the filthy foreign devils aren't cheating us requires being there in person. Does that appeal to you?'

Felix shrugged. 'I've never been much of a one for haggling.'

'Hmmm,' said Otto. 'Well, we also provide guards for our convoys, and we've expanded that service to providing guards for the convoys of other companies. Perhaps you'd like to be involved in the recruitment and training of these fellows. That sounds more in your line.'

Felix was trying to think of an appropriate answer when he overheard an exchange from a group of young men who were passing their table.

'That looks nasty, Gephardt. Get your hand caught in some lady's window when her husband came home?'

'No. Burned it. Stupid, really. Left the poker in the fire by mistake, and when I grabbed it I seared myself.'

Felix looked around at the speaker as the young men laughed. He was a wiry youth with the unlaced doublet and tousled bedroom hair that seemed popular among the more fashionable university students that year. He wore lavender and cream velvet, and had a bandage around his left hand.

'Ha!' said a chinless lad in pink. 'When I leave my poker in the fire too long, it melts! Ha ha!'

Nobody laughed.

'My *poker*, you see,' said the boy in pink, giggling. 'In the *fire*.'

'Do shut up, Kalter,' said the youth with the bandage.

Felix watched him walking away. Burned his hand, had he? And was it Felix's imagination, or was he hiding a limp? He tried to imagine that sly, sneering voice raised in command. It might have sounded something like one of the voices he had heard in the burning cellar, then again it might not, and he needed to be sure. It would be a cruel trick to set the vampires on an innocent man.

He turned to Otto. 'Who is that? The young man in purple and white?'

'Eh?' said Otto, looking up. 'What's this, now? Have you been listening to me at all?'

'Of course I have, brother, but that fellow looks familiar to me. Do you know who he is?'

Otto frowned, annoyed, and squinted across the room. 'Which one?'

'The one in purple and white,' repeated Felix, turning. 'Just now sitting down. He has a bandage on his hand, you see?'

'I see,' said Otto. 'The one next to the fire, yes? I've no idea. Why you would think I would pay attention to the spoiled ne'r-do-wells who frequent Wulf's I don't know. This is why I dine at the Hammer.' He sniffed. 'Looks a bit like old Gephardt, the wine importer, and he's wearing the colours of Gephardt's trading house. Might be one of his sons, I suppose. I couldn't say.'

Felix nodded. Gephardt was the name the youth's companion had called him. Give Otto credit for keen observation. Now the question was, was he a member of the Brotherhood of the Cleansing Flame, or had he only burned himself on a hot poker like he had said? If only Felix could get closer and eavesdrop on his conversation.

Gephardt looked idly around the dining room as one of his companions told a story. His eyes flicked past Felix, then came back. Felix looked away, heart racing. He had forgotten he was staring.

'So, does that appeal to you?' asked Otto, picking up their conversation again. 'Would you like to help us with finding men to guard our wagons? With all your experience fighting – ahem – ratmen and dragons, and so forth, I imagine you know a practiced blade when you meet one.'

Felix stole another look over his shoulder. Gephardt was staring fixedly at him, his eyes wide, whether in fear or anger Felix couldn't be sure. Felix turned back, heart sinking. Well, he had his answer. Gephardt recognised him. He must have seen him during the fighting in the Cleansing Flame's meeting house. Felix could have wished he had learned the information without revealing himself in the process. Now Gephardt knew he knew. Felix would have to catch him before he left Wulf's, or soon all of the Cleansing Flame would know as well. But how was he going to do that with his brother around? He couldn't very well say 'Excuse me, brother, I have to knock out and capture this young man. Do you mind helping me bring him to the College of Engineering so Gotrek can have a word with him?'

Perhaps his so called allies would help him. He looked over at Lady Hermione's man. He was getting up to leave, his gaze fixed on Gephardt. He must have seen the exchange of glances and deduced what they meant. Felix turned towards Captain Reingelt. He too was rising, eyes darting from Gephardt to Hermione's spy to Felix and back again. He knew too. But why were they leaving? Were the two of them going to go wait for Gephardt to exit the club, or were they off to their mistresses to tell them what they had learned? Whatever the case, he couldn't rely on either of them. He would have to take care of Gephardt himself, somehow.

'Felix? Did you hear me?' Otto was looking at him strangely.

'Er,' Felix said, struggling to remember what his brother had been saying. 'Er, yes, that, uh, certainly sounds like the most appealing alternative. I'll most definitely give it some thought. You make a compelling argument.'

Otto's chest puffed up. 'Well, you know, I pride myself on fitting the man to the job and the job to the man. Part of the secret of my success. Shall we order a sweetmeat for after? And a little more wine?'

'Yes, that sounds like a good idea,' said Felix. That would give him more time to come up with a way to kidnap Gephardt. Felix looked across the room again as Otto summoned the server. Gephardt was gone!

Felix's heart thudded violently. He hadn't expected the man to move so quickly! He was already on his way to warn his masters, no doubt. This was bad. He had to get back and tell Gotrek. If they moved immediately, they might be able to catch Gephardt before he talked to the Cleansing Flame.

Felix turned back to Otto. 'On second thought, perhaps we should be getting back,' he said. 'You've given me a lot to think about.'

Otto frowned. 'Are you well, Felix? You look a bit green.'

Felix swallowed. 'The duck, I think. I'm not accustomed to such rich food anymore.' He smiled weakly. 'I suppose I'll have to get used to it.'

A FEW FITFUL raindrops spattered the steps as Felix and Otto stepped out of Wulf's. Thick clouds hid the moons and the wind was cool and wet. Otto summoned his coach and it trotted up. Felix followed Otto into it, glad that it was covered. It looked like a storm was coming.

As they started up Commerce Street towards Kaufman district gate, Otto crossed his hands over his broad belly and burped contentedly. 'You're staying at the College of Engineering?' he asked. 'Shall I drop you there?'

'Thank you,' said Felix. The faster he got back the better. 'Very nice of you. And thank you for the dinner.'

'Not at all. Happy to. I'm just glad you've finally come around to deciding to make something of yourself. Once you start with the company we'll dine out like this all the time. Though I hope you don't want to go to Wulf's next–'

Otto was interrupted by a shout, and the coach slewed to an abrupt stop with a neighing of horses and a skidding of hoofs on wet cobbles. Felix and Otto flew forward out of their seats. Felix heard the bodyguards curse as they were thrown from their perches and tried to land on their feet on the street.

Felix pulled himself up and dropped his hand to his sword.

'Manni! Yan! Olaf! What is it!' called Otto.

'Men, sir,' came the coachman's voice.

'Men with swords,' said one of the bodyguards. 'Near a dozen.'

Fear gripped Felix's heart. Who was it? Hermione's gentlemen? Men from the Cleansing Flame? Had Countess Gabriella decided to kill him after all?

'Easy, gentles, easy,' said a Shantytown voice. 'We only want yer valuables, not yer lives. Hand 'em over peaceable and there'll be no need for violence.'

Felix gaped, amazed. Shallya's Mercy! Was it only a robbery? Could he be so lucky?

'Stand away, you ruffians!' retorted the other bodyguard. 'You'll get steel before you get gold.'

'No no!' cried Otto. 'Don't fight them! It isn't worth your lives. Stand down.' He pulled himself up and peeked out the window. 'Come forward, gentlemen. We'll give you what we have.'

'That's the way, m'lords,' said the Shantytown voice as boots approached the coach from either side. 'Nice and easy.'

'You watch yourselves,' growled a bodyguard. 'No tricks.'

'Sigmar's beard!' said Otto as he wiggled the rings off his fingers and started stuffing them under the cushions of the bench. 'The brass of these fellows. Right in the middle of Commerce Street! Where is the watch when they're wanted?'

Felix sat back on the bench as the bootsteps reached the coach's two doors. His hand went to his dagger. The coach rocked on its springs and two scarred, grinning faces appeared in the windows.

'Evening, gentles,' said the one on Felix's side, a swarthy fellow in a soft hat.

The other, who lacked a right eye, looked from Otto to Felix and back. 'Aye,' he said. 'These are the ones.'

The two robbers drew pistols from their doublets and stuck them through the windows.

Felix struck out in two directions at once, kicking hard against his door with the heel of his boot, while at the same time backhanding his dagger at the man in Otto's window.

There was a splintering of wood and both pistols fired, deafening Felix and filling the coach with smoke. Felix heard a cry, but couldn't tell who it was. He didn't think he'd been hit, so he hoped it wasn't him. He launched himself at his door and was gratified to feel it slam open and to hear a body hit the street.

The words, 'these are the ones,' echoed through Felix's head as he stopped and surged for the opposite door. He came up hard against it. The window was empty. He looked out. The one-eyed man lay on the ground, a messy hole in his throat, shot by his companion it seemed. Beyond him, more thugs were running forward. An ambush then, not a robbery. The only question that remained was, were these cultists from the Cleansing Flame, or hirelings of Lady Hermione or Countess Gabriella?

Felix turned to Otto, just visible now through the clearing smoke. He cowered against the back of the bench, eyes wide and darting, his fat chins trembling.

'Stay in the coach!' Felix barked. 'And defend yourself!'

He leapt out of the smashed door, and almost fell as his new boots slid on the wet street. The taller of Otto's bodyguards – Yan, his name was, Felix remembered – had killed the swarthy shooter and was turning to face the charging thugs. Felix drew his runesword and joined him.

One of the thugs fell before he reached them, a fletched bolt in his leg. Out of the corner of his eye, Felix saw Manni, the coachman, cranking a small crossbow.

Then Felix and Yan were surrounded, swords and clubs swinging at them from every direction. Felix knocked a cudgel from someone's hand and ran through a swordsman. He was relieved to see that Yan was a veteran. He did not flinch or panic. He met the greater numbers calm and alert, and though he made no touches, he took none either. It seemed that Otto had spent wisely when he had hired his guards.

Felix killed another thug, gashing his throat, then unstrung another's knee. The assassins wore no armour, and Karaghul was a heavier, keener sword than their rapiers and short swords. He batted them out of the way with ease. The greatest difficulty was keeping his feet on the slick cobbles.

A shout came from the other side of the coach, and then a shriek from Otto.

'Master Felix!' called the coachman. 'They're getting in!'

Felix cursed. 'Fall back with me,' he shouted to Yan, then flourished wildly with his sword and jumped back out of combat. Yan ran with him as he turned and ran for the back of the coach. Yan gasped and almost fell as a thug slashed him across the back. Felix caught his arm and they surged on, their three remaining opponents close behind them.

Olaf had acquitted himself well. Two corpses lay at his feet, and another was staggering away, trying to hold his guts in. But the bodyguard was slumped, motionless, against the coach door, his chest and face painted with blood. A thug kicked him aside and grabbed at the coach door. There were three more behind him.

Felix bellowed to get their attention, then barrelled into them, slashing left and right. One fell back, torso split from shoulder to hip, and the others dodged away, but one gashed Felix under the left arm and the cold shock of steel burned across his ribs. He grunted and stumbled aside.

Yan hacked the man down, then covered Felix as he turned. Felix's first thought, ridiculously, was that they had ruined his new doublet. Then the pain came in earnest and he forgot about the doublet.

There were seven assassins left between Felix and the coach. Seven against two, and he was wounded, blood running down his side. It would be quite a joke if, after persevering against nearly every horror the Old World had to offer, he was finally killed by common alley bashers on the high street in Nuln.

A thug at the back shoved some of the others forward. 'Hold them off while we kill the fat one!' he said, then screamed as a bolt from the coachman's crossbow punched down through his collarbone.

The others turned their heads at the noise. Felix and Yan charged instinctively. The thugs fell back, caught off guard. Felix and Yan pressed them against the coach, swinging wildly. Felix disarmed one and chopped another's club in half. Yan pinned one to the coach, but took a knife point across the cheek. Felix gutted the one he had disarmed, and clubbed another in the temple with the dragon-headed pommel of his sword.

The assassins had had enough. They broke and ran, scattering to the shadows on both sides of the street. Felix and Yan made no attempt to follow.

Felix put the point of his sword to the neck of the man who had taken Manni's bolt in the collarbone as Yan despatched the rest of the wounded with professional efficiency. 'Who sent you?'

The man spat at him, his eyes wild with fanatical ardour. 'You are dead!' he said. 'The flame will consume you! You and all your kind!' He pushed himself forward deliberately, impaling his neck upon Felix's sword, and laughed wetly as the blood pumped from his throat. 'Change is coming!' he hissed, then slumped back, dead. Felix shivered. Just like the one who had killed himself on Gotrek's axe. Their fanaticism was frightening. At least now he knew who had sent them.

'Is it over?' asked Otto, peeking out from the coach.

Felix nodded. 'It's over.'

He knelt down beside Olaf. The bodyguard was breathing, but only barely. Yan squatted down and the two of them picked him up.

Otto opened the coach door and they laid him on the floor. 'To Doctor Koln's house, Manni,' he said. 'Hurry.'

As Yan pulled himself onto his perch behind, Felix climbed back in the coach. He eased back onto the bench with a weary hiss and closed his eyes. The coach lurched forward, jarring his wound. He grunted, in pain, and opened his eyes.

Otto was glaring at him. 'This was no simple robbery.' he said. 'They were after us. After you!'

'I'm sorry, Otto,' said Felix. 'I...'

Otto wasn't listening. He was too angry. 'This has something to do with Gephardt's son, doesn't it? That's why you wanted to go to Wulf's! You had no interest in talking to me about working for the company. You were having one of your *adventures*, and now you've got me caught up in it! Sigmar! I might have been killed!' His face suddenly paled. 'Gods! I still might! Gephardt must have known me as surely as I knew him. He will come after me. He will come after Annabella and Gustav!' Otto's eyes blazed with fury. His round cheeks flushed red. 'How dare you! How dare you endanger my family with your mad antics!'

Felix hung his head. 'I'm sorry, Otto. I didn't think it...'

'Clearly, you didn't think!' shouted Otto. 'You are insane! Get out! Get out and don't come back!'

'I...' Felix felt like a daemon was twisting his intestines with both hands. It was true. He hadn't thought – not until it was too late. He had been so intent on finding the leaders of the Cleansing Flame that he hadn't considered fully the consequences for those around him. It didn't matter that Otto didn't know anything. The cultists had seen him with Felix, and would assume he was a threat. 'At least let me see you to your house,' he said. 'They might come back.'

'No!' said Otto. 'I don't want you near me or...' He hesitated, his eyes flicking nervously to the coach window, then nodded. 'All right, to my house. But never come again. I will not let you in my door.'

'I understand,' said Felix sadly. He couldn't argue. Otto was in the right. He brought wrack and ruin with him wherever he went. First he burned down whole neighbourhoods, now he had marked his brother's family for death. The hero of Nuln indeed!

THEY DEPOSITED OLAF with the doctor – and Otto waited impatiently as the old man salved and stitched and bound the long gash under Felix's arm as well – then hurried on under clouds that threatened rain, but did little more than spit.

As the coach pulled up to Otto's house, the front door opened, and young Gustav stepped out wearing a rain cloak over his scholar's robes. He had a lantern in one hand and a satchel in the other.

Otto practically leapt out of the coach. 'No!' he said, waving his hands. 'Back in the house! You're not going out!'

'What?' asked Gustav. 'Don't be ridiculous, father. I'm only going to–'

'No! You're not going anywhere!'

'But... but why?'

'Because your *uncle*...' Otto turned to glare at Felix as he stepped out after him, 'Has made us the target of some crazed madmen who he is at feud with!'

Gustav frowned. 'I don't understand.'

'Nor do I,' said Otto. 'Nor do I wish to. One moment he is asking questions about Linus Gephardt's son, the next we are attacked in the street by...'

'Gephardt's son?' asked Gustav, his brow knotted. 'You mean Nikolas? What does Nikolas have to do with–'

'You know him?' asked Felix eagerly.

'Nikolas? He is a classmate at university.' Gustav sneered. 'Fancies himself a pamphleteer. I've read better prose in an account ledger.'

'Do you know where he lives?' continued Felix.

'He lives at his father's house, just–'

'No!' cried Otto. 'I forbid it! He has already wound us too close to his folly. You will not assist him!' He turned on Felix and pointed towards the street with a shaking finger. 'You have hurt us enough. Go. Go and don't come back.'

Felix nodded sadly. 'Very well.' He bowed to his brother. 'I am sorry, Otto. And I will do everything I can to fix this.'

'I don't want to hear any more,' said Otto. 'Just go. Go!'

Felix sighed and started down the street towards the gate to the Neuestadt, his mind boiling with guilt and anger and a determination to honour his promise to Otto and make things right for him and his family. The rain picked up. He pulled up the hood of his fancy new cloak. It, at least, was still in one piece.

ELEVEN

FELIX WALKED OUT onto the roof of the College of Engineering, his brother's words still echoing through his mind. Bright lanterns pushed back the night, making the flat green copper roof and its crenellated edges appear to be a island in a dark and endless sea. Slanting raindrops slashed past the lanterns like little comets.

Students were rolling barrels of black powder out from the stairwell and stacking them in piles beneath the *Spirit of Grungni*, which hovered above them like an iron cloud. A winch was lifting a net full of barrels up through a hatch into the belly of the gondola. Another net was spread out on the rooftop and barrels were being placed in its centre. Beyond all the activity, a gyrocopter sat like the withered husk of some gigantic insect, chains securing it to the roof.

Malakai stood by the net, supervising the loading. Gotrek was with him. Felix limped towards them. There was nothing wrong with his legs, but his wounded side was so stiff he could hardly walk straight. It throbbed with blunt, insistent agony. All he wanted to do was dull his brain with ale and try to sleep, but the Slayer needed to hear of the night's events.

The two dwarfs looked up as he approached.

'Evening, young Felix,' said Malakai.

'You must have found something,' said Gotrek. 'You've been fighting.'

'Aye,' said Felix. 'I found out what a fool I can be.' He cast a distracted eye up at the barrels that were disappearing into the hatch. 'I don't dare to hope that you've recovered the powder in my absence.'

Malakai shook his head. 'This is the new powder, bought with Lord Skinflint-Keppel's money. But what happened tae ye?'

Felix sighed. 'I went to Wulf's. One of the cultists we fought last night wore–'

'Aye, a wolf's head pendant. Ah noo a' aboot it,' said Malakai. 'Gurnisson told me all o' what went on in yon cellar. Nae need tae explain. Go on.'

Felix frowned, uneasy. How much had Gotrek said? Had he mentioned Ulrika? Countess Gabriella wouldn't like that. Well, he couldn't very well ask Gotrek that in Malakai's presence, could he? He coughed and continued. 'Well, I saw a man at the club with a burned hand. Unfortunately he saw me too, and he sent some thugs to waylay me and my brother on our way back to his house. There was a fight. My brother... my brother has told me to never come back to his house.'

'And why, pray tell?' asked Malakai.

'He blames me for getting him involved and bringing trouble to his door.' Felix sighed as the daggers of guilt stabbed at him again, almost as painful as the cut in his side. 'And he is right. I should have found some other way into Wulf's. Now the Cleansing Flame are after him as well. And his family. I fear I have doomed them with a death meant for me.'

Gotrek and Malakai snorted in unison.

'Men,' grunted Gotrek, contemptuously.

'A dwarf would have added his axe tae his brother's and faced his enemy at his side,' said Malakai.

'Did you catch this burned man?' asked Gotrek.

'No,' said Felix. 'But I learned his name, and where he lives.'

'Good,' said Gotrek, turning towards the stairs. 'Let's go.'

'Gurnisson!' snapped Malakai. 'Don't be an ass. Can't ye see the lad needs a wee lie doon?'

Gotrek stopped and looked back, glaring at Felix's blood-soaked shirt. He seemed offended that Felix had got himself wounded. 'There's no time. These fools could use the powder tonight. And the *Spirit of Grungni* leaves in less than two days.'

'I'm fine,' said Felix, though he felt anything but, in body or soul. 'But I don't think we'll be able to reach him tonight anyway.'

'Who says we won't?' Gotrek snarled.

'He's a rich man's son,' said Felix. 'He lives at his father's house in the Kaufman district. The city watch doesn't let commoners through the Altestadt gates at this time of night. Particularly not when they are wanted criminals such as ourselves.'

'Then we'll take the sewers,' said Gotrek. 'Come on.'

The mention of the sewers and of their outlaw status reminded Felix of the encounter they had had with the watch under the Gunnery School earlier that day. He turned to Malakai. 'Did you get a visit from the watch today about us?'

'Oh, aye,' said Malakai. 'I told Gurnisson o' it already. They came asking after ye.'

'And?'

Malakai shrugged. 'I told 'em I didnae know where ye wis, which was the truth. And I told them I'd tell ye, if ye returned, no' tae dae it again.' He grinned. 'So, dinnae dae it again. And dinnae tell me who this rich laddie is, or where his house is, neither. A dwarf niver lies.'

Felix gave a half-hearted chuckle, then groaned and pressed his ribs.

Malakai clucked his tongue. 'Ye shouldnae be goin' anywhere, laddie, except to yer bed.'

'I'll sleep when this is over,' said Felix, and turned after Gotrek. *If I'm still alive*, he thought.

FELIX WALKED BESIDE Gotrek as they travelled again through the stinking brick tunnels towards the Altestadt district, his head down and his mind churning like a stew on the boil. A thought would come to the surface like a mushy onion or a bit of meat or carrot, and then sink back down into the depths as another one roiled up, demanding his attention – his culpability in his brother's danger, his responsibility for the fire in the Maze, the threats of the countess and her even more vicious rivals, the doom that would come upon the Gunnery School if they failed to find the powder, the fact that, not two weeks back in the Empire and they were once again outlaws.

He looked over at Gotrek, striding along with his beard jutting forward, his brow lowered, a picture of unwavering determination. Did he ever have doubts or second thoughts? Did he ever have regrets? Then he recalled the Slayer hunched over the body of his friend Hamnir, whom he had just killed. Of course he did – more than Felix would ever know of, no doubt.

Felix shook himself and tried to clear his mind for the task ahead. 'So,' he said at last. 'When we get there, is your plan to beat this Gephardt until he tells us where the powder is and who his leaders are?'

'Aye,' said Gotrek. 'What else?'

'I don't think it will work.' said Felix. 'The orator we captured in Shantytown yesterday cut his own throat on your axe rather than talk. And the leader of the men who attacked my brother's coach did the same thing when I tried to question him tonight. He threw himself on my sword and died laughing at me.'

Gotrek grunted. 'They're not cowards, at least,' he said.

'No,' said Felix. 'They're mad.' He hissed as the cut over his ribs flared again. 'I think our best bet is to watch Gephardt, and follow him until he brings us to the leaders of the cult.'

Gotrek shrugged. 'All right. But if he doesn't lead us to them before the *Spirit of Grungni* is ready to leave, we'll try it my way.'

'Fair enough,' said Felix.

They walked on, the flow of sludge in the sewer channel was higher and quicker than usual from the rain, and in every direction Felix heard the rush and splash of water pouring down through iron gratings. The brick walls were slick with moisture.

A little further on, Felix slowed and looked around as a familiar fetid smell reached his nostrils. He inhaled deeper, trying to separate it from the pungent background odour of the sewer. Was it? Yes it was. There was no mistaking it – the rancid musky reek of ratman – faint but unmistakable. Was it some old spoor he and Gotrek had stumbled over, or had the skaven returned to Nuln?

Gotrek was turning his head back and forth like a dog sniffing the wind. He caught Felix's eye. 'Aye, manling. I smell it too. But we've no time for diversions.'

He strode on. Felix shook his head as he followed. Only Gotrek could call those horrific abominations a 'diversion'.

A few tunnels on, Felix remembered what Malakai had said on the roof, and his heart thudded in his chest. 'Ah, Gotrek, did you tell Makaisson about our alliance with Ulrika?'

'Of course not,' said Gotrek. 'I might kill her, but I'd not betray her.'

Felix flushed. 'I didn't think so, but when he said you had told him about the pendant…'

'I kept her out of it.'

'Good.' Felix was relieved. That was one lump in his roiling stew of fears that could subside. He could confidently tell the countess and her compatriots that he and Gotrek had kept their existence a secret. Though whether that would matter to Lady Hermione and Mistress Wither he could not say. Their mistrust of men seemed to run too deep.

Gotrek looked up. 'We're under the Altestadt now. This way.'

He led Felix to a side tunnel with an iron ladder as if it had been yesterday that he had used it, not twenty years ago. Felix's wounded side ached as he pulled himself up. The rungs were wet, and a steady stream of drips rattled on their heads as they climbed. At the top of the ladder, Gotrek shouldered up an iron grate and helped Felix out into an alley behind a row of shops. The rain had finally started in earnest. It was pouring. They were wet in seconds.

Felix sighed. 'A perfect night for spying.'

THE GEPHARDT HOUSE stood in the middle of a row of elegant town homes: a four storey granite mansion with tall, narrow windows at each floor and a balcony over the front door. It was nearing midnight when Gotrek and Felix found the place, an hour when most honest Nulners were abed – *and the sane ones were out of the rain*, thought Felix miserably, as a drip ran down his nose – but there was a light behind one of the windows on the ground floor, and when they looked in, they could see young Nikolas pacing before a huge fireplace, and drinking deeply from a wine bottle. There didn't appear to be anyone with him.

The young man was nervous, but what about? Had his thugs reported that Felix and Otto escaped them? Was he frightened that he was going to be exposed? Had he sent his men back out to find Felix? Had they regrouped and gone after Otto? The thought made Felix want to run back to his brother's house and defend it, but Otto had said he didn't want him there and, truth be told, the best way of saving him and his family from the threat of the Cleansing Flame was to find the cultists and wipe them out. Felix just hoped that was possible.

They could not stay too long at the window. Unlike Shantytown and the Neuestadt, the Kaufman district was well patrolled. Gotrek and Felix heard the tap of the watch's spear butts striking the cobbles further down the block before they saw them, and retreated into a service alley, then watched as the men passed, looking wet and out of sorts, their captain carrying a lantern on a long pole before them.

After the watchmen had turned a corner and vanished again into the night, they returned to Gephardt's window. Nikolas was gone, and an old servant was covering the fire and tidying up the wine bottle.

'Around the back,' said Gotrek.

They circled the block. The alley behind the houses was not as neatly cobbled as the street in front and they splashed through puddles and muddy ruts until they came to the right gate. The back of the property was large, and divided into coach yard and garden. As they craned their necks to see over the wall, a light went out in a window on the top floor.

'Gone to sleep,' said Felix.

'Perhaps,' said Gotrek. 'Perhaps not.' He looked around. The coach house of the mansion across the alley from Gephardt's butted up against the alley. Gotrek crossed to it and started climbing the wall to the roof, which was low and partially screened by yew trees. 'I'll watch from here,' he said over his shoulder. 'You go back to where we were. If he leaves from the front, strike your sword against stone. I'll hear it.'

'And if he leaves from the back?' asked Felix. 'I don't have your hearing.'

Gotrek pulled himself up onto the roof and drew his axe. He held it up and grinned. 'You won't need it.'

Felix shrugged. 'All right. Let's hope he leaves quickly, though. I think I'm catching a chill.'

Gotrek snorted. 'Humans are soft.' He settled himself in a valley between the peaks of the carriage house roof.

Felix rolled his eyes, then trudged down the alley and back to the street.

IT SEEMED NIKOLAS might never leave. Felix stood shivering and sniffing in the service alley across the street from the Gephardt mansion for hours while the rain beat down on his head and his wound ached and itched as if imps were clawing at it from the inside. Nothing happened. Once every hour the watch walked by and Felix stepped further back into the shadows of the alley, but other than that, all was quiet. The rain rained, cats and rats prowled, very occasionally a coach rolled by or deposited someone at one of the grand houses – once even to the house he was hunched against – but none stopped at Gephardt's house.

After a time Felix's legs grew tired and he squatted on his haunches, but then his new boots cut off the circulation in his legs and he stood again, stomping away the pins and needles. At last he sat down on the driest cobbles he could find and tried to keep his eyes open while his seat got wetter and colder. Won't be long now, he thought. Any minute Gephardt's front

door will open, or the clash of Gotrek's axe will ring
out, and we'll be off and running. Any minute now.

Any minute now.

'WHAT'S ALL THIS?' said a voice in Felix's ear. 'Are you
well, m'lord?'

Felix flinched awake, blinking around in confusion.
Booted legs and spear shafts ringed him like a fence. A
square face with a broken nose was inches from his,
and a loud voice buffeted his eardrums, accompanied
by a gust of onions and beer and cheap meat pie. It
was still raining.

'Lost yer way home from the club, hey, m'lord?' said
the watchman, not unkindly. He offered Felix his arm.
Felix took it, and the man hauled him to his feet.
'Upsy daisy, m'lord. That's it.' He dusted Felix down
and smiled at him, revealing rotten teeth. 'Best to find
your own bed then, hey? You'll catch your death out
here in this wet.'

'Thank you,' said Felix, still trying to clear his head.
It appeared to be dawn, or almost dawn. How long
had he been asleep? Had he missed Nikolas leaving?
Had he missed Gotrek's signal? At least with his new
clothes they seemed to have mistaken him for a
nobleman and weren't suspicious of his being here.
'I… Well, I guess I'll be going.'

But where, he wondered? He pulled his sodden cloak
around his shoulders. Would they follow him if he went
around the block to find Gotrek? And what if Nikolas
slipped out before he could get back in position?

As he started towards the street one of the watchmen stepped to the sergeant and whispered in his ear.
Felix saw this and picked up his pace.

It was no good.

'Just a minute, m'lord,' said the sergeant from behind him.

Felix turned at the mouth of the alley. 'Yes?'

'Begging your pardon,' said the sergeant, 'but could you tell me your name? And where you live, exactly?'

'My name?' said Felix, panic rising in his throat. He tried an aristocratic sneer. 'And what business is it of yours what my name is?'

'Well, er, ye see, yer lordship,' said the sergeant, looking uncomfortable. 'Edard here thinks you look like a fellow what's supposed to be under house arrest in the College of Engineering. That one were described as having a sword with a dragon hilt, just like the one you're wearing, and, well…'

'Oh, sergeant,' came a silvery voice from above them.

Everyone looked up. A beautiful woman in green, with long auburn hair trailing out from beneath a shawl, was leaning out of a window of the townhouse beside the alley. She smiled down at them.

Felix stared.

It was Ulrika.

TWELVE

THE SERGEANT TOUCHED his fingers to his cap. 'Morning, m'lady. Terrible sorry if we woke you.'

'Not at all, sergeant,' she said sweetly, and without a trace of Kislev accent. 'But I must ask you to release this man, ruffian though he may be. I threw him out last night after we had a little lover's quarrel. He has pined beneath my window ever since, but I believe he has suffered enough, and I have forgiven him. Let him go and I will open the door for him.'

'Aye, lady,' said the sergeant, uncertainly. 'It's just that we have reason to believe he might be–'

'Nonsense,' said Ulrika, even more sweetly. 'He couldn't possibly be anyone you had any interest in. He is merely my poor, sweet, bedraggled lover, heartsick in the rain.' Her voice was as syrupy and cloying as honey, and her eyes seemed to have gotten very large and very deep. 'My poor, sweet, bedraggled lover,' she repeated. 'Heartsick in the rain.'

'Aye, lady,' the sergeant mumbled. 'Heartsick in the rain. Aye, of course. Thank ye. And we'll be going now.'

'Yes, you will,' agreed Ulrika. 'Goodbye.'

The watchmen turned and shuffled off down the street like sleepwalkers. Felix watched them go, then looked up at Ulrika again.

'How are you here…?'

Ulrika put a finger to her lips and motioned to the front of the house, then closed the window.

Felix walked around to the front door, giving the befuddled watchmen a wide berth. After a short wait, the door opened, and a grave looking butler bowed him in. As he was taking Felix's dripping cloak, Ulrika appeared at the top of a curved mahogany staircase and smiled sourly down at him.

'You see how much nicer things could have been if you and Gotrek had honoured your promise?' she said. 'Come up and I will find you some dry clothes.'

'I don't understand,' said Felix crossly, starting up the stairs. It was deliciously warm in here, and dry. The smell of eggs and bacon and spiced tea wafting from the back of the house was making his stomach growl. To think he had spent the whole night getting soaked in the alley, while right behind the wall he had slumped against, Ulrika was sitting in the lap of luxury. 'What promise did I not honour? And how do you come to be in this house?'

'You broke one promise, and Gotrek broke another,' said Ulrika, as she led him along the hall. 'You did not return to the countess and tell her what you had discovered.'

Felix scowled. 'Was there any need? Her besotted knight – what was his name? Captain Reingelt? He was there. He saw it all. As did one of Lady Hermione's dandies. They must have told their mistresses, else you wouldn't be here.'

'Aye, they did, but you forget what I said of the countess's nature of late. She would take even so small a lapse as a deliberate slight.' She opened the door to a bedroom and stood aside to let him enter. It was a comfortable room, with a large canopied bed on one side and a crackling fire on the other. 'But that is by the by. It is Gotrek whose treachery is unforgiveable.'

'Oh come,' said Felix. 'Gotrek has never broken a promise in his life!'

'Indeed he has,' said Ulrika, closing the door behind him and turning, her eyes suddenly as cold and hard as sapphires. 'And you know it.'

'What?'

'Mistress Wither followed you from Wulf's last night, at Lady Hermione's bidding. She was on the roof when you spoke to Gotrek and Malakai. She heard Malakai say, just as you heard him, that Gotrek had revealed my existence to him.'

Felix blinked, confused. 'What? He didn't.'

'Do you lie now too, Felix?' she asked, advancing on him. All her former humour had drained away as if it had never been. 'The Slayer speaks much about honour and keeping vows. Apparently he doesn't hold himself to so high a standard.'

Felix took an involuntary step backwards. She was terrifying. 'Wait! You have it wrong. It must be Mistress Wither that lied.'

'Did she?' she said, still coming forward. 'She reported to us that Makaisson said Gotrek had told him all about the pendant, and the whole truth about the fight with the Cleansing Flame.' She reached out and grasped his collar. 'And the whole truth includes *me*.'

Felix backed into the bed, banging his head against one of the posts. 'Wait! Listen! I can see how she might have construed Malakai's words that way. But she doesn't know Gotrek. He did not give you away. He told Malakai all of it but your part. He left you out.'

Ulrika was inches from him. Her sharp teeth glinted in the firelight. 'And how do you know this?'

'I asked!' Felix swallowed. She was going to kill him! 'It… it troubled me too! Gotrek doesn't do things like that, but knowing how he feels about you and your mistress, I thought perhaps…'

'You thought?'

'I was wrong!' cried Felix. 'He said he might kill you, but he would never betray you.'

Ulrika glared at him, her ice-blue eyes boring into his as if she could dissect his soul with them. Then after a long moment she sighed and backed away, shaking her head and chuckling. 'He might kill me but he wouldn't betray me? Ha! That does sound like the Slayer.'

'You believe me, then?' asked Felix, barely daring to breathe.

'Aye,' said Ulrika. 'I believe you.' Then she frowned. 'But this is unfortunate.'

'What is?'

Ulrika looked up at him apologetically. 'The countess believed Mistress Wither's story, as I did. Therefore she believes that you and Gotrek betrayed me. She is not pleased. In fact, she gave Mistress Wither, Lady Hermione and myself permission to kill you both if we found you.'

'Sigmar!' Felix's heart hammered. Three ancient, powerful, *insane*, vampiresses, all out for his blood! Could it get any worse? 'You have to tell them! You have to call them off!'

'Have no fear, Felix,' said Ulrika. 'I will repair the damage. I will tell the countess what you have said. All will be well.'

Felix swallowed and tried to calm his breathing. 'I hope so.'

'Worry not,' she said smiling reassuringly. 'I am her favourite, and Mistress Wither is a rival. She will believe me.' Her eyes dropped to Felix's clothes. 'But look at you! You're dripping on the carpet. What sort of hostess am I?' She crossed to a wardrobe. 'Let's see what we can find for you.'

Felix blinked at this quick change of subject and mood. Ulrika seemed to have dismissed the countess's death sentence without another thought, but he was having a hard time imagining that all would go as well as she seemed to think.

He looked around the luxurious room as she rummaged in the armoire. Gephardt's father's house was visible through the front window. 'How did you find this place to watch from?' he asked. 'Don't tell me the countess just happens to own a house directly across from Gephardt's?'

Ulrika pulled a dressing gown of blue Cathay silk from the wardrobe and held it out to him. 'Here. This should fit. Put it on.'

Felix took it and set it on the bed, waiting for her to withdraw.

She sat down in an armchair. 'As I mentioned once before, the countess has many clients among the nobility, and she is very good at...' She frowned at Felix. 'What's the matter. Get dressed. You'll catch your death.'

'Ah...' said Felix, colouring.

'Oh, don't be an idiot,' said Ulrika, rolling her eyes. 'It's not as if I haven't seen it all before, when we were...' She stopped as she saw Felix's expression, and snorted. 'All right, all right.' She stood and picked up the chair – a heavy oak and leather behemoth – as if it weighed nothing, then turned it to face the fire. 'Now, go on. I won't look. I promise.' She sat down in it and looked into the flames.

Felix glared at her back, then shrugged and began to peel off his sopping clothes.

'Where was I?' said Ulrika to the fireplace. 'Ah yes. The countess has many rich clients, and she is very good at getting them to do what she wants. Her voice can be very hypnotic when she wishes.'

'As can yours,' said Felix, recalling the befuddlement of the watchmen.

'I am learning,' said Ulrika, then continued. 'This is the house of Lord Jorgen Kirstfauver. When Captain Reingelt reported to the countess – that is, to Madame du Vilmorin – that you had revealed the son of Linus Gephardt to be one of the Cleansing Flame, she knew where he lived – Gephardt senior being of course another client of our house. So it was simplicity itself for her to call upon Lord Kirstfauver and invite him to sample the newest and youngest girls in the house, for as long as he liked, in exchange for the use of his house and servants for a day – with the greatest discretion, of course. Lord Kirstfauver is besotted with Madame du Vilmorin, as are all men, so he readily agreed.'

'And if we must wait longer than a day?' asked Felix, shucking out of his wet linen shirt and taking up the robe.

Ulrika chuckled. 'Time has a way of passing almost unnoticed in Madame du Vilmorin's house. Lord Kirstfauver will find that he was so bewitched by the beauty of his bedmates that the days just slipped away.' She paused, frowning. 'Where is Gotrek, by the way?'

Felix felt a hot flash of shame. He had been here talking all this time while Gotrek was still out in the rain, watching from the back alley. 'Sigmar! He's watching Gephardt's coach yard. As I should be from the front.' He started angrily for the door. 'You've lured me from my post. Gephardt may have gotten away.'

'Fear not, Felix,' said Ulrika. 'I have seven spies watching the house. We will know if he leaves.'

'Seven!' Felix stared at her. Seven spies? And he had seen none of them?

She spread her hands. 'You see? Had you told us as you should have, you might have slept in a warm bed tonight. Your stubborn insistence on going it alone soaked you to the bone, and the fox might have slipped away while you slept.' She smirked. 'Do you want to relieve Gotrek from his misery now?'

Felix flushed again. He did want to bring Gotrek in out of the rain, but the thought of the Slayer finding him in a silk robe in the company of Ulrika made him cringe. 'Yes, I'll… Just a moment.'

He crossed to his sword and unsheathed it. Ulrika looked alarmed until he stepped to the side window, which looked over the alley he had spent the night in. He opened it and rang the flat of the blade against the stone window ledge. Ulrika looked at him curiously.

'Our signal,' Felix explained.

He leaned out of the window until he saw Gotrek's squat form appear at the end of the block and look down the street towards Gephardt's house.

'Hssst!' said Felix.

The Slayer looked up, and Felix waved at him, then pointed to the front door. He saw a look of angry confusion cross Gotrek's face before he started across the street.

Felix and Ulrika reached the entryway just as the butler opened the door.

'What is this foolishness?' said Gotrek as he stepped through the door, water dripping from his beard in rivulets. 'You were only to signal if…' He stopped when he saw Felix's silk robe, then looked past him to Ulrika. He sneered. 'Ah. Not interrupting anything, am I?'

'Let me explain,' said Felix.

'Is it you explaining?' asked Gotrek. He closed the door behind him. 'Or is it her, jerking your strings?'

'I…' said Felix.

'Felix is not beglamoured, Slayer,' said Ulrika. 'I merely invited him in out of the rain, as I invite you now. Had you both come immediately to the countess when you learned about Gephardt, you might have waited out the night in comfort here instead of soaking yourselves out there.'

Gotrek growled. 'And who watches the house while we wait in comfort?'

'I have seven spies watching the house,' said Ulrika. 'Trust me, your quarry will not slip away while you enjoy the countess's hospitality.'

The Slayer grunted, apparently unhappy that all his questions had been answered so reasonably. For a moment he looked ready to turn around and walk back out into the rain, but finally he ran his thick hand through his wilted crest and flicked the water on the floor. 'Then get me a cloth and some food and a pint.'

Ulrika curtsied, her lips twisting into a sly smile. 'At once, sir dwarf. We live only to serve. You will find a fire in the parlour to your left.'

She turned and disappeared through a servant's door.

Gotrek crossed to the parlour door, then looked back at Felix. 'Go and sleep, manling. Alone.'

Felix stiffened. 'All these years, and you don't trust me not to be a fool?'

Gotrek looked as if he was going to snap back with some retort, then he paused and shrugged, looking almost contrite. 'I trust no human when one of those things is around. Now get some sleep.'

He turned and entered the parlour. Felix glared after him for a moment, then started up the stairs for the bedroom where he had left his clothes.

FELIX WOKE SLOWLY. The room was dark but for the low flicker of firelight. The big four-poster bed was soft and warm and enveloping. The patter of rain on the windows was soothing. The smell of fresh linen and wool was comforting. He yawned and stretched – and yelped like a trodden-on dog as the stitches in his side stabbed at him anew.

He curled up in a ball, hissing and blinking away tears. He saw a face in the blurred dimness. There was someone next to his bed! He jerked back and yelped again as the wound caught him once more.

'Good evening, Felix,' said Ulrika, laughing.

Felix glared at her, panting and sweating. She sat slouched in the arm chair, dressed in her manly garb again, looking as if she had been there for a long while.

'What… what… what do you want?' he finally managed. 'Is it time?'

'No no. Our fox has not yet left his den,' she said. 'But night has come. He may soon. I thought you might want to feed – sorry – to eat, before he moves.'

'Yes.' Felix sat up gingerly. 'Yes. That's a good plan.'

She stood and turned the chair around, as easily as before, then sat down again facing away from him and pointed to the chest at the end of the bed. 'Your clothes have been dried and mended, and there is a wash basin by the fire and a pitcher of water warming before it.'

Felix rubbed the sleep from his eyes, then grunted and hissed his way out of bed. He pulled on his hose and breeches and padded to the fire.

'You will be relieved to hear,' she said from behind him. 'That while you slept, I sent a message to the countess, telling her that you and the Slayer did not betray my existence to Makaisson after all, and asking her to call off Lady Hermione and Mistress Wither.'

'Thank you,' said Felix. 'And has she replied?' He poured the water into the basin. It was the perfect temperature.

'Not yet,' said Ulrika. 'She is unlikely to tonight. Most of her servants are busy, either at the brothel, or looking for the Cleansing Flame.'

Felix shivered as he soaped his hands and face. He was glad to hear that Ulrika had sent the note, but he would be unable to relax entirely until he knew the countess had withdrawn her order of execution.

'You look very young when you sleep, Felix,' said Ulrika. 'Like you did when we first met.'

Felix choked. He looked up, covered in suds. 'You... How long were you watching me?' The thought made him uneasy.

'Our kind do not sleep,' said Ulrika.

Felix frowned and splashed his face. That wasn't really an answer.

'Which is unfortunate,' she continued. 'For it leads to contemplation, and perhaps madness.' Felix heard her sigh. 'I was remembering how it was with us, when last we knew each other, and wondering if things would have been different – if this might not have happened – had you not lost interest in me.'

Felix snorted and water squirted painfully through his nose. He coughed and hacked, convulsing, tears streaming from his eyes and the wound in his side screaming. 'I...!' He wretched and tried again. '*I* lost interest in *you*? You left me for Max!'

She turned in her chair and looked at him, raising an eyebrow. 'Come now, Felix. That was long after things were over between us.'

Felix glared at her. He was surprised at how much the old wounds still stung. 'Is that so? I wish you had thought to tell me.'

'Maybe we didn't speak of it,' said Ulrika, then chuckled. 'We were very good at not speaking of things then, weren't we? But we both knew.'

'I'm not sure I did,' said Felix stiffly. 'I seem to recall your losing interest in me before I lost interest in you. Why else did you start all those pointless arguments? Why else the sullen moods? The sudden anger?'

Ulrika barked a laugh. 'You describe yourself!'

'I was only reacting to you!'

Ulrika's eyes flashed like a cat's, and she sprang from the chair to face him. Felix shrank back, suddenly aware that he was half naked and facing a well-armed and inhumanly strong monster.

Ulrika seemed to come to the same realisation, for all at once she deflated and sat down on the arm of the chair, hanging her head. 'I apologise, Felix. You are entirely right. I started many of those fights, and I did have bouts of sullenness and anger. But you did as well.'

'I… I suppose I did.'

'We were both very young then,' she said. 'Perhaps we still are.' She laughed bitterly. 'I certainly haven't gotten any older.'

Felix crossed to his shirt and drew it on as memories flooded back to him across the years. 'You were very hard to figure out,' he said. 'At times it felt as if you thought me an amusing commoner, not worth more than a summer fling. Other times you seemed to act as if I was your saviour – someone to lead you out of the oblast and show you the world. I didn't know what you wanted.'

'That is because *I* didn't know what I wanted,' said Ulrika. 'I wanted... I wanted...' She paused, her eyes far away, then laughed suddenly, a great guffaw of surprise, and stood, running her hand roughly through her short white hair. 'Shall I tell you when it was over?' She held up a finger. 'And this will prove that you were correct, and that it was me who decided to end it, though I didn't realise that that was so until this very moment.'

'All right,' said Felix, as he tugged on his boots, though he wasn't sure, now that she said it, that he did want to know. Had he said something ridiculous? Had he proved himself a peasant in some obscure manner?

'I set you a test,' she said, leaning against the mantelpiece and crossing her arms. 'Though I didn't know that was what it was at the time. And it was a test that you could not win, no matter your answer.'

'I don't understand,' said Felix. 'What test?'

Ulrika smiled. 'Do you remember, at Karak Kadrin, when I asked you if you would leave the Slayer and come away with me to Kislev?'

Felix's face hardened. 'I do remember. I said yes, I would. It is the only time I have ever betrayed my oath to Gotrek.'

'Yes,' said Ulrika, nodding. 'And because of that, you failed the test. From then on I began to think of you as a man who would go back on a vow, and I no longer had the respect for you that I had previously.'

'So,' Felix said, anger rising in him, 'I would have passed the test if I had said I would not go with you?'

'No! Of course not,' said Ulrika. 'Had you said no, it would have proved that you did not love me enough to go back on a vow.'

Felix blinked. 'But then it was…'

'Impossible. Absolutely!' Ulrika laughed. 'You see? Young and foolish! I thought myself a noblewoman, and a noblewoman must have a lover of unimpeachable honour – a man who would die before he broke an oath. And yet, at the same time, I wanted from my lover such passion and devotion that he would be willing to trample his honour in the mud and forsake his friends and family at my lightest word.'

Felix shook his head in wonder. 'Shallya's mercy, it wasn't Krieger who made you a monster. What madness!'

Ulrika flashed a sharp-toothed grin. 'There is no more dangerous monster than a nineteen-year-old girl with ideals.'

Felix laughed, then winced, and eased gingerly into his doublet. 'I… I must confess to a similar struggle.'

'Oh?'

Felix looked at her sheepishly. 'You were everything I ever wanted – a beautiful girl with spirit and intelligence, who loved life and adventure and…' He paused, '…and love. And yet, you were also everything I ever hated, a noblewoman who'd never done a day's work in her life. A sportswoman who would rather hunt than read, and whose idea of poetry was a Kossar drinking song.'

'Lies!' cried Ulrika, interrupting. 'I worked harder than you ever–'

Felix held up his hands. 'I know. I know. You were not really any of those things. Only a symbol of them. I knew it then too, but I couldn't help it. I spent all my school years being snubbed by the sons and daughters of nobles, and I held it against you. By loving you, I was betraying every ideal I ever held about overturning privilege and ending the tyranny of class, and so I felt guilty. But when I looked at you, and listened to you, and saw you for who you were, rather than what you stood for, I felt guilty for the pigeon hole I had put you in.'

'And so grew sullen,' said Ulrika.

Felix nodded. 'And angry.'

'And started arguments for no reason,' they said in unison, then laughed and caught each other's eyes.

A whole conversation flashed between them in that look. A recognition of regret, of longing, guilt, of understanding come too late – and a pain went through Felix's chest that had nothing to do with his stitches. He turned away, suddenly angry, though whether at Ulrika, or himself, or cruel fate, he didn't know. By the gods, the foolish nothings that drove people apart! It was all so unfair.

'Why couldn't we have had this conversation twenty years ago?' he asked.

'Because we were twenty years younger,' said Ulrika, sighing. 'And twenty years more foolish. And could not name our trouble to ourselves, let alone each other.'

Felix spun back to her. 'But think what those years might have held for us! Think how different our lives might have been if…'

'Aye,' said Ulrika, and the pain in her eyes was like an open wound. 'I do think on it. Often.'

Felix flushed. 'Ulrika.' He stepped towards her. 'Forgive me. It didn't even occur to me.'

He raised a hand to clasp her shoulder, but she flinched back, thrusting out a warding hand and showing her fangs. 'No! You may not touch me!'

Felix stopped, confused.

Ulrika turned away and stared into the fire, hugging herself. 'I could not bear it.'

Felix's hand dropped, his heart breaking. He wanted comfort her, but how? He stared at her back, unable to think of anything to say.

The door opened. Gotrek stood in it. 'He's leaving.'

Ulrika sighed. It sounded to Felix like a sigh of relief.

But all Gephardt did was go to dinner at a nearby restaurant, alone, and then, after an hour, return home, still alone. It was maddening. Felix was certain that somewhere in Nuln the Brotherhood of the Cleansing Flame was preparing to use the black powder for some nefarious purpose, and that something terrible might happen at any minute. But where? When? And what would it be? He had thought Gephardt would be part of it, and would bring them to it, but he appeared to be in for the night.

'Maybe I made a mistake,' he said. 'Maybe I picked the wrong man.'

Having returned from spying on Gephardt's dinner, he and Gotrek and Ulrika now watched his father's house from the window of Lord Kirstfauver's darkened front sitting room. Gephardt's lamps were on and his figure moved back and forth through the rooms.

'Maybe the look I saw in Gephardt's eye was nothing but indigestion,' said Felix miserably.

'You were attacked,' said Ulrika.

'It could have been some other member of Wulf's who recognised me and sent those men.'

'It's him,' said Gotrek. 'He is nervous. He paces. He drinks. He is waiting for something. Something will happen tonight.'

'It had better,' said Felix. 'The *Spirit of Grungni* flies at dawn.'

'And I will let it fly, if need be,' said Gotrek.

Felix looked at him, surprised.

'I will not leave until Heinz is avenged,' Gotrek rumbled. 'No matter how long it takes.'

Another hour passed.

'What if Gephardt's not part of what is going to happen?' said Felix, from where he slumped in a chair. 'What if he's only waiting to hear of the success of the plan? What if it has already occurred?'

Gotrek snorted. 'If somebody set off that much powder somewhere in Nuln, we would have heard it.'

Midnight came and went. Gotrek remained at the window, watching intently, apparently untiring. Ulrika prowled from room to room, restless.

Felix dozed fitfully, dreaming uncomfortable dreams of his times with her. It had been difficult to think of anything else since their conversation. Daggers of regret would stab him in the heart when he would turn his head and see her looking out of the window. Shards of memory would tumble through his mind, cutting everything in their path with their sharp edges. He would find himself thinking, there must be some way to fix this. There must be some way that, now that they knew each other and themselves, they could return to what they had, older, wiser, and forever. But there was no way. Ulrika had died seventeen years before, in the arms of Adolphus Krieger, and was given the semblance of life only by darkest sorcery from the mists of time. There was no way back from what she had become. There was no way to cure her but the stake or the fire or the sun.

Felix raged silently at the unfairness of it all. How cruel was fate to allow them such an epiphany decades too late? Had they talked then as they talked now, they might have shared their life together, travelling the world side by side, sharing life's wonders and horrors and joys. Instead they had both wandered alone among their companions, divided from each other by unbreachable walls of death, distance and misunderstanding. It was enough to make Felix want to weep, or fight something that would kill him.

It occurred to him that, had Ulrika not been turned by Krieger, Felix might have tried much harder and much sooner, to turn Gotrek back towards the shores of the Old World.

At last, almost three hours after midnight, Gotrek grunted, waking Felix from his fitful slumbers.

'A visitor,' said the Slayer.

Felix and Ulrika stepped to the window. A coach was pulling up before Gephardt's door. A man in a heavy cloak got out. Gephardt's door opened for him, and the coach drove off as he entered the house. It was Gephardt that ushered him in.

'Is he throwing a party?' asked Felix. 'At this time of night?'

'A hunting party, perhaps,' said Ulrika.

For another half hour Gephardt and his guest moved behind the windows, talking and drinking, then another man, this one on foot, approached the house. Again, the door opened before he knocked and Gephardt let him in.

Now, however, Gephardt did not entertain. The lanterns were quickly snuffed and the house went dark. Felix looked back and forth from the front door to the upper floors, expecting them to leave or retire above.

They did neither.

'They are leaving from the coach yard,' said Ulrika. 'I'm sure of it. My spies will tell me in a moment.'

She scanned the roofs of the houses to either side of Gephardt's house. After a second, a dark figure appeared and waved a hand, then pointed left.

'Ah. I was right.' Ulrika turned to the door. 'Come. They are heading south.'

THIRTEEN

IT WOULD HAVE been too conspicuous to follow in Ulrika's coach, so Gotrek, Felix and Ulrika trailed Gephardt's carriage through the Kaufman district on foot. With his short legs, Gotrek was at a disadvantage for this kind of work, but he plodded on tirelessly behind Felix while Ulrika sprinted ahead, disappearing into the shadows and keeping the coach in sight. Felix wasn't much faster than Gotrek. The day's rest had revived him, but it had also stiffened his wounds and tortured muscles. He limped and gritted his teeth with every step.

The night was cold and blustery. Shutters rattled and trees rustled. The rains of the previous night had tapered off to sporadic sprinkles, and the moons appeared and disappeared behind a herd of racing clouds that filled the sky like a stampede of grey bulls.

Ulrika soon vanished entirely ahead of them. Felix carried on in the direction he hoped she had gone, all the while wondering if she was leaving them behind intentionally – revenge perhaps for his not informing her and the countess about Gephardt. But then, after a few minutes, she reappeared in the distance, waving him forward.

'They're going into the Neuestadt,' she said, as he trotted up to her. 'Through the gate. I don't think the watch will let you through.'

'But you they will?' Felix asked, sceptical.

'I don't need the gate.'

'You have wings?'

'Something like that.'

Felix looked down Commercial Way. Gephardt's coach was stopped at the Altestadt Gate while his coachman talked with the guards. How were he and Gotrek going to get through, and do it fast enough to keep the coach in view?

Gephardt was the son of a rich man, with all a rich man's trappings. He had the coach and coachman, faultless clothes, well-bred friends. If he said he was going to some brothel or gambling hall in the Neuestadt, the watch would touch their caps and bow him through. Would they do the same for Felix and the Slayer?

Felix looked down at himself, taking stock. He was dressed well enough at the moment, and was well shaved, and that counted for something – the guard had woken him politely enough when they had found him in the alley this morning, instead of driving him out of the district with kicks and head-knocks – and even though he and Gotrek were being sought by the watch, his face was ordinary enough that he might be able to pass without them giving him a second glance, but Gotrek…

Gotrek could not be called ordinary – not even by Slayer standards. If the guards at the gate had been given a description of him – and Felix had no doubt that they had – he would be recognised in an instant. They would be stopped. There would be questions, and most likely violence. Innocent men would be hurt and Gephardt's coach would get away.

Maybe they should go via the sewers again. But that would take too much time. Gephardt might be anywhere by the time they resurfaced.

Gotrek strode up. 'What's the trouble?'

'They're going into the Neuestadt,' said Ulrika.

'The watch isn't going to let us follow,' said Felix. 'They'll question us. Arrest us.'

The gates were swinging open, and Gephardt's coachman was whipping up the horses.

Gotrek growled. 'If they want to arrest us, let's give them a reason.'

'We can't do that. We…' He paused and gaped at Gotrek. 'Wait! That's good. They want to arrest us. We'll let them.'

'Hey?' said Gotrek.

Ulrika cocked an eyebrow.

'Just long enough to have them take us through the gate.'

'Ah,' said Gotrek. 'Good thinking, manling. Lead on.'

Felix turned to Ulrika. 'Keep them in sight. We'll catch you up on the other side.'

'I'd rather stay and see this,' said Ulrika, grinning. 'But very well. Good luck.'

She turned and ran down a side street, then disappeared into an alley in the direction of the wall. Felix stared after her. Her merry grin had gone through him like a hot poker.

'Well, manling?'

'Right,' said Felix, snapping out of it. 'Sorry.'

He and Gotrek started towards the gate.

'We can't just turn ourselves in,' he said, out of the corner of his mouth. 'They'd know something was up. We need to look like we're trying not to get arrested.'

'And how are we going to do that?' asked Gotrek.

'HALT!' CALLED THE watch sergeant, holding up a hand. He had six stout spearmen behind him, standing in front of the gate, all in breastplates and helmets. 'State your business, sirs.'

Felix and Gotrek halted. Gephardt's coach was still just visible through the bars of the gate, trundling down Commerce Street as it curved east through the Handelbezirk.

'Open the gates, my good man,' said Felix in his snootiest voice. 'I have urgent business at the Gunnery School.'

'At this hour, sir? The school don't receive visitors at this time of night, sir,' said the sergeant as he looked them over in the light of the guard house lantern. 'And no one goes through this gate until sun up.'

'Don't be ridiculous. You let a coach through just now. Let us through.' Felix waved an imperious hand.

'The gentleman was known to us,' said the sergeant. He couldn't seem to keep his eyes off Gotrek. 'And often has business at this hour.'

And slips you a healthy bribe every night, thought Felix.

'I demand you let us through,' said Felix. 'Countess Emmanuelle will hear of this if you don't!'

The sergeant shot a glance back at his men and they began to spread out. 'I'll have your names sir. You and your companion.'

'*My* name?' said Felix. 'Damned if I will. I'll have your commission, you lout. Let me through!'

'Your *names*, sirs,' growled the sergeant.

'My name is… is… Lord Gesundheit, damn your eyes! And this is my servant, ah… Snorri Nosebiter.'

The sergeant blinked for a moment, then shook his head in wonder. 'Gesundheit and Nosebiter. Those are the worst false names I've ever heard.' He turned to his men. 'Take their weapons and put them in irons. I believe these are the "Heroes of Nuln" who are meant to be locked up in the College of Engineering just now. We'll put 'em in Universitat station house until someone can be sent for tomorrow morning. Open the gate!'

'How dare you!' said Felix, as the guards started forward, spears at the ready. He saw Gotrek stiffen. 'Play along!' he muttered out of the corner of his mouth.

'Aye aye,' grumbled Gotrek.

'Your weapons, sirs,' said a watchman.

Felix sighed and unbuckled his sword belt as the gate began to swing open. 'This is a great indignity,' he said, as he gave the dragon-hilted sword to a young watchman.

Gotrek took his rune axe off his back, then paused as if he was reconsidering, his eye blazing. It looked like he might slaughter the watchman instead of handing it over. At last, with a reluctant grunt he held it out. The young watchman took hold of it, then stumbled to his knees, his arms nearly wrenching out of their sockets as Gotrek let go. It clanged off the cobbles.

'Don't dent it,' Gotrek grumbled.

The watchman struggled to lift the axe as he stared wide-eyed at Gotrek. He finally got it up to his chest and cradled it like a man carrying a barrel.

'Your wrists,' said the first watchman.

Gotrek and Felix put their hands behind their backs and a third watchman slipped horseshoe irons around them and locked them.

'Right,' said the sergeant. 'Four of you with Kulich. March!' He bowed slyly to Gotrek and Felix as four watchmen prodded them forward through the gate, followed by the boy who was carrying their weapons. 'Your lordship,' he murmured with mock respect. 'Master Nosebiter.'

Felix could hear the sergeant's men laughing as the others led them into the Handelbezirk. Gotrek rumbled in his throat, but said nothing.

Felix looked ahead. Gephardt's coach was just disappearing around the curve of Commerce Way, far in the distance. They needed to hurry, or they would lose them, but they couldn't act until they were out of sight and earshot of the gate. He hoped Ulrika had made it over the wall as easily as she had said she could. Her scouting was essential.

'Dorfmann, take this axe!' rasped the young watchman, after a few streets. He was staggering under the monstrous weight of the ancient weapon. Even in the dark of the street Felix could see that his face was beet red.

'Yer doing fine, Mittleberger' said another watchman, chuckling. 'Be there before you know it.'

The others laughed.

'I mean it,' whined Mittleberger. 'It's slipping.'

The watchmen only laughed harder.

Felix looked over his shoulder. The gate was five blocks behind now, and edging out of sight. 'Now,' he said quietly.

'About time,' said Gotrek. He shrugged his massive shoulders and the chain between his shackles snapped like a pretzel.

The movement was so small and calm that for a second the guards didn't notice. It wasn't until he stepped to the struggling Mittleberger and plucked his axe and Felix's sword from him, that they turned and cried out in surprise.

Gotrek butted Mittleberger in the solar plexus with his forehead. The boy fell back, gasping like a landed fish.

Two guards rushed the Slayer's back. Felix lurched right and shouldered into them. One stumbled into the other and fell. The other continued on. Gotrek spun and chopped through his spear, then shoved him to the cobbles.

The other watchmen hopped back, lowering their spears and shouting at Gotrek to drop his axe. Gotrek slashed down at Felix's back. Felix flinched, but the Slayer's aim was true. The axe blade parted his chains with a *ching*, and he was loose. Gotrek tossed him his sword.

Felix caught it and brained the fallen guard with the scabbard.

The last two guards charged Gotrek. He sidestepped one and knocked aside the other's spear, then upended him over his shoulder.

Felix cracked that one over the head too, then did the same to the one with the halved spear. That left only the one who had charged past Gotrek still on his feet and fully conscious.

Felix and the Slayer turned to face him. He stared at them for a moment, then turned and ran back towards the gate, screaming for the sergeant. Two steps later he staggered sideways, squawking, and fell on his face, unconscious. A bolt with a blunt fowling tip clattered to the cobbles beside him.

'Who…?' said Felix, looking around.

A movement above him caught his eye. He looked up. Ulrika saluted from a nearby rooftop, a mere silhouette against the grey clouds, then waved them on.

'Onward,' said Gotrek, and they hurried down Commerce Street, leaving the dazed watchmen moaning and writhing behind them. Felix rolled his head around on his neck. He felt better. The fight had loosened him up a bit.

A FEW BLOCKS past the Reik Platz, Gephardt's coach stopped and one of the men got out. His face was now hidden behind a yellow mask, but Felix could tell it wasn't Gephardt. This man was too short and broad.

From the shadow of a trading company office, Gotrek and Felix watched as the man nodded to the coach, then vanished down an alley between two tenements.

'Do we follow him, or the coach?' murmured Felix.

'Gephardt is the leader,' said Gotrek. 'The others came to him. We follow him.'

Felix nodded and they continued down the street as the coach started forward again. Far ahead of them he saw a blur of shadow leap from one rooftop to another, an impossible jump. He shivered. Whatever remnants of her old self remained, leaps like that proved that Ulrika was no longer one of his race. The shiver was followed by a sigh. If only the rest of her were as alien, he might find it easier to accept that what had happened to her was irreversible. But she was still too human – much too human.

A while later the coach turned north into the Weston district. Felix and Gotrek hurried to the corner, then peered around it. The coach was making a left into a side street. They trotted to the next corner. The coach turned again.

From another rooftop, Ulrika waved to get their attention, then motioned for them to hold. Felix saw the wisdom of this. The streets were wider and straighter in this stolid, burgher neighbourhood, and there were fewer places to keep out of sight. If they followed too closely they might be seen.

After a few moments, Ulrika waved them ahead and they moved to the next corner. They travelled for a while in this stop and start fashion until the coach pulled up at a genteel looking tavern, dark and apparently shuttered for the night. Another man got out of the coach and rapped on the tavern door – two short knocks, a pause, then three knocks, another pause, then two short knocks again. It opened and he slipped in.

Felix looked at Gotrek, for the man had been tall and thin, like Gephardt.

The Slayer shook his head. 'Too thin in the shoulders.'

Felix nodded. Gotrek had a better eye for scale and proportion than anyone he knew. If he said it wasn't Gephardt, then it wasn't.

They made to follow the coach again, but it doubled back on them and they had to scramble to find a hiding place in the shadow of a deep door well as it turned onto their street. They held still as statues as it passed them by and continued on the way it had come.

With Ulrika motioning them ahead at every corner, they trailed the coach south again until, after crossing Commerce Street, it entered the Shantytown district and stopped at last at a long wooden warehouse a street away from the wharves.

Gotrek and Felix hid in the shadow of the arched gate of a boatmaker's yard, and watched as Gephardt descended from the coach. And it was Gephardt. Felix recognised him by his strutting walk. The masked youth knocked, using the same rhythm as his companion had at the tavern, then slipped into the warehouse. The coach pulled away and started back in the direction of the Altestadt again. Felix frowned. Whatever Gephardt was up to, he didn't intend to return home tonight.

'This is his final stop,' he whispered.

Gotrek growled. 'More final than he knows.'

Ulrika dropped down beside them, as silent as a falling cloak. 'A big gathering,' she said. 'I smell many scents.'

'Good,' said Gotrek. 'My axe thirsts.'

'We should learn what they're up to first,' said Felix.

Gotrek grunted, impatient, but then nodded. 'Aye.'

Felix turned to Ulrika. 'Can you hear them through the wall?'

'Not well enough, but I have a better idea.'

'Yes?'

She nodded over his shoulder. 'Look.'

Felix turned. Two men in masks and cloaks were walking down the street towards the warehouse. They would soon pass their hiding place.

'Disguises?'

She grinned. 'Aye.'

Felix's skin prickled. He didn't like disguises. So many things could go wrong. 'And how will we disguise Gotrek? A mask and a cloak won't be enough.'

'I need no disguise,' Gotrek said. 'When the fighting starts, I'll come in.'

And what if you come in too late, thought Felix? He and Ulrika could be overwhelmed before the Slayer arrived. But he kept it to himself. It would sound like whining.

'There are skylights on the roof,' said Ulrika, then looked Gotrek up and down. 'If you can get to the roof.'

Gotrek growled. 'I'm a dwarf. There are no better climbers.'

'Shhh!' said Felix. 'They come.'

Gotrek, Felix and Ulrika stepped further back into the arch of the boatyard's gate. The two men walked past, looking nervously over their shoulders, but not into the shadows beside them.

Gotrek reached out and grabbed one by the belt. Ulrika took the other by the collar. They yanked the men into the archway and broke their necks with brutal efficiency. Felix winced in sympathy, then pulled their masks and cloaks off. He recognised neither of them. They looked like shopkeeps.

As Gotrek heaved the bodies over the boatyard gate, Felix handed a mask and cloak to Ulrika and donned the other himself. His mask smelled of sausage and sour sweat. He fought down nausea and looked at Ulrika and Gotrek through the small eyeholes.

'Ready?'

'Ready,' said Ulrika.

'Aye,' said Gotrek.

They stepped out of the archway and started towards the warehouse, Felix and Ulrika making for the front door, Gotrek angling for the alley that ran between it and the next.

When they reached the door, Felix stretched out his hand to knock, then paused. What had it been? Ah yes. He rapped sharply on the door twice, then three times, then twice again.

The door opened, and a short, masked man in workman's clothes looked up at them. 'Welcome, brothers. The password?'

Felix froze, his heart thudding. There was a password? Sigmar, they were sunk before they had begun!

'Er,' he said, for want of anything better to say.

'We have already told you the password,' said Ulrika, speaking in a husky voice and stepping forward.

'You have? said the cultist, his brow crinkling. 'No you haven't. I would have heard.'

Ulrika pressed her mask close to her face so that he could see her piercing blue eyes. 'We have already told you the password.'

She took another step forward. Felix followed her lead and advanced as well. They were in the door now.

'But…' said the man stepping back unhappily. He sounded like he was going to cry. 'But…'

'Don't you see? We must have told you the password,' said Ulrika, soothingly, as she eased past him.

'Or you wouldn't have let us in. You are not to let anyone in who doesn't know the password, correct?'

'That's right,' said the man. 'And…'

'And you are a stalwart man who would not forsake your duty, aren't you?'

'Of course I am! There are none more loyal to the brotherhood than I.'

'Yes. You are dutiful and loyal, and would not have allowed anyone in who hadn't told you the password.'

'Never,' he agreed.

'So since we are in…?' she let it hang.

'I… I suppose you must have told me the password,' said the cultist. 'Yes, of course you did. Why else would I have let you in?'

'Yes,' said Ulrika softly. 'Nothing else makes sense.'

'Yes.' He sighed, glad to have it all resolved. 'Nothing else makes sense.' He pointed to the door at the back of the small office they were in. 'The others are in the back.'

'Thank you, brother,' murmured Ulrika.

Felix shot her a look as they stepped to the inner door. Her eyes behind the mask twinkled with amusement. Felix swallowed. He hadn't seen anything amusing in the exchange. He felt like he had just watched a cat toy with a mouse and then eat its head.

The warehouse beyond the office was dark but for a flicker of lantern light that glowed from somewhere beyond a blocky mountain range of stacked barrels and crates. Low murmurs disturbed the dusty silence. Felix and Ulrika followed the voices around the towering piles of cargo and found a group of men sitting on and standing around a ring of rolled carpets, in the centre of which stood a figure that Felix was nearly certain was Gephardt. There was a lantern at his feet.

'Brothers, welcome,' said the figure. It was indeed Gephardt. 'We will begin shortly. We wait only for two more.'

Felix and Ulrika nodded, but said nothing. They joined the men leaning against a wall of crates at the edge of the circle, staying as far out of the lamplight as they dared. Felix glanced up at the roof. Through the rafters that supported it he could see a line of square skylights. He did not see Gotrek.

After a few minutes, another man came in, and right after him, the guard who had watched the door. Felix counted nineteen in all – twenty-one including Ulrika and himself.

'Good,' said Gephardt, as the door guard took a seat on a rolled rug. 'Now we are complete. And soon our plans will be complete.' He stood straighter and spread his arms. 'Brothers,' he said. 'The time of the rising of the Brotherhood of the Cleansing Flame has come at last. All over the city our fellows meet. Tonight is the last night of Nuln. Tomorrow comes the change!'

The men murmured soft cheers. Felix and Ulrika followed suit.

'I will now tell each of you your target. When we have finished here, go to it and wait in secret until the signal. This will come in a few short hours when the men of the school test the last cannon they shall ever make. When that gun fires, our brave leader will light the powder that will blow the Imperial Gunnery School to the heavens. That explosion is your signal. When you hear it – and have no fear, you *will* hear it

– you will set fire to your primary target, then, when it is burning well, light as many nearby buildings as you are able. The houses will burn! The foundries will fall! The manufactories will collapse!' He raised his fists. 'We will raise such a cloud of smoke that Nuln will know no dawn today, and no tomorrow ever after.'

The men cheered.

Gephardt raised his voice to be heard over them. 'The flames of the city will light the way for Tzeentch's glorious armies as they march across the broken empire that will be theirs, and ours!'

The men cheered louder. Felix's heart almost stopped in his chest. By all the gods, they meant nothing less than the destruction of the Empire! For, though they intended to burn only Nuln – only! – Nuln was more than a city. It was the Empire's armoury! Out of it came the cannons and black powder and hand weapons that kept her strong and secure. If Nuln's forges were destroyed and her foundries stilled, no amount of men could defend the Empire's borders, for they would have no arms to do it with. The hordes of Chaos that even now assaulted their northern borders would lumber south unimpeded, and everything that Felix called home would be ground to pulp beneath their iron-shod hooves. The enemy was striking from within, far from Middenheim and the front, and unless he and Gotrek and Ulrika could prevail, no one in power would know it until it was far too late.

Gephardt lowered his arms and motioned for quiet. 'Brother Matchcord!' he called.

'Aye?' said a sturdy fellow at the front.

'Your shift at the granaries starts in an hour, yes?'

'Aye, sir.'

'Go to work as usual, but when the signal comes. Light the silos.'

'Aye, sir! All glory to Tzeentch!'

'Brother Candlewick!'

'Aye,' said a stooped older man.

'Handelhoff's livery stables. Start in the hayloft.'

'Aye, sir.'

'Brother Lampblack!'

'Here, sir!'

And so on through the assembly – Brother Flint, Brother Tinder, Brother Flame, Brother Brand, with each being given a target in the general vicinity of Shantytown. Felix's heart lurched as he all at once realised that they would soon call *his* name, and he didn't know what it was! He looked at Ulrika and she nodded and shrugged. They both glanced towards the ceiling. There was still no sign of Gotrek. What was keeping him? Had he met with some accident? Was he already here?

'Brother Torch!'

There was no answer. The men looked around.

FOURTEEN

'BROTHER TORCH!' REPEATED Gephardt, scanning the crowd.

'H-here!' said Felix at last.

Gephardt looked at him, his eyes seeming to burn through Felix's mask. 'You are not Brother Torch.'

'Who says I'm not,' said Felix, remembering belatedly to affect a Shantytown accent.

'Wait a moment,' said the door guard, shaking his head as if waking from a dream. 'Wait a moment. They're the ones who told me they gave me the password when they didn't. I knew something wasn't right about them!'

The masked men all stood, drawing daggers and cutlasses and cudgels from under their cloaks.

'Friends,' said Gephardt. 'You have made your last mistake. Get them!'

His followers surged towards Felix and Ulrika in a mass. Felix threw back his cloak and drew his sword.

Beside him, Ulrika did the same. Two versus nineteen, thought Felix grimly. Ulrika might survive it, but he would not. There were too many. If only Gotrek were here.

"Ware below,' grated a familiar voice from above, as the cultists slammed into them.

Felix didn't dare look up. He was too busy blocking and parrying a dozen attackers. But then a groaning of tortured wood followed the words. He stole a glance over his shoulder. The cliff face of crates was leaning precariously out over their heads. Felix yelped and dived left, his stitches tearing as he batted aside the cultists' blades and hit the floor, hissing with pain.

Four big crates toppled down on the masked men just as they realised what was happening. They screamed, and more than half a dozen of them were caught under the crates as they exploded on the floor in an eruption of planks, splinters and brass chamber pots, one of which bounced and clonked Felix on the head.

Gotrek leapt down from the gap he had made, bellowing Khazalid war cries, and cut down three cultists with two swings. Felix surged up unsteadily, the pain from his reopened wound making him dizzy. He slashed around himself, half blinded by his mask, which had turned askew. He tore it off and hacked at a cultist who was engaged with the Slayer. The man screamed in pain and turned, swinging a hand axe at Felix. Gotrek decapitated him without looking around. Beyond the Slayer, Ulrika ran the door guard through the stomach. He squealed as he died.

'Kill them!' cried Gephardt, from behind the pack. 'They know all! They cannot be allowed to escape!'

The cultists pressed forward, calling on their heathen god. Gotrek roared as they came, cleaving one down to his guts, then turning on three more. Felix slashed left and right to keep the ones he faced at bay, then ducked instinctively as something bright flashed overhead. It was Gephardt's lantern, sailing over the heads of the attackers to smash behind Ulrika. It splashed her back with flaming oil. She shrieked and dropped, rolling to put the flames out. A cultist stabbed her through the leg. Another smashed her in the chest with a huge mallet.

'Ulrika!' Felix cried, and tried to scramble through the jumble of crates to reach her. He mis-stepped, and jammed his foot in a chamber pot. He slipped as the pot skidded on the wood floor. The fire was spreading across the floor. The wreckage and the wall of crates were catching.

Gotrek growled, annoyed, but pushed towards Ulrika, fanning back her attackers with his axe. Felix tried to free his foot, but three cultists were on him. He smashed one's sword out of his hand, but slipped again. A cultist with a cutlass lunged in, trying to take advantage. Felix parried desperately and nearly fell. Beyond the melee he saw Gephardt and another man disappearing around a mound of crates.

'Gephardt's running for it!' he said.

'Well, get him!' said Gotrek, holding off four cultists as Ulrika rolled behind him, still smouldering.

Felix grunted. He could barely stand with this foolish piss bucket on his foot, let alone run. He blocked a smash from an iron-shod club and kicked the cutlass wielder in the face with the pot. The brass split from the impact, and the man dropped like an empty sack. Felix shook his foot as he blocked another bash from the club, but couldn't free it. Curse it! He'd just have to run with it. He bulled past his three attackers, knocking two to the floor, then ran in the direction Gephardt had gone, clanking ridiculously with every step, his attackers in hot pursuit.

As Felix rounded the mound of crates, he saw a door open in the far wall and Gephardt and the other man's silhouettes fill it. He raced towards them as fast as he could go, *clang, thud, clang, thud, clang, thud,* which wasn't very fast. He could feel blood trickling down his side from his torn stitches. He heard his pursuers gaining on him and glanced back. He'd have to fight them before he could fight Gephardt, curse it.

He turned to face them, but as he did, a black shadow dropped down behind them, sillhouetted against the glow of flames from the front of the warehouse. A bright spike of steel sprouted from the last one's ribs. Ulrika! The others turned and cried out as the vampiress laid into them. She was still smoking slightly.

Felix turned and clanked on, his caught foot cramping terribly. Gephardt turned and paused in the door.

'Go!' he called over his shoulder. 'Spread the word! There may be more spies among us! Tell the others to start the fires early!' He tore off his mask and drew his sword, glaring at Felix with wild eyes. 'I'll handle this fool.'

Felix charged at him, swinging, but Gephardt backed out of the door, and Felix's sword bit into the wall beside it. Gephardt lunged through the frame, forcing Felix to twist ungracefully aside to avoid his point. His stitches ripped further. He cursed through clenched teeth. The little snot had him at a disadvantage. Karaghul might be a runesword and a dragon killer, but it was a slashing weapon, not made for quick thrusts, whereas Gephardt's weapon was a slim rapier, a courtier's weapon, made for the lunge. Felix couldn't get a good swing in, with the door frame in the way.

He thrust, but Gephardt parried easily, and returned a riposte that pinked his arm. Felix fell back, his trapped foot slipping sideways and wrenching his groin. Curse this stupid pot, Felix thought. He kicked savagely to try to dislodge it. It flew off his foot and through the door, glancing off Gephardt's forehead.

Felix leapt forward before the cultist could recover, and ran him through the belly, tearing it horribly. Gephardt flopped back in the mud of the street, gasping and staring at the ropes of his intestines as they slithered out through the hole in his abdomen.

Felix raised his sword to put the man out of his misery, but a black form blurred past him and shoved him aside.

'No!'

Ulrika straddled Gephardt's chest and thrust her head forward, baring her fangs. 'Burn me, will you?' she snarled, then sank her clawed fingers into his neck as if it was soft butter. Gephardt sputtered and thrashed, but could not throw her off. She ripped his oesophagus out with one hand and showed it to his dying eyes. 'Burn in your master's flames, fool.'

She tossed the mess aside and wiped her hand on Gephardt's beautiful cloak, then caught Felix's horrified look. She shrugged. 'I don't like fire.'

Gotrek appeared in the door. 'Was that the last?'

Felix shook his head and looked up and down the empty street. 'There was one more. And we must catch him. Gephardt sent him to tell the others to start the burning early.'

'Which way did he go?' asked Ulrika.

'I don't know,' said Felix. 'I…'

He paused as he saw something on the ground. He picked it up. It was a mask. He groaned. They were sunk. The man could be blocks away by now, and they didn't know what he looked like. Half the city could be aflame within the hour.

FIFTEEN

'GIVE ME THAT,' said Ulrika. She snatched the mask from Felix's hand and covered her nose with it, inhaling deeply. After a moment she lowered the mask and tucked it away in her doublet, then crouched like a cat on the prowl, sniffing the air and the ground. She took a few steps north, then nodded and stood.

'I'll find him,' she said. Then she sprinted off into the night.

'This is bad,' said Felix, as he helped Gotrek carry Gephardt's body back into the warehouse. The place was filling with smoke from the rapidly spreading fire. 'Did you...' He coughed violently. 'Did you hear their plan?'

'Not all of it,' said Gotrek.

'They are going to blow up the Gunnery School after all, the minute the last Middenheim gun is test fired, and the explosion will be the signal for the rest of the

Cleansing Flame to start fires all over Nuln.' He shook his head. 'We'll never stop them all.' He looked despairingly at the inferno that raged at the far side of the room. 'We won't stop even this one.'

'We don't have to stop them all,' said Gotrek, 'just the explosion at the school. Then their signal will never come.'

'But we can't just let this burn!' said Felix. 'We already burned down this neighbourhood once! I won't do it again.'

'Better one neighbourhood than all of them,' said Gotrek. He started for the door. 'Come on, manling. No time to waste. If that gun is ready, they may fire it before dawn.'

Felix followed, reluctant and heartsick. Though he knew in his head that it was the cultists who were responsible for the fires, he also knew that they wouldn't have been set if he and Gotrek hadn't come sticking their noses in. And yet, had they not investigated, they would not have learned that the cultists meant to burn the whole city.

As they stepped into the street they saw Ulrika approaching, wiping her face with the cultist's yellow mask. Her lips and chin were smeared with blood, and her eyes glowed with feverish life.

'I found him,' she said, tossing the mask aside. She licked her lips clean.

Felix shuddered. Gotrek spat, then stumped forward, pushing past her as if she weren't there. Ulrika fell in behind him.

Felix made to follow them, then paused and turned, looking back at the burning warehouse. He couldn't just leave and do nothing. His eyes turned to the surrounding tenements. 'Fire!' he shouted. 'Fire in Pappenheimer's Warehouse! Fire!'

Gotrek and Ulrika stopped and looked back at him.

After a second, Gotrek raised his voice too. 'Fire!' he bellowed. 'Wake up! Fire!' He banged on a stone post with the flat of his axe, making a horrendous racket.

Ulrika joined them, her voice high and clear. 'Help! Help! They're burning Shantytown again!'

Felix heard shutters opening and voices calling questions in the tenements around them. They ran on. It wasn't much. But at least it was something.

'I DON'T UNDERSTAND,' said Felix as they trotted through the Neuestadt towards the Universitat area. 'We searched the school and the watch searched under the school. And they've been patrolling down there ever since. The powder hasn't been found. Where has the Cleansing Flame hidden it?'

'Somewhere we didn't look,' said Gotrek.

Ulrika laughed.

Felix rolled his eyes. He was going to say something snide, but he saw that Gotrek was deep in thought, and so kept quiet.

'The skaven tunnels,' Gotrek said at last. 'The ones that the vermin came out of when they attacked Nuln. These lunatics must have found them.'

Ulrika frowned. 'But would powder placed all the way down there be enough to bring down the Gunnery School?' she asked as the three of them entered the Reik Platz and passed by the Deutz Elm, continuing west.

'Aye,' said Gotrek. 'If it were set correctly. The sewers run under the school. If they found tunnels that run under the sewers, they could cave the sewers into the tunnels. The school would sink like a ship.' He growled deep in his throat. 'They must have an engineer among them.'

Felix groaned. 'But how are we to stop it? If we go down there and try to warn the watch, they'll only try to arrest us again, as they did last time. They won't listen to anything we have to say. Damn Wissen for a thick skulled fool.'

'I'll beat it into their heads,' rasped Gotrek, but then he sighed. 'No, you're right, manling. Arguing with those fools would only slow us down.' He paused and looked around, then started down a side street. 'Come. We will find a rat hole here that will take us under the sewers to the powder.'

Felix and Ulrika followed him half a block to an iron grate set in the street. Gotrek heaved it up and held it open.

'In,' he said.

'Wait,' said a voice behind them.

Gotrek, Felix and Ulrika looked around. Gotrek dropped the grate back into its frame with a clang and pulled his axe off his back.

Ulrika drew her sword and went on guard. 'What do you want?' she asked.

Striding towards them from the main street was a phalanx of dark figures. Some Felix recognised from his visit to the countess's brothel – the tall, impossibly thin shadow of Mistress Wither, hidden entirely within her trailing black robes and impenetrable veil; the beautiful, cold-eyed Lady Hermione, who wore a hooded cloak over her dark blue attire, and who was followed by a handful of her swaggering, immaculately dressed heroes, who were now clad in perfectly polished breastplates and morion helmets.

Beside them were persons Felix had never seen before – a cluster of skulking villains led by a voluptuous, coarse-looking vampiress, fairly bursting from the low-cut red bodice and hitched-up red skirts of a street trull. She might have been ravishing, were it not for the scar that pulled up the left corner of her mouth into a permanent leer. Her followers were just as unnerving – vicious-looking doxies and alley bashers, all scarred and wild-eyed, and armed to the teeth with daggers, cheap swords and iron shod cudgels. A more disreputable collection of human scum Felix had never seen. One of them towered above the rest, a filthy, bearded giant of a man who carried a stone-headed hammer in a huge, hairy fist. Felix could smell him from twenty paces away.

'Good evening, friends,' said Lady Hermione sweetly.

Gotrek growled low in his throat.

Ulrika did not lower her guard. 'Are you here to fight us?' she asked. 'Have you not spoken to the countess?'

Lady Hermione smiled. 'Fear not, sister. The countess informed us of your message, and has sent us to aid you.' She cast a sideways glance at the vampire harlot beside her. 'Madame Mathilda has added her support as well.'

Ulrika frowned, suspicious. 'You're here to help?'

'And why shouldn't we be?' asked Madame Mathilda, in a low accent. 'It's our city as much as it is yers.' She grinned and nodded at Felix. 'This yer lover boy, Kossar? Right sweet little buttercup, ain't he? Worth turnin', of a surety.'

'We do not turn men, Mathilda,' said Lady Hermione with a sniff. 'It only weakens the line. As dearest Gabriella learned to her cost.'

'No!' said Gotrek suddenly. 'I won't do it!' He glared at Ulrika. 'I've stood for you, Ulrika Ivansdaughter. You were a good companion once, and your father a Dwarf Friend and Oathkeeper, but these... these...' He couldn't seem to find a word vile enough to describe the assembled vampires. 'These will die by my axe before they fight by my side.'

'You haven't time to fight us, Slayer,' said Lady Hermione calmly. 'And you waste time arguing.'

'The lady's right, dwarf,' said Mathilda, scratching herself intimately. 'Don't waste yer energy fighting the likes of us when we want the same as you want. It ain't common sense.'

'Damn common sense!' snarled Gotrek. 'You die here, or I do.'

He dropped into a fighting stance. Hermione's handsome swains and Mathilda's ragged bashers did the same. Mistress Wither rattled like dead leaves in a wind. Ulrika looked from one side to the other, as if uncertain who to help.

Felix cursed under his breath. This fight couldn't happen. He was no happier fighting on the same side as Lady Hermione and Mistress Wither than Gotrek was, but there was no time. Win or lose, the fight would slow them and possibly wound them so badly that they would not be able to win the fight that mattered. He hated to play on the Slayer's sense of honour. It seemed a low thing to do, but as regrettable as it was, the vampires were right. 'Gotrek. Did you not vow vengeance on the Brotherhood of the Cleansing Flame for the destruction of Heinz's tavern? Did you not say that you were even willing to give up going to Middenheim to defeat them? Will you then let the Cleansing Flame triumph in order to fight a street brawl with unworthy opponents?'

'Unworthy?' snapped Hermione, but no one paid her any attention.

For a long moment, Gotrek remained glaring at the vampires, his massive chest heaving and his huge fists clenching. Then, at last, he let out a breath and lowered his axe. 'You're right, manling. You're always right.' He turned back to the sewer hole. 'One of these days it will be the death of you.' He wrenched up the grate and tossed it aside as if it weighed nothing. 'Let them follow if they can,' he said, then jumped down into the hole.

UNFORTUNATELY FOR GOTREK, the vampires and their minions followed him with ease. Though he trotted through the foul brick tunnels at a brisk clip, the Slayer was a dwarf, and his short legs were no match for human strides, let alone the vampires' inhuman vitality. And Gotrek wasn't able to travel as fast as he might like, for he stopped to examine the walls and walkways as he went, though what exactly he was looking for Felix wasn't sure. Felix could hardly see his footing in the uncertain light of the lanterns that Lady Hermione's gentlemen carried, never mind signs and traces.

The Slayer spared not a single glance for their companions, only trotted on with his axe in a death grip, all the while cursing bitterly in Khazalid under his breath.

Nathan Long

'Ain't no sewers in the Faulestadt,' said Madame Mathilda from behind them. 'More's the pity. Nothing like a sewer for sneaking about, I say.'

'How sad,' said Lady Hermione. 'You'll have to make do with the gutter.'

Madame Mathilda laughed, the echo booming down the tunnel. 'Now now, dearie. No fighting in front of company.'

Ulrika rolled her eyes and gave Felix an apologetic shrug at this exchange.

'Who is Madame Mathilda?' he asked, leaning close to her ear.

'Another of the countess's rivals,' replied Ulrika quietly. 'She rules the slums south of the river as Countess Gabriella rules the Neuestadt. Her web of spies stretches through the mobs and gangs and brothels of the Faulestadt as Countess Gabriella's stretches through the noble houses and the palace. A very dangerous woman.'

'That much I gathered.'

'Whispering sweet nothings, are you?' said Mathilda with a dirty chuckle. 'Ain't they just darling.'

Felix and Ulrika drew apart.

After a few more minutes, Gotrek stopped suddenly and faced the tunnel wall. 'Ha!' he said, then, 'Hmmmf! Even humans could have done a better job.'

'A better job of what?' asked Felix.

He could see no difference between this and any other part of the tunnel, but he had long ago given up trying to see the subtleties of construction and design that were as obvious to the Slayer as the differences in the prose styles of two different authors were to Felix.

Gotrek didn't answer, only stepped up to the wall, reversed his axe, and swung the blunt side at it. It smashed right through, and a fall of crumbling bricks clattered to the floor, leaving a ragged black gap. A cold wind blew from it that reeked of skaven. Felix gagged.

'You say the skaven bricked this up?' he asked.

'Aye,' said Gotrek. 'Hiding their tunnels.' he sneered. 'Or trying to.'

Felix shrugged. He would never have found the tunnel, and it didn't appear that any other human had either.

Gotrek swung again and the hole widened. Felix joined him, kicking at the wall with his boot. Ulrika did the same.

'Here, Pinky,' called Madame Mathilda. 'Give it a go.'

The hairy giant edged forward, pushing his foul stench ahead of him. He swung his stone-headed hammer wildly, nearly taking Felix's head off, and knocked a huge hole in the wall.

Gotrek ignored even this, merely widening the hole with a few more strokes of his axe and stepping through as if the others weren't there. Felix and Ulrika followed him. The others crowded in behind.

The skaven tunnels were round and irregular, like the animal burrows that they were, the walls cross-hatched with claw marks of the vermin that had dug them. The air inside was cold and stale. Spider webs hung like drifting lace from the curving ceilings. Felix scanned ahead nervously, looking for signs of recent usage, but did not see any fresh dung or rotting garbage. Perhaps the tunnels had been abandoned since their attack on Nuln had been driven back. But if so, why was the smell of them still so present?

Though the tunnels twisted and turned and rose
and fell and branched like the roots of a tree, Gotrek
stumped through them as if he had walked through
them a thousand times before. He did not pause at
intersections. He did not stop to get his bearings. He
just turned left, then right, then up, down and back
without hesitation. Felix was thoroughly lost in minutes, and it seemed their companions were too.

'Are you certain we go the right way?' asked Lady
Hermione imperiously.

'If yer leading us into a trap,' said Madame Mathilda.
'Ye'll get more than ye bargained for, dwarf.'

Gotrek only grunted.

Felix translated for him. 'You are more than welcome to go your own way.'

'Ha!' barked Mathilda. 'No fear! Ye'll not lose us in
this stinking warren.'

'You don't feel at home?' sneered Hermione.

A few minutes later Felix found himself walking
beside Ulrika, who was apparently deep in thought.
Her profile, in the low light, was heartbreakingly
beautiful. He looked quickly forward and back.
Gotrek was ten paces ahead of them. The vampires
and their minions were a ways behind, bickering with
each other in low tones.

He leaned in towards her. 'Ulrika.'

She looked up. 'Hmmm?'

He hesitated and licked his lips. 'Ulrika, I just…'

'Don't, Felix,' she said, looking away. 'There is nothing to say.'

'But…'

'Please,' she said. 'Don't you see? There is no way to
fix it. There is no way to go back and change our fate,

so talking of it – of what might have been – will only make it worse.'

Felix paused, his mouth open, wanted to contradict her, but he couldn't. He hung his head. 'Aye, I suppose you're right.'

'In fact,' said Ulrika, 'it might be better if we never saw one another again.'

'What?' Felix looked up at her. But he had only just found her again! 'That... that seems cruel.'

'Seeing you is crueller, for then the wound stays open, and will not heal.'

Felix hated the cold logic of it, but she was right. Remaining in her presence would only be torture. It would only remind him of what he could never have. And yet separating from her again was just as intolerable. What a choice. What a...

He looked back at her suddenly, struck by a thought. 'This isn't another test, is it? Some impossible conundrum of honour that I cannot hope to win?'

Ulrika smiled, then looked at him wryly, her eyes gleaming sapphires in the torchlight. 'No, Felix. It's not a test. We've outgrown that, remember. It's just the cold, sad truth. We need to find our happiness among our own kind, where...' She paused and took a deep breath. 'Where it is possible to find it.'

Felix sighed and nodded. 'Aye. Though at the moment the possibility seems hard to imagine.'

'When the wound heals, Felix,' she said. 'When the wound heals.'

'Hssst!' said Gotrek suddenly. He held up a hand and cocked his head down a cross tunnel.

The others fell silent.

Felix strained his ears. At first he could hear nothing but his own breathing, but then, at the very edge of his hearing came the faintest chittering and squeaking. It might have been rats, and then again it might not have. As he listened, it faded away.

'They're still here?' asked Lady Hermione, her voice rigid with disgust.

'Oh, aye,' said Mathilda. 'We see 'em now and then, or rather their spoor, but not much, and not often. Think they're still scared of Nuln – thanks to handsome here, and his grumpy little friend.'

Felix heard Gotrek's teeth grinding as he started forward again. It sounded like he was chewing rocks.

ABOUT HALF AN hour later, Gotrek slowed. 'We're close to the school,' he said to Felix. 'Tell them to cover their lanterns.'

Felix turned back to the others. 'Cover your lanterns,' he said.

Hermione motioned to her gentlemen and they closed the slots of their lanterns and hid them under their cloaks. Felix cursed inwardly as the tunnel went black. He didn't want to bump around blindly in the dark, but at the same time, asking Gotrek to guide him in front of Ulrika and the others was embarrassing. But then, just as he was about to give in and ask Gotrek for his shoulder, he realised it was in fact not entirely dark. Far ahead there was a faint red glow on the wall of the curving tunnel.

Gotrek crept forward, his axe at the ready. Felix put a hand on the wall and followed along behind him, Ulrika at his side. The others came after them, moving with uncanny silence.

As they got closer to the red light, Felix began to hear sounds of activity – low voices, thuds, clunks, scrapes, and intermittent hammering. There were more cross tunnels in this area, and even to Felix's untrained eye, it seemed apparent that some of them had been shaped by men, not ratmen. There were wooden support beams holding up the ceilings of some of them, and unlit lanterns hung from the walls that appeared to be of human make.

Just beyond one of the branching corridors, the tunnel slanted steeply down, dropping eight feet in roughly ten paces, then turned sharply to the right and out of sight. Reflected light flooded the base of the slope from around the corner, and the sounds of activity were much louder. A wave of sewer smell made Felix wrinkle his nose.

Gotrek, Felix and Ulrika crept down the ramp, then edged forward and leaned out around the corner. Gotrek grunted as he saw the source of the sounds. Ulrika hissed. Felix choked.

Before them was a large, low-roofed chamber, longer than it was wide, crudely hollowed out of the earth and lit by lanterns hung from hooks pounded into the rock walls. The roof was supported by two rows of rough pillars – no more than thin columns of rock that had not been dug out. Felix was amazed that they could hold up the weight of the earth above them at all. They seemed much too slender. The floor was a muddy soup, dotted with puddles of water that dripped constantly from the roof.

Figures moved among the pillars, roping barrels of black powder to them, drilling holes in the barrel tops, and spooling out long lengths of match cord that they laid on top of planks set on the ground to keep them out of the mud. Most of these figures were human, but others were not – not anymore. The sight of the worst afflicted among them made Felix want to gag.

A flash of green drew his gaze away from a hideous woman with a head like a rotten apple. Between the rows of pillars a pair of mutants – one huge and covered in maroon fur like that of a long-haired cat, the other a translucent blue thing like an upright, man-sized frog – walked from barrel to barrel. The furred beast carried an iron cauldron that glowed from within with a pale green light, and at each barrel, the blue frog dug its webbed hand into the cauldron and pulled out a fistful of glowing green embers. He trickled the embers into the hole that had been drilled in each barrel top, then used a mallet to pound a wooden plug into it and walked to the next, licking glittering green dust from his claws with a tongue like a snake.

Felix's heart thudded as he and Gotrek and Ulrika pulled back into the tunnel and climbed back up the steep slope to where the others waited.

'Well,' said Felix with a shudder. 'We've found the powder.'

'And the cultists,' said Ulrika.

'A crude bit of sapping,' said Gotrek. 'But it'll do the trick. The chamber runs under the sewer that runs under the Gunnery School. When they blow those pillars, everything comes down.'

'But what were they doing with the warpstone?' asked Felix. 'Will it worsen the explosions?'

Gotrek shrugged. 'It might. But worse; it will poison the ground for centuries. Anyone living above will end up twisted and corrupt.'

Felix swallowed, sick and angry and afraid all at once. The Cleansing Flame wasn't just planning to kill Nuln, they meant to mutilate its corpse as well. The city might never be inhabitable again.

'How many are there?' asked Lady Hermione, stepping to them.

Gotrek growled and looked away from her.

'About fifty, lady,' said Ulrika. 'Nearly half of them mutants.'

Madame Mathilda laughed. 'Only that? We're more than enough, then. Let's get to it.'

'Yes,' said Felix. 'But how do we keep them from lighting the powder?'

The vampires paused at that.

'Oh,' said Lady Hermione.

'They won't light the powder,' said Gotrek.

The others turned to him.

'Not if we attack now, before they're set,' Gotrek continued. 'They can't risk a partial explosion. The school might not come down.' He turned back towards the chamber. 'Come on, manling.'

'Slayer, wait!' hissed Ulrika. 'Let us all–'

She paused suddenly and looked into the branching passage. The other vampires did the same. Gotrek and Felix followed their gaze. A glow of lantern light was bobbing towards them, and in it, Felix could see the shadows of walking men.

Quicker than winking, the vampires and their minions vanished silently into the darkness of the tunnel. Gotrek and Felix started after them, but before they got two steps, a voice rang from the passage.

'Who's that?' it said.

Gotrek stopped and turned back. 'Not him,' he groaned.

'Him?' asked Felix. 'Him who?'

Out of the passage came Ward Captain Wissen of the city watch, six watchmen at his back. He gaped when he saw Gotrek and Felix. His men went on guard.

'You!' he said loudly. 'What are you doing here? What have you…?'

'Shhh, captain!' hissed Felix, looking uneasily down the slope towards the big chamber. 'They'll hear you!'

'Eh?' said Wissen, just as loudly. 'Who? What do you…?'

'The cultists,' whispered Felix, pointing. 'Down there, around the corner. They're priming the powder.'

'No wonder he never catches them,' said muttered Gotrek. 'Stomping around like a drunk ogre.'

Captain Wissen blinked, apparently confused, then his eyes narrowed. 'The powder? Here?' He smiled. 'So you were right after all, eh? They're going to blow up the Gunnery School? How many of them are there?'

'Fifty or so,' said Felix.

'Hmmm,' said Wissen. 'Too many for us. Are you alone?'

'Too many?' Gotrek snorted.

Felix looked up the tunnel in the direction Ulrika and the other vampires had gone, searching for some sign of them. They were nowhere to be seen. Had they lost their assistance because of this interruption? Would they not show their faces with Wissen around? Dangerous and uncertain allies they might have been, but given the choice of them or Wissen and his men, there was no question who he would rather have had fighting by his side. He sighed. 'Ah, yes. We're alone. Listen. Maybe you'd better go back and get reinforcements. We'll… we'll keep an eye on them.'

'What?' sneered Wissen. 'And have you burn down the city again with your clumsiness?' He waved a hand. 'Show me where they are. I want to see for myself.'

Gotrek rumbled in his throat. Felix shot him a warning glance. He didn't like it any better than the Slayer did, but starting a fight with Wissen would only alert the cultists. 'This way.'

Felix and Gotrek led the way down the slope, then slipped around the corner and edged towards the opening of the chamber with Wissen and his men shuffling behind them. It looked like the two mutants had finished seeding the barrels with the green embers, and the others were nearly done laying all the match cord. Felix swallowed, anxious. If they didn't attack soon they would have to worry about the cultists lighting the powder after all.

'You see?' whispered Felix, pointing to the pillars. 'They mean to bring down the sewer, which in turn will bring down the Gunnery School. And if we don't attack right away…'

'Brothers!' cried Wissen at the top of his voice. 'Look! Brave heroes have come to stop our villainous plan!'

SIXTEEN

FELIX AND GOTREK spun around. Wissen's six watchmen had levelled their spears at them. Wissen stood with them, grinning and tugging at the buckles of his breastplate.

Felix blinked, uncomprehending. 'What did you say?' He looked over his shoulder into the chamber. The cultists were turning and starting towards them, mutants of every size and description intermingled with their human comrades. He looked back at Wissen. Had the man gone mad?

Gotrek lunged forward, slashing at Wissen. 'Pawn of Chaos!' he spat.

Wissen's men jumped in front of him, stabbing at Gotrek and Felix as the captain stepped back. Gotrek chopped through spear shafts and arms. Two men fell. Felix blocked a spear and ducked another, still off balance by this bizarre turn of events.

'Pawn?' Wissen laughed. 'I'm a knight, at the least.' He let the breastplate fall. For such a trim man, his stomach bulged obscenely. In fact it seemed to be expanding as Felix watched. Then Wissen's shirt split, and angular black shapes ripped through it, unfolding as they thrust forward.

Felix recoiled, his gorge rising. Wissen was a mutant! Black mantis arms grew from his chest where his nipples should have been. They were covered in coarse fur and tipped with cruel pincers. They darted for Gotrek over the shoulders of his men. Gotrek lashed out at one, but it jerked back, faster than the eye could see. The Slayer missed.

The thud of approaching boots was loud in Felix's ears. He and Gotrek whipped around. The cultists from the chamber had reached them, mutants to the fore. Gotrek lurched to one side and gutted a giant humanoid slug as it lumbered past. It squashed Wissen's remaining watchmen as it fell, an evil smelling, custard-like ooze pumping from its belly wound. Felix ducked the claws of a thing like a skinned ape, then chopped through its corded neck with his runesword and ended up back to back with Gotrek in the centre of a frenzied sea of men and mutants. Swords, clubs, pincers and tentacles came at them from every corner.

Wissen laughed maniacally from behind his comrades. 'You see? You should have stayed with Makaisson! I tried to save you.' He lashed out again from behind the others. 'Kill them, brothers!' He seemed to have no interest in leading from the front.

Gotrek roared with something that sounded suspiciously like joy as he lashed out all around him, doing terrible damage to all who came near. Felix, on the other hand, fought down a rising surge of panic. They were surrounded. Two against more than fifty. Gotrek might have faced such odds before and won, but Felix was wounded and weary, and hadn't the Slayer's strength, quickness or stamina to begin with. He was quickly becoming overwhelmed. Where in Sigmar's name was Ulrika? Would she come at all? Would the other vampiresses?

The press of the cultists' attacks pushed Gotrek and Felix into the big chamber. The massive, cat-furred mutant swung at Gotrek with the glowing cauldron. Gotrek dodged back and the mutant kept spinning, the weight of the cauldron pulling it around. It clobbered a handful of its comrades with it, staggering wildly. Felix ducked the huge pot as it came around again and felt his skin crawl and his mind twitter as it breezed past him. The warpstone inside it radiated Chaos like a fire radiated heat.

Gotrek darted in and buried his axe in the furred mutant's spine. It shrieked like a scalded baby and crashed to the ground, its cauldron bouncing noisily away into the chamber, sprinkling warpstone embers as it went.

Felix cut down a thing with legs like a stork, then whipped around to parry attacks from two normal-appearing men. He found that his left hand was bleeding, but he wasn't sure from what. He hacked madly in all directions, though there didn't seem to be any point. The tide of men and mutants was endless.

But then the cultists at the edges of the melee began to cry out and turn. Through clawing limbs, Felix saw Lady Hermione's gentlemen charging from the dark tunnel, swords high. Madame Mathilda's villains were running forward too, led by a huge black wolf bitch with a scar twisting one side of her long snout. She leapt at a massive mutant and ripped out one of its throats. The giant bearded alley basher waded into a pack of cultists, swinging his stone-headed hammer mightily. Mutants and men flew left and right, their heads and ribcages crushed to pulp.

Felix exhaled, relieved, though it was a strange feeling to be glad for the arrival of a host of thralls and a skin-changing vampiress. It was even stranger to realise that his life had become so filled with madness and horror that he could accept the fact that Lady Mathilda had changed into a wolf with little more than a shrug.

Ulrika vaulted a squat cultist, impaling him with her rapier in mid-flight, then dropped beside Felix to guard his back.

'Cut it a bit fine, didn't you?' Felix said over his shoulder.

'I apologise, Felix,' said Ulrika. 'The others paused to discuss, er, "tactics".'

'Ha,' barked Gotrek.

'And where are Lady Hermione and Mistress Wither?' asked Felix dryly. 'Is their tactic to hide?'

'Their skills are not in the art of cut and thrust,' said Ulrika, hacking off the head of a woman with hair like writhing vines.

Felix heard Wissen cursing from somewhere to his left. 'Where did these come from?' he cried. 'This is taking too much time! Leibold, Goetz, Zigmund, break off. Finish setting the charges. We must be ready.'

Three cultists broke away and ran back towards the barrels of black powder. There was no way Felix or

Gotrek or Ulrika could go after them. The madmen were four deep around them, fighting with the fearless fervour Felix had noted in them earlier. They seemed to care not at all if they lived or died, so long as the will of their master Tzeentch was done. Some threw themselves on Felix's sword merely to weigh it down so that others might get a strike in.

Gotrek fought an enormous, naked, bloated thing that smelled like rancid cooking oil. It had the head of a kindly old grandmother perched atop a mountain-ous, wobbling torso. The hands at the end of its fat arms were like mittens, unable to hold a weapon. The fight should have been over before it started, but every time Gotrek swung at the thing, a gaping, shark-toothed mouth opened in its skin wherever Gotrek had aimed, and bit down on his axe, trapping it, while the heavy arms clubbed him unceasingly. It didn't matter where Gotrek swung – at the thing's arms, its stomach, its side – a mouth opened there and snapped at his weapon.

'Little boys shouldn't play with axes, dearie,' it said, in a sweet, quavery voice as it bashed him in the head.

Gotrek swore and slashed at it again, and again a mouth caught his axe.

Beyond this fight, Felix saw the black wolf clamp down on one of Wissen's insect arms. He slashed her horribly with the other, but then she didn't let go. Wissen screamed and flailed at her with his sword. She paid the blows no mind.

'Doctor Raschke!' Wissen called, his voice tinged with panic.

'Aye, aye, coming!' said a harsh voice. 'Turn about, damn ye! Turn about!'

Felix stole a glance towards the voice. A towering woman with the plump, powerful body of a farm girl was tottering slowly towards the melee on thick legs, a look of blank idiocy on her moon face. Surely it couldn't have been her that had spoken. She looked slightly less intelligent than a turnip. Then he noticed she had some sort of basket strapped to her back.

'Turn about, ye great lumbering cow!' the voice said. 'Turn about, or I'll rend your fat for soap!'

Something thin slapped the giantess on the left shoulder and she shuffled in a circle until she was facing away from the battle. There was indeed a basket on her back, and strapped into it, like an infant in a bassinet, was a wizened old man with shrivelled limbs and an enormous bald head that seemed much too heavy for his wrinkled chicken neck. His pale blue eyes flashed with an evil intelligence, and his teeth had been filed to points. He held a horsewhip in one hand, and wore what appeared to be a fortune in gold and lapis lazuli necklaces, pendants, bracelets and rings.

'Now, skin changer!' he cried. 'Feel the wrath of Tzeentch!'

The old man pointed his whip at the black wolf and began to chant in a grating sing-song. A ball of blue and gold light swirled into existence before him. Or perhaps it was a hole in the world that opened into a blue and gold inferno. Felix couldn't tell. He looked deeper into it. It was fascinating.

A hook gashed Felix's arm. He blinked and tore his eyes away, cursing, then hacked at the man with the hook. Gods, he hated magic.

With a shriek, the warlock pushed violently at the swirling ball with his splay-fingered hands, and it flew at the black wolf – and entered her.

The wolf leapt back, rolling and howling like she was being attacked by bees, and suddenly she was Madame Mathilda again, screaming and writhing naked on the floor. She came up snarling to her feet, voluptuous curves swaying, and glared at the sorcerer. 'Ye'll pay for that, witch-man,' she snarled.

'I have the warlock, sister,' called Lady Hermione from the shadows of the tunnel mouth. 'Get the others.' She raised her hands, murmuring under her breath, and squirming shadows began to weave around her fingers.

'Ta, Missy,' said Mathilda. She snatched up a sword and launched herself into the fray again, naked from head to toe. Her guttersnipes and doxies charged after her, howling.

The shadows around Lady Hermione's hands grew solid and stretched out towards the warlock. The old man lifted his voice in a counter spell and the air flexed and stiffened between them. A look of strain appeared on Lady Hermione's face. Her shadow snakes faltered and nosed around as if they had hit a wall. She forced her words out through tightened lips.

'Brother Wissen!' cried a wounded cultist. 'They are too strong! Light the powder now! We cannot risk them defeating us!'

'No!' shouted Wissen. 'Not before the signal! Hold your ground! Only a few more moments!'

Why was it so important to wait for the signal, Felix wondered as he fought on. What was so important about test firing the gun? Were they also going to blow up the testing range? He didn't understand it.

Beside Felix, Gotrek pulled his axe free from another of the blubbery grandmother-thing's mouths. He staggered back, swiping around him to fan back more cultists.

The grandmother-thing bobbled after him. 'Give to mommy,' it said in its kindly old voice. 'Be a good boy.'

'Eat this!' snarled Gotrek, slashing again.

Another mouth opened under the thing's left breast, but this time, just as it bit down, Gotrek twisted the axe so that the blade was facing up. The razor-sharp metal cut through the roof of the closing mouth. Gotrek jerked back hard, and ripped the axe out through its belly flesh in an eruption of meat and gore. The thing squealed like a stuck pig.

Gotrek slashed again, and this time found meat. Felix joined him, hacking off one of its arms. Gotrek split its head, and they turned to face new opponents as the battle swirled around them.

Ulrika killed a mutant with a face like an eel. Mathilda's hairy giant spattered the walls with a cultist's brains, but he was breathing heavily, already exhausted from wielding his too-heavy weapon. Lady Hermione and the shrivelled warlock continued to strain back and forth, neither able to gain any advantage. Dead mutants and cultists lay everywhere, mostly in a ring around Gotrek, but the fight had not been entirely one-sided. Only half of Hermione's gentlemen were still on their feet, and less than half of Mathilda's gutter trash.

Felix found himself fighting a man who looked in every aspect like a counting house clerk, from his spectacles to his buckle shoes, except for the huge, tentacled tumour that grew from his neck. The thing rested on the clerk's shoulder, as big and lumpy as a sack of laundry, pushing his head aside at an awkward angle. He staggered under its weight and apologised meekly as the tentacles lashed out at Felix and everyone else around him.

'Terribly sorry,' the clerk said with each attack. 'Can't control it. Not my doing. Sorry.'

The tentacles sparked with violent black energy wherever they touched. One of Hermione's men fell, twitching, as one slapped him across the face. One of Mathilda's doxies jumped back and dropped her carving knife as another caressed her neck. Cultists killed the stricken before they could recover.

Felix hacked at a tentacle as it snaked towards him. A shock ran up his blade and for an instant his whole body stiffened. He staggered back, arm spasming uncontrollably, numb to the shoulder. Ulrika pushed forward to cover him.

'Apologies,' said the clerk to Felix as the tentacles reached for Ulrika. 'I don't care for it any more than you do.'

'No iron!' cried Felix as he massaged his arm and ducked away from more cultists.

Ulrika nodded and whipped her rapier out of the way, then snatched up a fallen spear instead as Felix took his sword in his clumsy left hand and stepped in to defend her flanks. He flailed awkwardly at a mutant as Ulrika swung the butt end of the spear at the clerk. The tentacles caught it. With difficulty, she wrenched it from their clutches and swept the clerk's legs out from under him. He went down in a heap, tumour first, and she thwacked it with all her strength. It burst, spilling stinking red jelly, and the tentacles slapped at the clerk, shocking him over and over again as he twitched convulsively. Ulrika ran him through. The tentacles flopped, limp, to the floor.

There was no time to take a breath. More cultists attacked them from all sides. Gotrek fought a mutant with axes in each of its four hands. Their fight sounded like a busy foundry. Mathilda's giant staggered as the transparent blue frog-thing clawed out his eyes from behind. The giant roared and dropped his hammer to grab for it. The frog tore his throat out. The giant toppled, blood pouring down his filthy jerkin from under his beard.

All around them the vampiresses' thralls were dying at the hands of the cultists. Felix's heart sank. It seemed they would not be enough to turn the tide after all. He gripped his sword two-handed as the feeling tingled painfully back into his right arm. His blocks and attacks were weak and soft. He wouldn't last long.

Then a chorus of shrieks brought his head up. The cultists and mutants nearest the entrance were screaming and backing away. Felix craned his neck. What could frighten a mutant? And then he saw them – shambling figures with long, shadow-eyed faces, clad in rags and scraps of armour, staggering out of the darkness of the tunnels and reaching for the cultists with cruelly curved claws.

Felix gaped, and had to parry desperately as an axe nearly blindsided him. Skaven! The chisel-toothed heads were unmistakable, but there was something wrong. They were painfully thin. More than thin! He risked another look. They were skeletons! By Sigmar, had the vile ratmen invented some new way to conquer Nuln?

'Skaven skeletons?' he choked, incredulous. 'Were the mutants not enough?'

'Fear not,' said Ulrika, blocking a meat axe. 'They are Mistress Wither's work.'

'She… she raised them?' Felix swallowed. 'Ratmen?'

Ulrika shrugged and ran her opponent through. 'She must use the materials available to her, I suppose.'

Felix heard Gotrek curse viciously in Khazalid. Felix knew how he felt. How had they ended up on the same side of a battle with a necromancer? They had fought against necromancers and their minions whenever they encountered them for as long as he could remember. And yet here he was, almost relieved as the undead servants of one of his allies came to his rescue. How had this happened? What had led him to this mad outcome?

His eyes slid to Ulrika, fighting valiantly beside him. It was she who had brought him here. These were her allies. If he accepted her as a friend, did it mean he must accept her kin as well?

The skeletal skaven swarmed the cultists, clawing and snapping and rattling like dice in a cup. They were not fast. They were not strong. Nor were they difficult to kill. A few bashes and they were reduced to bone shards and powder, but there were hundreds of them. Cultists were dragged down by their sheer numbers, or died at the hands of Mathilda's villains or Hermione's heroes while they were distracted by some meagre scratch or bite from behind.

Felix was aghast at how many of the things Mistress Wither had found to raise. The tunnels must be full of dead skaven. He remembered helping the citizens of Nuln kill hundreds of ratmen in the streets during their invasion, but he couldn't recall anyone taking the fight to the tunnels. What had killed them down here?

The cultists fell back before the skeletal horde, panic rippling through their ranks. Seconds ago they had outnumbered Gotrek and Felix and their allies three to one. Now they were outnumbered ten to one, and more cultists were falling every moment.

Felix crossed swords with a man who had strange, circular burn scars all over his face and hands – a few of them still a fresh, angry red. Felix frowned as he turned the man's thrust and made one of his own. He looked familiar. Where had he seen that face before? In the burning cellars below Shantytown? On the street? During the riot on the bridge?

A dim memory was just coming to the surface of his mind when a man in the uniform of a Gunnery School guard ran into the chamber from the far end.

'Brothers! Master Wissen!' he cried. 'Rejoice! The cannon has sounded! The test was successful! They are loading it on the airship now!'

The cultists cheered. Felix heard Wissen sigh with relief.

'At last!' he said, then raised his voice. 'Liebold! Light the fuses! The rest, hold these meddlers where they are! We will take their souls with us when we go to meet Tzeentch!'

The cultists shouted exultantly and attacked Gotrek, Felix and the vampires with renewed fury as a cultist with a mane of black hair ran for the far end of the room, where the ends of all the match cords came together.

'Push through!' shouted Gotrek. He began surging forward, butchering the cultists in front of him.

Felix cursed as he gutted the man with the half-remembered face and slashed left and right to drive back half a dozen attackers. It seemed the lunatics were willing to die here to make sure their enemies died as well. They were madder than Gotrek – all gleefully looking forward to sacrificing themselves for the greater glory of their daemon god.

Gotrek hacked down four cultists and tried to push past six more. He wasn't fast enough. The black-haired cultist took up a torch and began lighting the ends of match cords, all laid out in a line before him. Sparking flames raced across the floor in all directions as the cords burned towards the barrels.

'Kill the bastard!' shrieked Madame Mathilda.

'Forget him!' roared Gotrek. 'Get the cords!' He battered aside a trio of cultists and tried to run for the nearest barrel, but a broad shouldered mutant with plates of orange, coral-like armour growing from its skin got in his way and swung a fist like a huge, barnacled club at him. Gotrek blocked and slashed back, sending orange gravel flying as he chopped into the crusty armour.

Ulrika hissed a Kislevite curse and leapt over the wall of cultists with a gazelle-like spring. But before her feet touched the ground, a translucent appendage shot out and caught her around the ankle. She fell flat on her face and the blue frog thing jumped on her back, clawing at her with webbed talons. It had been its tongue that tripped her.

Felix cursed and shoved forward, hacking right and left to reach her. He swung down at the frog-man. It rolled away and shot out its tongue, jerking Felix forward by the wrist while slashing at his face with his claws. Felix blocked with his free arm and the talons tore bloody trenches in his forearm.

Ulrika surged up and aimed a cut at the frog-man's back.

'No!' said Felix, kicking the frog in the stomach and catching one of its arms. 'The fuses! I have him!'

'Right.' Ulrika turned and sprinted for the furthest barrels. Madame Mathilda was right behind her, breaking free of a clutch of mutants. The two vampire women began snatching up match cords and yanking their ends out of the barrels.

'Stop them!' shouted Wissen. 'Put the cords back! They must all go up at once!'

Cultists broke away from the main fight to protect the barrels. Wissen scuttled after Ulrika, using his mantis arms as an extra pair of legs, and launched himself at her back. She spun around and sheared off one of his pincers. He shrieked, but lashed at her with both sword and remaining claw. She parried and returned his attacks.

The frog thing raked Felix's arms again. Felix hissed in pain and punched it in one of its saucer-sized eyes. It squawked and its tongue let go of his sword arm. Felix slashed at it, but it dodged back, out of range, clutching its eye. Felix raised his sword, then ran for the closest barrel instead. This was no time to fight. He pulled out the cord, then hurried to the next.

The vampires' surviving minions swarmed all over the room, chopping through fizzing match cord or ripping it out of the barrels as they fended off cultists and mutants. Gotrek stepped over the corpse of the coral mutant and ran to do the same. The skeletal skaven lurched forward as well. Only Lady Hermione and the wizened warlock remained where they were, still frozen in their contest of wills.

By Sigmar, we're going to do it, thought Felix as he tugged out another match cord and started for the next. The frog-man's tongue caught him around the neck and slammed him to the ground, knocking the breath from his lungs and his sword from his grip. He clawed at his neck, but the tongue was already gone.

The frog-man sprang, slashing at his face with its talons. Felix rolled over, hunching, and the talons shredded his shoulder and back. He grabbed his sword and swung it in a wild arc. The frog-man hopped away.

Felix scrambled up and faced it. The frog-man was between him and the next barrel. The flame was racing closer along the match cord. The frog-man crouched. Felix went on guard.

'No, Rombaugh!' screamed Wissen. 'Pull out the cord! One blast will only ruin us. We must kill these villains first to keep them from interfering! It's all or none!'

The frog-man backed up, eyes on Felix.

'Stop him, manling!' said Gotrek, pounding towards them. 'Let it blow!'

Felix hesitated, confused by this sudden change in objectives. Let it blow? Why? The explosion would kill him.

The frog-man pulled the cord out and sprang away with it. Felix lunged after him, but too late.

'Now kill them!' shouted Wissen. 'Kill them all so we can reset the charges!' He leapt at Ulrika again, snarling with fury. 'Cursed spoilers!'

'I will set the charges!' rasped a voice from behind them.

Everyone turned. It was the wizened warlock. All Felix could see of the old man behind the fat farm girl's bulk were his outstretched arms, trembling with tension. Glowing blue light stretched towards Lady Hermione from the lapis lazuli on his gold bracelets, and wove a pulsing net around her. Felix could see that the vampire sorceress was fighting to escape the cage with all her might, but it was not enough. Her strands of shadow were dissipating like smoke in a strong wind. She was curling in on herself, her face twisted with agony and impotent rage.

'Lady!' cried Hermione's last remaining gentleman. He rushed towards her. The skaven skeletons ran at the old man. Mutants ran to intercept them.

The warlock clashed his wrists together and the net of blue light tightened around Hermione like a noose. She jerked and dropped, unconscious, flickers of glowing blue fire crawling over her like scuttling rats. Her handsome thrall cried out in anguish as he tried to fight past two mutants.

The warlock cackled, triumphant, then raised his voice in a climbing wail of tortured syllables. Purple clouds began to coalesce over his head. The farm girl just stood there placidly, staring straight ahead.

'No you don't, sorcerer,' Gotrek growled. He ran towards the warlock, knocking aside the skaven skeletons and the mutants as if they weren't there.

Felix ran too. He didn't know what the warlock meant to do, but it had to be bad. He saw Ulrika and Mathilda converging on him too, cultists in hot pursuit. The purple clouds were boiling across the roof of the chamber like smoke.

Something grabbed Felix's ankle and he fell flat. The damned frog! Its tongue dragged him back. He whipped behind him with his sword and chopped the tongue in two. The frog-man fell back on its arse as its tongue snapped back into its mouth. Felix scrambled up and ran on.

Wissen spidered in front of Ulrika, slashing at her with his remaining claw. She fenced with him. Mathilda and Gotrek angled around them, neck and neck, and closed in on the farm girl. Felix didn't want to look. The poor girl hadn't a brain in her head. Killing her would be like killing a puppy.

Gotrek raised his axe. Mathilda raised her sword. But just as they reached her, the girl, as blank as ever, opened her mouth and vomited, spraying Gotrek and Mathilda with vile green liquid that hissed when it touched their skin.

Mathilda fell to the ground, shrieking and writhing as the bile burned her naked flesh. Gotrek stumbled back, cursing and mopping at his bubbling face with his hand, then surged forward again, his left arm shielding his head. The warlock's voice reached a screeching crescendo as Gotrek chopped through the girl's leg, severing it. She toppled sideways, her piteous little-girl cry lost in the foul torrent of the old man's words.

A sound like thunder rumbled overhead as the girl pawed feebly at the ground before Gotrek. Felix ran up in time to see the shrivelled little warlock grinning up at Gotrek from the basket on her back. 'I have done it,' he giggled, his eyes shining. 'The master's will is done.'

'And so are you,' snarled Gotrek. He slammed the rune axe into the warlock's face, splitting his enormous head in two and sinking the blade deep into the girl's back. Her struggles ceased.

The thunder rumbled again and Felix felt something hot on his back. Then on his arm. He looked down. His cloak was on fire. Tiny pink flames dotted it in a dozen places. He beat at them. They didn't go out! Where had they come from?

Beside him, Gotrek cursed as he slapped at his arms and shoulders. There were shouts and squeals behind them. Felix spun around. He gaped.

The warlock's purple clouds hid the roof of the chamber from end to end, and were raining a steady shower of tiny pink candle flames. Wherever they landed, fire spread. The cultists, the mutants, Wissen, Ulrika, Mathilda, her guttersnipes and Lady Hermione's last gentleman were all crying out and running for cover, swatting madly at the flames that burned their clothes and skin. The top of every black powder barrel was burning with little pink blazes, and the wood was starting to blacken. It would be mere moments before the fire burned through the wood to the powder.

'Sigmar save us,' said Felix in a hollow voice as he backed towards the tunnel with Gotrek. 'We'll never put them all out in time. This is the end.'

'Fah!' said Gotrek. 'We need to fight fire with fire, is all.' His face and forearms were a mass of hideous, pus-filled blisters, and he still stank of the farm-girl's viscous vomit. He seemed to feel none of it.

'Fire with fire?' said Felix, confused.

Gotrek put his axe on his back and looked around the floor, then barked a pleased laugh as he saw Mathilda's giant lying dead where the frog-man had ripped out his throat. The Slayer crossed to the giant and picked up his ridiculous stone-headed hammer. He had less trouble lifting it than the giant had. But what did he want it for?

'Into the tunnel, manling,' said Gotrek. He began to spin in a circle.

Ulrika heard and dragged Lady Hermione towards the tunnel mouth. Madame Mathilda's guttersnipes did the same for their barely conscious mistress. Wissen and the cultists had taken cover in an alcove on the far side of the room.

The barrel tops were blazing like torches now. Gotrek turned, faster and faster, holding the huge hammer at the very end of the haft. Was he going to fling it at Wissen, wondered Felix as he backed out of the chamber. What good would that do?

'Back, I said!' Gotrek roared, and let go of the hammer. It flew straight for the closest black powder barrel.

Felix ducked back, gaping with shock as Gotrek dived toward hims, laughing madly.

A huge explosion rocked the tunnel. A fist of hot air punched Felix in the chest and popped his ears painfully. It threw Gotrek into him and sent them rolling backwards into the tunnel. They came to rest in a heap next to Ulrika and Mathilda at the base of the sloping ramp. Pebbles and dust rained down on

Felix's head and blistering heat washed over him in a wave. He tensed, waiting for more explosions. They didn't come. A loud roar came from the chamber, but it wasn't an explosion. It was a strange sustained thunder. And what was that horrible smell?

'Ye madman!' screamed Mistress Mathilda, sitting up and glaring at Gotrek. 'What did ye do?' Her face and shoulders where the farm-girl's vomit had splattered them were as blistered as the Slayer's.

'Saved your sorry, undead arse,' rasped Gotrek. 'More's the pity.' He turned to Felix. 'Up, manling. Or you'll be swept away.'

Felix groaned and pushed himself painfully to his feet. 'Swept away?'

A knee-high bow-wave of frothing brown water rushed into the tunnel, nearly knocking him off his feet. Corpses and bits of shattered barrel floated in it, and it reeked of excrement and garbage. Mathilda and Ulrika staggered and braced themselves against the tide, which was rising swiftly. Lady Hermione's last gentleman lifted her unconscious form in his arms and held her above it. He began carrying her up the slope, out of the water. Madame Mathilda and her last few guttersnipes followed wearily.

Felix and Ulrika slogged forward against the current and looked into the chamber, eyes wide with wonder. There was a crumbling hole in the roof directly above the place where the barrel had been, and through it poured a solid, tree-thick column of brown water that was filling the chamber like a teapot filled a tea cup. The tops of the barrels were still burning with pink fire, but the water was already three-quarters of the way up their sides, and climbing fast.

'What a terrifying race,' breathed Ulrika.

Felix nodded, mesmerised. The barrels could still explode at any second. They should all be running for high ground, but he couldn't tear his eyes away.

Then another explosion, far back in the chamber, knocked them back into the tunnel as a ball of fire billowed out across the roof.

Ulrika shook her head as she picked herself up out of the water. She looked at Gotrek. 'It was a good try, Slayer,' she said. 'But not enough, I think.'

'Never doubt a dwarf, bloodsucker,' said Gotrek, grinning as he pushed past her. The water was up to his chest now, and his beard was beginning to float. 'Look.'

Felix and Ulrika followed him back to the door of the chamber. There was another hole in the roof now, above where the second barrel had exploded, and another thick column of water was pouring down. The tide was rising twice as fast. Even as they watched, it began lapping over the tops of the barrels. One by one the pink fires began to wink out.

'Sigmar's hammer,' said Felix, shaking his head in wonder as floating corpses and barrel staves bumped into him. 'We did it! Er, you did it. Ah, it's done.'

Ulrika inclined her head to Gotrek. 'Never again will I question your judgement, Slayer.' She wrinkled her nose. 'Now come. Let us find higher ground. It stinks.'

With a gasping scream, the body floating next to Felix reared out of the water. It was Wissen! He lunged at Felix, his remaining pincer crushing Felix's arm and pulling him close while he clamped his hands around Felix's throat.

'You ruined it!' he screamed, his eyes afire with fanatical hate, his face pock-marked with little circular burns from the rain of pink fire. 'You ruined it all! Our glorious future, drowned in a tide of shit! I'll kill you! In the name of Tzeentch, I'll...'

Felix punched Wissen in the nose. Ulrika ran him through. Gotrek swung his axe underwater and bit into him somewhere below. Felix could feel the brutal impact through the hands that clutched his throat.

Wissen's fingers slackened, and his eyes glazed over as the water around him began to swirl with red. 'At least there is still the master...' he murmured. His skin, around the circular burns, was turning white from lack of blood.

Felix frowned. The burns. The circular burns. Like the man he had killed earlier. Like the... His heart slammed against his chest as realisation dawned. Now he knew where he had seen the man with the circular burns before! He hadn't recognised him at first without his leather robes. He had been one of the Sigmarite priests at the pouring of the last cannon. The initiate who had fainted. The one who had poured the ashes into the molten iron!

Felix grabbed Wissen by the collar. 'Wissen! Don't you die, you fiend! The cannons! What did you do to the cannons?'

Wissen's eyes regained some of their focus and he chuckled weakly. 'Too... late. They have flown.'

Felix shook him. 'What did you do to them?'

'Tainted. All of them,' he said, dreamily. 'Warpstone... in the iron. Once on the walls of... Middenheim, the master will... wake them. Their crews... driven mad... turn them against the gates of the Fauschlag... shot down from... within. Archaon will enter... Chaos... triumphant at last!'

Felix stared at him, stunned. His arms sagged and Wissen slipped beneath the filthy, bloody water.

Gotrek stepped forward and hauled the captain up again. 'The master!' he growled. 'Who is the master?'

Wissen's head tipped back, a blissful smile on his lips.

Gotrek shook him. 'Grimnir curse you! Talk, vermin!'

Wissen's extremities swayed loosely in the current. His eyes stared at nothing.

Gotrek swore furiously and let Wissen's body submerge. He started up the slope of the tunnel, angling towards the side passage Wissen and the watchmen had entered from. 'Hurry, manling,' he said. 'We have to stop Makaisson before he flies.'

Felix nodded and followed, though he was afraid it was already too late. The *Spirit of Grungni* must certainly have lifted off by now. Still, they had to try.

Ulrika joined them. The three of them pushed forward, rising slowly up out of the water, their clothes soaking and smeared with filth. At the top of the rise, between them and the side tunnel, Lady Hermione, Madame Mathilda and Mistress Wither looked down at them. Lady Hermione propped herself against her gentleman. Mathilda stood naked and blistered and dripping, hands on her hips. Mistress Wither was a tall shadow behind them.

'Get out of the way,' said Gotrek.

The vampire women didn't move.

'Our apologies, Slayer. Herr Jaeger,' said Lady Hermione. 'You have saved Nuln, and we are grateful.

But you have also betrayed the countess, making her existence known to Makaisson, the engineer, and perhaps others.'

'I did what?' growled Gotrek.

'For this oathbreaking,' continued Lady Hermione, as if he hadn't spoken, 'she has ordered your death.'

'What!' cried Ulrika.

Behind the three vampiresses, the corridor began to fill with a numberless throng of skeletal skaven.

SEVENTEEN

'COME AND DIE, then!' snapped Gotrek, raising his axe out of the water.

'Wait, Slayer, please!' said Ulrika, sloshing ahead of him.

'There's no time,' Gotrek rumbled, pushing forward. 'Make for the side tunnel, manling.'

Felix joined him. Lady Hermione's gentleman took her up in his arms and backed away with her. Madame Mathilda and her guttersnipes edged away. Mistress Wither drifted back like a ghost and pointed a bandaged hand at them. Her army of dead skaven advanced, sounding like a thousand marionettes all rattling together at once. They crowded down the slope towards Gotrek and Felix, wading into the water and clawing at them.

Ulrika glared up over the advancing horde at Hermione as Gotrek and Felix chopped into the first wave. 'I don't understand, sister! You said that the countess had sent you to help us! You said the countess understood that I was mistaken – that the Slayer had not mentioned her or myself after all!'

'I said she had received the message,' said Hermione. 'I did not say that she believed you.'

'What? Why?' cried Ulrika backing into the water, as the skeletons advanced.

'She thinks that your loyalties are in conflict.' A sneering smile curled Hermione's lips. 'That you are besotted with cattle.'

Ulrika stiffened with outrage. 'I am a woman of honour, the daughter of a boyar and kin to royalty. I do not lie. I do not break oath.'

Gotrek and Felix advanced another step up the slope, leaving shattered bones and rusted weapons sticking up from the water behind them. The skeletons were pitiful foes, but there were so many. It was maddening. The side passage was only five strides above them, but it seemed they might never reach it.

'Perhaps not,' Hermione continued. 'Perhaps you only believed what you wished to believe. It is a common *human* failing. But...' she said, raising her voice over Ulrika's protests and the sounds of battle. 'Whether you lied or were lied to, the Slayer and the poet must die.'

Felix frowned. Would the countess truly say this? 'Ulrika!' he called, as he shattered a dirt-caked skaven ribcage with a savage cut. 'What if it is Hermione who lies? What if the countess believed you?'

Ulrika looked at him, the light of hope kindling in her eyes, but then, just as quickly, it died. 'But if she didn't, then I would be going against her.' Her eyes narrowed. She turned back to Lady Hermione. 'And I? Am I to die as well?'

Hermione shook her head. 'A mother does not so easily cast aside a daughter. Even an adopted one.' She smiled. 'So that you do nothing to interfere, you are forgiven, and, were you to kill them yourself, why, I believe the countess could never have cause to mistrust you again.'

Ulrika's glance flicked to Felix and then away again. 'I... No! I cannot betray my friends.'

'But you can betray your mother?'

'I did not betray her!' wailed Ulrika. 'Felix and the Slayer did not expose her! They do not deserve her wrath!'

'Whatever they deserve,' said Hermione coolly, 'their death is what the countess wishes. Did you not swear to serve her when she saved you from Krieger? You who claim to never break an oath. Will your vow to her shatter at its first testing?'

If vampires could cry, Ulrika would have been weeping. She stood paralysed, knee deep in sewer water, her face contorted in anguish. Felix cursed Hermione under his breath. There were two battles being fought here, and he could not say which was more savage.

'Ulrika...' he said.

'Don't bother, manling,' said Gotrek. 'She's made her decision. Or she would have killed the bitch already.' He stepped back from the avalanche of skaven and slashed backhanded at Ulrika. 'Defend yourself, bloodsucker.'

'No! she cried, splashing away up the slope through the skeletons. 'No!' She turned at the top and looked into Felix's eyes, her beautiful face twisted with

322   *Nathan Long*

misery. 'I'm sorry, Felix,' she said. 'I will not fight you, but I cannot go against my mistress.'

'But perhaps you don't!' cried Felix, frustrated. 'Perhaps it's all a lie!'

'I… I cannot take that chance,' said Ulrika sadly. 'I am alone in this world without the countess. She saved me. She is my mother.'

And with that she turned and ran down the tunnel, pushing through the army of dead ratmen, and into the darkness. Felix's eyes stung, and he found it hard to swallow around the lump in his throat. No matter. Fighting would fix that.

He ploughed up the slope with Gotrek, wading into the skaven with fevered fury. Suddenly he wanted to see Lady Hermione dead more than anything in the world. The conniving bitch had broken Ulrika's spirit and divided her from Gotrek and Felix as neatly as an executioner lopped off the head of a traitor. She needed to die by his sword. If only these cursed skeletons would get out of the way.

'These puppets won't stop 'em,' snarled Madame Mathilda. 'Come on, me brave ones.'

She dropped into a squat, then launched herself at Gotrek, transforming in mid-air – her body twisting and sprouting black hair, her jaw lengthening, her fingers clumping together into yellow-clawed paws. Her few remaining guttersnipes charged down the slope behind her, howling.

Gotrek hacked off Mathilda's left foreleg as she hit him in the chest. They tumbled backwards together into the water.

Mathilda's half-transformed limb splashed beside Felix, and then her doxies and alley bashers were on him, pushing through the skeletons to stab at him with knives and cutlasses and hooks. He blocked and parried as best he could, but quickly lost all the ground he and Gotrek had won.

Beside him, Gotrek and Mathilda fought under water in a churning froth of limbs. He glimpsed wolf teeth, then Gotrek's axe, then a tail, a foot.

Then he could look no more. He was surrounded. The bashers and doxies and dead ratmen hacking and lunging at him from all sides. He could do nothing but spin in an endless circle, weaving figure eights in the air with Karaghul. It kept them at bay for now, but how long could he keep it up? He felt like he had been fighting for hours. The water dragged at his legs, and the footing was uncertain. Skeleton limbs splintered and spun away as they reached for him and met his blade. A snaggle-toothed harlot gashed his arm with an ice pick.

'Gotrek?' he called.

There was nothing but thrashing behind him.

A basher leapt at him, trying to bring him down like his mistress had Gotrek. Felix sidestepped him and he splashed into the water behind him. Felix stabbed down into the water and found flesh. The skeletons and bashers closed in, hemming him in on all sides. Claws caught his legs and arms.

'Gotrek!'

There was a yelp from behind him, and a great splashing, and the black wolf charged up the slope on three legs, shouldering the skeletons out of her way.

'Cursed wolf bitch!' roared Gotrek, surging up out of the water and charging past Felix, his arms and shoulders running red from a dozen deep wolf bites.

The skeletons and bashers turned away from Felix to stop him. The Slayer slashed all around at them. Dead ratmen exploded in showers of bone. The bashers merely died.

Felix breathed a sigh of relief and took up his usual position behind and a little to the left of Gotrek, chopping down any skeletons or guttersnipes that got past him. This was how things worked best – Gotrek taking the brunt and Felix cleaning up behind him. Now they might get somewhere.

Gotrek pressed forward relentlessly against the tide. The last of the alley bashers fell and things went quicker. The Slayer destroyed half a dozen bone skaven with every swing. They were almost out of the water. Felix craned his neck, trying to find Lady Hermione beyond the skeletons.

Just then, what little light there was in the tunnel winked out all at once. They had been seeing by the reflected glow of the lanterns from the black powder chamber. Now everything was black.

'What happened?' he called. Had the water risen high enough to snuff out the lanterns high on the walls? No. That was impossible. It was still only rib deep.

A skeleton ripped at his chest in the dark. He swung blindly at it and heard it shatter. More clawed at him. His skin crawled at their touch and he lashed out. He heard them snap and smash all around him, but still there were more. Gotrek's axe whooshed and whizzed nearby, crushing more of them.

'Sorcery,' grunted Gotrek. 'I can't see.'

Felix gulped. If Gotrek was blind it was indeed sorcery. He had known the Slayer to be able to see in lightless mines.

'What do we do?' said Felix, fighting off panic. He hacked all around him, but kept his strokes tight, afraid of hitting Gotrek.

'Press on, manling,' said the Slayer. 'The passage hasn't moved.'

Felix nodded, then realised that that was foolish in the dark, and opened his mouth to speak. But just as he did, something slithered around his neck and choked him, constricting his windpipe and cutting off his air. He cried out and clawed at his neck, expecting to find some slimy tentacle wrapped around it. There was nothing there!

Teeth and claws continued attacking him in the dark. He flailed about one-handed with his sword, futilely clutching at his throat with his left while panic consumed him. He tried to call to Gotrek, but could only hiss.

'What's that, manling?'

'Chhhikik,' said Felix. 'Chhhht bttthhhh.' Dim stars flared before his eyes. His sword strokes were weakening. He fought to take a breath.

A hard hand gripped his arm and he almost stabbed towards it before he realised it was Gotrek. Something heavy whipped past his ear, and then his other ear. The breeze ruffled his hair. Gotrek's axe! Was he attacking him? Was he mistaking him for an enemy?

Teeth and claws bit his arms and legs. He tried to scream in pain, but only rasped.

Gotrek cursed and, with a swish and a clatter, the teeth and claws fell away.

The Slayer's huge hand moved to his neck and felt around. Then a snarl. 'More sorcery. Fight her, manling. And keep moving.'

The callused hand grabbed his arm again and tugged him forward. Felix stumbled after him, swinging his sword in weak arcs and trying to force down the panic that was consuming him as, all around him, came the sounds of clattering movement and the whoosh and clash of heavy steel chopping bone.

Fight her, Gotrek had said. Fight who? The image of shadowy snakes spilling from Lady Hermione's hands flashed through his mind – stretching out, reaching, strangling. The evil witch. She had snuffed out Ulrika's will with a word. Now she was trying to snuff out his life with black sorcery. He waved his sword in front of his throat, as if doing so could sever the coils. Nothing.

He staggered on behind Gotrek, weak-kneed, the stars in front of his eyes blooming into fireworks, bursting one after another in purples, pinks and yellows. He tried to picture the black coils dissipating into candle smoke. Tried to feel them relaxing their grip on his neck. They remained as tight as ever. The ground beneath his feet became level. They had reached the top of the slope. Gotrek jerked him left. His shoulder hit the wall. He felt a cross-breeze on his cheek. The clatter of exploding skeletons filled his ears.

'Move!'

Gotrek shoved him towards the breeze, and all at once there were no skeletons around him.

It didn't matter. He was suffocating to death. He couldn't lift his sword anymore. He could barely put one foot in front of the other. His pulse was pounding in his ears like a hammer on an anvil. He could no longer hear anything else. His chest was going to implode for want of air. His tongue was swelling to fill his mouth. His fingers pawed weakly at his throat.

Something hard hit him in the stomach and he was lifted off his feet. His head flopped down towards the ground. His sword dragged on stone. The hard thing bounced him up and down and swayed him from side to side. He could hardly feel it anymore. All he could feel was the pain in his chest and the coils crushing his windpipe, constricting tighter and tighter. If only the bouncing would stop and let him die in peace.

Then, slowly, peace came, black and soft. The bouncing faded. The pain in his chest eased. He had the sensation of drifting down, like a snowflake, through a sweet murmuring darkness. This wasn't so bad. No pain. No loud noises. No horrible smells.

A hard bounce jolted him awake. It knocked the wind out of him. He gasped. Sigmar! He had gasped! There was air in his lungs! He tried again. It was like trying to suck air through a clogged pipe stem, but he was breathing. It hurt like swallowing glass.

Another hard bounce. Another gasp. The world flooded back around him – pain and noise and stink. His head throbbed. His stomach screamed. His chest felt like it was filled with rocks. His ears were battered with thuds and grunts and clanks. His nose was assaulted by the reek of sweat and sewer sludge. He looked around. For a moment he could see nothing. Then came movement and shadow. A dim glow of torches – all upside down. It slowly came to him where he was and what was happening to him. He was draped over Gotrek's shoulder, and the Slayer was running hard. An earthen floor blurred past, inches from his face. They were in a lantern-lit tunnel. Beyond that he didn't know.

'Got… rek,' he mumbled.

'Alive then?' said a harsh voice. 'Good.'

Felix frowned. How was he alive? How could he see? Had he fought off Hermione's sorcery? Had he willed the snakes away? Had Gotrek done it? Had the Slayer's brutal jostling broken the spell somehow? Had the duel with the warlock weakened her so much that she couldn't prolong the spell? Had they simply gotten too far away?

Gotrek stopped and set him down. He groaned in agony. Somewhere in the distance came a clicking and clattering. Gotrek did something off to Felix's right. A breeze puffed on Felix's cheek, and more sewer smell filled his nose. He looked towards the breeze. A secret door. Into the sewer tunnels.

Gotrek leaned over him and took his arm.

'I… I can walk.'

'Not fast enough,' said Gotrek, and hoisted him over his shoulder again. Felix's bruised stomach throbbed with agony.

As Gotrek carried him through the door Felix saw movement behind them, a milling throng of wedge-skulled skeletons shuffling towards them. And there were darker figures among them, pushing through them, past them.

Gotrek kicked the door closed, then ran on. The dim grey dawn filtered down into the sewer from above. Felix looked at the sewer channel as they jogged past it. The stew was very low. He had never seen it so low. A gummy brown tide mark was drying high above a sluggish trickle. The holes Gotrek's black powder trick had blasted into the channel must have emptied the sewers. He chuckled. That would take some fixing.

A crash behind them. Felix twisted his head awkwardly to look back. A broken door was toppling into the channel. Two dark figures emerged from the hole in the wall. Or was it three? They surged forward.

'Grimnir take them,' cursed Gotrek. 'No time. No time.' He ran on.

Felix looked back again. The dark figures were closer – much closer. Gotrek turned a corner into a small square space and stopped. He lifted Felix off his shoulder and steadied him against the wall. A set of iron rungs ran up it.

'I hope you can climb,' said Gotrek.

'I hope I can too,' said Felix.

Gotrek started up the rungs. 'Come on. Right behind me.'

Felix nodded and pushed himself away from the wall. The world swirled vertiginously around him. He clutched a rung and held on. The world steadied. He began to climb. One rung. Two rungs. He heard a soft thudding. It got louder. Was it his heart?

Above him, Gotrek reached the top of the ladder and put his shoulder to the grate. A shaft of weak sunlight slanted in and lit up a square of bricks beside the ladder. The Slayer pushed the grate up until it fell aside with a clang.

Felix kept climbing. Halfway there. His vision dimmed. His head pounded. Or was that the thudding sound, growing louder still?

Gotrek climbed out of the hole.

Felix looked back. A black wolf bounded into the room from the tunnel, a petite woman clinging to her back. The wolf had four legs, but one was pale and shiny and had no fur. Behind the wolf and rider was a looming shadow, as thin as a dead tree.

Felix climbed faster, at least he tried to, urging his legs to extend, his arms to pull and grasp. He was sweating like a pump.

'Come on, manling!' called Gotrek from above. He held his hand down into the hole.

The wolf shook off its rider and leapt at him, snapping. Her teeth clashed shut an inch from his ankle. Felix climbed another rung. Only three more! The wolf howled angrily, and transformed. The howl became words as the paws became hands and clambered up the ladder behind him.

'No ye don't, pet!' said Madame Mathilda. 'Haven't had my dinner.' She grabbed his ankle in a grip like a steel talon and yanked down, hard.

Felix's slick fingers slipped off the rungs. But just as he fell, Gotrek's meaty hand grabbed his right wrist and pulled up, hard. Felix barked in agony. He was being stretched like taffy. Another few stitches popped. Every wound on his body screamed.

'Your other arm!' rasped Gotrek.

Felix threw up his left arm. Gotrek caught it and pulled, his legs braced on either side of the hole. Mathilda hauled back the other way. Felix groaned with pain.

Below Mathilda, Lady Hermione was standing wearily and making gestures with her hands and Mistress Wither was floating upwards like a dry leaf, scrawny, bandaged fingers stretching out of her drooping sleeves towards him.

Felix kicked Madame Mathilda in the face with his free foot. She snarled and grabbed his other ankle, pulling with all her weight. Above him, Gotrek heaved mightily. Felix felt his spine pop. His muscles tore and spasmed. But he was rising, slowly – too slowly. Mistress Wither was closing fast.

Gotrek pulled harder. Felix's legs raised up into the slanting shaft of sunlight. The edge of it touched Mathilda's fingers. She screamed and let go, her hands smoking.

Felix came up all at once, scraping his shoulders on the frame of the hole as he shot through it and landed on top of Gotrek. He groaned, in too much agony to move.

Gotrek shoved him off and staggered up, pulling his axe off his back, his eye fixed on the sewer hole.

'Not coming out, maggots?' he called.

There was no answer.

He shrugged, then turned back to Felix and hauled him to his feet.

Felix hissed, nearly passing out from the pain. 'Easy.'

'No time for easy, manling,' he said, starting away. 'Come on.'

Felix looked around as he limped after the Slayer. They were in a side street next to the Imperial Gunnery School. Gotrek's uncanny sense of direction had come through again.

Halfway to the corner, a faint, echoey voice reached his ears. 'It won't always be daylight, heroes.'

GOTREK AND FELIX limped through the gates of the Imperial Gunnery School and headed for the broad flat lawn that stretched along its west side. Men of the College of Engineering and of the Gunnery School were working together to dismantle a tower made of steel beams and guy wires. Other men loaded the pieces onto the backs of a line of wagons and made them secure as the dray horses stamped the grass and snorted steam into the cold morning air.

Off to one side, Lord Groot stood talking with Lord Pfaltz-Kappel and Lord Hieronymous Ostwald. They looked up as the poet and the Slayer approached, then gasped.

'The *Spirit of Grungni,*' barked Gotrek. 'Where is it?'

'You… you have missed it, Slayer,' said Groot. 'Look.'

Gotrek and Felix followed Groot's finger as he pointed west. At first Felix could see nothing but the towers and roof peaks of the city, outlined in pink by the light of the rising sun. But at last he found, just between the sturdy mass of the town hall and the sharp spires of the University of Nuln, a small black oblong shape nosing north and west before a high bank of lavender clouds.

Gotrek's shoulders slumped. He cursed.

Felix groaned. They were too late. The tainted cannon were on their way to Middenheim, to wreak havoc on the Fauschlag's defences from within. But maybe it wasn't too late. Maybe there was some way to warn them, to call the airship back – carrier pigeons or flares or some such.

He turned to Lord Groot. 'My lord…'

Groot, Ostwald and Pfaltz-Kappel were all backing away from them and covering their noses, their eyes wide with dismay and apprehension.

'Did you fall in the sewer, Herr Jaeger?' asked Lord Ostwald, gagging.

'Were you in a fight?' asked Groot.

'Are you diseased?' asked Lord Pfaltz-Kappel.

Felix looked down at himself, then over at Gotrek. He could understand the lords' reactions. He and the Slayer looked a mess. Felix's beautiful new clothes were torn and bloodied and smeared with filth, and he was still bleeding from the gashes the frog thing had torn on his arm. The Slayer was worse. His body was a mass of bleeding wounds. His bandages were soaked and partially peeled away, revealing his healing burn scars, his crest and beard were singed black in places and clotted with sewer muck, and his face, neck and shoulders were covered in angry, pus-filled blisters from the farm girl's vomit. He looked like he had contracted some virulent plague and was in its later stages. Well, perhaps their battered condition would add urgency to their words.

'The sewer fell on us,' said Felix. 'But listen, please, my lords. Something terrible has occurred. The cannon...'

'Another secret plot like the last one you invented?' sneered Pfaltz-Kappel, waving his handkerchief in front of his face. 'The Gunnery School seems to have failed to explode.'

'We only just stopped it from happening, my lord,' said Felix. 'Down in the sewer. Hence our, er, disarray. But please listen...'

'What!' said Lord Groot. 'You say someone was trying to blow up the school after all?'

'Yes, my lord,' said Felix, impatiently. 'Ward Captain Wissen. He was the leader of the Cleansing Flame. He and his followers...'

'Captain Wissen a cultist?' said Pfaltz-Kappel. 'Preposterous. No more zealous defender of the public good exists in Nuln.'

'That was how he covered his actions,' said Felix. 'But who perpetrated the plot isn't important anymore. Wissen has been defeated and his bombs defused. What is important is the fact that the cannons...'

'Wissen has been "defeated"?' asked Lord Ostwald, raising an eyebrow. 'What do you mean by that?'

'We...' Felix paused, suddenly realising how awkward this could become. He shot a look at Gotrek, but the Slayer was staring fixedly at the ground, mumbling to himself. He didn't seem to be listening at all. Well, it would all come out in the end. And it had to be told. 'We... we fought and defeated him and his followers, in order to stop the destruction of the Gunnery School. But unfortunately, part of their plan has succeeded. You see, the cannon...'

'Do you mean you killed him?' pressed Ostwald.

'Er,' said Felix. 'Well, he was killed, yes. But as I say, we discovered part of his plan too late, and...'

'You killed Captain Wissen!' cried all three, stepping back from them.

'And did you also assault the guards of the Altestadt Gate last night?' asked Lord Ostwald.

'And also one of the patrols Captain Wissen placed in the sewers the day before?' asked Lord Pfaltz-Kappel.

'My lords, please,' Felix pleaded. 'I can answer all these charges later. But you must hear me about the cannon. They have been...'

But Lord Groot was waving over a detail of Gunnery School guards as Ostwald and Pfaltz-Kappel continued to back away, hands on the hilts of their swords.

'Herr Jaeger,' said Ostwald. 'I am very disappointed in you. I believed you to be a true and noble knight, a defender of humanity against the horrors that besiege us from all sides, but these actions of yours are very disturbing – assaulting the watch, killing a ward captain of the watch, Sigmar only knows what other villainy. I am afraid I will have to place you under arrest until these matters can be investigated further.'

'Fine!' said Felix angrily. 'Lock us up! Do what you will! Only let me finish what I have been trying to tell…'

Gotrek's head snapped up. 'The gyrocopter!' He barked, then started across the lawn towards the front gates. 'Come on, manling. We've no time to lose.'

'Stop them!' shouted Lord Ostwald. 'Arrest them for the murder of Ward Captain Adelbert Wissen!'

EIGHTEEN

GOTREK GLARED AROUND, pulling his axe off his back. 'What's this?' he growled menacingly as the Gunnery School guards began closing in.

Felix drew his sword. 'I tried to explain about the cannon, but they wouldn't listen. They won't believe that Wissen was a cultist, and...'

'Never mind, manling,' said Gotrek. 'There's no time for explanations.' He lashed about with his axe, making the guards dance back. 'Stay clear if you want to live!' he shouted, then looked around. 'Here, manling,' he said, trotting off. 'Hurry.'

Felix limped after the Slayer and saw that he was heading for the line of wagons from the College of Engineering. Good. As fragile as he felt at the moment, the idea of sprinting to the college with a troop of guards at his heels didn't sound appetising, or possible.

The guards moved with them, maintaining a cautious distance from their weapons, but when they realised Gotrek and Felix were heading for the wagons, they blocked their way, drawing their pistols and resting them across their forearms.

'Shoot, then,' growled Gotrek, without breaking stride. 'But aim well, or it will be the last thing you do.'

'No!' shouted Ostwald. 'Don't shoot!'

'What, my lord?' cried Lord Pfaltz-Kappel. 'They are murderers. Groot! Tell them to fire.'

'No, Groot! Hold!' said Ostwald. 'There is a story here that may have bearing on the security of Nuln, perhaps all the Empire, and I will hear it.' He glared at Pfaltz-Kappel. 'And witch hunters have difficulty wringing confessions from dead men, my lord.'

Gotrek slashed at the guards and they danced back out of the way. He and Felix climbed on the first wagon. Felix took the reins.

Groot stepped in the way of the wagon. 'Be reasonable now, sirs. Turn yourselves in.'

'And face the witch hunters?' said Felix, flicking the reins. 'No fear.'

The horses started slowly forward.

Groot backed away, then paced them. 'But you cannot hope to escape the city.'

'Want to bet on it?' said Gotrek.

'Hoy!' said an engineer as he noticed the wagon moving. 'What are you doing? That's the property of the College of Engineering! Get off of there!' He ran at them and tried to climb on board.

Gotrek shoved the man down. Felix slapped the reins again and the horses picked up speed. More engineers started running forward, joining the guards as they ran after them. Gotrek stood wide-legged in the wagon bed, snarling back at them as the wagon bumped and bounced.

'Close the gates!' called Groot, waving towards the front of the school. 'Call for the watch! Call for the army!'

The gate guards frowned and cupped their ears, momentarily uncomprehending, as the horses pounded towards them across the lawn.

'Close... the... gate!' screamed Groot.

The guards understood him at last and scrambled into action, running to the iron gates.

The wagon jolted over a low curb and fish-tailed through the gravel of the drive as Felix pointed the horses at the entrance. The guards pushed on the gates. They groaned, closing slowly, but picking up speed.

'Faster!' shouted Felix, and slapped the reins again.

The horses strained forward, stretching out into a gallop. It was going to be close.

'Hold on!' Felix called over his shoulder.

Gotrek grabbed the back of the driver's bench.

The horses shot the gap easily. Unfortunately, the sides of the wagon stuck out more than a foot to either side of them. The left front corner caught the closing edge of the left gate with a splintering crack, bending the ironwork and ripping away the wagon's left side. The wagon swerved crazily, banged sideways against the right gate, then straightened as the horses plunged into the street, screaming with fright and trying to get away from all the noise and violence behind them.

Felix pulled left on the reins and they careened down Commerce Street as students and labourers and fruit sellers scattered before them in terror. Faint and far behind he heard Groot calling, 'Open the gates! Open the gates!'

At the end of the street Felix turned left again and they thundered down the Wandstrasse, which paralleled the Altestadt wall. The gallop came to an abrupt end just before the Emmanuelleplatz, where it passed through the Great Gate into the Altestadt. The way was blocked by merchants and tradesmen in carts and on foot, all waiting to get through the gate to service their rich clients on the other side. Gotrek and Felix's stolen wagon could go no further.

Gotrek jumped down. 'Come on, manling.'

Felix hissed and climbed down gingerly, looking back down the Wandstrasse. Bobbing helmets glinted at the far end. The Gunnery School guards were still coming. He limped after Gotrek as he turned left onto the Emmanuelleplatz. The towers of the College of Engineering loomed over the street, half way down, casting a long shadow over the tenements on the other side. Gotrek and Felix crossed the street, pushing through the crowds, and hurried to the entrance to the college.

The sergeant at the gate stepped out as they entered. 'Professor Makaisson is gone, sirs. Left with the airship. I'm afraid I can't...'

'It's all right, sergeant,' said Felix, over his shoulder as Gotrek stumped on unheeding. 'We... we're just collecting our belongings. Won't be a minute.'

He pressed after Gotrek before the sergeant could reply.

Inside the main building they wound their way through the maze of corridors and stairwells towards the roof.

As they passed near Makaisson's workshop, a few of the students gave them cheery salutes, then stared after them when they saw the condition they were in.

Gotrek pointed his axe at one. 'Where's the clumsy one? The blind one?'

The student shrank from the axe, and undoubtedly from the smell and Gotrek's blisters as well. 'Who? D'ye mean Petr?'

'Aye. Him. Where is he?'

'He, ah, he went with Professor Makaisson,' said the student, quaking. 'In the airship.'

'You'll do, then,' said Gotrek, advancing on him. 'Is the gyrocopter fuelled? Is it ready to fly?'

'I… I don't know.' The student cowered back against the wall. 'Professor doesn't let us touch it.'

'Where is the black water stored?' Gotrek barked.

'On the roof,' said the student. 'Please don't kill me.'

Gotrek grunted and pushed past him, striding towards the stairs.

'But it's locked up!' the student called after him. 'You have to get the key from the supply steward.'

Gotrek snorted and started up the stairs. As he made to follow, Felix heard a commotion coming from outside – raised voices and angry argument. It sounded like the Gunnery School guards had reached the college and were arguing with their counterparts at the college gate. He hurried on, groaning with each step. There was no place on his body that didn't hurt.

Three weary flights later he stepped panting onto the long, narrow roof. Gotrek was waiting to close the door.

'They're coming,' Felix gasped.

'I heard them, manling,' said Gotrek.

The Slayer looked around the roof. A sturdy cart loaded with heavy brass tanks labelled 'Heberluft' sat at one side. He stepped to it, grasped the handles, and pushed at it, angling it around. Felix pushed too, though he wasn't sure he was helping. Over the sound of the wheels grinding across the copper sheeting he heard a swarm of footsteps pounding up the stairs. Gotrek pushed harder, wrenching on the handles to bring the cart into position.

Just as they eased it side-on to the stairwell door, the door banged open half an inch and slammed against the cart. Fists pounded and knocked on the wooden panels.

'In the name of Countess Emmanuelle, open this door!' said an angry voice.

'You are under arrest!' bawled another.

Gotrek laughed and stumped to a padlocked shed halfway along the roof. He slashed at the lock with his axe and it fell in pieces.

Felix looked back as he heard banging and smashing behind him. The men in the stairwell were attacking the door. It rattled and shook.

Gotrek entered the shed, then returned a moment later carrying two brass tanks and a tin funnel. He lugged them to the gyrocopter, which was tied down with ropes at the far end of the roof. Felix followed, eyeing the flimsy-looking machine warily, as Gotrek chopped through its ropes and threw them aside. The thing only had one seat.

'Are you certain this will carry both of us?' he asked.

'No,' said Gotrek.

He uncapped a brass tank behind the pilot's seat, stuck the funnel in, and began to pour in the black water. The smell made Felix's eyes burn.

'We might not have enough fuel either,' said the Slayer, squinting towards the western horizon. Felix followed his gaze. The *Spirit of Grungni* had disappeared behind the clouds.

Gotrek looked in the cockpit. 'Take out those grenades,' he said, pointing with his bearded chin. 'That'll shed some weight. And find me a spanner. We'll have the cannon off too.'

Felix looked back at the door again. 'Do we have time?'

'The boiler takes ten minutes to build up steam,' said Gotrek, setting down the empty fuel can. 'We can't leave before then.'

'Ten minutes!' Felix cried. He had vague memories of what a boiler was from the lessons Makaisson had given him long ago, but couldn't remember exactly what it did. Whatever it was, he didn't think it was going to do it fast enough. He looked to the door again. An axe blade bit through timbers. It would never last ten minutes. 'We'll be knee deep in Gunnery School guards by then.'

'Just find a spanner.'

Gotrek pulled flint, steel and a curl of tinder paper from his belt pouch as Felix limped back towards the shed. Felix cringed as he heard a *whump* of flame, but when he looked back, Gotrek was closing a door in the side of the machine as if nothing was amiss.

There were no spanners in the fuel shed, but as Felix stepped out again, he noticed a half-dismantled contraption just to his left. It looked like some sort of telescope, or perhaps an experimental catapult. Rusty parts and tools were scattered all around it like fallen leaves. Felix hurried to it and scooped up as many tools as he could carry.

He ran back and spilled them at Gotrek's feet. 'Will these do?'

'Aye, fine. Now remove the grenades.' Gotrek took up a spanner and a pry bar and rolled under the front of the gyrocopter, from which a stubby cannon sprouted. 'And watch the gauge on the side of the tank,' he said as he reached up into the machines innards. 'When the needle points straight up, we're away.'

Felix peered at the gauge. The needle pointed left, parallel to the ground, but was rising slowly, in quivering starts and stops. He looked back to the door. There was a long, narrow hole in it, and axes and swords hacked at it from the other side.

Lord Groot's voice came through it, rising over the clamour. 'Come now, Herr Jaeger! Herr Gurnisson! Give yourselves up! You have no chance of escape!'

Felix swallowed as he leaned into the cockpit and began gingerly taking the heavy black iron spheres from the racks that held them. He set them carefully on the roof. He remembered too well how deadly and unpredictable the little bombs were. Images of Borek's bespectacled nephew Varek handling them as if they were harmless toys flashed through his mind and made him shiver. And thinking of Varek reminded him of how the young dwarf scholar had died – by crashing a gyrocopter just like this one into the flank of a Chaos-twisted dragon. Felix's shiver turned into full-fledged trembling.

Under the gyrocopter there was a clang, and Gotrek cursed. 'Give me a bigger spanner, manling. And a hammer.'

Felix sorted through the tools and put a huge spanner and a ball-headed hammer into Gotrek's outstretched hand. They disappeared under the gyro-copter and it began to shake as a deafening banging rang across the roof.

Felix checked the gauge again as he resumed unloading the grenades. He moaned. The needle hadn't raised more than a hair's width, and the guards would be through the door at any moment. Of course, they would still have some difficulty after that, having to climb over the cart or under it, but just one man with a pistol would be enough to end Gotrek and Felix's flight before it began.

He looked at the grenade in his hand. That would be one way to solve the problem. One grenade under those lift-gas tanks and everything on that side of the roof would be blown to the four winds. If only it were orcs or mutants or ratmen on the other side of the door instead of Imperial citizens. If he were the black-hearted villain Ostwald and Groot and everybody else in Nuln apparently thought he was, he would have had no qualms about killing them all. Alas, tempting as it was, he was no killer, at least not of innocent men – at least, he thought with a shudder of guilt as he remembered the columns of smoke rising over Shantytown, not on purpose. He was not going to change that now.

He sighed and placed the grenade next to the others, then paused and looked again towards the door. So the men behind it thought him a bloodthirsty killer, capable of anything, did they? Why not use that to his advantage? He grinned and picked up the grenade again.

'I'll be back,' he said, then started to the door.

Gotrek just grunted. The banging from under the gyrocopter continued.

Felix stopped about ten paces from the lift-gas cart. The hole in the door was bigger than a Verenan tome of law now. 'Groot!' he called. 'Lord Groot! Show yourself! I want to talk!'

There was a babble of voices behind the door, and the chopping and banging slowed to a stop. After a second, Groot's face appeared behind the hole, eyes wide and nervous.

'Herr Jaeger?' said Groot. 'You wish to speak to me? Did you wish to give yourself up?'

'No,' said Felix. 'I just wanted to say goodbye.' He raised the grenade so Groot could see it, then mimed jerking the pin out, and rolled the bomb under the cart.

Groot shrieked and disappeared from the hole.

'A bomb! A bomb!' came his scream. 'Down the stairs! Down the stairs! Hurry!'

The sounds of bedlam came through the door – bellows and shouts, the clank and clatter of dropped weapons, the thud of boots and falling bodies.

Felix laughed, then felt ashamed. It was a cruel trick, but when the alternative was murder? He shrugged and limped quickly back to the gyrocopter.

The needle was climbing steadily. It was less than the width of his finger away from straight up. Felix quickly removed the remaining grenades, then looked over the machine again. He frowned. Lightening the load was all very well, but there was still only one seat.

'Where am I to sit?'

'On your arse,' growled Gotrek.

A heavy thud came from under the gyrocopter. Felix looked down. Gotrek was rolling out from under it. The cannon lay on the roof, surrounded by brass lugs.

The Slayer stood and scowled at the gyrocopter, scratching his scalp through his matted crest. 'Hmmm. You'll have to sit behind me, or the balance won't be right.'

Felix looked into the cockpit, frowning. 'But there's no room behind your seat.'

'Aye,' said Gotrek. 'You'll have to sit on the cowling.'

'The cowling?' said Felix. He didn't know the word. 'You mean on top of it? On the outside?'

'Aye,' said Gotrek again. 'It's the only way.' He checked the gauge. 'It's ready. Get on.'

'No no!' said Felix. 'I won't! The airship was bad enough! I'm not going to flit through the sky clinging to the back of a mechanical dragonfly! It's impossible!'

'Use some rope, then.'

'Rope! And what if we crash? Or explode? How will I get away?'

'Stay behind, then,' said Gotrek, starting to climb up the wooden step ladder to the cockpit. 'Do what you want. I'm flying.'

There was a loud crack and something whistled past Felix's ear. He ducked behind the gyrocopter and looked towards the stairwell door. The muzzle of a long gun was withdrawing through the hole.

'Try to blow us up, will you?' came an angry voice. 'Fiends of Chaos!'

Felix groaned. His ruse hadn't bought them as much time as he'd hoped. Another gun poked through the hole, and another ball whizzed past.

Felix swallowed convulsively. 'I'll… I'll get the rope.' He darted out from cover, snatched up one of the ropes that had held down the gyrocopter, then clambered up onto the machine, feeling horribly exposed. He sat down on the skin of it, his back against the column from which rose the spindle that held the three very flimsy looking lift blades. He started lashing himself to it as Gotrek lowered the second canister of black water into the cockpit and climbed in after it.

There was a splintering crash from the far end of the roof. Felix looked up. The door had come down at last. Men with swords and guns were squirming under and over the lift gas wagon.

'Hurry!' he said.

'Easy, manling,' said Gotrek, situating himself and running his hands over the controls. 'I haven't flown one of these in over a century.' He murmured to himself. 'Gear engage. Rudder. Forward down. Backward up. Aye, that's the way of it. Right.' He reached forward, released a lock, and pulled slowly back on a lever. 'Hold on.'

With a hiss of steam and a clunk of pistons, the blades over Felix's head began very slowly to spin. Too slowly.

More guards were pushing out from under the wagon. They stood and fired their guns. Balls whistled past on all sides of Felix. One ricocheted off the fuel tank.

The blades turned faster and faster, making the machine rock and vibrate like a living thing. The first guards knelt and reloaded as more crawled under the cart onto the roof and ran towards them.

Up up up, thought Felix to himself, willing the gyrocopter to fly. *Up up up, damn you!*

As Gotrek pulled the lever all the way back, the rhythmic thump of the blades smoothed out into a steady roar. The gyrocopter shimmied and danced, like a kite straining against its string in a high wind.

The handgunners were standing and aiming again, shoulder to shoulder. A guard ran directly at Felix, sword held high.

'Up!' shouted Felix, terrified.

The long guns cracked. Gotrek pulled backward on the rudder stick. The gyrocopter leaped sideways up into the sky over the bullets. The runners clubbed the sprinting guard to the roof.

Felix flopped over to one side, clutching futilely at the machine's smooth exterior. The ropes cut painfully into his wounded ribs, but at least they held. Gotrek corrected his tilt and the gyrocopter zigged violently back the other way, throwing Felix against the ropes on the other side.

'Controls are a bit sensitive,' shouted Gotrek over the prop wash.

'Really?' moaned Felix.

Vertigo churned his guts as the machine veered over the edge of the roof and his eyes zoomed down the side of the building to the court yard below. With a sickening lurch the gyrocopter dropped and the ground shot up at him. He screamed. He and Gotrek were too heavy. They had overburdened the thing. The blades couldn't keep them airborne. They were going to smash on the flagstones and die!

Gotrek pulled back on the rudder and brought them up short, about twenty feet above the ground. Felix's crotch slammed painfully down onto the fuselage. The world dimmed as he curled forward in agony.

'I think I've got it now,' called Gotrek over his shoulder.

'Oh… good,' said Felix, clutching himself.

He sagged wearily against the ropes as Gotrek manipulated the controls – more gently this time – and the gyrocopter wobbled forward, glancing off a chimney as it rose over the tenements across from the college and started unsteadily across the city.

AFTER A WHILE even terror gives way to boredom.

At first Felix flinched at every dip and swoop that the tiny airship made, his stomach and bowels threatening to void themselves with every midair shimmy. Gotrek might have been the greatest warrior of his age, but he was a middling pilot at best. He flew dangerously close to spires and towers, and seemed to have difficulty staying high enough to clear the rooftops.

Things got better once they passed over the Nuln city walls and started flying above the countryside – there were fewer things to hit – but the machine seemed to be straining to carry them, and Gotrek constantly had to correct their altitude so they wouldn't plough into the tops of trees.

Flying like this was infinitely worse than flying in the *Spirit of Grungni*, Felix decided. He had hated that too, at first – terrified of the unnatural feeling of floating high above the ground – but once he had understood how the cells of lift gas worked, and how resilient the gondola was, he had accepted the fact that it probably wouldn't fall out of the air at a moment's notice, and had come to enjoy it. This horrid contraption was another matter entirely. Here he was exposed to the wind and the cold and the weather, and the only things that held him up were three delicate spinning blades powered by a steam engine that might stutter and die at any moment. That was what had been so reassuring about the *Spirit of Grungni*. Even if its engines stopped, it would remain floating in the air. If the gyrocopter's engines stopped, it would plummet to the ground like a cow dropped from a battlement.

But after the first hour, his terror faded to a dull tension that settled in his shoulders and made them ache. He watched listlessly as the endless green of the Reikwald scrolled past below them and the sun rose higher behind them. His mind, which until they had risen off the roof and out of the clutches of their pursuers, had been entirely occupied with either chasing or escaping their various enemies, began to think back over recent events and link together things that had, at the time, seemed unconnected.

The tainting of the cannons with powdered warpstone explained so much. The Gunnery School guard who had been hanged as a mutant, and the other who had gone insane and said that the cannons were looking at him – the poor fellows must have been warped by the tainted guns they had been guarding. The cannon that had exploded on the testing range – the addition of the warpstone dust must have caused a fatal flaw in the casting. The riot on the bridge that had ended with the cannon being pushed into the river – the Cleansing Flame must have orchestrated it so that the smiths of the Gunnery School couldn't examine the cannon closely and discover the taint. Wissen's insistence that the cultists wait until the new gun had been test fired before blowing up the Gunnery School – he wanted to be sure the last tainted gun didn't blow up like the other had, and so would be able to do its evil work in Middenheim.

It occurred to Felix that the explosion of the cannon on the testing range must have been just as frustrating for Wissen and the Cleansing Flame as it was for Gotrek and Malakai and the others. If the gun had fired successfully, the *Grungni* would have been away that same afternoon, and the shipment of tainted cannon would have reached Middenheim days ago. Had that happened, the mountaintop city might have already fallen to Archaon's hordes!

For a moment Wissen's other actions puzzled Felix. Why had the leader of the Brotherhood of the Cleansing Flame, in his guise as Ward Captain of the Nuln Watch, persecuted the Cleansing Flame so strongly? Why had he gone into Shantytown and beaten and arrested so many people? Was it only to deflect suspicion that he might be a cultist himself? Felix didn't think so. No one had had any reason to suspect Wissen anyway. On the other hand, what better way to make the people rise up against the brutality of the watch than to command the watch to commit worse and worse brutalities? The common people who Wissen, when he wore the yellow mask of the Brotherhood of the Cleansing Flame, stirred up against 'the vicious bullies of the city watch', had no idea that, unmasked, he was the very same Ward Captain Wissen that rousted them out of their beds and beat and arrested their sons for crimes they didn't commit. It was a brilliant scheme. Wissen had driven the common folk towards Chaos with a gauntleted right hand, and then changed masks and lured them to it with a welcoming left hand.

One thing Felix could still not explain. Magus Lichtmann had said that he had sensed no magical energy at the testing range after the cannon had exploded. Why hadn't he sensed the warpstone? Had another sorcerer cloaked its presence somehow? The old man in the basket perhaps? Or was it that Lichtmann wasn't much of a sorcerer? He had seemed more of an engineer to Felix.

'When will we catch up to them?' Felix called to Gotrek.

Gotrek shrugged. 'Not soon. It will take hours even after we see them.'

Felix nodded glumly. And what if they never saw them? It was hard to believe they were travelling fast enough. And what if they were blown off course? What if the *Spirit of Grungni* had been? It had happened before. Twice! He said none of this to Gotrek. He would only get sarcasm in return. He sighed. Hours. His rump and legs were already aching abominably, not to mention the rest of his battered and bruised and sewer-drenched body. He glared enviously at the comfortable cushioned seat Gotrek sat on. It was going to be a long flight.

'MANLING, WAKE UP.'

Felix moaned and opened his eyes, and yelped! He was falling! The ground was a mile away! He… No. No. Now he remembered. He was on the dwarf gyrocopter. He and Gotrek were flying, not falling. He was hanging sideways, leaning against the ropes that held him to the spindle column. He sat up with a groan. Every bone and muscle in his body ached, as if he had been beaten to within an inch of his life. He paused.

That was probably because he had been beaten to within an inch of his life. When had he last slept? In a bed? With pillows? Ah, pillows. Pillows were nice. Those clouds looked like pillows.

'Manling!'

Felix jerked. He had drifted off again. 'Aye?' He blinked around. They were still over the Reikwald – or was it the Drakwald now? From the position of the sun, it appeared an hour or so before noon. His cheeks burned from wind and sun. In front of him, Gotrek was wrestling the canister of black water out from between his legs. He lifted it over his head one handed and reached it back towards Felix.

'Take this and fill the reservoir,' he said. 'You'll need the funnel.'

Felix grabbed the canister, and almost dropped it! It was ridiculously heavy.

'Easy!' barked Gotrek. 'We're sunk without that.'

Felix hugged it to his chest like a lover and took the funnel that Gotrek handed back to him. He held onto it with one hand, then leaned forward against his ropes and stretched out his hand. The fuel reservoir's cap was almost out of reach. He unscrewed it with the tips of his fingers, and then fumbled it. It fell, then jerked to a stop and dangled at the end of a chain. Felix breathed a sigh of relief. Dwarfs thought of everything.

He stuck the funnel in the tank, then leaned out to the limit of his ropes and inched the canister forward, resting it on the fuselage. Any sudden moves and he would lose his grip. He tipped it down and black liquid poured from the spout and gurgled into the funnel.

'Ha!' said Gotrek.

Felix jerked and almost dropped the canister. The stream of black water splashed everywhere. 'What!' he said, looking around. 'What's wrong?'

'The *Spirit of Grungni*,' said Gotrek.

Felix raised his head and scanned ahead. Far in front of them and a little to their north, a long black oblong shape hung in the air, just below the clouds.

'At last,' said Felix. He let out a breath he hadn't known he was holding. They had found it after all. He returned to filling the reservoir.

IT TOOK AN agonisingly long time to close with the *Spirit of Grungni*, and the frustration was made worse because it was *right there*, directly ahead of them, and yet never seemed to get any closer. The sun climbed to its noon apex and sank an hour past it and they were still miles away. He kept hoping to see it turn about, or to see some other signal that the crew had spotted them, but it didn't happen.

Felix realized that he had been thinking of the *Spirit of Grungni* as their journey's end, but it wasn't, was it? What did they do then? Did they return the cannons to Nuln? Did they fly due west and drop them in the sea? How did one safely dispose of a warpstone tainted cannon anyway? Did they go on to Middenheim and try to discover who this 'master' was that Wissen had mentioned?

Felix wondered who the master could be. He would have to be a fairly powerful wizard to bring the guns to life the way Wissen had described. Someone already in Middenheim? A sudden thought made Felix's heart lurch. Max Schreiber! Malakai had said their old companion was there, helping with the defences. Could it be him? Felix had always been slightly suspicious of him. Certainly he had always seemed to fight on the side of the Empire and humanity, but there was also no denying he enjoyed his power, and had seemed at times tempted to use it for personal goals, rather than for the good of all. Had the years and his constant contact with the winds of magic twisted him in some way? Had he succumbed to the lure of Chaos at last? Felix shivered. Max must be a Wizard Lord by now. He did not look forward to facing him in a fight, and if he had turned traitor, Felix had no doubt that he would indeed be fighting him, because Gotrek would not suffer him to live.

At last, with the sun half way down the sky and glaring in Felix's eyes, the *Spirit of Grungni* loomed ahead and above them like a great black cloud.

Felix gazed up at it in wonder as Gotrek tilted the rudder stick back and they rose slowly towards it. He had never seen it like this before. He had been in it, looking out, and seen it flying from the ground, but there was something beautiful and wonderful about seeing it as a bird would, passing under the riveted brass gondola, rising up beside it, like a salmon pacing a whale, hearing the thrumming of the cables that fixed the gondola to the rigid balloon above it. Who could have imagined that so incredible a thing existed in the world?

Gotrek angled the gyrocopter to cross in front of the *Grungni's* gondola, then held it steady as best he could before it. Felix waved at the large viewing ports that looked into the command deck. He saw young men shouting and pointing at them, and then the broad, squat figure of Malakai stepped to the port and stared out, a look of confusion and concern on his usually cheerful face. Magus Lichtmann joined him at the glass. He gaped, his eyes agog behind his spectacles.

Malakai turned and barked some order to his human crew, then waved at Gotrek and Felix and motioned for them to circle behind the airship. Gotrek saluted, then turned the gyrocopter and angled off to buzz down the airship's side.

In the stern of the *Spirit of Grungni*, a brass door like a drawbridge was lowered on chains, revealing a narrow hangar constructed of bare metal bulkheads. Another gyrocopter was parked on the metal deck at the far end. Felix didn't understand how it had got in there, for the door looked barely big enough to admit two men walking abreast, let alone a contraption almost as tall as two men, with a wing span considerably wider than that. None the less, Petr, the wild-haired young engineering student, was waving them on as if he had every confidence that they would fit though the gap.

Gotrek tipped the rudder stick forward and they approached it rapidly, too rapidly!

'Slow! Slow down!' cried Felix. 'You'll wreck us!'

'I know what I'm doing,' Gotrek muttered, but he eased back on the stick a little just the same.

The door appeared to get slightly bigger as they approached, but not by much. Felix held his breath as Gotrek nosed the gyrocopter ahead in little fits and starts, raising it and lowering it, then raising it again, as he judged the height of the door and Petr waved his hands this way and that. Finally the Slayer pushed in decisively, and almost precisely.

There was a great clanging racket and the gyrocopter slammed to the deck hard enough to snap Felix's teeth together. He covered his head and looked up. One of the rotor blades was bent, and the whole rotor assembly wobbled in a slow off kilter circle. He looked back at the door. There was a bright gouge in the metal of the frame on the right side.

'Welcome, sirs!' cried Petr, hurrying forward with a wooden step ladder. He tripped over a riveted seam in the deck and the ladder flew out of his hands as he tried to regain his balance. He fetched up face first against the gyrocopter's flank. 'Sorry. Sorry. No harm done.'

He scrabbled under the fuselage, found the ladder and set it up next to the cockpit. 'Welcome to the *Spirit of Grungni*, sirs.' His forehead was bleeding.

'Ah, thank you, Petr,' said Felix. It was a wonder the airship hadn't gone down with all hands, with this walking disaster on board.

Malakai slid down a ladder into the hangar, then turned, scowling as he crossed towards Gotrek. 'What in Grimnir's name is this? Did ye come all this way just tae wreck yin of my flyin'…?' He choked when he got a close look at the Slayer's face. 'By my ancestor's ancestors, what's happened to ye, Gurnisson? Ye don't look well.'

'Mutants,' said Gotrek, as he climbed stiffly down from the cockpit. 'Now, turn about,' he said. 'The guns are sabotaged.'

'Whit?' said Malakai, raising a shaggy eyebrow. 'Sabotaged? What dae ye mean? They were tested. Passed by the school.'

Magus Lichtmann came carefully down the ladder behind him, his one hand letting go of one rung, then quickly catching hold of the next before he fell.

'Tainted,' said Felix, untying himself from the spindle pillar and sliding down the fuselage to the deck. His stiff muscles screamed as he landed, stabbing pain shooting through them and almost dropping him to his knees. He clutched the side of the gyrocopter for support. 'Warpstone, mixed into the molten iron. We saw it happen, though we didn't know it.' He stood straight, wincing and grimacing. 'The initiate who poured the ashes of the gun captain into the crucible was a secret cultist, a member of the Brotherhood of the Cleansing Flame. There was powdered warpstone mixed into the ashes.'

Petr and the other crewmembers who were lashing Gotrek and Felix's gyrocopter to the deck gaped, horrified.

Malakai looked aghast. 'Can it be true? But why would they dae it? To whit purpose?'

Felix shook his head wearily. 'I don't know many details. Wissen died too quickly to tell us, but...'

'Captain Wissen is dead?' asked Magus Lichtmann, stepping forward alarmed.

Felix nodded. 'Aye. Another cultist. One of the leaders of the cult. We stopped him and his minions from blowing up the Gunnery School.'

'Did you?' said Lichtmann, all agog. 'By the gods!'

'Wissen was a cultist?' said Malakai. He made a face. 'Ah, weel, never did like the wee stuck-up numpty, anyhow.'

'He said that some "master" was to wake the guns once they were in place on the walls of Middenheim,' continued Felix. 'And that the guns would drive their crews mad and cause them to turn them on the defenders.'

'Wake the guns?' Malakai gaped again and turned to Gotrek, as if for assurance. The Slayer nodded.

The engineer opened his mouth and closed it a few times, momentarily unable to put his horror and outrage into words. 'It's no' right!' he said at last. 'Befouling cannon wi' black sorcery! Makin' instruments o' Chaos out o' the purr wee things! The villains! I'll no hae it! It's as bad as the Dawi Zharr and yon daemon gun!' He turned and started for the ladder, his jaw thrust forward. 'Right. We're turnin' about. Make all fast.'

'Professor Makaisson,' called Magus Lichtmann after him.

Malakai stopped and looked back. 'Aye, what is it, magus? Make it quick.'

Magus Lichtmann unpinned his empty right sleeve and pulled it up to his shoulder, revealing a stump tightly bound in linen bandages. 'We will not turn back,' he said calmly. 'We will continue on to Middenheim, and deliver the guns as we have been contracted to do.'

'Whit?' said Malakai. 'Are ye saft in the heid, laddie? Have ye no' heard what's jist been said? Why would ye wannae dae that?'

'Because,' said Lichtmann, tugging at the bandages, 'I am the master.' There was a ripping sound, and the bandages loosened, then uncoiled and dropped to the floor. Beneath them was, not a stump, but something black and dry and crusted. It unfolded with sinewy grace, revealing itself to be a skinny black arm, which crawled with lines of glowing red, like an embered log. Flame yellow claws tipped each of the long, skeletal fingers.

Felix stared at the unnatural appendage, as did Malakai and his crew.

Gotrek cursed, and started forward, head lowered, drawing his axe off his back. 'Warlock,' he spat. 'You die here.' With his face blistered and his body burned and covered in scabbing wounds and filth, the Slayer looked like something escaped from hell.

'I think not.' Magus Lichtmann stepped back through the door that led to the cargo hold and thrust his claw forward. The air before it rippled like waves of heat rising from a tar roof. The fuel reservoirs of the two gyrocopters exploded in billowing balls of flame.

NINETEEN

FELIX FLEW HEELS over head and slammed into the bulkhead as fire blossomed above him. His head rang like a gong. Burning shrapnel rattled against the metal walls and rained down on him, starting his clothes on fire. He was too stunned to beat out the flames – too stunned to move. He felt like he had been slapped by a giant. His whole body throbbed. Gotrek lay on his back beside him, his one eye blinking up at the roof, his beard and crest smouldering.

The boiling fire dissipated as quickly as it had come, but the ruin it had caused remained. Three of Malakai's crew, who had been standing next to the *Spirit of Grungni's* gyrocopter, were dead, blasted into chunks of meat that were strewn across half the hangar deck. Had Felix and Gotrek not expended almost all of their machine's fuel chasing the airship, they would have been dead too. As it was, the explosion of their gyrocopter was miniscule compared to the fully fuelled one.

Felix raised his head and looked around. Petr lay in a heap beside him, struggling to get up, a deep laceration opening his left forearm to the bone. In the ceiling above, crewmen on the upper deck were gaping down through the ladder hatch at the carnage and calling out to Malakai. The stunned Slayer engineer was in the clutches of Lichtmann, who stood in the cargo hold door, hauling him to his feet with surprising strength. He put a long flame-shaped golden dagger to Makaisson's neck. The edges of it shimmered like heat waves over a hot roof.

'I regret the destruction of such fine machines,' said the magus. 'But no one must be allowed to bring word before we reach our goal. Now, Makaisson, have these two heroes thrown out of the door and maintain course to Middenheim, or I shall be forced to kill you.'

Malakai laughed up at him, eyes wild. 'Ye eejit! I'm a Slayer! D'ye think ah care if ah die?'

He lashed out with a booted foot and kicked Lichtmann between the legs. The magus squeaked and staggered back against the railing of the landing that looked over the cargo hold, gasping and holding himself as more of Malakai's crew slid down the ladder from above, armed with swords, hammers and huge spanners.

Felix saw Malakai stride through the cargo hold door and punch Lichtmann in the jaw with his massive fist. Lichtmann flipped backward over the rail and dropped out of Felix's sight, hitting the floor of the cargo hold with a satisfying clang. Malakai's crewmen pushed through into the hold to stand at their captain's side.

Gotrek staggered up and started after them. The runes on the head of his axe glowed cherry red.

Felix groaned and levered himself up to follow. Lichtmann. Why hadn't he thought of Lichtmann? Perhaps because the man had hardly seemed a sorcerer – more a scholarly engineer. The hangar spun sickeningly around Felix, and he had to steady himself against the bulkhead as he limped forward to the cargo hold door. Beside him, Petr picked himself up, moaning, and started after him, clutching his wounded arm.

The cargo hold was as wide as the airship, almost as long, and two decks deep. The door from the hangar opened onto a metal landing with stairs on the right that led down to the deck below. Just below the landing the cannons and mortars were chained to the deck in neat rows, and with their wheels securely blocked. Beyond them were crates of cannon balls, grape shot and other supplies, and beyond those, stacked against the far wall and roped in place, were the barrels of black powder. A pair of crewmen stood among the cargo, looking with wide eyes towards the action at the door.

Magus Lichtmann was just picking himself up behind a row of chained-down cannons as Felix limped into the hold behind Gotrek. The warlock's spectacles were smashed, and his gold-flecked green eyes, behind them, flashed with fury.

'You will come to regret that, engineer,' he said.

Gotrek made to launch himself over the rail, but Malakai threw out a hand.

'No! This yin's mine.' he said, taking a hammer from one of his crew. 'I want this two-faced gowk's head on a platter.' He tsked angrily and started for the stairs. 'Callin' me friend. Takin' an interest in my designs…'

Lichtmann opened his mouth and spat out a stream of harsh foreign syllables, his black hand twisting and thrusting at Malakai and Gotrek. Felix and the students cringed away as a blast of pink fire shot at the Slayers. Felix felt the edges of the spell, flames of fury and madness that boiled up in his head and made him want to kill everyone around him, but Gotrek and Malakai didn't even flinch. The Slayer laughed.

'Ye fool,' sneered Malakai. 'Will a dwarf succumb to magic? Bah!'

Lichtmann backed away, squeezing through the next rank of cannon. 'Then I must try more pedestrian means. Grieg!'

Malakai frowned and looked around. One of the engineering students cracked him between the eyes with a heavy spanner as long as a sword. The engineer staggered and the student caught him again hard over the ear. Malakai hit the floor in a loose flop.

'No!' cried Petr, and leapt at Grieg. The other students followed.

Gotrek roared and launched himself over the rail at Lichtmann, axe held high. The magus fell back, crying out a vile word, and a shimmer of purple snapped into existence between him and the Slayer. Gotrek strode towards him.

On the landing, Petr tripped, knocking the traitorous student into the railing as the murderous spanner swished over his head. The other crewmen swarmed Grieg, and it seemed that the effects of Lichtmann's spell still lingered, for they hacked at him unmercifully with their hatchets and tools.

Gotrek's axe smashed into the warlock's magical barrier and it exploded in pink sparks. Lichtmann flew back a dozen paces at the impact, as if hit by a wave, and crashed to the deck behind another rank of cannon. Gotrek started after him. The crewmen who had been crouching amidst the crates moved towards the sorcerer too, drawing hand axes. Felix crept down the stairs and started edging along the right bulkhead.

Lichtmann lurched up beyond the second line of cannons, glaring at Gotrek, his spectacles gone and his eyes glowing with a hellish inner light. 'That is indeed a mighty axe,' he said. 'It deserves a mighty opponent.'

He spread his arms and raised his voice in an ear-gouging screech of arcane verse. The flame-shaped dagger glinted and rippled in his left hand. His blackened right hand glowed red from within. Flickers of purple and gold light flashed in the air around him.

Gotrek clambered over the line of cannon as the two brave crewmen leapt at Lichtmann's back, hatchets high.

Lichtmann spun like a dancer, dodging their attacks, then lashed out at their throats with two graceful flicks of his golden dagger, all the while screaming his vile incantation. The men staggered past him and, as Felix stared in horror, their heads toppled from their necks and great jets of blood sprayed from the stumps in all directions, showering the nearby cannons and mortars in a red rain before their bodies collapsed to the deck. How could so slight a blade and so thin a man have made such horrible wounds? It seemed impossible.

Gotrek charged, roaring and swinging his axe. Lichtmann dodged nimbly back around a mortar and the

Slayer's blow glanced off iron. He continued after the warlock, slow but implacable.

Felix started forward too, but as he moved closer, he heard a strange hissing and bubbling. His eyes followed the sound to the guns, and he stared at what he saw, the hairs rising on the back of his neck. The blood of Lichtmann's victims was sinking into the iron. The cannons and mortars were absorbing it like sponges, and a green glow began to shimmer from them. The chains that held them rattled and shook.

'Gotrek?' Felix called, uneasily.

Gotrek ignored him. He was too busy stalking Lichtmann through the maze of guns.

The warlock's incantation was reaching a crescendo. He gashed his unmutated arm with the gold dagger, then raised both arms over his head as blood welled from the cut. With a final cataclysmic syllable, he pressed his arms together. The blackened flesh touched the bleeding wound. There was a sizzling hiss, and the scent of burned flesh, and Lichtmann cried out, doubling up in pain.

Gotrek rushed him, but the sorcerer threw himself backward over a cannon and crashed down behind it. Felix hurried forward. Lichtmann was down. This could be their chance.

But before he could reach him, he gagged and stumbled, eyes watering. The air was suddenly full of the scent of sulphur and spoiled meat, and there was a noise in the centre of the room like stew on the boil.

Felix looked up through his tears. Gotrek turned.

The blooded guns were glowing brighter now – a pulsating green corona that hurt the eyes. Arcs of arcane energy leapt between them, humming and crackling, and growing stronger by the second. Felix's skin crawled as the feeling that the guns were looking at him overcame him. Their malevolence was tangible.

Gotrek spat, 'Sorcery.'

There was movement in the midst of the guns. The bodies of the men Lichtmann had sacrificed were twitching and flopping like dying fish as blood gushed from their severed necks in arcing streams. There was too much blood. Gallons of it. Human bodies did not contain so much blood. It made a spreading pool on the deck in the centre of the big guns.

Felix stepped back involuntarily as the pool began to bubble and splash. The smell of sulphur and death got thicker, and Felix's sense of foreboding became a cloud of oppression that threatened to crush his soul. Foul whispers tickled his brain. The splashing blood rose higher and higher, like some grisly ornamental fountain, until it was the height of a man, and still it rose. At the same time, it became more viscous, like red honey, and the streams became ropy and thick. The students on the landing screamed in terror and scrambled for the door.

'Sigmar save us,' choked Felix. 'What is it?'

'Food for my axe,' said Gotrek. He started towards the thing, growling deep in his throat.

Felix wanted to scream and run as the students had, but knew that he could not. His vow to Gotrek wouldn't allow it. He clamped down on his sanity, willing the mad whispers to be silent. He looked to where Lichtmann had fallen. The warlock was gone.

Felix turned, on guard, searching for him, and found him circling on the other side of the Chaos thing, laughing maniacally. The shapeless horror picked up the two dead crewmen with two dripping pseudopods, then drew them within the frothing, flowing column of blood that was its body. The gore flowed all around the corpses, taking on their structure – arms, legs, torsos – and thickening them with layers of red putrescence until the thing looked like a pair of hulking, headless conjoined twins, fused at the spine, made entirely of running red candle wax. Faces and mouths formed on every part of the four-armed, four-legged horror, then melted away again to appear elsewhere, and Felix heard screams of unimaginable anguish join the vile whispers in his brain. The thing had not just consumed the crewmen's corpses, but their souls as well. He shuddered.

'Malakai told me that you have been seeking your doom for many years, Slayer,' Lichtmann called. 'Well, now you've found it.'

'Promises, promises,' growled Gotrek, pushing through the ranks of cannon.

For once, Felix had reason to share Gotrek's scepticism. As huge and horrible as the thing was, he had seen the Slayer destroy bigger daemons before with little trouble. The daemon-powered siege towers that had threatened the walls of Praag during Arek Daemonclaw's invasion, for instance, had literally exploded at the merest touch of the his axe. This thing looked puny by comparison.

Gotrek charged it, slashing, and opened a great trench in its torso. The horror howled in agony as its gelatinous blood boiled away from the touch of the axe. Felix leapt back, expecting an explosion of gore and pink fire.

It didn't come. The wound melted together again as if it had never existed.

Gotrek blinked, nonplussed. An arm like a sack full of wet sand backhanded him across the face. He flew back, drenched in clotted red mucus, and slammed against a gun carriage. Felix ran to him, aghast. What had happened? The daemon should have vanished in a burst of brimstone.

'All right, Gotrek?'

Gotrek lifted his head. Stinking red slime ran down his face. He growled savagely, glaring at the thing with his single eye. 'Nothing's right with this filth.'

'You will not banish it so easily from this plane, Slayer!' cried Lichtmann from behind the horror. 'Not when the warpstone in the guns strengthens it. Not when the souls of the greatest sorcerers of the age will it to remain!'

Sorcerers? Felix didn't understand. He looked around, almost expecting a phalanx of wizards to step out from behind the cargo crates like the villains in a pantomime. 'What sorcerers are these?'

Gotrek wiped his blistered face with the back of his hand. 'They're in the guns, manling. More foul sorcery.' He pulled himself slowly to his feet.

'In the guns?' Felix said.

Lichtmann laughed. 'Do you think we would sully such fine weapons with the bones of mere soldiers? Some of the most powerful sorcerers of Tzeentch have sacrificed themselves to join with these guns. It was their ashes that were added to them. It is their wills that will turn the gunners of Middenheim against their brothers and bring the Fauschlag down from within.'

As Lichtmann spoke, the bubbling horror reached out its massive, constantly mutating arms to four of the glowing, pulsing cannon, while at the same time a ropy tentacle stretched out from its chest towards a mortar. As the dripping limbs touched the guns, their flowing crimson flesh spilled down over them, covering them, ingesting them. The arms and the tentacle strained and bulged. The chains that held down the cannons snapped, and the horror lifted them out of their carriages as if they were enormous armoured gauntlets. The long tentacle retracted, settling the mortar between the thing's powerful shoulders. Streams of crackling green bale-fire arced between the mortar and the four cannons, forming a glowing cage of eldritch power around the horror. It roared a challenge from a dozen melting mouths as the mortar swivelled towards Gotrek and Felix like the eye of a cyclops. Felix could feel its hate like heat from a furnace.

Gotrek ran at it. Felix gulped and followed, praying to Sigmar for strength. The daemon swung an iron arm. They slashed at it together. Felix's sword clanged off ineffectually and his hands throbbed painfully as it touched the green energy, but the Slayer's axe struck home. The thick slime of sulphurous red matter that covered the gun splashed away from the runed blade like mud after a stone has hit it, showing a bright wound on the cannon's polished surface, then flowed closed again instantly.

Two more iron arms struck down. Felix lurched back, barely in time, but Gotrek ducked them both, slashing for the horror's torso. The axe bit deep, finding white ribs beneath crimson flesh.

The horror howled and fell back. Behind it, Lichtmann thrust out his twisted arm and a ball of fire exploded around Gotrek. The Slayer staggered in the midst of the flames, and a third cannon grazed the top of his head, knocking him flat. He rolled away, smoking, as two more arms slammed down, smashing deep creases in the metal deck. He scrambled back out of range, putting the horror's massive bulk between him and Lichtmann.

'Kill the warlock, manling,' he said out of the side of his mouth. 'The daemon is mine.' A purple bruise was spreading across his scalp to the left of his crest.

'Aye,' said Felix, though he was less than enthusiastic about facing Lichtmann one on one. He looked around, hoping the others might be able to help, that Malakai had perhaps recovered. He had not. Petr and the other students were carrying the engineer's body through the door into the hangar. A thrill of fear went through Felix. Could Makaisson be dead?

Gotrek charged the horror again. Felix summoned his courage and sprinted at Lichtmann, hoping to run him down before he could complete another spell. No such luck. The warlock's charred arm blazed, and a blossom of flame shot at Felix.

Felix yelped and dived aside, crashing down behind a stack of crates and covering his face as the fire billowed above him. The cloud of fire evaporated. He raised his head. All around him the crates were burning. He rose to a crouch, sword at the ready, and looked through the flames. How was he supposed to kill Lichtmann if he couldn't reach him?

On the other side of the crates, Gotrek once again dodged through the horror's slime-covered iron arms and slashed at it, but this time he didn't aim at the limbs or its chest. This time he chopped at the arm just above one of the cannons. The axe hacked through the muck as if it was water, and the cannon dropped to the deck with a clang, flashing and sparking.

The daemon howled in agony, and for the merest instant its crimson flesh became translucent and insubstantial and all the other cannon it carried drooped, as if they had become too heavy for it. The green nimbus around them flickered and hissed. Gotrek pressed his attack, his eye gleaming feverishly.

Lichtmann screeched, horrified, and began carving symbols in the air.

Felix charged him, sword raised. Sigmar's blood! They were going to do it.

Lichtmann saw him coming. He made a circle with his black hand and suddenly a roaring ring of flame sprang up around him. Felix skidded to a stop, throwing up his hands as a wave of heat rushed over him.

Gotrek hacked off one of the horror's legs, then another. Its flesh became nearly transparent. It toppled, cannon dropping. Gotrek tried to spring clear, but one of the falling guns caught him a glancing blow on the shoulder, knocking him sprawling. Another cannon arm smashed through a crate. Cannon balls spilled across the deck. The horror landed on top of the wreckage, all its form lost.

Felix lunged at Lichtmann with his sword, trying to stab him through the wall of fire. He jerked back as the flames seared his arm. Lichtmann ignored him, his eyes on Gotrek. He began another incantation. Felix cursed and looked around for something to throw through the flames. There! One of the dead crewmen's hatchets lay on the deck not ten paces away. He ran towards it.

Gotrek pushed himself up, his shoulder torn and bloody. On the deck in front of him, bathed in the pulsing energy of the possessed guns, the horror was reassembling itself, its legs reconnecting with its torso and its arms once again absorbing the dropped cannon. The cannon balls it had fallen upon were disappearing into its flesh as well.

Gotrek stood and limped forward, hurrying to attack the thing before it completely recovered.

Felix picked up the hatchet as Lichtmann pointed his black claw at Gotrek, the embered cracks glowing.

'Gotrek! 'Ware!'

Gotrek looked up.

Felix hurled the hatchet at Lichtmann through the curtain of fire. It was a clumsy throw. The flat of the axe hit the warlock in the back. He stumbled, but still loosed the fireball.

The Slayer dived aside, rolling behind a mortar. The flames exploded above him.

Lichtmann turned on Felix, flames playing around his right hand. 'It's a pity we do not fight on the same side,' he said, starting forward, his circle of flames moving with him. 'Your bravery and resourcefulness are unquestionable.'

Felix backed away, dodging behind another stack of crates. 'It's a pity you fight on the side of ruin,' he called. He looked towards the Slayer, trying to see if he had survived the blast.

'What choice did I have?' Lichtmann asked, following. 'I would be a loyal son of the Empire yet, had my hand not begun to change. I did nothing to make it occur. I read no proscribed books. I learned no profane rituals. I followed my teachers' instructions to the letter, and *still* I changed.' An edge of anger crept into his voice.

Felix ran behind a pile of barrels.

Across the room, Gotrek staggered to his feet, beard and eyebrows smouldering.

The horror rose before him, once again solid and complete, its pulsing corona of balefire glowing brightly. It lumbered towards him, the cannon balls it had absorbed boiling and subsiding under its skin like black bubbles. It was as if Gotrek's axe had never touched it. The Slayer growled and rushed to meet it, undaunted. Steel rang on steel. Felix groaned as he watched. They were back where they started, only worse for wear.

Lichtmann stepped around the barrels, his ring of flames setting them on fire. 'Could I go to my professors and tell them my plight?' he continued conversationally, as Felix ran and dodged before him. 'Could I ask for mercy at the Temple of Sigmar? No. The only mercy the Empire gives its twisted children is the axe. What could I do? I wanted to live. I did not want my great mind to go to waste merely because one of my limbs had betrayed me.'

Felix squeezed in between two rows of crates as the sound of Gotrek's battle rang in his ears. This was madness. There was nowhere to go. The hold was too small.

Lichtmann circled the rows, looking for him. 'So when Archaon began his march south, I saw that, though I loathed him and his uncultured barbarian

followers, his triumph was my only hope for sur-
vival.'

A loud clang made both Felix and Lichtmann turn.
Gotrek was flying backwards through the air. He
crashed down, shoulders first, on the barrel of a cannon, then slid to the floor, dazed.

As the horror slogged after him, the mortar that
served it as a head sank into the roiling red proto-
plasm of its chest, like a bucket disappearing into a
swamp.

Felix frowned. He didn't understand what it was
doing.

Gotrek struggled to his feet and backed away
through the guns while he recovered himself.

The mortar pushed up out of the horror's neck and
swivelled towards Gotrek, strands of crimson slime
clinging to it.

Felix still didn't understand. Then green fire flickered in the mortar's breach hole, and all became
horrifyingly clear.

Gotrek saw the flash too, and dived away just as the
mortar fired in a billowing burst of smoke and noise.
The cannon ball smashed through the right wheel of
a cannon and punched a ragged hole in the deck right
where the Slayer had been. Sunlight shone up through
it.

'No!' shouted Lichtmann.

Felix could barely hear him over the ringing in his
ears.

'Do not damage your brothers,' Lichtmann cried to
the horror. 'They must be whole or they will not be
placed on the walls of Middenheim.' He looked
around the hold at all the fires he had started with his

magic. 'In fact, we have caused too much damage already.' He stretched out his blackened claw, and the fires snuffed out one after the other.

Of course, thought Felix. Lichtmann has to protect the cannons or his plan won't succeed. And that made them perfect cover. Felix sprinted for the cluster of guns and ducked down behind one. Neither the warlock or the horror would dare to fire at him if he stayed among them.

Gotrek seemed to realise this too. He was back on his feet, beckoning to the daemon with a meaty hand. 'Come on, you overgrown nightmare. Come and face me steel to steel.'

The horror obliged him and waded into the maze of cannon, howling its fury from a multitude of mouths. The dwarf and the daemon clashed together deafeningly.

Felix turned and saw Lichtmann striding towards him, his flame-shaped dagger in his human hand. Felix readied his sword. This might be a fight he could win.

'Die, foul sorcerer!' shouted a voice from behind him.

Felix looked back. Petr and a few other students had returned to the landing, long guns and pistols levelled at Lichtmann. They fired.

Lichtmann threw up a warding hand and the bullets ricochetted off the air in front of him. Felix ducked. One went through his shirt sleeve. Several thwacked into the torso of the horror, to no effect. Others shot off at wild angles, bouncing all over the hold.

'Don't fire, curse you!' shouted Felix. 'You'll kill us all!'

Lichtmann laughed. 'Two can play at that game, fools.'

He sang out a string of profane words and raised his twisted arm. Fire flared from its embered cracks. The horror turned its mortar-head as its arms continued to batter at Gotrek.

'No!' shouted Felix. He ran at the warlock, sword raised.

The students saw what was coming. They made a mad dash for the door, fighting each other to get through it. Petr slipped and fell, then struggled to his feet again.

Almost as one, Lichtmann and the daemon loosed their attacks. A mortar ball punched through Petr's body, bursting him. A mess of limbs and viscera showered down on the guns below the landing, blood splashing everywhere. The students caught in the door were enveloped in Lichtmann's fire. The lucky ones screamed and ran into the hangar, beating at their flaming clothes. The others collapsed where they were, writhing and burning like torches.

Felix slashed down at Lichtmann, enraged at the death of earnest, clumsy Petr. The warlock sideslipped and stabbed backward with his dagger. Felix squirmed aside, barely avoiding its point. A horrible heat radiated from the shimmering blade.

Lichtmann lunged again, lightning quick. Felix swiped with his blade and jumped away, still off balance. He backed into a cannon and put a hand on it to steady himself. The iron tingled to the touch. He glanced back at it. Petr's blood was sinking into it and, just as had happened with the others, it was beginning to glow and crackle with poisonous green energy, as were the rest of the bloodied guns.

Lichtmann smiled. 'Yes, Herr Jaeger. More of my brothers wake. And I will use your blood to wake the rest.'

Felix backed away, flinching as the whispers returned, more strongly than ever, worming their way into his mind. He could feel the rage of the dead war-locks, their lust for his destruction. For the destruction of all his kind. They probed his mind with tendrils of corruption, they ripped at it with thoughts like claws.

Pulsing streams of balefire leapt from cannon to cannon as the spirits within them woke, forming a crackling, criss-crossing lattice of sorcerous energy that made the whole room thrum. The energy arced to the daemon's cannons, and they flared and fizzed with power. The daemon roared and raised its arms. It seemed to grow larger as Felix watched.

Felix's heart sank. The guns were feeding it, making it stronger. They were doomed.

Lichtmann came on, stabbing again. It was all Felix could do to lift his sword to block his attack. He couldn't think. His mind was too full of voices. He wanted to drop his sword and tear at his scalp to make the whispers stop.

To his left Felix saw Gotrek go down hard, a bloody gash across his massive chest. The horror edged through the cannons towards him. Felix knew he should do something, but he couldn't think what. He couldn't think at all.

Lichtmann slashed again with his dagger. Felix's arms wouldn't answer him. He could do nothing but stumble helplessly away through the cannon. He tripped over something and landed beside Gotrek. The sorcerer continued after him. Panic rose in Felix's throat. The whispers told him there was no hope, that he should just give up, that he should offer his throat to Lichtmann's shimmering blade.

Gotrek rose to his hands and knees beside Felix, shaking his head. He glared at Lichtmann and the horror, now only paces away, then grabbed Felix's arm. 'Come on, manling. Get up.'

Felix tried to get his limbs to move. They wouldn't. The whispers were in the way.

'Wake up, Manling!'

Gotrek slapped him, hard. The crack was deafening. Pain exploded through Felix's jaw, knocking the voices from his brain.

The daemon loomed above them, raising the hellish cannons. Gotrek yanked Felix aside as they smashed down. They missed Felix's legs by inches and ripped gaping holes in the metal deck. Felix scrambled up, his muscles finally responding, and followed Gotrek, who was charging straight for Lichtmann. The horror crashed after them.

'Thank... thank you,' he said through aching teeth.

Gotrek grunted.

The sorcerer backed away from them, then turned and ran as Gotrek lashed out at him with his axe.

To Felix's surprise, Gotrek didn't pursue him, but continued on towards the stairs to the landing.

'Where... where are we going?' asked Felix.

Gotrek started up the stairs. Felix swallowed. They were leaving the cover of the guns. Lichtmann would be able to blast them!

And he did.

Gotrek shoved Felix forward onto the landing and dived after him as a ball of fire exploded above the stairs. A cannon ball whistled overhead, then another. They blasted huge holes in the bulkhead.

Felix looked around. Two shots? The horror was firing with its arms as well as its head! It was bringing the other two cannon to bear.

Gotrek hauled Felix up and pushed him through the hangar door ahead of him. Felix stumbled over the burning bodies of the students that lay across the threshold, and sprawled face first on the hangar deck as Gotrek dived past him. A mortar round smashed a hole in the door frame behind them.

'After them, brothers!' came Lichtmann's voice. The airship shook as the horror stomped towards the landing.

'What are we doing?' asked Felix, getting up. He looked around the hangar. The wreckage of the gyrocopters was still burning. The remaining students were cowering in the far corner. Malakai lay prostrate on the floor at their feet. 'Are we running away?'

Gotrek snarled derisively as he smashed open a locked cabinet and pulled out two canisters of black water. 'We're taking the daemon away from those iron-befouling dead warlocks.' He handed Felix a lantern. 'Outside.'

'Outside?' But they were in the middle of the sky.

Felix glanced back through the door into the cargo hold. The horror was pulling itself onto the landing. The metal groaned under its weight.

'Up the ladder, manling.' Gotrek pushed Felix towards the rungs that were set in the wall beside the door, then picked up a piece of the burning gyrocopter's wooden frame.

As Felix started climbing the rungs, Gotrek split one of the canisters of black water with his axe, then heaved it out into the cargo hold. It bounced off a cannon, splashing black water everywhere. Gotrek pitched the burning wood after it, then clambered up the ladder after Felix.

There was a huge ear-popping *whump* from the cargo hold as the black water caught fire, followed by a blast of heat and orange light. Then a shriek from Lichtmann.

'No!' he cried. 'The guns!'

'That's only the beginning, sorcerer!' shouted Gotrek, climbing. 'A Slayer is not afraid to die. I'm setting fire to the balloon and killing us all!'

Felix stopped, heart pounding. 'You… you're what?'

'Keep moving, manling!'

The horror pushed two cannon arms through the door and started oozing in after them. Felix yelped and scrambled up the ladder, terror in his guts but his mind awhirl. Was Gotrek serious? Was he really going to blow up the airship? It would certainly finish off Lichtmann and foil his plans, but it would kill not just Gotrek and Felix, but Malakai and all his surviving students as well.

Felix clawed up through the circular hatch into the upper deck's central gangway, then took the canister of black water from Gotrek as he heaved himself up through the hole.

The airship shook violently as one of the horror's arms smashed the ladder just inches below Gotrek's boots.

Gotrek lurched up and grabbed the canister. 'Run, manling. The ladder to the roof!'

They ran, though Felix wondered if there was any reason. Could the huge daemon even fit through the hole to chase them?

With a noise like a steam tank crash, one of the cannon arms ripped up through the metal deck, tearing it as if it was paper. The impact knocked Felix off his feet. Gotrek picked him up and shoved him ahead. He looked back. A second smash widened the hole. Two glowing, muck-covered cannons snaked up through it and the horror pulled itself up, deforming like hot wax to fit into the cramped confines of the gangway. Lichtmann appeared behind it.

'Your fire is out, Slayer,' laughed the sorcerer. 'I foiled your little sabotage.'

The horror thundered towards them on four iron legs.

Felix sprinted on, sweating with terror. The ladder to the roof was just ahead to the right. He reached for it and glanced back again.

The mortar burst through the churning skin of the daemon's chest, the wide barrel aiming ahead. Green flame flared in its breach.

'Look out!' Felix threw himself against the right bulkhead. Gotrek did the same.

The mortar fired, battering Felix's ears with its roar. The ball ripped past, inches away, as the gangway disappeared in smoke and flame. Somewhere glass shattered and a man shouted.

Felix groped in the smoke for the ladder. He found it and hauled himself up, blinded and numb, the lantern he held banging off every rung. Gotrek clumped up behind him. The bulkheads vibrated with the thudding steps of the approaching horror.

'Faster, manling!'

Felix's head banged into the heavy hatch above him. He fumbled for the lever as something slammed into the ladder below. He shouldered the hatch back. Sunlight and cold wind slapped him in the face. He scrambled out onto the surface, then turned to take the canister from Gotrek again.

The Slayer squeezed through the hatch and rolled to one side, coming up on his feet with his axe at the ready.

Felix set the canister and the lantern down in a metal box that looked like it was meant to hold grenades, then drew his sword. He faced the hatch with Gotrek. Nothing happened. There was silence from below. Had the horror got stuck in the tight gangway?

Felix glanced around. The surface of the gondola was flat, with a low rail at the edges where the metal curved down on all sides. A score of taut metal cables stretched from sturdy rings in the roof up to the enormous expanse of the balloon, twenty feet above their heads. There was a ladder next to the hatch that rose, encased in a circular safety cage, up to a hatch in the belly of the balloon. All around them was blue sky and sunset clouds. Felix felt almost as exposed and precarious here as he had on the gyrocopter. The last time he had stood on this deck, he had faced the dragon Skjalandir. Memories of that night did not ease his mind. This was not the first place he would have picked for a fight to the death.

'Light the lantern, manling,' said Gotrek. He didn't take his eyes from the hatch.

Felix swallowed. He got out his tinder and flint and knelt, then opened the lantern's door. 'But this is just a ruse, isn't it?' he asked as he sparked a flame.

'If I kill the daemon and the sorcerer, it's a ruse,' said Gotrek. 'If I find my doom first, then it's not. You'll have to finish it.'

Felix lit the lantern, then looked up, following the ladder up to the balloon with his eyes. To be certain of destroying the airship, he would have to enter the envelope, pour the black water from the canister all along the catwalk that ran through the centre of all the lift-gas cells, then light it. He shivered. That would be the last thing he did in this life, for when the gas cells caught, the explosion would vaporise him.

'And if I die before I have the chance?'

'Then Sigmar and Ulric have mercy on their Empire,' said Gotrek. 'For Middenheim will fall.'

A glowing cannon shoved up out of the hatch at the end of a thick red tentacle, swaying like an iron-headed snake.

Gotrek lunged forward instantly and slashed with his axe, decapitating it with a single blow. Green sparks showered and gore splashed as the cannon dropped to the deck with a deafening clang. It bounced towards the side, hit the low railing and flipped over it, spinning off into space. The slithering voices in Felix's head rose in a keening wail of rage and loss.

'Ha!' said Gotrek. 'You won't get that one back, dae-mon.'

The beheaded tentacle flailed at the Slayer wildly. He dodged back, continuing to watch the hatch. Felix backed away, a spark of hope flaring in his heart. For once they had the horror at a disadvantage. If it had to push its cannon out through the hatch one by one, Gotrek might be able to cut them off as they came. He could destroy it without a fight.

A second cannon-tipped arm pushed up through the hatch. Gotrek dodged around the first tentacle and hacked at it. It too clanged to the deck, flashing and sputtering. Gotrek stepped back as it bounced past him and crushed a section of the railing before tipping and sliding down the side of the gondola and away. The voices wailed again.

The two headless tentacles shuddered and for a moment grew translucent, their corona of green energy flickering and dimming. But before Gotrek could take advantage, they grew solid again and lashed at him. He hacked at them and circled the hatch.

Felix's heart surged. By Sigmar, it was going to work! Only two more cannon and the mortar to sever and the horror would be so weak that Gotrek would be able to vanquish it with a mere touch of his axe.

A third cannon tentacle shot up through the hatch. Gotrek sprang for it, ducking the attacks of the other two and lashed at it. It reared back and he missed. He lunged forward again, but all at once he was hanging upside down in the air. The first tentacle had him by the ankle.

'Gotrek!' Felix ran forward and slashed the thing with his sword as the Slayer flailed and cursed. The attack did nothing. He drew back for another swing, but the second tentacle clubbed him to the deck.

The first raised Gotrek higher, swinging him about. It meant to throw him off the gondola! Felix struggled to rise. He was going to be too late.

With a violent twist, Gotrek chopped backwards at the tentacle, just below his foot. It parted in a spray of gore and sparks. The Slayer flew across the deck and crashed down on the railing, then rolled over it, sliding towards oblivion.

'Gotrek!'

The Slayer made a one-handed grab and caught the railing. Felix ran to him and offered him a hand. Gotrek took it and pulled himself back onto the roof. They turned.

In the interval, the horror had emerged fully from the hatch. It stood on four tree-trunk legs, its constantly flowing skin glistening in the crimson sunset light as moaning mouths formed and melted away all over it. Its two remaining cannon hung at its sides, the bright ends of their muzzles poking out from the muck that held them and green energy coursing back and forth between them. The other two tentacles rose from behind its back like twin cobras. Its mortar head turned towards Gotrek and Felix menacingly.

The Slayer lowered himself into a fighting stance. He ran his thumb along the blade of his axe, drawing blood. He grinned savagely. 'Now, daemon, you die!'

He charged towards it, roaring a Khazalid battle cry. Felix ran after him, commending his soul to Sigmar.

The red horror came to meet them, clubbing down at them with its iron arms and smashing great dents in the gondola's metal skin as the tentacles snaked forward to grab at them. Gotrek met it blow for blow, bashing at the cannons and hacking through a tentacle. It grew back instantly. Felix hacked at the tentacles too, hoping to keep them away from Gotrek so that he would be able to take off another of its arms. His sword barely scarred them. It was like chopping at a tree limb.

Suddenly he saw green fire flash at the back of the mortar.

'Gotrek! Look out!'

Gotrek looked up, then threw up his axe as the mortar belched flame and smoke. He caught the cannon ball on the flat of the axe and it glanced away to skip off the deck and out into thin air. But the force of the blow was too much. It slammed the back of the axe into Gotrek's temple and he stumbled, his legs buckling.

The horror knocked him flat with a tentacle and the Slayer slid across the riveted plates on his back. Felix ran back to him as the horror thundered after them.

The Slayer lurched up instantly, but his balance was shot. He shook his head to clear it and nearly fell again. A bleeding lump was growing over his patched eye. The horror swung in again, raining down crushing blows. Gotrek staggered back, blocking and ducking, but only at half strength. Felix backed with him. The horror pressed forward, pushing them back towards the nose of the gondola.

Beyond the battle, Lichtmann climbed from the hatch, his eyes blazing with fury. 'The cannons you just cast away contained the souls of Magister Valintin Schongauer and Magus Ermut Ziegel – greater men than you will ever be. You will pay for their loss!'

'I'll pay you in steel, warlock!' snarled Gotrek, ducking another cannon blow. He was still unsteady on his feet.

Lichtmann sneered. 'Yes. You will. I will take your axe, and I will melt it down as an offering to Tzeentch.'

He raised his charred claw, intoning a spell. His hand flickered with fire.

Felix flinched back, terrified, and almost stepped into a tentacle's grasp. One blast from Lichtmann and the balloon might erupt! Wait! That was it. He looked to the sorcerer, pointing up. 'Do it!' he said. 'Do it and finish us all!'

Lichtmann paused in his incantation. He looked up at the balloon and frowned, then shrugged. 'No matter. There is more than one way to shape a flame.' He started for the fight, drawing his gold dagger with his left hand and murmuring a new incantation. He balled his black claw into a fist, and the flames that wreathed it grew brighter.

Felix eyed him warily. A man armed only with a dagger should not have concerned him, but he had seen Lichtmann sever the heads of two men with that dagger, as easily as he might have clipped a rose from its stem. He had felt the heat that radiated from it. At least with Karaghul he had reach on him.

But just as the thought formed in Felix's head, the flames around Lichtmann's fist extended from it to become a blazing sword. The warlock charged him.

Felix stepped back and parried, almost colliding with Gotrek as the Slayer ducked a whistling swipe from the horror. The sword of flame smashed into Felix's runesword, embers splashing from it like water. He was showered with hissing sparks. Felix staggered, the flames pricking his hands and face. The fire blade had weight! It hit like a great sword, and Lichtmann seemed inhumanly strong. The gold dagger darted for Felix's stomach. Felix twisted away from it, and was knocked sideways by a tentacle. Felix slashed around him blindly, trying to keep Lichtmann at bay until he recovered himself.

The sorcerer laughed and pressed his attack. 'You are running out of roof, Herr Jaeger.' His eyes glowed. In fact his whole aspect was changing. His reddish hair was now flame orange and growing long and wild, and his once hairless face was sprouting curling orange moustaches and a beard.

Beside him, the horror battered at the Slayer with a whirlwind of glowing iron and red tentacles. Arcs of Chaos energy flared all around. Gotrek blocked every attack, his axe seeming to be in six places at once, but he was still not fully recovered, and could not penetrate the thing's defence. He took a step back, and another, his muscle-knotted torso red to the waist from the deep gash across his chest.

Felix beat aside Lichtman's sword of flame and lunged for his chest. The warlock turned the thrust with the gold dagger then stabbed it for Felix's face. The vile weapon hissed like a snake. Felix jerked back from it and brought his sword up, opening Lichtmann's forearm.

The warlock howled in pain and slashed furiously at him. Felix parried desperately and took another step back. Something pressed against the back of his legs. He glanced back. He was at the rail. Beyond it, the green carpet of the Drakwald spun vertiginously far below him.

Gotrek threw himself back as one of the daemon's iron arms slammed into the deck, tearing a huge trench in the brass plates. He bounced off one of the wrist-thick cables that held the balloon. He too had nowhere to go.

'Ha!' cried Lichtmann. 'Goodbye, brave fools!'

He and the horror attacked as one, Lichtmann lashing out at Felix with both sword and dagger, the horror swinging its iron arms at Gotrek's head. The Slayer dived left. Felix dived right, landing on his face. There was a *spang* like an enormous guitar string snapping, and the roof lurched under him.

Felix rolled over and looked up. Lichtmann was staggering back from the edge, his arms in front of his face, one of the steel cables loose and whipping around behind him.

The horror plunged after Gotrek, who was rolling to his feet beside the rail. Its cannon arms swung again. The Slayer ducked. Two more cables snapped.

Lichtmann fell to his knees as the roof jolted down a foot, broken cables lashing like snakes. The horror staggered sideways, almost tipping off the edge of the slanting gondola, then caught itself with its tentacles and continued after Gotrek. The remaining cables creaked and groaned alarmingly as it moved along the edge.

'No, brothers!' shouted Lichtmann, trying to stand on the metal slope. 'Do not damage the ship! We must make it to Middenheim!'

The horror didn't appear to hear. It swung again. A fourth cable snapped and Gotrek slammed to the deck, blood spraying from his forehead. The nose of the gondola sank further, tilting the roof alarmingly. More cables creaked and stretched.

Felix heard things shifting and thudding below him, deep inside the airship. He pushed himself to his feet and ran to the Slayer. His feet slipped on the slope and he fell again.

The Slayer pushed up, his burned and blistered face a mask of blood, which poured from a gash like a white smile across his forehead. Felix gagged as he realised he was seeing Gotrek's skull.

The horror howled and raised its two iron arms to smash the Slayer to a pulp, but it lost its balance and slid back towards the edge.

With a roar of fury, the Slayer threw himself down the slanting roof at it. It flailed wildly at him with its two cannon. Gotrek ducked them and swung his axe up from below. He chopped through the left arm at the root, severing it in a flash of green fire. The huge cannon dropped, and crashed down right on Gotrek's head and upraised right arm, mashing him flat to the deck, then it rolled off him and bounced down the slanted roof to tumble off into space. Gotrek slid down the slope on his face after it, unmoving.

Lichtmann and Felix stared at Gotrek's body as it bumped to a stop against the rail at the prow end of the gondola and lay there motionless. Felix was frozen in shock. By Sigmar, had he just seen the Slayer's death?

Lichtmann laughed triumphantly and grinned at Felix. 'A good trade, wouldn't you say, Herr Jaeger?' he asked. 'An arm for an enemy's life?' He turned to the horror, who stood beside him. 'Throw him over the side.'

The thing swayed down the incline, tentacles reaching out for the Slayer.

Felix's heart slammed against his ribs. He had to do something. He had to stop it! What could he do?

'At least the Slayer won't have died in vain!' he cried, then turned and scrabbled up the slanting roof towards the ladder. His feet slipped and skidded with every step. 'Prepare to burn, sorcerer!'

'Stop!' shouted Lichtmann, and then, 'Stop him!'

Felix heard the thudding steps of the horror coming after him and looked back, not daring to hope, then groaned with relief. Gotrek still lay at the rail. Lichtmann and the horror had left the Slayer behind to chase him.

Now if only Gotrek would wake up and finish them off, thought Felix, all would be well. He wouldn't have to go through with his threat. He wouldn't have to blow up the airship. He wouldn't have to die. He... he wouldn't have to face the fact that the Slayer was dead.

He looked back again. The horror was gaining, driving its remaining cannon down into the metal of the roof for purchase as if it was a cane, leaving a trail of ring-like dents. Lichtmann was right behind it, lit from below by his sword of flame.

Felix reached the hatch and snatched the fuel canister and the lantern from the grenade box, then ran to the ladder. He started up it one-handed, as fast as he could, which, in his current condition, wasn't terribly fast. The canister clanged off the bars of the safety cage with every step, slowing him.

'Are you certain you want to make this sacrifice, Herr Jaeger?' called Lichtmann. 'You are no Slayer.'

Felix cursed and tried to climb faster, but his battered body didn't respond. The fiends were going to reach the ladder before he reached the top. He was still a dozen rungs away. He felt like weeping. 'I can still die doing the right thing.'

Ten more rungs. Nine.

'Very noble, Herr Jaeger,' called Lichtmann, pacing the horror. 'A sacrifice worthy of Sigmar.'

Eight. Seven.

'A grand gesture to be sung about for all eternity.'

Six. Five.

Lichtmann and the horror reached the base of the ladder. Lichtmann sneered. 'If only you had succeeded.'

The daemon's iron arm swatted the ladder with a horrendous crunch, mangling the safety cage and pinching it shut at the base. Felix lost his grip and slipped several rungs, dropping the fuel and lantern. They rattled through the bars to the deck and clattered away down the slant.

Felix climbed frantically on. Six again. Five again. Oh gods!

The horror smashed the ladder again, and this time ripped it free of the bolts that held it to the belly of the balloon. With a scream of tortured metal, the cage and ladder toppled sideways towards the nose of the gondola, Felix trapped inside. The air exploded from his lungs and pain blasted the wits from his head as his prison slammed to the roof, then rolled towards the side and hit the railing. For a moment it seemed that it might stop there, but then inertia pushed it up and over. Felix clawed up the ladder towards the open end of the cage as he felt the twisted bottom half dip earthward and start scraping down the side of the gondola.

With a last desperate surge Felix pushed his head and shoulders free of the cage and threw out a hand. The gondola's railing smashed against his palm as he slid past it. He clutched at it, caught it, then lost it, and was dragged with the cage down the side of the gondola. He screamed and scrabbled with his hands at the smooth surface. There was nothing to hold on to.

A sharp ridge cracked him under the chin. He grabbed at it – a porthole – brass, and studded with rivets. His fingers clung to it with hysterical strength and he stopped his slide as the ladder and cage fell away, dropping down through wispy, sunset-pink clouds towards the ground far below.

Felix's legs swayed and banged against the side of the gondola as he held on to the porthole. The wind whipped at him, and his fingers were slick with panic sweat. He wouldn't be able keep his grip very long. Already his fingers were cramping. He didn't dare look down again, or the view would paralyse him, so he looked up.

That was no better.

Lichtmann and the horror loomed above him. Lichtmann shook his head admiringly. 'Such tenacity, Herr Jaeger,' he said. 'I do believe if I just left you to die, you would somehow find a way to climb back up and attack me again. I'm afraid I can't leave that to chance.' He looked to the horror. 'Brothers, Herr Jaeger and his uncouth companion have tossed three of our dear colleagues to the winds. I think it only fitting that you do the same for him.'

The horror howled from its melting mouths. The hateful whispers in Felix's head joined the chorus. The mortar and the cannon that were all that were left of the thing's armaments crackled with haloes of scintillating green energy. The mortar sank down into the churning mass that was its chest, and a cannon ball floated up to meet it.

Felix swallowed, eyes wide. By Sigmar, it was going to shoot him point blank! He looked down and to either side. There was nowhere to go. The skin of the gondola was smooth until the next porthole, more than a body's length away.

The mortar rose again from between the horror's shoulders, breaking through the pulsing red flesh, then swivelled down towards Felix like a dead black eye. Green fire flared at its breach.

Lichtmann smiled. 'Goodbye, Herr–'

There was a blur of movement behind the daemon, and then a bright flash of steel appeared under the mortar, slashing through its fibrous crimson neck. The mortar toppled from the horror's shoulders, turning as it fell.

It fired.

The deafening report almost shook Felix's fingers from the porthole. He cringed. Was he hit? No. He looked up, and ducked. The mortar clanged off the deck just above his head and bounced down and away.

The smoke from the explosion cleared, revealing the scene on the roof. Lichtmann was staring down at himself, an expression of disbelief on his chinless face. His blackened arm was gone, blasted away by the cannon ball. Blood gouted from the stump in a torrent. With a weak whimper the sorcerer tottered and fell to the deck.

Beside him, the headless horror was turning and swinging its sole remaining cannon at something behind it, its multitudinous mouths roaring in fury.

Another bright flash of steel and the last cannon separated from the daemon's arm in a burst of green fire, then sailed out far beyond the edge of the gondola before plummeting out of sight.

The thing shrieked. Its tentacles lashed forward to snatch something up and raise it high. It was Gotrek, axe raised and drenched in blood, roaring with wordless rage. He swung down one handed, and buried the axe deep in the daemon's chest.

It exploded.

Crimson gore spattered everywhere, then evaporated into a sulphurous pink cloud that whipped away on the wind. Out of the dissipating cloud fell the mangled wet bodies of the two crewmen it had ingested. Gotrek fell with them, hitting the deck in a loose jumble of limbs. His axe flew from his fingers and slid a little way down the slanting deck. Felix craned his neck. Was the Slayer dead? Had defeating the daemon taken the last of his strength?

No.

Gotrek was moving. He could just see him over the curve of the gondola, struggling to rise.

'Gotrek?' called Felix weakly. 'Gotrek. Down here.'

The Slayer didn't seem to hear him. He slowly pushed himself to his feet, wincing and pressing his ribs with his left hand. His right arm hung useless at his side. He swayed unsteadily on the angled deck.

'Gotrek!'

Gotrek stepped out of Felix's line of vision, then returned, dragging his axe behind him to stand over Lichtmann, who lay huddled by the low railing at the edge of the roof. Gotrek raised the axe with his left hand.

Felix couldn't see the sorcerer's face, but he saw his remaining hand rise in supplication.

'Mercy,' whispered Lichtmann. 'Mercy, I beg you. I don't want to die.'

'Ask your master for mercy, sorcerer,' rasped Gotrek, spitting blood.

He let the axe fall. Felix heard it chunk into meat, and there was a spray of blood. Lichtmann twitched once and lay still. Gotrek stared down at him, his face blank, blood from his horrible scalp wound dripping from his nose and matting his orange beard.

'Gotrek,' called Felix. 'Gotrek, get a rope.'

The Slayer swayed and took a step, then toppled backwards out of sight, his one eye rolling up in his head.

TWENTY

FELIX GROANED AND his head drooped forward to press against the glass of the porthole. His fingers screamed with agony. They were slipping slowly but inexorably down the curve of the rim. Of all the cruel jokes. Gotrek had killed the sorcerer. The airship, though wounded, was still air-worthy, and had not been blown to flinders, and Felix had miraculously survived it all, but now that it was all over and the day was saved, he was going to die, with no one to see or care.

For all he knew, Gotrek might be dead above him. He might have met his doom at last, and as heroically as he could have wished, saving the city of Middenheim from the most devious, destructive sabotage imaginable. And, wonder of wonders, Felix was alive to record the doom... for perhaps another minute. He giggled hysterically at the ridiculousness of it all, and almost lost his grip. Perhaps he could compose Gotrek's epic on the way down, crafting the final rhyming couplet just before he slammed into the ground. Bizarrely, the verses began to flood into his mind. He knew exactly how it would go. He could see it all transcribed on the page before him. A tear trickled down his cheek. It was all so sad. His greatest work, lost before it was written. No one would know his true genius.

Voices rang out above him.

'Hurry! Hurry! Out! Out!'

'I'm hurrying, curse you! Come on, hand them out.'

'Look! The Slayer!'

'And the sorcerer!'

'Sigmar's hammer! He did it! He killed the dirty traitor!'

'I think he killed himself as well. Tears of the Lady, look at the state of him.'

'And where's the swordsman? Jaeger.'

'Professor! Come up! They're up here! Look!'

'Help,' whispered Felix. And then, 'Help!' as he caught his breath. His fingers slipped another inch. His arms trembled with fatigue.

'Grimnir and Grungni,' came a familiar voice. 'They snapped the cables. That's the cause of it. Here noo, see to the Slayer, and gie him a...'

'Help!' cried Felix again. 'Malakai! Makaisson!'

'Hsst!' said Malakai. 'Dae ye hear something? Wis tha' my name?'

The voices stopped.

'Help!' bellowed Felix.

'Over the side,' said someone.

Malakai's round, bewhiskered face appeared over the curve of the gondola. He had a lump on his forehead as big and purple as a plum, and another over his ear. His eyes grew wide. 'Why, Herr Jaeger, what are ye doin' doon there?'

He turned away before Felix could say anything, and was back an instant later with a weird leather bag that looked something like a backpack, but with long, looped straps that would have the thing banging around your calves if you tried to wear it. Makaisson held onto one loop and flipped the other down towards Felix. It slapped against the side of the gondola just above his head.

'Catch ahold of tha', young Felix,' he said. 'And haud on tight.'

Felix was almost too terrified to let go, but there was nothing for it. He threw a desperate arm up and hooked his hand through the loop. He couldn't grasp it as he normally would. His fingers were too cramped to close. He inched his hand forward until the loop was firmly in the crook of his arm.

'Pull,' he gasped.

Malakai pulled, two of his crew holding onto his shoulders to steady him. Felix began to slide slowly up the curve of the gondola, groaning with both relief and pain. His fingers felt like they were on fire. At last strong hands reached out and pulled him over the railing and he collapsed gratefully on the roof, panting like a dog.

He lifted his head and looked around for Gotrek. The Slayer was standing, barely, supported by several of Makaisson's crew. What were they doing to him?

'No time for a kip, young Felix,' said Malakai. 'We hiv tae abandon ship. Now!'

Felix squinted up at him, confused. 'Abandon ship?' He didn't understand. And why were all the young men who stared down at him wearing the strange sagging packs?

Malakai pulled him roughly to his feet and handed him the pack he had pulled him up with. 'Aye. Put this on. Some burning crates slid into the black powder barrels when the gondola tipped. We cannae put it out.'

Felix gaped as he mechanically put on the pack. The powder would blow the ship to pieces and the fire would set the gas cells alight. 'Then we're all dead.'

'Nae, nae. Not at a',' said Makaisson. 'My newest invention will get us all safe tae the ground. But we have to go, *noo*.'

New invention? Felix looked around the roof, expecting to see some weird contraption – a ten-man gyrocopter perhaps. There was nothing. What was Makaisson talking about?

The engineer turned to Gotrek, who leaned wearily against the railing, trying to get his limp right arm through the strap of one of the packs. 'Are ye ready, Gurnisson?'

One of Makaisson's crew took the Slayer's arm, trying to help.

Gotrek winced and shoved him away. 'Leave off,' he growled, then forced the arm through the strap, gritting his teeth. 'Ready,' he said. Something white glinted halfway up his forearm. It was the jagged end of a bone, sticking out from the Slayer's skin.

Felix blanched at the sight. He had never seen Gotrek so hurt. Then again, Gotrek had never fought a daemon with arms of iron before. Could even the Slayer recover from such grievous wounds?

Malakai stepped to the Slayer and shook a brass ring that dangled from the pack's left strap. 'Once ye jump, ye count tae five, then pull the ring. Aye?'

Gotrek nodded. He picked up his axe. 'Aye.'

Malakai looked back at Felix. 'Ye have it, young Felix? Count to five and pull?'

'Count to five and pull,' repeated Felix, not understanding in the slightest. The pack? The pack was the invention? 'But what is it? What does it do? What does it carry?'

Malakai put a foot up on the rail. 'It's a wearable air-catcher. Ah call it a "reliable".' He took a last look around at the battered gondola of the *Spirit of Grungni*, and the balloon that rose above it. 'Ach weel,' he said with a shrug. 'Ah always did want tae build a bigger one.' He lowered his flying goggles and waved a hand over his head. 'Awa, lads. Awa!'

And with that, Makaisson jumped off the gondola and dropped out of sight. His few remaining crewmen gave each other wild-eyed looks, then shrugged and leapt after him, screaming 'Awaaaaay!' at the top of their voices.

Felix swallowed as he watched them plummet towards the earth. He turned to Gotrek. The Slayer was lifting a stiff leg over the railing. 'Come on, manling. It's a long walk to Middenheim.'

Felix put a foot up on the rail, then hesitated. A muffled explosion rocked the gondola, jolting him sideways. Another followed right on the heels of the first.

Gotrek leapt into the air, bellowing a dwarfish war cry. Felix jumped after him, a prayer to Sigmar on his lips that, whatever it was supposed to do, the 'reliable' he had strapped to his back was more of a success than Makaisson's 'Unsinkable,' or his 'Unstoppable.'

He dropped towards the ground at an alarming rate. The landscape rushed up at him like something out of a dream – rivers and fields and trees growing larger and more clear with every passing second. It was mesmerising. Sigmar! He had forgotten to count! Had it been five yet? Had he waited too long?

With a loud whump, a huge white shape blossomed beside him, then whipped up out of sight as he shot below it. That was Gotrek! The Slayer would not have forgotten to count. With panicky fingers, Felix fumbled at the ring and pulled.

Another whump, and something grabbed him roughly under the arms and jerked him to a stop in mid-air. It was agony on his wounds, and he nearly blacked out. The pressure lessened quickly and he looked up. A giant white mushroom cap as big as a tent floated over his head. Felix blinked. He was dangling from it by a score of thin silk cords. An aircatcher. Astounding. He looked down. More mushroom caps were floating lazily down towards the trees below him in the golden, late-afternoon light. There was no sound. The beauty of it all took his breath away. How strange to feel so peaceful so high up, with nothing under his feet but air.

An explosion like a hundred thunderclaps punched his eardrums and knocked him down and sideways in the air. Heat like a hammer slammed the left side of his body. He looked up. Beyond the shadowing white circle of the air-catcher, a black cloud of smoke was blotting out the sun. He heard a rushing crackle like coach wheels riding over dry leaves.

As the hot wind buffeted his air-catcher to the side he could see more of the sky above. The gondola of the *Spirit of Grungni* hung nose down from the balloon by a handful of cables, a huge hole blown in its belly. The balloon pointed up towards the sun, its underside on fire.

Why doesn't it explode, thought Felix?

It exploded.

A continent of fire erupted into existence above him, filling the sky, and a tidal wave of sound and heat smashed into him, knocking him up, down and sideways, as if he was a ship caught in a storm. Debris pattered down onto the cloth of the air-catcher above him, then something struck him violently above the temple and his vision dimmed. The last thing he saw was the *Spirit of Grungni*'s gondola plummeting nose-first towards the ground, and Gotrek's reliable drifting past below him, covered in smouldering black rubbish.

Then he knew no more.

IN HIS PRIVATE quarters deep below the city the surface dwellers called Bilbali, the ancient grey seer poured over the correspondence he had just received from Skavenblight, the words inscribed by an elegant paw on the finest man-skin vellum, sealed with the insignia of the Council of Thirteen. He snarled to himself and crumpled the scroll between his claws, then threw it on the fire.

It mattered not how beautiful the vessel, if what it carried was poison. How could they deny him again? How could they refuse him his rightful position in the aristocracy of the greatest of all skaven cities? How could they ask that he continue this exile, this banishment, this insult of a proconsulship in this forgotten backwater, so far from the hub of skaven society? Weren't all his failures – rather, the failures that vile betrayers had falsely called his – almost twenty years gone? Couldn't the council put it all behind them? Couldn't they forgive and forget? Twenty was more years than most skaven lived to see. Had he not lived almost three times that number? Was he not therefore three times – nay, three hundred times – more wise? Was he not the keenest mind of three generations?

Oh, he knew he had little to show for it. All his greatest plans had been stymied, all his certain triumphs brought to crashing, calamitous ruin. But how could they blame him? Was it his fault that he had always been cursed with incompetent underlings? Was it his fault that his colleagues had been jealous backstabbers who had claimed his best ideas for their own, and sabotaged those they could not take advantage of? Was it his fault that he had been stalked by two of the most ruthless, relentless, remorseless enemies ever to cross the path of skaven-kind?

The mere thought of those fiendish beings sent him scrabbling through his papers until he found the stoppered bottle of powdered warpstone. He uncapped it with shaking paws and took a generous snort up both nostrils, then sank back with a sigh as he felt the mellow warmth of it trickle soothingly through his veins. There was nothing like it to calm his nerves. These last years would have been unbearable torture without it.

At least the two monsters were gone, he thought happily. He hadn't heard even a rumour of them for almost twenty years. It had been the one solace of his long exile that they had ceased to plague him. Of course it would have been far more pleasurable to have had them under his power, running them through his maze, testing experimental poisons on them, making their every waking moment a living hell of...

A scratching came at his door.

'Who is it?' he snapped, angry to have been disturbed from such a delicious daydream.

'Only I, oh most ancient of grey seers,' said an obsequious voice. 'Your humble servant, Issfet Loptail.'

'Come come,' said the grey seer. 'Quick quick.'

The door opened and a scrawny skaven with a foolish, simpering look entered, his head bobbing respectfully. He stopped a respectful distance from the grey seer's desk and swayed in place. He was a pitiful thing. He had lost his tail in a raid on a human farm once – to a female no less – and no longer had any balance. But he was smart, and listened well, and – most importantly – obeyed his master's orders without question.

'Speak speak, simpleton,' squeaked the grey seer imperiously. 'Your master is busy. Very busy.'

'Yes, oh pernicious one,' said Issfet, bowing and almost falling over. 'I have news from Nuln.'

'Nuln?' said the seer sharply. 'I wish to hear no news from that ill-favoured place. Have I not told you that I...'

'You have told me always to listen for certain rumours, master, no matter where they spring from.'

'Rumours? What rumours?' the seer asked. 'Speak! Quick quick!'

'Yes, your superfluousness,' said Issfet. 'I discovered a report from our outpost there. Two warriors were seen in our tunnels, travelling with a group of blood drinkers. One of the warriors was a dwarf, with one eye and fur the colour of flame. The other…'

The grey seer reeled back in his chair and nearly fell. He grabbed the stoppered bottle again and upended it on his tongue. 'My nemeses!' he moaned as he swallowed the warpstone snuff. 'My nemeses have returned! Horned Rat protect me!'

'Master!' said Issfet, a look of concern on his snaggle-toothed face. 'Master, wait. Listen further. The news is perhaps not as bad as it seems. There comes a further rumour that these same warriors were killed in an explosion upon a dwarf airship.'

'Killed?' said the seer, rising from his seat, his eyes blazing with weird green light. 'Killed? Those two? Never! I am not so fortunate.' His claws clutched convulsively. 'No. They are not dead. But they soon will be. This time I will be certain of their destruction!'

'Yes, oh most impotent of skaven,' said Issfet. 'How could so wizened, so devoid a grey seer fail to destroy such lowly creatures?'

'How indeed?' said the seer, thinking back with a shudder to his previous encounters with the dangerous pair. 'How indeed.' He turned to the fire, gazing into it. 'Go go,' he said without looking around. 'Disturb me not. I must think.'

'Yes, master.'

'Oh, and Issfet,' the seer said, turning as the crippled skaven backed towards the door.

'Yes, master?'

'Speak of this to no one. There have been times in the past when my rivals have used these two against me. It will not happen again.'

'Of course not, oh most parsimonious of masters,' said Issfet, bowing low. 'None shall hear of it. My snout is sealed.'

'Good good,' said the grey seer and turned back to the fire as his servant backed through the door and closed it behind him. He warmed his cold paws over the flames, then paused and looked over his shoulder, squinting suspiciously. Had there been just the faintest hint of slyness on Issfet's face as he bowed? Had there been the shadow of a cunning smile?

Perhaps the tailless little spy was too smart. Thanquol would have to keep an eye on him.

ABOUT THE AUTHOR

Nathan Long has worked as a screenwriter for fifteen years, during which time he has had three movies made and a handful of live-action and animated TV episodes produced. He has also written three Warhammer novels featuring the Blackhearts, and several award-winning short stories. He lives in Hollywood.

THE BLACK LIBRARY

GOTREK & FELIX
THE COLLECTED ADVENTURES

Read the exciting adventures of Gotrek & Felix
in these two amazing omnibus editions -
each containing three action-packed novels!

The First Omnibus
ISBN 13: 978-1-84416-374-8
ISBN 10: 1-84416-374-1

The Second Omnibus
ISBN 13: 978-1-84416-417-2
ISBN 10: 1-84416-417-9

Visit www.blacklibrary.com to buy these books, or read
extracts for free! Also available in all good bookshops
and games stores.

READ TILL YOU BLEED

THE BLACK LIBRARY

GOTREK & FELIX

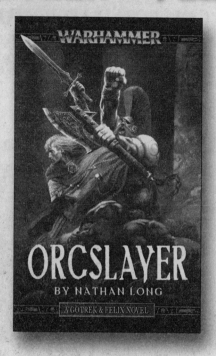

Also from Nathan Long

Our heroic duo are back in this amazing
tale of honour, bloodshed and revenge!

Orcslayer
ISBN 13: 978-1-84416-391-5
ISBN 10: 1-84416-391-1

Visit www.blacklibrary.com to buy this book, or read the first
chapter for free! Also available in all good bookshops and
games stores

READ TILL YOU BLEED

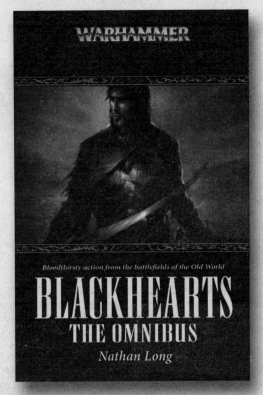

Also from Nathan Long

Forced to carry out the most desperate and suicidal secret
missions, the Blackhearts encounter Chaos cultists, ratmen,
dark elves, rogue army commanders and more.

Blackhearts the Omnibus
ISBN 13: 978-1-84416-510-0
ISBN 10: 1-84416-510-8

Visit www.blacklibrary.com to buy this book, or read the first
chapter for free! Also available in all good bookshops and
games stores

THE BLACK LIBRARY

BRINGING THE WORLDS OF WARHAMMER AND WARHAMMER 40,000 TO LIFE

MANSLAYER

Check out all the action happening on the Black Library website!

All the latest news, downloads, special offers, articles, chat forums, online shopping and much more.

Miss it and miss out!

WEB STORE

Pre-order new titles, buy available products and exclusive Collector's Editions.

NEWSLETTER

Sign up for all our latest news and special offers!

DOWNLOADS

Free first chapters of all our novels, wallpapers and loads more.

FORUM

Chat with fellow Black Library fans and submit your own fiction.

Visit :: www.blacklibrary.com